THE
351 BOOKS
OF
IRMA ARCURI

THE
351 BOOKS
OF
IRMA ARCURI

--->*<---

DAVID BAJO

VIKING

VIKING
Published by the Penguin Group
Penguin Group (USA) Inc., 375 Hudson Street, New York, New York 10014, U.S.A.
Penguin Group (Canada), 90 Eglinton Avenue East, Suite 700, Toronto, Ontario,
Canada M4P 2Y3 (a division of Pearson Penguin Canada Inc.)
Penguin Books Ltd, 80 Strand, London WC2R 0RL, England
Penguin Ireland, 25 St. Stephen's Green, Dublin 2, Ireland (a division of Penguin Books Ltd)
Penguin Books Australia Ltd, 250 Camberwell Road, Camberwell, Victoria 3124, Australia
(a division of Pearson Australia Group Pty Ltd)
Penguin Books India Pvt Ltd, 11 Community Centre, Panchsheel Park,
New Delhi – 110 017, India
Penguin Group (NZ), 67 Apollo Drive, Rosedale, North Shore 0632, New Zealand
(a division of Pearson New Zealand Ltd)
Penguin Books (South Africa) (Pty) Ltd, 24 Sturdee Avenue, Rosebank,
Johannesburg 2196, South Africa

Penguin Books Ltd, Registered Offices: 80 Strand, London WC2R 0RL, England

First published in 2008 by Viking Penguin, a member of Penguin Group (USA) Inc.

1   3   5   7   9   10   8   6   4   2

Copyright © David Bajo, 2008
All rights reserved

LIBRARY OF CONGRESS CATALOGING IN PUBLICATION DATA
Bajo, David.
The 351 books of Irma Arcuri : a novel / David Bajo.
p.   cm.
ISBN 978-0-670-01929-8
1. Mathematicians—Fiction.   2. Missing persons—Fiction.   3. Man-woman
relationships—Fiction.   I. Title.   II. Title: Three hundred fifty-one books of Irma Arcuri.
PS3602.A578A615 2008
813'.6—dc22   2007040430

Printed in the United States of America
Designed by Nancy Resnick

For Elise

For Esme

ACKNOWLEDGMENTS

No real books were destroyed or damaged in the making of this novel. All Cervantes quotes use Edith Grossman's 2003 rejuvenating translation of *Don Quixote* (Ecco). The Pepys cookbook that Irma restores is based on Christopher Driver and Michelle Berriedale-Johnson's clever compilation *Pepys at Table: Seventeenth century recipes for the modern cook*. The pulp western she transforms is taken from Peter McCurtain's *Carmody* series. All anagrams were configured by Esme Bajo. If anyone alive can find Irma Arcuri, it's Markus Hoffman, who carried this book around the world with such enthusiasm and success.

I admit to being nothing more than a transcriber. This story would be much less than it is without Joshua Kendall and Peter Steinberg. For any life found in these pages, I thank Elise Blackwell.

THE
351 BOOKS
OF
IRMA ARCURI

Z E D

He held the parchment to the window light. He did it to cast its color on her, to see how its soft ink shadows and yellow translucence would play on her form as she reclined on the disheveled bed. Her feet toed a stray pillow. An arm extended over the edge. Her hip tilted toward him. She rested her head to her shoulder, exposing the side of her neck where it paled beneath her ear. She mistook his intent.

Which story do you want?

He gave her a puzzled look as he shifted the parchment to move its shadows along the dip of her waist and the cusp below her rib. To her lips she held a kind of rock candy, quartzlike *dulcitas* made from sugared coffee, sold by cane vendors in the bus cutout. She lifted the sweet away from her lips and pointed it at him, at the parchment he held to the light.

There are at least two there. She pointed the candy toward the paper. There's the one you see in transparency, the one whose words you're moving over my tits. And then the one you'll see when you drop it away from the light.

He dropped the parchment from the light. It then felt rigid, appeared rusted, the gray ornate lettering gone and replaced by faint scripts like water stains. Even if it were in a language he could understand, he would not be able to read through the script fades, erasures, and webbing. He slid her parchment onto the sill of the recessed window, treating it as something you weren't sure you were going to keep, maybe left for housekeeping to sweep away. The light fell on her now unobstructed and she turned herself to it, stretched in it, her breasts lifting. She twirled the candy like a smoky prism in her fingers and then caught him watching. He turned away to face the window but still felt, undeniably, her gaze on him, as palpable as the most intimate stroke.

Outside the window were the twin volcanoes with late morning light flooding down their chutes. The older one, Nevado, stood quiet and softened and slightly arrear, snowcapped as always. The younger one, Volcán, billowed steam from its snow-lipped caldera, a sharpened look to it. The volcanoes accounted for the odd clarity and focus of the light, shaping and throwing it, the younger one's steam thickening it. The two mountains still had a freshly sprung look to them, the colors of seashells, and from their peaks she had shown him the Pacific.

They roomed together in this old coffee finca converted to an inn for those who wanted to explore the volcanoes. They had only known each other for seven years and had traveled here to purge false starts and loves from their lives. They were making adjustments. We can go together, she told him, but apart. The room now held an uprooted smell, from what they did after hikes and climbs.

The sound of her skin brushing over the sheets, of her breath arcing through her, lured him away from the view. He looked back over his shoulder. She had just begun to look beautiful to him.

Turn, she said. Show yourself.

If I do, I'll miss everything. I'll miss the whole day.

He was so young then.

Instead he dressed quickly, pulling on jeans, shirt, and sandals, combing his hair back once with his fingers, to show her he could resist. He hurried to catch the bus. He wanted to see the fiddlers and mask dancers in a town at the foot of the mountain, something that didn't interest her. They're not real, she told him. They're not real anymore.

I'll see you here at five, he told her as he left the room, not daring to look back.

Maybe, she said.

But he didn't get off the bus in Suchitlán to watch the fiddlers, and instead kept riding toward the city of Colima. Going on because he sat near the front of the bus, where he could see the road disappear beneath the huge windshield each time the driver swung them around another dramatic turn along the mountain road. Because that was how he was beginning to feel with her—thrown above a green and plunging world, maybe with enough wing and agility, maybe not. They would have to see. Together but apart. And so he patted his passport and wallet and in his mind willed to her his abandoned clothes, his boots and toothbrush.

In the midway town of Comala he impulsively left the bus and found a taxi on the little zócalo. The driver, dressed in a wedding shirt with stained collar, promised he could take him to where the optical illusion was, where the stalled taxi would seem to roll uphill through lava fields. En route, he dozed and then was awakened by the sound of her long breath and hiss of sheets, and this made him ask the driver to return to the zócalo. From there, he took the bus back up the green foothills of the volcanoes, to the coffee fincas.

It was already evening. The volcanoes now reflected the setting sun. He had wasted the entire day sweating on buses and taxis, making decisions that didn't need to be made, fretting in a land where she claimed fretting would be laughable. He felt her laughing. In the common area of the finca, among tattered chairs for smoking and reading, he mistook someone else for her. All appeared dimmed by stained glass and he was late. Her hair was dark, the same length, parted the same, the brown tip of her shoulder familiar. She was considering—not reading—a broken book taken from one of the common shelves. When from behind he touched the stranger's arm, she looked up, startled, and he apologized swiftly and hurried on to the room.

Everything was almost the same. The window light was now reflected and deeper, colored more by the volcanoes. She sat on a stiff chair by a little fire she had made and wore one of her thin dresses, the yellow one. She could roll them as small as baseballs and carry three in a handbag. Her look was the same he had turned from, direct and full-bore. It seemed almost as though she hadn't left the room. But there was a clean mineral scent, water on stone. She had run the volcano and showered.

Sorry I'm late.

You're not late, she said. You're returned. You ran. You left.

He feigned confusion.

It's all about you, she said. Your eyes taking me back in. The tufts in your hair where the sweat has dried, where you kept trying to push your thoughts with your fingers. The way you are just half turned toward me. You left, then tried to go somewhere else, but found yourself heading someplace we talked about going. Maybe you made it there before you turned back.

She moved from the chair to the edge of the bed and hiked up her dress as though to cool her legs. You came in here with apology still struck across your face, still curled in the press of your fingers. But not for me, really. So you must have apologized to someone out in the hall.

He felt a breeze and realized she had managed to pry open the window a bit, somehow found a way around the warps and swells of the wood. Her parchment was gone from the sill and he peeked worriedly out the window for it.

I burned it, she said.

What? You *acquired* it. It's so old.

Some bloodied grocery list of a conquistador scribbled over the bleached-out chants of a monk. Who needs it? I used it to make the fire.

She pulled up her dress farther, knotted it between her breasts. We'll put its light to good use.

I don't believe you.

She drew back on the bed, her knees going up then over together. He stepped to her, without thinking, in her draw.

I brought that book to its end, its completion, its unbinding and decay. To dust and ashes, Philip. I gave it more than it deserved. Just like you. Right now.

But you're angry, he said. He could see it easily in her eyes, stilled also in the dark waves of her hair around her brow.

That will make this all the better. My anger. And don't forget yours.

He straightened, drew a breath that kept him from the bed just a moment longer.

Don't start now, she said. Don't start being afraid of what I can know about you. Of what I can tell. I've hardly begun. I know so little. Just more than you.

His desire to press himself to her swept upward through him, cupped his senses toward her, a shell to his ear. His hands, already shaped to grasp beneath her arms, ached. He felt dizzy, but with some direction, as though tethered and spiraling into her. She looked to the fire, her arms above her head, fingers locking. Though she then remained still, a quickening seemed to gather about her, a drawn and held strength.

But when *I* go, she whispered hard into his ear as he fell across her and pushed the knot of her dress up to her neck. She rubbed herself against the stiffness of his clothes. When I go, I won't return.

And as the light of the fire took over the light of sunset, he sensed everything in her skin. Everything that could happen, that might happen. Everything.

But you must forgive him here, then. There is so much he doesn't know.

ONE

Irma Arcuri bequeathed her book collection, all 351 hardcovers, to Philip Masryk. Within the collection were the five novels she wrote and bound herself. Two were published and three were not, but he never cared which ones made it through that process. She always gave him copies she bound herself, versions that slid into his hands like cool pieces of marble, weighted and balanced. And she always hand-delivered them, no matter where she had to travel. Philip received notice of this final bequeathment in an e-mail from her mother in Santa Barbara. He reread the message as he rode the morning ferry from Philadelphia to Camden. The spring mist rising from the Delaware dampened the printout. He held the message with both hands so the early sun could shine through the paper. Other commuters along the rail held the opaque *Inquirer* to block the sunrise, mist, and bowspray. It was cold.

He stopped driving the Franklin Bridge and started riding the ferry after his second ex-wife won both cars in their friendly settlement. Letting Beatrice have both cars was not as amicable as it may have seemed to her and her lawyer. In the thirty seconds it took her attorney to utter the request, Philip accurately calculated the economic and temporal impacts of parking two cars in downtown Philadelphia.

He accepted. He had a certain way of seeing things—a tilt—and so he trusted her and her anger toward him. She took ownership of their flat near Rittenhouse Square. She compensated him for this, but in terms of what the place was worth when they bought it together, not in the inflated terms it was worth now.

After the ferry took him to Camden, he went to work just long enough to resign and then walked along the riverfront to the aquarium. He spent the day there, learning that the glass separating him from the fish was eleven inches thick. He waited until eleven to call the Arcuris, so that it would not be too early an hour on the West Coast. He called them from the aquarium's promenade.

Mrs. Arcuri answered on the third ring. She answered ninety-seven percent of the time, so Philip was expecting her voice. He asked her about the bequeathment and didn't that imply some kind of death or vanishing. He listened to Irma's mother for five minutes before his cell phone was cut off, the interruption informing him that the insurance company he quit earlier had removed him from their service. He understood their anger and was relieved by the abrupt ending it gave to his conversation with Mrs. Arcuri. She stopped liking him twenty years ago when she realized that he was not going to marry her daughter. She remained polite, treating him through the years as a sort of family member, one known as the man who would not marry our daughter. Whenever he had Thanksgiving with the Arcuris, he was seated next to whoever was Irma's current lover, like the next figure down on her mother's evolutionary scale of suitors.

Irma, he learned from Mrs. Arcuri's abbreviated chat, was only figuratively dead. If she had actually died, Mrs. Arcuri assured him, she would have called him in person. But he could tell by the erosion in her voice—her verb-to-total-word ratio diminishing from sentence to sentence—that this figurative death was almost as distressing and final as a literal death. Irma was gone. Her figurative suicide note, left on a pillow in a *pensión* in Seville, mentioned a secular mission, the sacrifice of one's dreams. Most tragically, it declared an end to her writing. Mrs. Arcuri cried during this sentence. The cell phone cutoff occurred amid her tears.

Philip wandered back into the dark knot of the aquarium, to the jellyfish display, where he watched one small tank for a long time. The jellies were only a few centimeters long, but they were colorful and phosphorescent in their black water. They were from the deep-sea trenches off the Philippines.

The jellyfish took turns undulating themselves upward, then parachuting softly through the dark water. This was how they gathered microscopic food, Philip read from the descriptive plaque. Some lit up like neon, others were hardly visible, membranes in ink. At the bottom of the plaque, Philip saw that his insurance firm—his now ex-insurance firm—sponsored the jellyfish. He briefly calculated the cost of this sponsorship: the ichthyologists, their collecting grants, the specialized boat and equipment, permission from the Philippines, tank maintenance. All for a few centimeters of sea life, wisps of vellum that were barely even there. The plaque understated the firm's generosity.

His resignation had not been bold. The cell phone cutoff aside, he was reasonably certain they would take him back; his talent was rare enough. Depending on whose research you followed, there were approximately ten thousand to twenty-five thousand like him in the world. Perhaps a thousand of those lived in America. Of those thousand, only a few hundred had their talent discovered because they were in ideal socioeconomic situations, fewer had taken the time and effort to cultivate it through higher education, and roughly a third of those were of working age. He knew numbers. Others called it calculation, but usually there was no calculation necessary, certainly not in the simple math of addition, subtraction, multiplication, division, square roots, and exponents. If you gave him a set of numbers and told him what to do with them—add them, cube the result, and then give the square root, for example—he could do it in his head in the time it took you to input.

Useless, you might think, in the advanced Age of Technology. But he was always ahead of computers. Like them, his speed was only limited by the input. Like them, he could process the numbers through any equation or formula. He would always—always—know the most efficient formula or set of formulae to use in any given situation. In a day, he saved his firm a year's worth of work by five lab technicians. We have these numbers, Philip, what should we do with them? Where can *you* start with them? They found him, collected him. They put him in a nice office and called it a lab. They sponsored him.

The famous insurance firm, which spearheaded Camden's riverfront renaissance and enjoyed the tax breaks that came with it, did not use him much for risk assessment. That was for the number crunchers who worked on the lower floors. Philip worked primarily on the investment end of things, with the portfolio managers on the top floor, which rose just a little higher than the dome of the aquarium, the other bookend on the riverfront renaissance.

Beatrice once worked for them, too. She was a systems analyst, expert on both human and procedural structures. She loved trying to understand the way he saw things, the way he thought. After recommending quite sincerely that the insurance firm remove its entire second tier along with most of the first, she quit, and quickly found consulting work waiting for her. The companies and clients who used her called her Satan. As in, "Let's conjure Satan." As a gift, Philip had some business cards made for her: Satan, with the *t* shaped into a little pitchfork. She was tall and dark. Sometimes all we have is the sex, she would often tell him; and then she would consider this, systems analyst that she was, and seem to decide it acceptable, ideal perhaps. They had two dishwashers in their Rittenhouse flat: one for dirty, one for clean, and no shelving in between. He was pretty sure she had a photographic memory.

The jellyfish took turns feeding, convulsing upward, parachuting gracefully. They drifted in a waiting line near the bottom of their tank as one descended; then the next would propel gently upward. Philip mimicked them with his hand raised to the tank. He dangled his fingers, pursed them, then opened them into an umbrella and lowered his hand along with a jellyfish.

"Are you high?" asked the security woman behind him. "Because if you are, I will have to ask you to leave the building. I will give you a certificate of return and a number you can call to seek help."

He turned to face her because her voice sounded pleasant, gravelly but young. Her face was black with an Italian nose. Beautiful New Jersey. Her expression was sincere, concerned, fixed, a relief from the ephemeral jellyfish.

"I'm not high," he told her. "I'm unemployed."

His resignation had not been that bold, but it was bold enough, with enough reckless imprecision to react to his divorce and to pay homage to Irma's disappearance, to her gift. He could say to her mother, only from afar, I have resigned, I have changed, I am devastated, look what I've done with my life. From Irma, it would only elicit a lift of an eyebrow, maybe a folding of her arms across her chest and a cock of the hips as she waits to see what he does next.

The books arrived in one week, two refrigerator-sized boxes with protective packaging. They were packed alphabetically, impact-guarded, and marked fragile. He shelved them the way she shelved them— alphabetically, with no consideration of history, nationality, genre, or theme. They transcended these divisions, and Philip knew—somehow understood—that this was why she'd had them. They were splendorous together, in their cloth and leather bindings of jewel-toned yellow, green, red, or blue, or the more austere black and burgundy. No jackets, with titles embossed in gold, silver, brass, or iron. Most she had re-bound or restored herself, using period materials and tools. This was easy, she told him, because we use tools similar to those used since the fifteenth century. I could walk into an eighteenth century bookbinder's shop, she explained, and have no trouble sewing up Defoe's first volumes. Her shop and her mentor's shop looked like museums, with their mallets and presses, awls and knives. Their work floors held the smells of old leathers, parchment, and linseed. Sometimes in their dark corners he would find a jar filled with a petrified volume soaking in amber linseed, the book's fused pages beginning to separate like petals. If he lingered too long by one of these jars, she would crouch behind it and peer at him through the xanthic oil, her face magnified, tinted, and swirled around sharply focused eyes. Eyes aimed at him, not the sloughing book fossil. If we stir it softly with a wooden spoon, she taunted, it will all dissolve like a sugar cube in tea.

Her five novels stood among the first, in the *A*'s right before Austen, two blue, then one red, one green, and one yellow. The first book he drew from the collection after he had completed shelving all 351 volumes was her novel *The Theory of Peter Navratil*, finished when she was thirty-eight. He was Peter Navratil. She never denied this to him or any of her friends who noted it. It was about a private-sector scientist who searches for a woman in Michoacán, Mexico. Bound in green, embossed in silver, the book smelled like a new baseball mitt and crackled upon opening.

In his heightened state of self-indulgence, Philip read his own story. Numbers were his first language, she told the reader. A truly bilingual child, Peter's two languages hindered each other's early development to the extent that he was at first termed learning disabled—retarded in those days—by concerned teachers and pediatricians. But during the second grade, after a night spent reading his mother's astronomy book, his two languages cross-pollinated, and then bloomed. He suddenly could speak and read English like everybody else in his class. But numbers were different. Through numbers, his first language, he saw and interpreted the world. He became the trick pony of his school. A conspiracy of teachers would challenge him with fast, long sequences of spoken equations, mixing addition, subtraction, multiplication, division, exponents, and square roots. His answer was always correct and delivered immediately at the end of the spoken sequence. The teachers would spend nightly hours devising these sequences, double-checking their accuracy, and computing them carefully with pencil and paper and new electronic calculators. And little Peter would dash their efforts in less than a second every time. School auditoriums applauded. At first he enjoyed the applause. Then it began to make him feel like an oddity. He began to sense the applause as a kind of pounding by the audience, a tactile shove that said stay away from us. He retreated from the demonstrations.

His talent had limits. As a boy, he excelled at most cerebral challenges, such as chess. But Peter played that game numerically, applying number values to the pieces—a queen equaled nine pawns, a bishop and knight equaled three—and envisioning their movements as numbers of squares on a grid of 64. This approach conquered good players, certainly most grade schoolers. But it lost against any spatial wizardry. His understanding of written English was higher than average, but only because he attributed numerical quantities and patterns to parts of speech and other grammatical measures. He knew verbs, nouns, adjectives, and adverbs because he needed to count them and place them in ratio-to-word totals.

By the fifth grade, he could diagram any sentence by approaching it as an equation. His sentences were perfect. His literal comprehension was perfect. He could make sentences clearly define his thoughts, but he could not use them to lead his thoughts. His essays were true, precise, unblemished, and entirely unprovocative.

The child excelled in music, but only up to a point. His parents, overjoyed initially when his piano teacher mentioned *prodigy*, were flattened when they heard his surgical playing style next to the music played by other boys and girls in competitions. Peter's father, the music scholar and yet more adoring parent, confessed to having a jaded ear for his son's playing. Some judges loved his playing, and he won two medals. I could not say for certain how far Peter carried his mathematical understanding of life. Did he measure his emotions in equations? Was love passion divided by sadness over the square root of time? Did he count his breaths? Did he count her tears?

Philip winced and snapped the book closed. He knew this narrator and recognized her anguish. He slid the book into its space on the shelf, the second to last of her five beautifully bound novels. She had sewn five copies of each one and dispersed them carefully among friends. The last of her books, and now it was final, he found inaccessible. Entitled *Slip*, it did just that as you tried to read it. Scenes often changed midstream. Passages then repeated themselves later, only to be changed yet again by those immediately following. Sentences returned, trying to clarify themselves. There was a character based on him in this novel, too, though he never read far enough to find out what happens to him.

In that week waiting for the books to arrive, he prepared his new apartment, which he secured on a monthly lease in a three-story brick row, directly above Baum's Clothing, along the old trolley line. Street noise helped him sleep. Throughout his life, his sleep was always a series of dots and dashes spaced by frequent wakings. Street noise, the sounds of others moving in the night, served as his most effective tranquilizer. The Eleventh Street line and the calls, whispers, coughs, and drunken laughs of its passengers as they boarded or disembarked caressed him back to sleep in his new place. Even after the trolley finished its final one a.m. run, the line's parallel bars embedded in the asphalt seemed to magnetically attract the night stragglers of Philly. And if sleep continued to elude him, Philip could draw his jacket over his sweats and walk around the corner to Finn McCool's or Ludwig's on Sansom and drink a whiskey in the three a.m. taper. The bartenders would play exercise equipment promos with the TV volume off and fill faux-wooden bowls with hard salted peas. The single whiskey, the knowledge that nothing was really disappearing in the night, the cold walk back to his apartment, and the mannequins wearing Eisenhower-era suits in Baum's display windows would combine to escort him back to sleep. A one-room studio with tea stains on the white stucco walls, the apartment held what he needed. He purchased a bed, a table, and a chair. From the Salvation Army in the Italian Quarter, he purchased an aqua-blue Naugahyde recliner for reading, and a tin stand to hold a lamp and a drink. He enjoyed the sound of glass on metal each time he returned his drink to the stand. The heavy-bottomed whiskey glass he purchased at the same thrift store. And, of course, he purchased bookshelves. These he bought new. Solid maple, no nails or glue, crafted by Mennonites near Harrisburg, the shelves cost more than all of his purchases combined, including the lease and security deposit for the apartment.

The insurance company let him keep his laptop now purged of all information. It came with a supplementary keyboard, with its right-hand side dominated by numbers and mathematical and trigonometric signs. This laptop he placed on the bare table along with a tin coaster he took from a bar on South Street. Could you write a story in numbers? she once asked him. I could then help you translate. She translated Spanish, Portuguese, some French and Italian, though insisted she spoke none of them very well.

Also in the days waiting for her books to arrive, he took long runs along Penn's Landing overlooking the Delaware and its docks, shipyards, and museumed sailing vessels. Or he would ride the subway up to Penn and run along the Schuylkill with its sycamore-canopied greenways. Still dressed in his running clothes, he would then stand beside the frog sundial in Rittenhouse Square, where he would watch workers hurry to their lunch spots. Then he would have his own lunch after the rush, eating plain yogurt or soup in an inexpensive teahouse while reading math and physics theory. If he found a teahouse that served borscht, he would have that and spatter the equations with brilliant flecks of beet juice. During the last spring snow—it had to be the last—he ran along the Schuylkill and watched the white flakes disappear above the grass and the new sycamore leaves, and then ran a second time that day along the Delaware as well, watching the snowfall evaporate over the tide-warmed water. The ferry to Camden cut a slight wake through the snowfall, a contrail that spun the flakes sideways before melting them.

As soon as he set up his e-mail, he received a request from the insurance firm for his consultation services on a brief investment project. He accepted on condition that he could work strictly from home. His second e-mail came from one of the firm's main competitors, asking for the same service on an amusingly similar investment project. He politely declined due to conflicting interests. How do you add risk to your life? she asked him in a moment of frustration. The numbers always fall in place for you, because that's what numbers do. I know it's more complicated than just that. That often equations take weeks to unwind, that they are marked by peaks and valleys and little mysteries here and there, and that they involve experimentation. But you need to go somewhere where they speak another language, where you have to think in another language. Where you end up dreaming in another language. Come with me. I could translate for you. He was married at the time, to his first wife Rebecca, a mathematician as well, who agreed that the simple equation was always worth attempt.

The third e-mail was an invite from Nicole, his stepdaughter from that first marriage. Her message was curt as usual: Be there. And although he had not heard from her in two months, he knew of what and where she spoke. And he knew she must be in the midst of one of her so-called sea changes, and that her family was troubling her, and that she needed to clear her head. He even knew there would be some shift in her look. A freshman at Rutgers, she would take the brief train ride down from New Brunswick to see him, to race him. Philip wondered if and how others could sense change in him. And would she—Nicole or Irma—deem this shift in his life a sea change. It isn't a change in the sea, his stepdaughter once informed him, but transformation brought about by the sea. The very atmosphere around me would look different, feel different, if you were paying attention.

So on the Saturday in the middle of that preparation week, after fifty minutes of morning consultation work, he ran the River to River 10k through downtown Philadelphia with Nicole. He clocked his personal best for that distance, beating the time he had set twenty years ago at the age of twenty-one, when he ran next to Irma for most of the race, before kicking away at the very end, counting all 243 of his final strides and all 48.6 exhalations. Divide strides by five and you get breaths in a decent kick.

At the starting line to the River to River, Nicole did not appear until just before the gun sounded. Her timing was so close, he knew she must have been hiding in the crowd, watching him search for her, trying to note whether he was looking forward to seeing her, or put out, or just indifferent, concerned with nothing more than running well. She approached from behind, surprising him with a shove to his shoulder. She smiled at him, lifted her brow, then nodded him forward just as the starter raised the gun and fired. She beat him by thirty-seven seconds, an eternity, and he never saw her during the race. In the strain of the run, as he pushed against the pain in his lungs and thighs, he had only that glimpse given to him before the start. Her smile and lift and nod. He never saw Nicole as much as he wanted to, after her father came back into her and Rebecca's life. Isn't that like losing the race after you've taken the lead in the final stretch? Irma asked him. You'd be nothing more than a change of mind, really.

Nicole found Philip as he emerged, gasping but grinning, from the finish chute. Together they had bagels and pineapple juice provided by the race sponsors beneath a tree alongside the river. She stretched on the grass as if it were summer rather than spring. She was already tan, and light from the early sun formed in shards along the sinews of her legs and shoulders. Her hair had an out-of-season shine and streak to it, as though she had been swimming a lot, and it was gathered in a less sporting ponytail, almost a chignon. He knew never to ask her about herself, about any of her troubles, if you truly wanted to learn anything. Engagement with Nicole was elegantly, mercilessly Heisenbergian, and this fact only grew more definitive as she matured.

"Do you remember Irma?" he asked as his breathing lightened.

"Your book friend. Sure. You took Sam and me on picnics with her. We'll always remember those. But they weren't much as picnics. More Frisbee than food. Sam always worried that Mom would lose you to her. Ha. He'd always point and say, 'See!' when you'd sit alone with her. Whenever she came over to the house, he'd spy on her."

Philip was surprised by her response, by the amount of words. "Did he ever see anything?"

"I don't know," she answered. "But I know she caught him once. She barred him with her arm—she was stronger than she looked. She told him if he wanted to spy, then he better make sure he was prepared for whatever he discovered. That scared Sam."

She continued her stretches, straightening one leg and pulling the tip of her shoe with her fingertips, concentrating there, unconcerned with any words—hers or his. Philip felt his own muscles beginning to cool and stiffen as he sat on the grass. He waited for her to ask why he brought up Irma, someone long out of her life, someone possibly forgotten. But she acted as though they had been discussing the weather. The more precisely the position is determined, claims Heisenberg, the less precisely the momentum is known in this instant, and vice versa.

"She's disappeared," he told her.

Nicole stretched her back, arching it, touching forehead to knee. He was not sure she heard him. Then—

"You mean you lost contact?" She sustained her stretch, fingertips touching balletlike above the tip of her shoe, her nose just over her knee.

"No. She very much contacted me. She's sending me all her books."

She lifted herself gracefully, spreading her arms, angling her hands upward, ninety degrees at wrist. She slowly looked at one hand, then the other.

"All?"

"All three hundred fifty-one of them," he replied.

"That's not very good disappearing. What will you do?"

"Read them," he answered.

"I meant about *her*. Are you going to *look* for her?"

"When I figure out how one would do that."

"You just start. I hate mathematicians," she said as she twisted away from him, lifting her arms and bringing her fingertips together above her head. "To think I once had not one, but *two* for parents." She stretched her neck backward, the morning sun on her face, eyes closed lightly, almost disdainfully. But there was sadness there, too, in the overdefiant lift in her chin, the tremble in her eyelashes. He would not have been surprised to see her chin quiver. He felt very much the stepfather—the ex-stepfather—without license to pry. Probably there was some boy trouble, some questioning of her place in the world, the college world, new paths presenting themselves. All of the above, he thought. Unlike most, she and her brother both never tried to talk their way toward revelation. If pressed, they would lead you and themselves astray, like ill-chosen formulae in a longer proof.

Nicole was eight and Sam was seven when Philip entered their lives. He did not know what to do with them, and so he taught them how to play sports. He bought them baseball gloves, took them to the Sourland fields, and hit infield to them into the twilight. Nicole and Sam took turns fielding second and shortstop, but he could see, in the enthusiasm of her crouch, that Nicole preferred short. They found a suburban basketball court on the grassy banks of the Raritan River and he perfected their jump shots. He taught them how to run the 100-, 5,000- and 10,000-meter races. He was quarterback to their receiving when the Jersey woods turned color. And then Nicole developed a strong arm and took turns at quarterback. They designed plays and pass patterns in the infield dirt and then ran them in the outfield grass. He showed them how to pitch horseshoes and throw a Frisbee backhand, forehand, and overhand. He never helped them with their homework and never spoke math to them. Their schoolwork suffered, but for the first time in their lives, their mother told him, they were sleeping soundly. Their questions still aren't answered but their bodies are tired.

His two ex-wives left him for the same two reasons. One, they felt excluded by his way of perceiving the world—them—in numbers, ratios, and equations. Rebecca, the math professor, experienced this exclusion intensely, the way an anthropologist might begin to feel among her field subjects once she began understanding the intrinsic and irremovable bones of their culture. Was it envy, relief, befuddlement, emptiness, or something else that she felt? Two, they found him too understanding. Though they could spur all other passions in him, they could never spark his anger. Perhaps this had something to do with the first reason, his inherent embrace of numbers and the rationality they provided. But because he *always* understood Rebecca and Beatrice, they felt that he did not understand them deeply enough. Everyone wants to have something internal that cannot be understood, but he denied them that. Irma writes in *The Theory of Peter Navratil* that he never put himself in his own equations.

This, she notes early on in the story as Peter Navratil takes the long train ride to Michoacán, went back to the limits of his talent. He understood math theory well. In fact, he understood any good theory well because he could transpose its elements to numerical values, its logic to equations. He often fine-tuned the formulae and equations of new math theory, which he read as soon as it was published, and sent these elegant adjustments back to the authors. Once or twice a year he received a manuscript from an author or editor seeking his review of the math. But, Sylvia the narrator notes, he could not do theory himself. This, according to her own theory of Peter Navratil, was because he could never put himself in his own equations. He would never develop into a theoretical mathematician. He could only be the best calculator, the best statistician, the best vessel of comprehension. The only real way to feel him, understand him, maybe love him, was to use him. But only, the narrator claims, in the way he uses his most precious numbers—not to manipulate, but to follow and see.

After he and Nicole cooled down from the race, Philip treated her to brunch at Carman's off the Eleventh Street rail, where they discussed her chances of making the Rutgers basketball and softball teams. In Carman's, the waiters and waitresses always introduced you to other patrons—then conversations were open to all. It was on this afternoon then that Nicole received advice on her jump shot from a Penn history professor who took everybody back to the black-sneaker days of Bob Pettit. Over his omelet and sweet potato hash browns, he demonstrated the exact arm position before release. Carman herself, beautiful as a Roller Derby queen, pantomimed the precise motions of Pettit's jumper as the history professor talked her through it. The attention and its tangent was exactly what Philip had hoped for Nicole when he brought her here. And though Nick did not quite smile, she did lift her face to them with an angle of interest and consideration. When they were done eating, Philip left her to enjoy the city on her own for the rest of her Saturday, believing that was what she wanted. On the sidewalk outside the café stood a blue doghouse. Over its little archway, a painted sign warned that the dog inside was "not necessarily nice." Philip peered inside the arch. Nicole came up beside him, returning from somewhere down the sidewalk. She pressed her hands together in front of her lips, prayerlike.

"Run with me some more?"

He had underestimated her sadness. There was anxiety in it, a circumference to it. It outlined her, stood her ready to be cut away. He groaned and rubbed his back. His hips ached from the morning race, his calves and hamstrings had tightened, and his left instep burned with tendonitis. His stomach was full and sleepy. Thin wintry clouds were stretching across the sky, cooling what began as a warm spring day.

"Please?" she asked. "Just an easy five?"

A simple but important request by someone he cared about divided by time plus ability. With the heel of his hand, he kneaded his right hip flexor.

"Sure, Nick. An easy five. I'll show you my new route." He opened his hand to her, only to usher her along. She surprised him by taking hold of it, wordlessly, without smile, without looking, but with a firmness and tether that concerned him.

That first time he took Sam and Nicole somewhere, on his own, at their mother's insistence, they existed for him as nothing more than two numbers representing their ages—7 and 8 alone on a cloudy afternoon at the

Sourland playing fields. They did not speak to him and they did not look back at him as they moved around on the grass infield in aimless, slow ricochets, a cell-like Brownian motion. He gave them their new Phillie ball caps and mitts, his entry gifts to them, and they both put their gloves on the wrong hand. Sam almost immediately placed his glove over his face and watched his sister through the gaps. Be nice, she shushed. She pushed the mitt away from Sam's face and straightened his cap. Philip showed them where to position themselves between the bases. When he hit the first grounder, it passed softly between them on its way to the outfield as Sam and Nicole, with only a casual turn of their heads, watched it. Nicole understood everything first and took the initial step toward the ball. But then, after that one step, she halted, let her little brother grasp the entire concept and scamper toward the ball. His first throw, a natural, went right to his sister, who caught it with a similar ease of motion. They were either fooling him with a brother-sister revenge on their mother's suitor or they were untapped infield prodigies, pure as whole numbers. Philip did not care. He was fascinated by them, by their little interactions. By Nicole taking that first hint of a step, then letting her brother go. Let him go and be the one. They began immediately to become undiscovered numbers to him, she tangential to wariness, he signified by experimentation, but both at work within the same proof.

When Irma's books finally arrived on a dark Monday afternoon, he did shelve them alphabetically, the way she had packed them. But he planned to approach them using 3, 4, 7 sampling. This, he often explained to Irma, was one of the simplest and most effective formulae for achieving a representative sample of any finite collection. 3 was the first prime number, excluding the unique case of 2, and 4 was the first true composite and their sum was 7, another prime. The integers—3, 4, 7—functioned like magnetic prompts in a pendulum's swing. Irma never let him fully explain the formula, rolling her eyes at the first point of boredom (the first variable n), then groaning, then finally pretending to gasp for oxygen. The first calculation, the first swing of the pendulum applied to

Irma's collection, brought him to Borges's *Ficciones*, the translated version. He noted that the preceding volume on the shelf was the original Spanish text and he remembered her telling him once that Borges would have wanted it that way. Philip had no idea what she meant by that. He knew nothing about the author, except that he was blind. He had never read anything by him.

He placed the Borges on the tin stand by the Naugahyde recliner, fetched a bourbon and ice in his recently acquired whiskey glass, adjusted the lampshade, and then sat down. He raised the glass of bourbon to Irma and her collection.

"It is certainly pretty, if nothing else," he said. These were Irma's favorite words of approval. Just then he felt a rush of sadness, the surprising draw of a gathering wave, and it did not let up. *I leave my books to Philip.* He quietly cried for her, the suddenness and finality of her collection there on his maple shelves. He wondered if he could ever figure what happened. Where she had gone. Her hiding place would include anywhere books gathered, in any language, any form. And its location might change with her mood and whatever discoveries she made. It puzzled him anew that she would leave the books to him. At first he figured that he was the only one of her friends who did not already have most of these works. She would certainly argue that he was the one person she knew in the world who most needed to read the books. But the value of them, their own inherent worth and their value to her, was what struck him now, preparing to move through his 3, 4, 7 formula, a sampling that if carried out to its fullest extent would hit upon all 351 selections in seemingly random order, but without repeating one.

He opened the Borges.

Welcome to my world, it said in pencil on the flyleaf. Far beneath this was Borges's autograph, also in pencil. The lead in Borges's scrawl appeared heavier. The space between the greeting and the signature seemed to indicate, too, that the two inscriptions had been written separately, at different times by different hands. But Borges was blind. Maybe he lost his sense of location on the page as he hurriedly autographed the text. Philip held the page to the light. The handwriting, between greeting and signature, seemed comparable to a degree. Using his bookmark, which was a ten-centimeter copper ruler, he measured the millimeters between letters. He turned the page. Another flyleaf and another penciled inscription: *It doesn't matter.*

He moved to rise from his recliner, then hesitated, took a sip of the bourbon, and leaned back. He read the volume's eighteen stories over the six following days. He loved them. Borges was a mathematician. *He could write a story in numbers.* Philip wanted to ask Irma, at the end of each story, Why didn't you insist that I read these? Why, as we sat around a table with your friends, didn't you turn to me and say, "You really need to read these, Pip"? She always used this name when they drank together, with her friends, and she needed to turn to him to help them all resurface from the murky depths of their arguments concerning writing and purpose. She was aware of how much the name irked him and he was aware of how much she was irked by her and her friends' need to turn to him, the only one of them still afloat in these sessions.

His favorite from *Ficciones* was the third story, "Lichen," the tale of the gravedigger in Alcala de Henares who discovers first a code amid the epitaphs of the headstones, then another contained in the cosines of the headstones' arches, then finally another in the death dates. The grave-digger frightens away his fiancée as he tries to show her what he has discovered. What exactly the gravestones lead him to is lost, however, when he discovers the final stone through the careful triangulation of the three codes. The final stone's inscriptions have been eaten away by a beautiful spread of lichen whose bright edges contain the story itself. Borges, at least the man in the story identified as Borges, ignores the gravedigger's declaration of defeat and is left desperately trying to scrape away the lichen.

The story left Philip sleepless, even more insomniac than usual. He considered first a night run, an easy five under the lights of Penn's Landing. But "Lichen" had rendered him somewhat frightened, afraid of the dark—and the banks of the Delaware would be dark. He took a walk down Fourth and joined the crowds and lights of South Street. People on the sidewalk were opening their dark coats, slowly realizing that the air was warming to spring, unveiling bright and loose clothes beneath dull wool and felt. He saw cleavage and tattoos on black skin. He smelled sweat, perfume, and tobacco. People spoke loudly, laughed to punctuate their sentences, and ignored traffic signals and crosswalks. Still, there was hesitation in their motion and noise as every other breeze brought a chill with it. The music clubs and theaters were letting out and people were searching for ways to extend the night.

Philip entered the TLA, slipping through the crowd exiting the music club. He chose a stool from the many empty ones around the angled bar. Night air blew through the wide-open doors. The music the roadies had chosen to listen to as they packed up the stage was Sampson's "Demeter in the Grass," he guessed. The trumpet was soft, a rest for their ears. A blue stage light colored it all. He ordered a bourbon with ice and as he playfully dialed the glass on the bar top, a woman who reminded him of Irma left her place along the adjacent side of the bar and took a seat next to him, though one stool removed. She placed her bottle of beer between them like a declaration.

Her resemblance to Irma increased—to a heart-fluttering level—as she leaned toward the bar in the bluish light. But he wondered now if anyone remotely similar would gain semblance in Irma's slipstream, if that was one of many small prices he would be forever paying, his eyes following her colors and impressions, seeking the grooves left in his senses. The woman gave him a suspect look, maybe reading some of his thoughts, ready to get up and go before he uttered the most common of bar lines. Instead, widening her eyes playfully at him, she turned squarely to him, then lifted her chin in a kind of challenge.

"I just like it better when the show's over," he told her, compelled by her look to explain his late arrival.

"Aftermath," she said, looking at the bar mirror, savoring the word with its end lightly between her teeth.

"Yes," he replied as she returned her gaze to him. "What we do in it."

"Most people leave it. That's what makes it aftermath. That's what makes it worthwhile." She lightly adjusted her beer on the bar top, using thumb and middle finger. Then she reached to lift his drink, tilted it to her nose, and replaced it precisely into its water ring. She looked at him as though she knew him that much better.

"I didn't mean . . ." He drew his whiskey closer. "I didn't mean *we* as other people."

"You meant it as you and I?" she said before he could go on.

"Not exactly. I . . ."

"Then you and someone else? You and everybody else?"

He sipped his drink, then set it down gently, turning it once. Then adjusted her beer likewise, the two drinks aligned. "You and I," he said. "Here."

Eventually, he told her about the Borges story. She played with a Chinese finger puzzle woven of straw and painted the colors of the Mexican flag. Her two index fingers were trapped in the puzzle ends as she listened or did not listen to Philip. Though dumbly ensnared, her hands looked elegant, fingers evenly spaced, in adagio. Her dark hair was loose except for a small, neatly braided lock that was bleached white, blue in the stage light. She looked Mexican or Italian or Puerto Rican or Jewish or Lebanese or just from New Jersey. She could smile with one side of her mouth.

"I have seen you before," he paused to tell her during his summary of the Borges. "I have." He hoped that embedding this in his retelling of the story would render the line genuine. She seemed, at least, amused.

"I know you're not the kind to come home with me now," she told him when he was done with the Borges and done explaining how it had made him afraid of the dark. She freed her fingers from the woven tube. "So my number is on this," she said, handing him the toy.

Her scent, fresh tar, lingered after she eased herself from the bar. She left with a series of movements that brought her body close to his face and then suddenly away. He walked the thinning crowd of South Street to Eleventh. The last trolley was an hour gone, and he was resigned to walking in the apocalyptic glow from the empty stops. The woman from the bar found him. She pulled alongside him on a Vespa.

"I thought you were afraid of the dark," she said.

He took the ride she offered and gently held her waist as she buzzed them down Eleventh Street. At each red light she pushed her lower back into him in order to brace the bike with her leg. He knew she could feel his erection, which did not diminish between stops, and in fact began to rise in anticipation of each approaching red light.

"Sorry," he said after the fourth stop, sensing her half-smile.

She dropped him in front of his brick apartment building.

"Call," she reminded him before she buzzed away. "You have my finger puzzle."

T W O

The second calculation, according to the formula's design, swung him toward the end of the collection, Turgenev's *Sketches from a Hunter's Album*. He set the volume on the tin stand and fingered the soft leather of its burgundy binding. The book was flexible, like a missal. He could almost roll it up and tuck it in a pocket. He wondered if Irma had re-bound it and taken it backpacking somewhere, and after he read the first sketch he decided that she most definitely had done this. He read the first sketch standing beside the lamp. He had meant only to sample the first sentence or two before fetching his bourbon and settling himself in the recliner.

He read the next two sketches sitting in the recliner. Philip was drawn by the hunter's guileful movement between the solitude of his excursions and the company he found in country homes and camps. But Turgenev's work with light struck him most profoundly. Dusk, dawn, gathering storms, distant windows, campfires were all deftly lit by the economical prose. Light often drew the hunter's course or carried his final thoughts and impressions of a place with its color and wane. The light in the Turgenev eased the fear of dark created by the Borges story. But still, after reading the first three sketches, Philip went back to the Borges and read "Lichen" once again, perhaps to restore that fear. There was a palpable, if undirected, desire in that fear. In the Borges story, he found that the description of the gravedigger's fiancée resembled the woman from the TLA. Josefina had a way, writes Borges, of speaking while not facing you, then finally turning to you when her words were finished. Everything she said this way. Sefi's arms and legs were long and elegant and the considering expression in her eyes and mouth constantly pulled you toward embrace. She wore a small braid that was not the same color as the rest of her black hair. It seemed a tiny coif, a gesture, too young for her, an artifact from an age she had left or was always in the process of leaving.

This description, out of context from the whole story, drove him to Irma's fourth bound manuscript, *The Theory of Peter Navratil*, and its description of the character of Ofelia—Feli for short—a stage actress who performed in some street theater in Pátzcuaro and who bore an ever-shifting resemblance to the woman Peter Navratil sought. She spoke to the lake, then looked at him. She spoke to the lake isle, then looked at him. She helped him release the salamanders they had rescued from the market, and tapped the moist head of each amphibian with a delicate finger, sending them on their way into Lake Pátzcuaro. One small lock of her black hair remained dyed red from her last stage performance.

He failed to sense any connection between Sefi and Feli until he had met the woman at the TLA. The equation was simple: Irma had borrowed, knowingly or unknowingly, from Borges; Philip's own exposure to both fictional characters led him to project them both onto the real-life character of the Vespa woman. She was $(n-1)$. After three more of the Turgenev sketches, he remained afraid of the dark and decided to call her.

But the Chinese finger puzzle offered him nothing. He examined its sides and inner edges yet could find no writing. He assumed a piece of paper had fallen from it or that the woman never had any intention of giving him her name and number. "I know you're not the kind to come home with me now." How did she know to say this? He turned to another description of Peter Navratil. The narrator, Sylvia, remarks that he was never one to have sex with a woman immediately or even soon after meeting her. He had to date her first, even if those few dates were pure ritual, ceremonial pretexts to blunt expressions of physical desire. At Santa Cruz, Peter dated or did not date me for three years before we undressed each other one afternoon and did just about everything in the open sunlight of my boyfriend's one-room surf shack. The plain light aroused us and kept arousing us. After we were finally done, there was no hiding what had taken place in the room and we just left. We did leave a window open, but the salt and seaweed air smelled much the same as the feral steam we left in the room.

Philip returned to the TLA, arriving again in that hour between the show's end and the club's closing, but did not find Vespa. The rest of the night his sleep was more broken than usual and he ended up running the banks of the Schuylkill as dawn broke through the angles of the Philadelphia skyline. His desire to solve the equation of Feli, Sefi, and Vespa was indivisible from the want to fit himself behind her again.

Unshowered after the long run, he read more of the Turgenev while the city worked. Turgenev's sketches left him restless, dislocated, and vaguely guilty. He found no math in them, but nonetheless felt compelled to move from one to the next, following the hunter's journey. The ever-varying light in the sketches continued to mesmerize him; that he did feel and quantify. By late morning, sticky in his running clothes, he felt the way he had in college after morning lab—accomplished, silent, and not responsible while the city around him worked to create the day's noise. During a similar spring hour, more than twenty years ago, he found Irma in the same condition in the plain morning light of her boyfriend's studio in Santa Cruz. She and Philip left the windows open when they were finished.

Showered and dressed as if for work, he took the Turgenev to lunch at a teahouse and read more, a bowl of borscht and a cup of plain yogurt beside him. When the Living Relic first appeared in the sketches, the book finally became a wonderful, complex equation for him, eloquent and pliable as a work of calculus that emerges with the first appearance of e. He spent the rest of the afternoon with the book, carrying it with him, finally taking it back to his recliner where he could ease completely into the language. Turgenev shone a fire-colored light on the old woman, projecting her image back through all of the earlier sketches. When the hunter finds the Living Relic, he finds that which he has been searching for, without knowing that there was something to seek, without knowing he was ever searching. With her appearance the order and composition of the sketches, seemingly random, become necessary and illuminating.

A two-word (when and where) message from Nicole, challenging him to an evening run, prevented him from completing the book. Tired, stiff, and sore from his dawn run, he agreed to meet her atop the Walnut Street walkover at Penn's Landing, where his route began. He felt as though he could promise her nothing.

He never became anything like a father to them. He rarely advised Nicole or Sam about anything outside of athletics, and even that he gave only when asked. Any needed math help came from Rebecca, who was the better teacher. Who was the strongest mathematician remained arguable among all of them. Whenever he found himself alone with one stepchild, they would discuss the progress of the other. Sam would tell him about Nicole winning her first cross-country race and how she would not say anything to anyone afterward; Nicole would tell him about Sam racing kids years older than he, about his freckled face turning red with frustration, anger, tears, even if he won. Sometimes it looks like he's imagining someone ahead of him, Nicole would say, even when he's far out in front. And Philip would respond by taking them to another sport, a new one, even. Rebecca found him once working on his stepfather formula, Philip not moving quickly enough to obscure the pages. She found it sweet and posed some adjustments to the asymptotes. They'll take you to infinity, she warned him.

The sun was already behind the skyline when he found Nicole on the Walnut Street walkover stretching her calves and back, her hands pressed to the brick railing as she stared over the twilit Delaware. Her empty expression filled upon seeing him, rose somehow without actually smiling. He was limping from the tendonitis in his left heel and shortening his stride due to the tightness in his right hip flexor. He waved off her concern and asked what brought her to town.

"Just this," she answered.

She turned again toward the broad Delaware and then shifted her gaze to his face and spoke to his questioning expression.

"Running with you—if I'm ahead, behind, tied—it's so silent, Philip. I know you're there counting your strides, even though you say you don't. And it's so quiet."

He squinted upward, the way he did whenever offered an equation that took more than the usual second or two. In Nick's little equation, quiet seems to appear twice as a variable, Q. You can watch him calculate.

You can't resist watching, as his sincerity makes him handsome. In this equation it is an easy mistake to equate silent with quiet. Q is not s. He is getting better at translating words into numbers, perhaps from the reading. Silent implies there is something to say. Quiet implies completion. In Nick's equation, what's in between s and Q is his spatial relationship to her, then her cognizant relationship to him along with his vain attempt to deny his own nature. Yes, numbers do have natures specific to them. The nature of e is different from that of i or π. The closeness in nature of e and π, in fact, indicates that they are nonetheless different and that a spectrum of characteristics exists among them all.

Philip replied to Nicole without words, quiet rather than silent. Her father, Andrew—the one who reclaimed the lead from Philip—was not overly talkative; he was kind, not loud, but he had a way of speaking as though he were always quoting something, as though he were pulling knowledge and observations from a ready source, an invisible stream of abiding that flowed through the air between you and him. He often turned his hands in it as he spoke, offering some of it to you. It could be quite comforting. Poised to race atop the walkover, Philip merely cleared his throat, smiled, and nodded to Nicole, knowing that she would not smile in return. He then kicked into a run, jumping the gun on her and gaining a sizable lead as he banked off the ramp and onto Penn's Landing. She cried out with a playful anger he was happy to hear along with the rapid pop of her strides behind him.

In *The Theory of Peter Navratil*, Sylvia says of Peter: His father was a music professor who defected from Czechoslovakia in 1964, the year Peter was born. His father was also the Slovak 3,000-meter steeplechase champion, but was denied appointment to the Olympic team that year because he taught Janáček as insurgent. Tomas Navratil defected during a meet in Switzerland. His defection was more or less shepherded by the team and the Czech government, though Tomas learned to play up the drama of it all when he told the story in later years. I could sense he wanted me to write about it, Sylvia tells the reader. His mother was a U.S.-born physics professor who was always watched with suspicion during her university tenure in Bratislava. This accommodated the defection. She then taught under the suspicion of the U.S. government during her tenure in California, and her adopted accent grew more pronounced in defiance. Of Slovak descent also, she ran a twelve-minute 3,000-meter steeplechase only a month after giving birth to Peter. Tomas still disputes this time and questions the staggering of the hurdles.

The 1964 Tokyo Olympics were televised in brand-new Mondovision, broadcasting live events to all parts of the world. Tomas and Anna watched the 3,000-meter steeplechase on a small black and white TV in a friend's home in Berkeley.

Gaston Roelants of Belgium took the gold medal and Maurice Herriot of Great Britain won the silver. The Soviet Ivan Belyayev, a man Tomas raced against but never came close to beating, won the bronze medal with a time of 8:33.84. After the race, Tomas turned to Anna, who was nursing infant Peter, and announced that Europeans would forever be eclipsed by the great Kenyan runners he had seen in Switzerland that year. Forever is a rather extreme claim, Anna replied. In the 1968 Olympics in Mexico City, Amos Biwott of Kenya won the gold medal in the 3,000-meter steeplechase and his compatriot Benjamin Kogo took the silver. Kenyans would win the event in each of the Olympics in which they competed through 2004 (they did not compete for political reasons in 1976 and 1980). In 1968, right after Biwott won the gold, four-year-old Peter Navratil was walked through his first 3,000-meter steeplechase by his mother and father on a track in Palo Alto, California. He laughed when they splashed him in the water hurdle.

Philip quickly lost his stolen lead to his stepdaughter. She passed him with another brief yelp and continued to stride away as he winced through the pain in his heel and hip. When his muscles loosened, he veered off the path and hurdled some stone benches. He had to step on the bench tops as he cleared them, a move perfected by Biwott to conserve energy without losing time. As he veered back to the path, he could see Nick far ahead of him, her ponytail swinging over vigorous strides. Her figure shone coppery in the settling twilight and under the filtered lights of the walkway. He cleared three puddles left by spring rain as he tried to make up some of the distance.

A woman riding a motor scooter merged off Dock Street and banked onto the harbor road beside him. The drone of her bike subsided as she dropped her speed to make the turn. He stutter-stepped and looked over his shoulder. But even in the waning light, he could see that the banner of hair beneath her helmet was too long and light. The curve of her back was familiar, though, and he watched it arch as she crouched into acceleration and vanished into the sparkle of streetlights. A hundred meters ahead of him on the walkway, Nick's bright form glided beside the ancient tall ships crowding the dock. And as Philip reached the cluster of tall ships, their white masts and yardarms bare and thin against the darkening sky, he found himself in another silent cry for Irma, the pace of his breath slightly hitched. Irma ran best with a hangover and often competed in a Saturday morning 10k that way, usually beating him. She called it running on fumes. After a race, she would crack open a cold beer—race sponsors often doled out free cans back then—and sit on the grass and smile at him as he caught his breath. She would make fun of his postrace stretching, remind him that he was not preparing for the Olympic 3,000-meter steeplechase, that they were just running poseurs and there was no need to call any more attention to this fact with awkward body positions. Relax, Pip. We're young. And he would drink the rest of her beer after her first sip harshly reminded her of the night before.

Irma narrates in *Slip*, through the character of Alma, in a present-tense voice criticized in several publishers' rejections for creating too much artifice and distance. She narrates: He holds the gift he unwraps for me. He holds it between us, our breath thrumming the ends of the handmade wrapping paper. He unwraps it for me because he is so proud of the gift, because he finds the Prague blue oil in a tiny supply shop in Tijuana, because he is afraid I will love—in this moment—the gift more than I will love him. I deepen the Prague blue with black to attain the precise color of a tabletop in a Jersey diner. One publisher told Irma to make her characters less removed. For the fifth time over the course of fifteen years, he rejected one of her novels. The letterhead on each rejection reflected his steady ascent through the ranks of the publishing house, from assistant editor to publisher. She sent him a response to this final rejection. I wonder. What if you came to my shop and saw what I do to books? How I tear out their innards sometimes, only to transplant them. How I make them look the way they once looked, or even better than they once looked. How they thought they looked once, when your predecessors first released the scent of their linen and leather. Philip warned her about bridge-burning. But I really do wonder this, she told him. Where would his eyes fall first? Where might they linger? she asked as she sat before her press, her bare instep against a book fossil she was using as a footrest. She always visited the East Coast while one of her manuscripts was being submitted and Philip would get many chances to see her. Then he, in turn, would visit west during her binding of the manuscript. Binding them herself was the only way she could keep herself from continuously changing them. "I can never get them quite right," she told him. The books she made appeared more beautiful and singular than any of the published versions and he could never remember which ones had made it "out there" and which had not.

Philip visited Irma in her shop to watch her sew the bindings for *Slip*. The wine smell of shaped leather filled the room. She remained wide-eyed, caught in battle, as she worked the awl through the compressed pages. She twisted the augers on her press tighter. It's like building their coffins, she said, smiling partially. We end up in beautiful coffins, more beautiful than our houses, more beautiful than our lives. She bound *Slip* in kidskin dyed with genuine indigo. She gave him a copy and he could never finish reading it. The gift-giving scene was rendered at least seven times through the course of the novel. In it, she imagines them as married, with an eight-year-old daughter.

Near the end of their run, he tried one more time to make up some distance on Nicole. Perhaps she sensed this from a hundred meters ahead and increased her pace. Or perhaps he was too old now, and any increased effort on his part only compensated for deteriorating skill and strength. The two of them glided along the bank, the black Delaware now in dusk and reflecting the lights of the two cities it divided. Only if you knew the two runners could you see how they were together, how they ran together. Following their run, he treated her to beer at Ludwig's, where the barmaid winked at Nicole's false ID, pretending to not quite see it in the dimness, and brought them a bowl of marble-sized pickled onions with their pitcher. Nicole seemed happy, at least in a momentary way.

She speared the little onions with a pickle fork, laughed at them, then ate them, making each one pop inside her mouth. She drained her beer with the ease one expects from a Rutgers freshman. He told her about the Turgenev and how he was reading Irma's collection. She feigned great interest. Oh, Philip. I'm glad you're reading something without numbers in it. Can I come see it? But before he could extend an invitation, she reversed. She gazed just to the side of him, imagining the collection, it seemed, its colors and breadth, a brittle trepidation in the angle of her brow. On second thought, no, she said. After a pause, she shook her head as if asked again.

And her responses remained no more than one sentence deep. Yes, she remembered Irma well. Even when she brought up Sam, in order to leave the subject of Irma and her books—which was beginning to bore and irritate her—her words dipped and trailed like a bird gliding just over water. It's strange and scary, she said, watching your little brother turn into a man, something with shoulders and thin whiskers, racing against real athletes. Like her phrasings she seemed resolved, flying fast and low for now, moving past everything in the whiskey light of an evening run along the landing. And he felt it was all he could do to let her go that way. Can you help me know them? he asked Irma once when they were his. Can you help them know me? No, she answered. Actually, I can't.

He finished *Sketches from a Hunter's Album* that evening, physically unable to do much more than sink into his recliner, turn pages, and lift his bourbon glass. The way Turgenev signed off at the conclusion, with "Good Night" instead of "The End," seemed fitting as well as amusing. The hunter says Good Night, closing the light of the sketches but letting the reader know it is possible he will see you in the morning. At the very bottom of the final page was a pencil sketch of a stick man running. Philip closed the Turgenev after staring blankly at the sketch for some time. He stacked the book on top of *Slip* and the Borges, which remained teetering on the little tin stand, vying for space with the glass and the lamp. Without dowsing the lamp, he pulled a cover over himself and remained in the recliner and drifted into a half-lidded doze, a point of consciousness where he could sense the early intrusion of dreams. The books on his shelf, with their gem-colored spines, together appeared as some calliope-like musical instrument. He believed he could play them by gently hammering the spines with wooden spoons. He reversed his two runs of the day, his mind's way perhaps of undoing the pain and injury inflicted on his body. He ran with Nicole, then alone, then he was running with Irma and she was young and swift and the only way he could keep up with her was to draft off her contrail. The ships and syca-more banks of the Philly riverfront interspersed with the surf shacks and cliffs of California's Central Coast. And then they were running along the wide stone paths beside the Guadalquivir River in Seville.

She coaxed Philip and Beatrice to travel there with her, to go as a trio. Beatrice remained suspicious and intrigued. Both suspicion and intrigue resolved on a night when they drank absinthe and opened the balcony windows to let in the warm air, the scent of wine-splashed stone and the music and calls of a city that did not seem to sleep. He believes Bea-trice made the first suggestive move, crossing her tan legs in a way that opened her robe. Philip believes he was the last to move, though his lack of movement on the sofa was what allowed the three of them to wrap themselves together. Beatrice and Irma first gazed at each other across him, then kissed above him, their breasts dovetailing, then pressing and trembling together. He remembers thinking, What does the third do? But this was answered when he joined his tongue with their tongues. He heard or felt a roar of wind as he tried then stopped trying to distinguish which tongue was Beatrice and which was Irma. He felt that arousing kind of jealousy when it was Beatrice who paused to choreograph their final climax, firmly taking hold of Irma's thighs while sliding her own hips beneath Philip and embracing him with her thighs. With a pitch of her shoulders, she thrust Irma backward, into his arms.

Irma left the next morning, taking the train to Córdoba before Bea-trice awoke. The first African wind blew into Seville that morning, marking the beginning of the Spanish summer and its building heat. He believes he caught the first scent of bruised orange petals coming through the still-opened doors of the balcony.

Irma traveled alone through southern Spain and Madrid and Barce-lona, sending postcards to their rental in Seville. She did not return until their month was nearly ended and the cusp between spring and summer had been decided by the unrelenting heat of the Andalusian sun and the Saharan winds. On the night of her return, it became clear that all three of them had thought of more things to do together. They spread the mattress on the floor and opened the balcony windows to the night heat, the brown Sevillan moon, the sleepless laughter from the streets and the scent of wine corks. It was even better this time, with no pretense or inhibition. They removed their clothes and then poured the wine. Once again Beatrice arranged them, understanding first that passionate fumbling and improvisation was good, but that firm and decisive holds and positions and commitments produced the most intense pleasure. It was the most fun she had ever had in a foreign country, she told him after Irma returned to the States.

He only saw Irma twice more after that, both during family visits west, when he went to her shop to watch her bind the five copies of *Slip*. He did not cheat on Beatrice, not with Irma or anyone. He and Irma spoke of Seville, though, as they sipped sherry in the cool of her workshop. And he wondered if those nights in Seville marked both the apex of his life with Beatrice and the beginning of the logarithmic spiral that defined the end of their marriage. In the upwelling heat just before siesta, he showed Beatrice and Irma the decorative patterns based on logarithmic spirals that had been hewn into the walls and archways of Seville's Town Hall by sixteenth century stonemasons decades before Napier even discovered logarithms. "Don't ruin it for us," said Beatrice.

Irma stayed outside the downward spiral of Philip and Beatrice's relationship. However, he could tell from phone conversations and e-mail exchanges with Irma that she paid some visits east without telling him. Math, higher and lower, was always good for filling in gaps. When she looked at him without saying anything, he could sense that she explored areas of his life without his knowledge, let alone without his approval. You do it to me, she argued. Just because you use math doesn't make you any better, Philip. You map the cosmos through math. Anomalies, mysteries, and holes are merely unfinished proofs for you. Your computations run dry, so you rub your eyes, take a break, and call it dark matter for now. How much of me is dark matter to you, Pip? Or worse—she looked hard at him, pausing with a needle drawn through a book spine—how little of you remains dark? To me. She drew the thread and cinched it with a violent tug.

Lulling toward sleep in his recliner, peering lazily at the spines of Irma's books, he considered for the first time that Irma may have been seeing Beatrice instead of him after their return from Seville. The thought seemed to fall randomly from memories of Spain and of Irma in her workshop. But this was not unlike the way the most complex mathematical problems were solved by the tumbling emergence of a key equation or number hidden in his musings and calculations.

The recliner groaned as he leaned into an upright position. The blanket fell away. He called Beatrice, suddenly wishing to wake her. She said his name with concern. Did you have an affair with her after we got back from Seville? he asked softly. She answered with the same note of concern. In Seville, too, she added, before we returned home. But it was best when it was the three of us. Now sleep, Philip, she told him as though she had just given him the loveliest of gifts, recognition.

He hung up the phone and fixed a fresh glass of bourbon before returning to the recliner. If you could somehow peer through the window of his third-story flat above Baum's, you would see that he was not such a bad sight. A runner at rest, reclined in aqua-blue comfort, three pretty books stacked within arm's reach next to his whiskey. In the farther reaches of the lamplight, his book collection glowed against leak-stained walls.

THREE

The third swing of the mathematical pendulum took him back toward the beginning of Irma's collection, to Cervantes. *Don Quixote.* It was the fattest book in the entire collection, bound in dimpled pigskin, dyed the color of topaz. Philip caressed the spine, four fingers wide. So Irma had returned intermittently to Seville from her solitary ventures in Córdoba, Granada, and the Manchegan countryside to have sex with Beatrice, to walk the city with her, to take siesta with her. Without him, they revisited Seville's Town Hall, to see the logarithmic spirals he showed them first. They fitted their palms to the curved stone almost hot enough to scald.

Philip called Beatrice again, this time at a more reasonable hour and at an hour when he figured she would have some privacy.

"Did you know she's missing?"

"Missing?" she asked.

"Gone. She's gone."

"Gone?" asked Beatrice. "What does that mean? She's always gone somewhere."

"Gone." Philip pressed the phone to his chest, wondered. "This is different. She's gone from life. Gone from her life."

"Can one do that? Leave her own life? How does one do that?"

He knew she was not that cold. People assumed that about her. But he found it appealing, how she automatically asked the right questions. The first questions. The Big Picture questions now, apologies and sympathies later, if needed.

"She left me all the books, B. That would be a start. For her. Wouldn't you say?"

There was a pause over the line, a thoughtful click of tongue. "Yes. I would say."

"I was hoping you could tell me something. Something she said." He bit his lip. "While you were . . ."

"Screwing?"

"I didn't mean that," he said.

"It's all right. That's what we did. Mostly." She paused. "She didn't say anything, Philip. She didn't say anything about disappearing. Here or in Seville. She had so much energy all the time. Her words were like sparks to me. She seemed like someone coming even more to life. Not like someone about to vanish."

"Then could you tell me a little more about Seville? I want to know some of the details," he said. "You owe me that."

Irma surprised her one night when Beatrice decided to walk the narrow, labyrinthine passageways of Seville's Santa Cruz Quarter. Alone, Beatrice wanted to see for herself what all the night noise was about, all the laughter and music and frank conversation that drifted up to their apartment window. None of the streets ran straight. They broke at new angles and changed names at random. Side streets, dark hallways really, opened suddenly from shadows and protrusions in the ancient Moorish brick. In these, she could spread her arms and graze both walls with her fingertips as she walked along. The sky, visible in the overhead channels created by the crowded buildings, seemed always dark brown and starless. The streets had mundane and comforting names like Glass, Wax, Water, and ominous names like Death, Ashes, and The Street Without Exit. Emboldened and curious, Beatrice ambled down The Street Without Exit, noting that it was a dead end. When she turned to look back from where she had entered, that, too, appeared to be a dead end. The brick lines and dimly lit mud hues of the Moorish walls all ran together. Pulse quickened, she reversed her direction. The long, zigzagging streets that seemed to run deep into the old Jewish Quarter began to comfort her. She passed others exploring the night—couples, tourists speaking

quietly in German, teens sharing enormous bottles of beer, children gig-
gling, and even other women walking alone. She came upon open con-
vergences in the streets, where café tables were filled with Spaniards and
tourists, young and old, drinking wine that looked black in the night. To
Beatrice they appeared as the dead come to life in these hours between
midnight and dawn, awake and dressed in these little pockets of Spanish
Brigadoon.

She reached Juderia Street, the bottom of the quarter, where it
butted against the fortress walls of the Alcázar. Two black archways
marked either end of Juderia. Standing in the low and dusty push of a
streetlamp, she watched couples emerge from the archway to her right.
Beatrice chose that direction and walked past a small, tiled fountain that
trickled through the Alcázar wall. The archway seemed a mistake when
she reached it; it was actually an unlit zigzag of a tunnel, drawing gray
light from either end, black and foreboding in its center. Irma emerged
from this black center and stood beneath a low brick arch. "Beatrice,"
she said. "What say you?" She wore a sundress and looked tender against
the rough brick.

"I thought you were in Córdoba," Beatrice said. The tremble in her
voice surprised her, and she pressed her hand to her chest. Perspiration
dampened her skin beneath the collarbone.

"I came back to spy," Irma replied.

"On whom?"

"On everything. I like to spy on my own life. How it might be without me in it."

"Then why reveal yourself now?" asked Beatrice.

"Because I'm horny."

She took Beatrice's hand and led her quickly into the black center of
the angled tunnel. She kissed Beatrice, first on the collarbone to taste,
then gently on the lips, then firmly on the lips. Irma had a way of align-
ing her lips to yours, sucking softly to create fusion, then opening your
lips along with hers. Her tongue then waited for yours to make the first
thrust. She pressed Beatrice against the brick and let her feel that she
wore nothing beneath the sundress. Then she took her hand and led her
out the other end of the tunnel and into the expansive plaza surrounding

the enormous cathedral, where lovers sat on the lip of the fountain and night tourists staggered in the light and shadows of the Gothic spires. The men and women who came to clean the streets were blasting the cathedral steps with a fire hose, their reflective vests flashing with insect-like glitter. The water on stone filled the night heat with an incense more stirring than any perfume.

Irma led her down a side street and into a corner bar named The Children of José Morales. There were no chairs or stools in the place, only an angled bar-front with a foot rail and two large barrels on the open floor for standing and drinking. A group of old friends drank beer around one of the barrels and took turns ordering little plates of artichokes, peaches, and almonds. A German-looking young couple sipped coffee at the bar and stared at a map. Irma and Beatrice ordered sherry and thought only of the softness and heat they would soon feel when they were done with their drinks and this audience. "There are some things I couldn't try with Philip in the way," Irma told her.

"Me, too," replied Beatrice. "I have some ideas."

A few from the barrel group, perhaps those who understood English, looked their way. The German couple lifted their collective gaze, then looked at each other. Beatrice turned her gaze away from everything in The Children of José Morales and stared at the night beyond the bar's arched openings. She felt Irma's hand on her wrist. She felt everything connecting to her, everything seeking her warmth. She imagined Philip back at their apartment sleeping fitfully on the floor mattress, the moonlight and shadow slanting through the open balcony and playing about his face, guiding his shallow dreams. And when Irma finally led her from the bar and across the cathedral plaza, now empty but for the intoxicating scent of wet stone, and to her little hostel room, Beatrice took that image of Philip with her. And she pictured him dreaming of the things she and Irma did together. Irma, naked on top of her, their legs together like interlocked scissors, kissed and licked Beatrice's closed eyes. Then, in a voice hoarse with pleasure, she whispered, "Open your eyes . . . look at me . . . stop thinking of him." She then thrust softly with precision to create a suction between their legs similar to her kiss. Beatrice opened her eyes wide and tried to muffle her roar and sobs in Irma's breasts.

Here, Beatrice paused to ask Philip over the phone, "Should I stop? Is this enough detail?"

He answered only with silence.

"Okay, then," she told him. "Just a bit more and then I need to sleep." She told him that in that small, hot hostel room that had once been a monk's quarters, Irma's damp breasts were like warm liquid on her face. She could breathe them.

"It never felt like cheating," Beatrice told Philip. "It always felt like an extension of things the three of us did together. At least in Seville. Maybe it felt like cheating those few times back here."

"Back here? Few?"

"Three," she replied in a voice understanding his mathematician's need for precision. "Actually, five."

He remained silent on the phone.

"Do you need me to come over now?" she asked. "I owe you that. I mean, you must feel pretty . . . loaded."

Again, his answer was silence.

"Wait there," she said and hung up. Wait there, as though he were in a bar and not in the Naugahyde recliner of his makeshift home. He wondered which of the two cars she would drive.

Peering through his third-story window from across Eleventh, you would see him not answer the door right away, see him walk first to the shelf of books, see him gently finger the spines as though seeking a particular volume. As he finally begins to move toward the door, he pauses again—this time in order to switch on his laptop, which rests on the otherwise bare table. The screen's blue glow pushes against the yellow aura of the reading lamp and the room divides in two with light. It is like watching a cell multiply, the way the two lights resist yet cling. When Philip opens the door, Beatrice greets him with a kiss on the cheek and then steps past him to survey his place. She removes her wool hat and shakes her straight dark hair, bending back slightly to let it fall and air. She looks at the bookshelf as she removes her overcoat. She is in yellow light. She tosses hat and coat onto the recliner. She wears a brown satin sundress and she is tan, the color of Spain and summer and not the cold spring of Philadelphia. Philip, still near the door, compliments her, earnestly, astonished, and she shrugs, lifts her hands, and steps into blue light. Beatrice leans toward the laptop and brushes her fingers over the keys. She is calling up music, you can tell, as she smiles and leans closer to the screen and sways her shoulders. Perhaps she finds a favorite, a violin and cello piece, John Adams's "Common Tones in Simple Time." She steps into the cusp between blue and yellow light, as though she can tell, and waits for him to come to her.

Philip tried to send her home, tried walking the way Gregory Peck walked toward Audrey Hepburn when they both knew, tried staying in the yellow light as Beatrice drew back into the blue and the music of Thomas Adès's "Visible Darkness." He placed his hands lightly on her shoulders and softly kissed the bridge of her nose, an angle she let him measure once. "Go home, Beatrice," he whispered. She bowed her head slightly as if to comply, then swiftly lifted her face to his and took his lips with hers, creating that precise fusion they had both learned from Irma. Her breath tasted of celery. And as her lips opened his, Irma was there in the rush of thoughts. She pressed her pelvis to him. "Oh, you're not going to last long," she whispered, "and that won't do. We want to last for a *little* while." She knelt, the scent of celery again in the wake of air from her drop. She undid his pants and his erection struck her forehead. She braced her hands firmly to the backs of his thighs so that he could in no way withdraw from her soft bite, the brush of her tongue, the push of her lips. She almost fell back from the force of his sudden arch, but she held on to his legs, keeping her mouth on him even as he staggered forward into the blue light. The blue light consumed his vision.

After he caught his breath, he lifted her, cupping her jaw. And he knelt this time, reversing positions. First, he did not lift her sundress, and pressed his lips and nose to the brown satin. He began to lift her dress and she helped him, hurried him, put both hands behind his neck and pulled his face hard into her. He worked his lips to create that vacuum, Irma's vacuum. She pushed herself into his face and arched over him, her eyes closed, mouth open, hair falling forward. "Common Tones in Simple Time" played softly. They finally parted, but stood close enough to remain within the membrane between yellow and blue light. They finished undressing, pragmatically, as though getting home from work. She saw that he was ready again and smiled, folding her hair behind her ear.

Philip awoke in the recliner, alone in his apartment, a gray and time-less light coming through the window. Beneath the blanket, he felt sore and sticky. Beatrice left the music on, Aleck Karis playing Cage's Sonata No. 9 on prepared piano. There was a message, as well. The marquee sliding across the laptop's screensaver said: *A much better way to settle things.* The bed was awry, its covers twisted, the mattress and box spring stacked like books on the floor. The big yellow Cervantes volume tee-tered next to him on the tin lamp stand. He could not remember fetch-ing the Cervantes from the shelf, but he could remember everything else. He pulled the volume to him and found its weight crushing. It was beau-tiful work by Irma. The dimpled pigskin was liquid soft and its yellow color looked apothecary. It felt cool and smelled of wine dregs. It will take me a year to read, he thought. He did not open it.

He forewent his usual routes and ran through the city that day, never registering the exact time, deducing from the urgent traffic that it was morning. The city's two rivers exchanged mists in the cold spring air, dragging a low fog across downtown. He enjoyed the steeplechase of Sansom Street, the sudden buckles in the brick sidewalk, dog leashes, scooters, bikes, newspaper bundles, and tree wells. The closeness of the buildings reminded him somewhat of Seville. He ran with great energy and speed, an extra spring in his hurdling of curbs and puddles. Cutting through the stillness of the fog increased his sensation of speed.

Philip ran hard to Irma's favorite bookstore—she had a favorite in every city. He caught his breath in front of Hibberd's dusty display win-dow. Shreds from the shop's tattered awning brushed his shoulders as he gazed at the display that had changed little over the past three years. The entire shop, in fact, had a sealed quality about it. Everything inside— the books, the shelves, the clerk hunched over an open volume, his hat and gloves stacked on the old register—looked part of a snow globe. If you shook it, flakes of old paper would swirl around the still figures. A book Irma restored and re-bound for the owner in exchange for credit still reclined in the lower left corner of the display, a middling edition of *Pepys at Table*, which was a culling of food-related entries from the famous diary.

Pepys, she once said to Philip. He could've been a mathematician.

She answered Philip's expression, the pause in the lifting of his drink. He used secret symbols and encryptions that were designed to be easily deciphered. It was a seventeenth century expression of freedom. Look at me. I'm writing in code. I'm being subversive, even as I tell you what kind of sandwich I'm having for tea today. Did you know he had a special symbol in his diaries for whacking off?

At table? asked Philip.

She squinted at him, meanly. Then she softened and gave him a sideways look. You know, she told him, whenever I read Pepys, I realize a sad and important thing. Most of us can't accept being the protagonist of our own lives. Whether we only watch TV or sports or read thousands of books, we're all just trying to find another protagonist for our lives. One besides ourselves. But Pepys accepted himself as the protagonist of his own life. She watched his reaction, Philip sipping his bourbon. I know what you're doing, she said. You're designing some equation for that. For the inevitability of being the protagonist of your own life. One's life $=n$ to the power of $x-1$ over i—or some crock of shit. You should write a story in numbers, Pip.

"Or something like that," Philip said to his reflection in the bookstore display window. He was catching a chill as the sweat from his run cooled fast along the collar of his shirt and the damp edges of his hair along his neck and temples. He stared at the Pepys volume in the display, and shivered.

He continued his run to the Schuylkill. In California, Irma would let him stay in her shop for as long as he wanted. The air inside felt distinctly different, contemporary. A panel register, running the length of one wall, kept the room at a constant temperature and humidity. The air had a clean, distilled taste, a lightness, but its smells changed according to Irma's current task. If she was shaping leather for a cover, there was the vinegar scent. If she was sewing volumes in the press, you smelled fresh laundry. That scent, he came to believe, was from her breath and tongue as she pursed the ends of the linen twine with her lips. Sometimes they would kiss at length in her shop, more often in the early days when she was just getting started, and he would taste that smell in her mouth, clean wet sheets twisting open. She worked in the coned brightness of a lamp, but kept the rest of the shop in natural light. If he was there at night, she would light a candle for him. Might the smoke cause damage? he asked, trying to show that he understood the delicacy and intricacy of her work. Particulates aren't the problem, she explained. Humidity and temperature fluctuations are the biggest threats. Especially here—she referred to Santa Cruz, where moss grew on telephone poles and where sea air encrusted the moss tips with icy crystals. These texts in this press right now could swell or contract significantly in the time it takes me to sew them. She had five copies in her press, the maximum it would hold.

When Philip and Irma were quiet, they could hear only the clean squeak of her awl twisting into the compressed paper or the whisper of drawn twine. He never grew tired of watching her meticulously fit books together, each process hinging on precision—the exactness of cuts, and shapes, and measurements as thin as parchment. He only sauntered away, or forced himself to find something else to do, because he did not want to physically admit to her or to himself that it was enough for him to be in her shop, to watch her in her shop, to taste its air and to breathe its scent. Her fingertips, the nails trimmed carefully so that they might serve as quick tools, would line up evenly on the back edge of a coverboard as she guided it slowly into its leather, or canvas, or muslin, or linen crease. She often held her bone folder lightly, the way a violinist holds her bow, and he was transfixed by the strength hidden in the delicacy of her movement. She smiled at him when she drew thread along a beeswax knob, getting ready for binding. From this task, she could look up. Sometimes she held the freshly scraped wax to his nose and he could still sense the honey.

What do you like more? he asked her, the wax knob still held close to his lips. Writing books, or making them?

Both. One makes me want to do the other.

Philip reached the banks of the Schuylkill feeling strong. The mist was dissipating and the gray coin of the sun above the Philly skyline was beginning to flicker with yellow. He ran three 800-meter speedplays along the river, enjoying the cushion of spring grass. Dewdrops fell from the sycamores, tiny cold splashes, one striking the bridge of his nose and feeling somehow tender. Easing out of the final 800, he felt the spring mist condense with the sweat on his face and neck and he believed he could run forever and live on whiskey and books. I knew something then, he thought, that I do not know now.

Later, he suffered from the run and the ambitious speed drills. That evening he sat in his Naugahyde recliner, legs elevated, a heat pad pressed to his hip and an ice bag wrapped against his left instep. The tin stand teetered with the weight of the Cervantes, Borges, and Turgenev, Irma's bound manuscripts of *Slip* and *The Theory of Peter Navratil*, a new bottle of bourbon, his glass, and the lamp. There was not enough room for everything on the small tin disk and so the books hung precariously over the edge. On the floor was an ice bucket at the ready, for refilling his drink and restocking the bag wrapped to the sole of his left foot.

Not knowing exactly which text he wanted, he reached toward the volumes anyway, perhaps to secure them. He drew *The Theory of Peter Navratil* to him, after fingering the dimpled spine of the Cervantes. He was amused to find that he had bookmarked the manuscript with the Chinese finger puzzle given to him by the Vespa woman. He remembered searching for passages that described Feli/Sefi. The passage he marked described, instead, Sylvia. Philip slipped the woven puzzle over his index finger and read.

I am the daughter of a Portuguese fisherwoman and an Italian fisherman who trolled the Monterey coast. The languages that fell about me on the docks and on the loading quays of the canneries sounded like music. Portuguese, Spanish, Italian, Russian, Japanese. I did not understand them as a child, and only came to learn the first two through study, but I happily listened to them in all their inflections and forms and volumes. My parents were very much a part of this world. All the families drank each other's basement wine and sampled and argued which one was best. And then sampled some more. But in three ways my parents acted independently of their community and that ended up making all the difference in my life. First, my mother continued to fish after I was born, which raised many immigrant eyebrows, except for those of the Mexican families, who mostly worked the canneries and the nearby strawberry fields and did not go out on the water, and who were always honest about which wine tasted best. Second, my parents saved a bit of money and purchased a cottage for $1,500, five years before I was born, but in preparation for my arrival. It was on a rocky little slope, facing away from the sea. On the top of the slope stood a Monterey pine, sprawling away from the wind, its low-growing limbs tapping the ground, its silhouette against the evening sky filling the view from our kitchen window. When the sea wind blew hard, the tree waved crablike atop the slope. Third, they studied English and spoke English to each other and to me. People in Monterey, who could not tell from my dress or speech that I was the daughter of cannies, could not tell if I was Portuguese, Italian, Mexican, or Russian. As a grown woman, in any country I traveled through, people took me for native or for colonial immigrant. In France, I was Algerian. In England, perhaps Punjabi or Egyptian or even French. In Australia, Indonesian.

My father, Clement Torano, did not make particularly good wine. But on our rocky little slope, he built a stonehouse partially embedded in the hillside between the back of the cottage and the pine. He did this because we did not have a basement. Here, he made and stored his wine and for this purpose it was better than any basement along the Central Coast. A Portuguese fisherman named Albuquerque Santos, who did make good wine, began storing his best bottles in our stonehouse. My mother helped herself to more than our share of Albuquerque's finest red. Apollonia Silva enjoyed wine, not to excess, but certainly to fulfillment, and it was not possible, she claimed, to drink inferior bottles when Albuquerque Santos's bottles were just outside her door. She did not try to hide or deny her theft and instead told Albuquerque Santos that his wine was too good to resist.

Despite the well-angled flattery, Santos demanded recompense in the form of us acquiring a nice concentrate from San Francisco and hauling it back. This led to my first expedition, at the age of nine, to this city of lights and books. I was, at first, completely intimidated by everything about San Francisco, and this intimidation was what sent me into a bookstore.

"Where would you like to go?" asked Mother while we waited for Dad to procure Albuquerque Santos's coveted concentrate. It was evening, the hills of the city sparkled, the windowed shops and cafés and taverns glowed. Psychedelic pop, sounding vaguely French, drifted from upper-floor apartments. The people walked fast and did not speak to us. I pointed to a softly lit place, where the silhouettes inside remained still or moved only in small increments—turn a page, pull a volume from a shelf, examine its front then back, replace it. A bookstore.

"There," I answered, still pointing.

My mother nodded. Perhaps she felt exactly as I did. And she was thrifty and primarily saw San Francisco as a place that wanted to inhale her hard-earned fish money. She must have been relieved that I pointed to a bookstore. The books inside were all used. The paperbacks cost a dime and the hardcovers sold for forty-five cents. I chose novels because I told the clerk I liked stories and he pointed us to the fiction section. I chose strictly by title and what it might promise. With the dollar my mother gave me in hand I selected paperback editions of *The Plague*, *Invisible Man*, *The Octopus*, *Far from the Madding Crowd*, *The Magus*, *The Possessed*, *The Sailor Who Fell from Grace with the Sea*, *The Moviegoer*, *The Naked and the Dead*, and *Carmody, Tough Bullet*. I knew none of these books, but they all had lurid, Technicolor covers depicting muscular thighs of men and women. My mother seemed to know some of the titles. The only one she checked was *The Naked and the Dead*. She pushed it across the counter toward the clerk, a skinny man with long brown hair, pookah shells, a failing beard, and a muslin shirt that hung like a curtain from his bony shoulders.

"Is this okay for her?" she asked.

With cocked wrist, he hooked the paperback Mailer away swiftly and said, "No—but not for the reasons you think."

He looked at me and whispered, "Perhaps another time."

My mother and I looked at each other.

"Try this," he said. He slid *Madame Bovary* across the counter toward us.

The title promised nothing for me—a boring story about a fancy lady. But the paperback cover sufficed. A woman with bountiful, swirling black hair, olive skin, cleavage over lace, thighs outlined in a burgundy wind-blown dress, a slightly openmouthed expression of intelligent anguish, stepping from a horse-drawn carriage. Inside the carriage you could only glimpse a man's open hand, fingers spent and releasing, wrist cuffed in lace.

I took the stack home. At nine, I was able to read only the pulp western. It wasn't really a western because it was set in New Orleans, but Carmody was definitely a cowboy. The copy on the back told me that "Carmody was looking for a good time in New Orleans. With eleven thousand in stolen money in his pocket, he figured to enjoy some good liquor and bad women before he headed back to Texas. But just as he was getting comfortable, he found himself framed for a brutal murder." Just like on the paperback cover, he had a scar on his lower right jaw, a small but muscular build, and a gun on his hip. The woman on the cover was named Minnehaha, and she was Creole with some Choctaw blood. She worked in a brothel and smoked opium and wore see-through blouses. On the cover her blouse was gauzy but her nipples were only shadows. Her hair, like Madame Bovary's, was thick and black and swirling in a wind that forever seemed to be blowing across these paperbacks. She turned out to be the villain in the end, the conspirator behind all the bad that Carmody had to shoot down. She seduces Carmody when she realizes he is on to her and then poisons him with opium wine. But she underestimates the amount of opium it would take to destroy the rawhide, scar-ridden, but still handsome body of Carmody, Tough Bullet. He accidentally kills Minnehaha when she tries to finish him off with a knife and he instinctively twists her wrist to reverse the thrust of the blade. Her Creole breasts remain perfect beneath the blood-soaked gauze of her see-through blouse. I would always love her.

At the age of nine, I could not understand the other paperbacks in my stack. I could not actually read them. But I often would hold one of them for long periods of time as I stretched out on my little bed after school. I read the copy on the back, the blurbs, flipped it over to view the cover once again, and then opened to some random passage and read that until enough incomprehensible thoughts and images piled together, fogging my brain and blurring the words on the page. I loved their dead leaf smell and the way some of the older paperbacks were beginning to brown at the edges. I began keeping them in order between two abalone-shell bookends my father made for me. The abalone he caught himself. The order of the books changed according to my mood and interest. For a long time, I kept them arranged according to the color spectrum. At the right bookend stood *The Plague*, a deep red paperback with a very handsome French doctor—he holds a black medical bag for house calls—on the cover. Because he's dealing with plague, his shirtsleeves are rolled up to his muscular biceps and several buttons are undone, revealing a wedge of his chest. Reclining along the bottom of the cover art is a woman on a bed, facing away from you and toward the handsome doctor. Her hip thrusts upward through a silky, pearl-colored nightgown. Standing against the left bookend at the end of the spectrum was the violet *Moviegoer*, with Binx Bolling and his secretary on the front cover. They are both facing away from you and toward some kind of cloudy, lavender netherworld. Binx has his arm across the secretary's back as he pulls her close and she leans her head to his shoulder. His hand presses low on her waist, almost ready to cup her curvaceous bottom. She wears a brown, clingy skirt and a pair of pumps that flex her athletic legs. I knew, by the age of ten, that the man on the cover was the hero Binx Bolling and that the woman was not the heroine Kate Cutrer. I knew this because Kate and Binx, along with the whore Minnehaha, became my first literary crushes. Over and over again I read Kate and Binx's final dialogue at the end of *The Moviegoer*. They were like emotional superheroes, the way they knew in detail what would happen to themselves in the near and distant future. I loved the way Kate rubbed, with her middle finger, the flake of skin that peeled from her thumbnail. She rubbed it to cause pain while at the same time conversing pleasantly with Binx.

I eventually held all the books long enough, sampled enough random passages from each, found all the scenes that roughly corresponded to the cover art, to reach the point where I could claim that I had actually *read* them all.

Philip wondered. He liked to match Irma's most autobiographical passages to what he knew to be her actual experiences. Here, Sylvia was virtually Irma. As author, Irma had moved the family slightly north, but kept the cottage, the Monterey pine on the hill, the stonehouse cellar, and some of the names. Philip replaced the Chinese finger puzzle to book-mark *The Theory of Peter Navratil* and hobbled to his bookshelf, the ice bag still strapped to the instep of his left foot. He carried his bourbon with him. He remembered some of the paperback titles from his unpack-ing and shelving of Irma's volumes, but he did not know any of the vol-umes' authors and thus could not search alphabetically through the 351 colorful spines. Mailer was the only author mentioned in the passage he had just read and he was not in her collection. The cold pain in his left foot rendered Philip too impatient to scan for the titles. He remembered the French name Flaubert and thus went to the *F*'s in hopes of finding *The Plague*, with its dashing, muscular, roll-up-your-sleeves, Gallic doc-tor. Instead, he found *Madame Bovary*, which was fine. Very near, still in the *F*'s, he found *The Magus*. Also near, in the other direction, he found Ellison's *Invisible Man*. He stacked the three books gently on the floor.

He remembered a Japanese author for the long, wonderful, and unforgettable title of *The Sailor Who Fell from Grace with the Sea*, but he could only remember it beginning with *Mi*, which was enough to find Mishima. Nearby, he found Norris's *The Octopus*, then, continuing, Percy's *The Moviegoer*. Philip noted that Percy's volume was bound in the same violet describing Sylvia's paperback. It was the only such tone of violet among all the volumes. He wondered, stepped back, scanned for color, found the spine of the deepest red, and pulled *The Plague* from the shelf. Here was her handsome French doctor.

Only three remained, but among those three was the one he was most curious about. Was the pulp western on his shelf? On the floor, he arranged the seven books he had found according to the color spectrum. There was a hole in deep orange. He scanned the spines on the shelf for this color and almost immediately found Dostoyevsky's *The Possessed*. The gap in light green was filled by a quick scan leading him to Hardy. *Far From the Madding Crowd*. He stared at the nine volumes fanned out on the floor according to the color spectrum. He sipped his bourbon and pressed his ice-packed heel to the floor, numbing his instep.

Looking in through his window from across Eleventh Street, you would see that he struck a rather elegant pose, though oddly dressed in a Rutgers sweatshirt given to him by his stepdaughter and a pair of mariachi pants he bought in Tijuana, many years ago, on a dare. The way he held his injured foot, extending the leg *en garde*, made him seem taller and well postured. The angle of his neck as he gazed down at the books rendered him much like a hero on the cover of a paperback, perhaps a rugged scientist about to ravage the beautiful Brazilian river guide who is leading him to the secret whereabouts of the medicinal orchid that will help stanch the plague. Her black windswept hair seems to coil upward, reaching to ensnare him. Or perhaps he is just Dr. Arrowsmith, austere and forever understanding.

Philip thought that maybe he could see a gap in the spectrum somewhere between green and cyan. And it would no doubt be a thin volume. He scanned for thin cerulean and, with more labor than he would have liked, he found *Carmody, Tough Bullet* by Peter McCurtin. Irma had bound it in elegant blue linen. Inside, she had mounted the original paperback front and back covers. There was Carmody, with the white chip of scar on his rugged jaw. And there was the beautiful Minnehaha in her see-through blouse and full mascara, part Creole, part Choctaw.

He imagined Irma as a little girl holding these books, ensconced in her tiny room. She liked to let in the breeze, no matter how cold and wet the sea air. The small casement window, set high on her wall, fit poorly in its warped frame and was difficult to open and close. She told Philip she used to eat a particular brand of cookies when she read after school, hard vanilla wafers with holes in their center and laced with chocolate stripes. She tried them once as a coed, shared one with him. He told her it was like eating wax. They nodded together and ate more. She took him on a drive down the coast one weekend in the middle of spring semester to show him where the house used to be. A golf course covered the hill, but the Monterey pine still stood, a dark crab against a veiled sky. She walked him over the fairway to show him exactly where the stonehouse had been and where her room had been. They ate some more of the cookies there, where her room once stood, until a foursome of golfers yelled at them and threatened to call the greens marshal.

But this is where I first read Hardy and Camus, she told them. She pointed up toward the Monterey pine. I lost my virginity under that tree.

Oh, if you could see how he performed in that moment, maybe from the view of one of the caddies, a son of Albuquerque Santos who also knew about the stonehouse and its treasure. You could see how Philip placed his arm across her back, like Binx Bolling assuring his secretary. The way he beamed at the irate duffers. He is one of us, they think, only longer off the tee. Tell me your scores, he said to the four golfers. And I'll multiply them all together before you can drop a tee. They were on the fifteenth fairway and the numbers were high: $68 \times 73 \times 67 \times 78$.

25,941,864, he told them.

How do we know you're right?

We'll be out of your fucking way by the time you figure it out, she told them.

And the square root is 5093.3156, Philip added. Roughly.

He led her up to the Monterey pine, like Binx leading Kate up Loyola Avenue in the aftermath of Mardi Gras.

We showed them, she said.

And a sad look played on his face as they approached the tree, an expression out of context, as though he somehow knew they would not see the ocean when they crested the hill, but only that cloudy lavender netherworld on the paperback cover.

FOUR

Philip returned to his recliner and once again drew *Theory* to his lap. He opened to the page marked by the finger puzzle and slipped the straw tube onto one index finger. He read Irma's description of the night train ride to Michoacán. How could she know what he had been thinking on that train, what he imagined, what he dreamed? Irma, through Sylvia's narrative, rendered his dream perfectly, the dream where she changed to various women as she rode him softly. He only mentioned it once to her, without elaboration. The final set of light patterns from the trolley moved across his ceiling, the last rectangle crimson.

While he read, he absently worked the finger puzzle, now inserting both index fingers into the tube and tugging gently. Irma's books, the ones she had bound or restored, always lay themselves open, carefully weighted to offer their pages to the reader. You could freshen your drink as you read them, knit, play with a finger puzzle. He traveled to Mexico with Irma before and after his first marriage. There's an equation in that, Rebecca told him later when they met for drinks in a New Brunswick bar to discuss her kids and her hopes for his continued friendship with Nicole and Sam. On their first journey to Mexico, he and Irma traveled as jilted lovers and spent most of their time around the city of Colima, exploring those old coffee fincas on the slopes of the volcanoes and also the untouched ruins along the decline to the Pacific. They traveled as friends, sworn to a celibacy that would cure their respective heartaches. Then, early in their monthlong excursion, they drank a pomegranate punch in the mountain town of Comala. They had sex during siesta and deliberately reenacted their ex-lovers' least and most favorite moves and positions. And then did to each other what they had been denied by their exes. Only later, back in Colima, did a cantina owner tell them about the Comala *ponche* and its legend. Honeymooners go to Comala to drink the *ponche*. And if you eat the seeds at the bottom you might as well reserve the nearest room for three days. Irma and Philip had eaten the *ponche*-soaked seeds. Every siesta after that was well spent. "Is it siesta yet?" she would ask, looking at him from across a table, a ruin, a pottery display, a sidewalk, a fountain.

A later journey through Mexico took them to the Michoacán high-lands and the Spanish colonial cities of Morelia, Pátzcuaro, and Urua-pán. They established no understanding on this trip, but agreed to avoid, at first, any native drinks. Irma loved the library in Pátzcuaro, a con-verted cathedral with no inside walls and no rooms—only shelves and shelves of books and, in the dim corners, a few Purépechan artifacts and odd collections of jarred animal specimens. People read together at the long, narrow tables dividing the cavernous library. The sex Philip and Irma had in Michoacán was furtive, restive, dutiful, hindered by their contrasting moods, and defined by long conversations, Irma doing most of the talking. She stopped going on morning runs with him and took up smoking these short black cheroots found in a Morelia tobacco shop. He would watch her talk and smoke as she sat naked on the bed during siesta. She would tell him about some great novel, about its characters and what they did and how he and she were like them. She would let the smoke spill from her mouth.

Sylvia narrates, near the end of *The Theory of Peter Navratil*: I felt him watching me as we climbed the cinder cone to the rim of the volcano, with me leading the way up the switchbacks. The surface was nothing but ash and pumice. Our feet and hands sank several inches deep with every step, grasp, and clamber. I felt him watching the stretch and push of my legs as he calculated the first and last angles of each thrust upward. He watched the whole of me and the composition of me and must have, at that steep angle of ascent, seen me pressed against the blue mountain sky. I think there, he finally recognized me. There, just below the lip of a volcano that grew and died within a span of just thirty years, still managing to smother two towns in the process. I felt his recognition as a sudden bloom of sweat turning cold in the high air.

Sometimes we are just too much like Port and Kit in *The Sheltering Sky*, only I'm him and you're her, Irma told Philip as she sat naked on the edge of the bed, legs crossed as though taking dictation. She drew on her cheroot and ashes fell and powdered her breasts and thighs. In Michoacán, it always felt as though she wanted something of him. Not something for herself, but something that would emerge from inside Philip, something for her to witness but not to take. One day, she told him as she crushed the cheroot in an ashtray, you'll read all these books, Pip. And then you will know everything.

Philip's index fingers were trapped in the straw puzzle. He tried drawing his fingers apart, but the tube ends only gripped tighter. When he tugged once more, stretching the weave of the puzzle, seven numbers revealed themselves along the tiny straw trapezoids: 339-9613. Vespa's phone number.

Once he had freed his hands from the puzzle—you must go in to get out—he called her. Only after entering the number, while listening to the ring, did he consider the lateness of the hour. He simply responded to the number, used it because he discovered it, followed it because that was what one did with discovered numbers. She answered before he could cut the call.

"It's me," Philip explained. "From the TLA. I have your finger puzzle."

"Oh, yes," she replied. "Borges. How nice. I thought I saw you running along the river the other day. I almost tried to stop and talk. You run fast."

"My parents were steeplechasers."

"I see," she said.

Her name was Lucia, which she pronounced softly. Philip agreed to meet her that night at the Latham Hotel bar on South Street. He changed his shirt but kept the mariachi pants. Spring had left again and a thin icy rain dampened the sidewalks and buildings of downtown. But the late-night crowds of South Street still pressed onward, perhaps a little quieter steeled against the weather, yet perhaps also a little more reckless because of the rain and the fact that they were in it. Philip sensed the recklessness, too, water as harbinger of possibilities and the unknown. As he neared the Latham, he removed his wool cap and let the sparse mix of ice and drizzle dampen his hair and bead his face.

The Latham bar was dark, spacious, and empty. The young bartender seemed glad to see him. Philip ordered a shot of bourbon for warmth and a nicer bourbon to sip neat. He shed his winter things, piling their wet felt smell on the stool beside him. A gigantic, floor-to-ceiling, orange, black, and white poster of a cartoon brewmeister loomed above him. The jolly brewer carried a tray of mugs with one hand; with the other, he downed the contents of one of the steins. Beneath the poster, the bartender busied himself by arranging cocktail glasses, filling his trays with lime slices and cherries, and then expertly shaving lemon peels into dainty yellow curls, all as though he were expecting a late-night crowd to arrive. He would glance at Philip and his drinks, anxious to see if the bourbon proved satisfactory. Prompted, Philip downed the shot and smiled and nodded to the bartender.

Lucia entered. She wore a sundress, sleeveless and perhaps orange, and a slight pair of espadrilles that clapped softly with her steps. She carried no coat or hat or purse. Her arms were free and she walked with her hands held in front of her waist, fingertips together as though turning a coin. This played her elbows at a curious angle. She moved directly to him, nothing coy or pensive to her step. She smiled as she neared him. Her skin seemed darker than he remembered. She raised a finger to the bartender and this sent him wordlessly to the task of fixing her a drink. Philip stood to greet her.

She cocked an eyebrow at the two glasses in front of him. She smiled with one side of her mouth.

"It's cold outside," he explained.

She took her seat at the bar, crossing her legs and pulling the hem of her sundress to the tip of her knee. She propped her elbow on the bar top, cocked her wrist, and waited for the bartender to slide her drink beneath expectant fingers.

"Do you own this hotel?" Philip asked.

"I've been living here for almost a month," she explained. She lived in hotels like these, months at a time, in different parts of the world. The Latham was perfect for her: a small independent hotel in the center of a downtown. She translated textbooks from Portuguese and Spanish. This she could do from anywhere, so she chose anywhere. Currently she was finishing up a Spanish materials science text. The hard sciences pay the most, by far, she told him. Usually she chose one city per translation, rented motor scooters to get around, showed the nearby bartenders how to fix her drinks. All she needed was her laptop and a nearby university library in case she had to track down an obscure reference or seek advice from a professor. Her favorite city was Seville.

"I don't make a lot of money," she told him. "But I don't have much. I don't want much."

"What about friends?" he asked.

"Funny," she said. "Most people ask more about the money first. They don't get to friendship."

"It just struck me," he replied, "that I could live like you. Starting now. But what about friends and the people in your life?"

"I have lots of friends. Good friends. They like me because I'm not around so much. And when I am around, I'm always keen to do something with them, be with them. They have fun tracking me."

"Where were you before Philadelphia?"

"Corsica." She fashioned a circle with her hands. "That's an island."

"Ajaccio?"

"Corte," she answered. "The university's there. You've been?"

"I helped look for books in a fort."

She sipped her drink, which looked like a tall glass of ice water. "You should've tried the library. You said you could live as I do. What do you do? Besides look for books in odd places."

"Do you know the math?" he asked.

"Math?"

"You said you were translating material sciences."

"Oh. I simply cut and paste the equations and formulas. I have no idea what they mean. I can tell you all about vibrating lattices, though. Except for the math."

"I know all about vibrating lattices," he replied.

"Are you physics?"

"No," he answered. "I do the math. All the stuff you cut and paste. That's me you're treating so coldly, with unknowing hands."

"We'd make a good team," she said.

He watched her sip her drink, in profile. He searched her dark hair for the bleached lock, could not find it at first, then saw that it lay underneath, bound by a plain rubber band that nonetheless matched her dress. She spoke most of her words looking away from you, then turning to look right at you as she uttered a final phrase or word, much like Sefi in the Borges and Feli in Irma's manuscript.

"I have a friend who translates," he told her. "She makes books, too."

"What do you mean—she makes books?"

"She writes them, then binds them herself. They're amazing. Beautiful. You might know her. You travel in similar circles, in similar ways. She can translate Portuguese and Spanish. Her name is Irma. Irma Arcuri."

She shook her head. "I don't know anyone who makes books. I wish I did. I deal with people who *sell* books."

"I think you do know her."

Math led him, as usual, and he did not stop to think outside that language. The sundress, the lock of hair, Seville, her way of speaking, her likeness in Irma's books—*her*. In math, it would be unreasonable not to seek connection among these hard impressions within the common denominator that was her.

She flexed her brow thoughtfully and shook her head.

"No, I'm sure I don't know anyone like that."

Philip did not believe her. But he did not want to risk pushing her away, so he distracted himself by imagining them on the cover of one of Irma's paperbacks. Without exaggeration, or even much elaboration, she presented enough curve and push to inhabit one of those covers. All she needed was an open door to let in the night breeze that would lift her dark hair into tendrils, press her thin dress close to her form. Her shoulder might lift seductively, yet the rest of her would appear enemy to the mathematician standing above her though clearly at her mercy. To solve the theorem, he needed the formula only she possessed.

"Paranoia suits you, though," she said.

"My mother immigrated from Brazil," she told him. "My father's ancestors came over on the *Mayflower*. He's from Trenton. I'm from Trenton, and you know, not many people will admit to that. They say 'New Jersey' or 'from around here' or from 'the New York area.' That one's my favorite. Anybody tells you they're from the New York area, they're from Trenton."

She opened her arms to him. "I'm from Trenton. There's nothing to be afraid of."

"Trenton Makes," he said, quoting the sign on the bridge bringing you into the city.

"The World Takes. That pretty much defines me," she said, speaking to the mirror behind the bar, then turning to face him after a brief pause.

"That way of speaking you have," he said. "How did you come to that?"

"You mean the speak-then-look," she said. "That—I think—comes from translating."

"Did you speak that way before you started translating?"

"I've always translated. My mother is a native speaker." She finished her drink, draining her highball glass and letting the ice slide to her lips. Then she balanced the glass on her knee. "You're very much a mathematician, you realize. I can almost hear the equations in your words and questions. What fits. What applies. What equals."

"You can't already know that about me."

Again she opened herself to him. She turned on her barstool, placed one hand on her hip, elbow out, shoulders straight.

"What is it that you suspect? That I've been following you, watching you? Or that I have been sent?" She lifted her foot and pointed an espadrille, considering it. "I hope it's the latter."

Her hotel room was small and wallpapered with Victorian flower prints. She had removed the drapes and the bedspread and folded and stacked them in a corner. They're covered with the same flowers, she explained. I can only take so much. Her laptop, a large coffee mug, and the materials science text she was translating were on a small table in one corner of the room. She dimmed the light, then clicked her laptop and some fado began to play softly, a woman singing mezzo-soprano to accordion and guitar.

"Irma listens to fado," he told her.

"Mm, so do many others." She walked to the uncovered window. The hotel was nestled low amid the downtown skyscrapers. Philip stood next to her, watching with her. The high-rise across the street filled their view. Even at the late hour, several of the windows, here and there along the grid, were lit. "Someone's always up somewhere," she said. "I hope they have telescopes."

She removed her dress by letting it slip from her shoulders. Naked, she stepped closer to the window, the downtown lights on her.

"Now you," she said, facing the city, eyeing the lighted windows of the high-rise across the street.

Philip undressed in front of the window without reservation. Before he turned forty, he would not have done this. But this loss of reservation was a distinct development of his age, and it went beyond the mere loss of inhibition. It represented, he knew, a sad revelation. People did not care. They may feel initially shocked, repulsed, aroused, angered, excited, even included. But, quickly, they ended up with no real concern for you, divided from you by the voyeuristic lens, perhaps empowered by it. It seemed such a simple gain in knowledge, the first time he realized this. He suspected that Lucia had learned it early in her life, sought to challenge or even refute those seeking comfort and power behind it. She gnashed at it.

Still gazing out the window, she took hold of his erection.

"That night, on my bike, you were at least this hard."

"Sorry," he replied. "It speaks for itself." He watched her hand on him. He noticed she still wore her espadrilles. This lifted him farther and she laughed softly, but gripped more firmly.

"You know one thing I do know from the math I cut and paste?"

She watched him try to answer as she pulled harder. "What's the matter? Cat got your tongue?"

He concentrated on the fado, the delicate control of the mezzo just short of a cry.

"What I do know from the math is that mathematicians and physicists are not nearly as clear and cold and rational as most people think. As I once thought." She paused with her hand, but did not release. "You're just as murky as the rest of us. More so, even. All those i's and e's. And π's."

He turned to her and gently took hold of her wrist, lifting her hand away. He placed his hands delicately on her shoulders and backed her to the bed. The gray light of downtown still reached them there. He sat her on the edge of the bed and knelt on the floor. He lifted her knees apart. Her lips remained open, her teeth together in a delicate bite.

"i, e, and π are infinite mysteries with exact . . . with exact locations," he told her. He put his face between her legs and touched her with the very tip of his tongue. He felt her lean back. He moved his tongue according to her groans and exhalations. She lifted her knees and hissed through clenched teeth. He slid his fingers beneath the espadrilles and cupped the soles of her feet. This made her groan loudest. He continued without pause. At first, it almost seemed like work as he concentrated on her sounds and the placement and movement of his tongue and fingers—he put his fingers between her toes. But then it became the best thing he could possibly be doing, and Lucia let him know this. Every new and incremental movement from his tongue, lips, or fingers brought deeper sounds and movements. "Again," she would sometimes say.

I worry that you're down there counting my orgasms, Irma once told him during their journey through Michoacán. She smoked a black cheroot as he held her thighs. They can't be counted, you know. Because often one negates the one before it. Sometimes five become one, then that one blossoms into seven.

Lucia placed her feet on his shoulders and finally pushed him away. She put her wrist to forehead and blinked, then rose from the bed. She walked by him as he remained kneeling on the floor. Her calf brushed his erection. She again stepped to the window, then leaned forward and pressed her hands to the glass, set her legs at a firm angle. She looked over her shoulder at him and waited. The city lights reflected off the damp curves of her shoulders, back muscles, and thighs. As he approached her, he could see silhouettes against the windows of the high-rise across the street.

"We'll break the glass," he whispered.

"It will hold," she assured him. "Hurry."

Pushing into her, he gripped the tendons of her hips, holding her to him, believing he could set the pace. But she flexed something inside, a kind of gentle pursing at the tip of his thrust, something learned and timed. Something she felt, too. He could tell. He could hear her, soft clicks in her throat, small releases there. She went up on her toes and then shoved against the glass to drive him farther in. He felt as though he might pass through her, into the wall of lights beyond the window. In the upward rush of pleasure, that audible quickening, he imagined the glass bending outward. She lifted her face to the view and he saw the pulse of her breath in plumes of mist on the pane. She groaned to gather and control her voice.

"Take us past this, Philip."

In the morning, he woke wanting to run. He lay on his side, facing the undraped window and its cloudy light. He could make out Lucia's hand-prints on the glass. His mariachi pants, dress shirt, and boots were piled on the floor by the window. He could not run in those. In these hotels, ask for what you want. Still reclining on the bed, he called the desk—quietly, so as not to wake Lucia—and asked if by chance they had sweats and shoes he could borrow. He felt Lucia's arm stretch alongside his as she lightly grasped his wrist to interrupt his call. Don't bother, she told him. I have some things you can use. In the bottom right of the ward-robe. She pointed and then pushed her hair back, holding it piled above her forehead. She glanced sideways at him. You want to stretch first?

Wearing a burgundy terry-cloth tennis outfit and snow-white sneak-ers, he ran two miles down South Street toward the Delaware. Pedes-trians grimly strode to work, openly irritated by Philip and his sartorial freedom. He weakened quickly and stopped for a coffee, which fueled him for a steady five miles along the river. The borrowed shoes blistered his toes and heels, but running, gaining speed in the cool moist air, felt too good for him to stop. The borrowed terry cloth held a trace of expensive cologne, reminiscent of melon rind.

In Seville, he ran almost every morning with Irma, unless she was off exploring the rest of Spain. He would leave Beatrice in her deep morning sleep and try to beat the Andalusian sun. He and Irma usually ran along the wide walkway overlooking the Guadalquivir, passing the Moorish lookout, the three bridges, the bullring, the Plaza de Armas. The cobblestone plazas just above the river were always strewn with the previous night's party litter and the sweepers would be pushing the bottles and napkins with their wide brooms. A few Spaniards still dressed for the night would be shambling off to work or finally off to sleep. It was not unusual to pass stragglers from a wedding party, caught suddenly in sunlight, blinking and beginning to sweat in their tuxedoes and gowns, considering a group plunge into the river. Running from the river to Barrio Santa Cruz, he and Irma would have to shorten and quicken their strides to navigate the pedestrian-filled sidewalks. "Does Beatrice think we're screwing?" she asked one time.

She veered into Maria Luisa Park, which was what she did when she needed to run more. The park offered an expansive maze of tree-shaded gardens, courtyards, plazas, pools, arbors, and groves, all connected by paths and clay roads. He could steeplechase throughout it, hurdling ninth century Moorish benches and little fountains barely rising from packed dirt, or he could bank around a circle of porcelain frogs the size of children. Philip stayed with her, which was his choice during their runs, whenever Irma would peel away from their expected route and leave him to think alone or think with her. If he stayed with her, though, he understood that it would be a challenge, that he would most likely get himself in trouble both physically and emotionally.

"No," he answered, hoping she would slow the pace. "But I think she's jealous of something else. About you."

Irma throttled down a half stride, listening.

"Love, togetherness, forever, children, nesting, growing old," he said, eliminating all unnecessary words to keep his breath.

"She doesn't understand why I—maybe we—don't care about such things?" she asked, throttling down a little more.

"Something like that," he replied. He swallowed and looked ahead to a long, shallow fountain. It stretched for fifty meters, nothing more than a narrow rectangle canopied by arcs of water running along either side.

"Is that why she married you?"

"I believe so."

"To join you in that understanding? Or to conquer it in you?"

"One of those," he replied.

"But why did *you* marry *Beatrice*? Why did you marry Rebecca? Why do you marry, Pip?"

He slowed, hoping she would continue at her pace. She slowed with him. The Sevillan sun had reached a scorching height already, even though their morning shadows were still long. They were in the dust, out of the trees, heading toward the long fountain. Spaniards in white shirts were moving along the shaded paths, but with some sense of the day, this one unique day in this one unique place composed of a hundred different settings for contemplation.

"You have your books, Irma. The ones you make, the ones you restore. You bring them into existence or restore them to life and they are beautiful."

"They're delusions, Pip."

"But isn't the act of creating them worth it anyway?"

"What is your equation for that?" she asked.

"You really want to hear it?"

She remained silent as they both began a hard kick to the fountain. He sensed her expression, a child's arithmetic wince.

"I thought not," he said.

"So I construct my delusions," she said. "And you join yours?"

They race to the water. Gray and white doves scatter in front of them, whipping up dust. The water is a few centimeters deep and they can run in it like steeplechasers. A tunnel of water arcs above them and the sun divides into thousands of tiny suns. He must crouch slightly into his run, to duck beneath the arc. And this allows her to see his expression and it slows her a half stride that ultimately costs her the race. His face, squinting against the water and sun and strain, is earnest—to the point of boyish, to the point of wanting. He is the protagonist of her life and there is nothing she can do to erase or end this fact.

FIVE

The plan, as Philip and Lucia saw it, was to have the simplest of dinners together, to begin showing each other their respective versions of the city. But from the start, the simple equation grew exponentially. To show him her version of the city, Lucia chose perhaps his favorite eatery at the time, a little taqueria on South Street called The Joint. This choice did not stand completely outside the laws of probability. The space was undemanding. You ordered at the counter, all the cooking was done behind the register by the Spanish-speaking men who took your request; the drinks all cost the same and you simply pulled them from the refrigerator—beer, wine, soda, juice, tea—then found yourself a table along the side wall or in the back. From the side wall you could watch South Street. In the back, you were cut off from everything. The back room remained unfinished, with exposed subflooring, inner walls, and ducts.

The taqueria fit her needs: inexpensive, good, slightly exotic, but still Philly, and with a choice between being seen or being hidden. It was named after the shape of the eatery's signature dish, a burrito foil-wrapped and twisted closed at the ends. But Philadelphia, even if you stayed within downtown, had at least twenty places that fit her criteria. South Street alone held five. So the odds of her choice also being his, though well within the laws of probability, were long enough to prompt suspicion.

The equation remained simple, but divergent. If she somehow knew of him, then choosing The Joint would have to represent an intentional overplaying of her hand. A play designed to distract a mathematician. Think like Philip. Here is where the equation diverges—for equations can diverge and then reconnect. The overplay, the choosing of The Joint, could indicate simple innocence. No intelligent player would make such an overplay except out of complete innocence. Or it could indicate audacity aimed to weaken his position by amplifying intrigue into paranoia. Or—and the motivation for this, M, remains unclear to him—it could represent an effective attempt to distract him, sending him, the mathematician, on divergent paths in the same equation. The equation of her. She knows something about vibrating matrices.

On his way to meet her, as some sort of talisman against physical desire, he lugged the big yellow Cervantes with him. How was he to know that it could only have the opposite effect. He was not a man of letters and he had yet to read it. He wore a long felt coat and pulled the collar up to ward off the river breeze and the cold night. If you saw him as he passed the old granite buildings of the Mütter Museum and the College of Physicians, with his long green coat and his big yellow book on a cold spring evening, you would guess that he was somehow *of* those buildings. Unless you could see that the book was Cervantes and not some ancient text on the identification and treatment of swallowed objects. And you knew that on his way to pick up Lucia at the Latham, he veered considerably off the direct route to stroll by those buildings, which he loved.

After they ate, along the sidewall where they could watch the stream of black youth along South Street, Philip and Lucia took fresh beers to the back room. The room was empty except for a group of four Penn girls drinking from small bottles of Chianti and showing each other their cell phone pictures. He hauled the Cervantes with him and plopped it on a tabletop. The little table keeled under the book's weight. Lucia motioned to the Cervantes with her fingers as she sat.

"May I?"

He pushed it toward her. She brushed the yellow leather, the soft dimples. She ricocheted the hard cover lightly between her fingertips, then perused the flyleaves.

"Where did you get this edition?"

"Irma gave it to me. She left me her books."

"Left?" Lucia gave him a slanted look.

"She quit," he told her.

"Reading or writing?"

"Everything," he explained.

"Can anyone really do that? Quit everything?" She spoke toward the pages of Cervantes. And she did not lift her gaze to him right after, the way she usually did. She continued to look into the pages, waiting for the answer to emerge. She looked up only in afterthought.

"I'm still trying to figure that out," he replied. "What she means. Can she really do that? I've done some quitting myself. To try to follow along. But I'm not nearly as bold as she is. I'm sort of trying to quit without really quitting. I could explain it better with math. In math we use experimental equations to plumb the surface of a larger proof. It's a way of going into someone else's proof without affecting it. And you can reverse it at any time."

"So you won't get lost in it?" she asked. "And wreck it? Like Theseus with his ball of string?"

"Something like that."

"Have you ever become lost in it?" With a look aimed just beneath the words, Lucia made it sound more beckon than question, a husky emphasis on *lost*.

"In this proof," he said, "I know that I would. If I followed in too far, too fast."

"You don't seem worried. About getting lost."

"But I am," he told her. "I read her books for comfort, understanding, direction. But their effect is always the opposite."

She opened her lips, chewed her tongue thoughtfully, gave him a look at once misanthropic and inclusive. As though there were always a back room she knew. "Your mistake is seeing it as a proof. As a ball of string. Losing yourself in another life, the labyrinth of another life, is more than strings and proofs. It's an act. A physical act, one that puts your body at risk, the very cords of it. But even dipping into it a little gives you life. When Theseus gets back, he and Ariadne go at it, don't you think?"

"Not even all the way back," he said. "Somewhere in the outer walls. Where she waits."

She nodded while examining the *Quixote* pages, as though she understood. But then the pages seemed to perplex her. She pushed her hair behind her ear and lowered herself over the book. He could see that this movement was habitual for her, a tumble of locks, a way of beginning her work.

"There's no translator," she said toward the pages, then peeked at him. "In fact, none of these credits and copyrights seem right."

"It's an old book. Doesn't all that stuff get muddled? Over the centuries? Over all those editions?"

She shook her head. "That's the one thing that doesn't get muddled over the centuries. Not when money is involved."

She perused the flyleaves, the copyrights, and the opening pages again, flipping back and forth through them, bending them to her gaze. Her lips parted and her eyelids relaxed, the gauzy light reflected in the curve of her dark lashes. She let the book open itself by delicately lowering its coverboards with her fingertips. She smiled at the way the weight and balance of the book spread the pages. She caressed the paper in a diagonal across one page, then the next.

"She believed books should require no hands," he told her.

"A translator's dream," said Lucia.

He reached across the table and placed his hand in the middle of the text, as though dipping it in a pool.

"Have you read it?" he asked.

"In Portuguese, of all things, for a translation class a long time ago." She covered his hand with hers, slipping her fingertips into the daedal cusps between his fingers. He knew about daedal cusps because in *Slip*, a photorealist painter falls in love with the hands of a pianist as she plays Ravel's *Tzigane*. Lucia pressed each cusp, one by one, in order, as if playing scales. With the edge of her thumb she caressed the curve of his thumb.

"There is a price," she said, "to dipping into the labyrinth."

"The blackening of our hearts."

"Not hearts. Souls. You think I'm joking?" She pushed his hand firmly into the book, his thumb into the soft cool crease. "It's in here, even. In this story there are absolutely beautiful women, strong women, whose souls darken as cost for the thrills they take, for their risky expressions of

their beauty. For their acts. But in Cervantes's fallen Spain a little darkness in the soul is forgiven, overlooked, unnoticed even. For a while."

He felt the heat of her palm against the back of his hand, and he felt
the marble coolness of the paper.

"Do you know where Ionic Street is?" she asked, then peered at him.

He nodded, but gave her a puzzled look.

"Go there."

"There is nothing there," he replied. "It's hardly even a street."

"Go there." She squinted at him and then nodded for him to exit.
"And don't forget your book." She sipped her beer as he left the table,
balancing the bottle with light fingers, lips softly to glass. The Penn girls,
in unison, lifted their brows to him.

While on one of his first evening runs in Philadelphia, just after mar-
rying Beatrice, he discovered Ionic Street. He veered into it because it
was far too narrow for cars. It was merely a brick passageway and he
could brush his fingers along both walls as he ran into its darkness,
wings spread. But he could tell right away that it connected somewhere
to the river. A warm breeze filled with the metal and water smell of the
Delaware streamed between the bricks. The passageway grew blacker,
seemed to dead-end, compress, then angled sharply toward an opening
that popped him into a sudden view of the piers and two entire cities
reflected as lights on water.

The old bricks, soaked with centuries of smoke, breath, sweat, and
blood, seemed to warm the air. They stacked three stories high on either
side and appeared to tilt toward each other as they held in the darkness.
No doors opened onto Ionic Street. It served no need anymore. Midway in, Philip leaned his shoulder blades to the brick and looked at the
bronze sliver of night sky above. A tidal breeze from the river, warmer
than the air, puffed through and then stilled. Pedestrian sounds rever-
berated from the narrow opening to Second Street, fragments of laughs,
conversations, and heel clicks. Her voice came from the other direction,
where it was dark, but from where the sapid breeze emanated. Put the
goddamned book down. He put it down and she opened it and knelt
on its tender pages. She unzipped his pants, reached in with cool fingers, and chuckled at how quickly he responded. She had trouble pulling

his erection free, but blew him immediately with a vigor that suspended him against the brick, something pressed ashore. Her lips were cool, her tongue warm. She made a humming sound that vibrated through him. A flashlight shone from Second Street. It found his face, then dropped down to her, where it stayed for a moment, before it was swept away by footsteps and the words of someone asking for directions. She never paused on him. Her lips were cool, her tongue warm, her throat hot. She twisted the base of his erection with her fingers. Her lips and tongue paused at the very tip of him. She inhaled and he thought that she was going to leave him there, unfinished. Then she took him in, clamping firmly, using her teeth. He bent forward, then back, pressed his shoulder blades painfully against the brick, and roared uncontrollably. He felt his throat go raw as his sound poured upward to the fissure of sky.

Beneath him, she vanished for a moment, as though never rising from her knees and sliding away in the dark. The book lay open on the alley floor. Then she was suddenly at his side, shoulder to the wall, smiling.

Your place is closest, she determined. They walked arm in arm the way he noticed mothers and daughters strolled together in the evening paseos of Michoacán. The Cervantes rode as counterweight against his hip. Lucia gazed like a tourist at the buildings they passed. She kissed him as a lover in front of the closed gates of the Bourse. In his room, she got him to the bed swiftly. Again he felt pressed ashore, the wave suspended on sand. She straddled him as she pulled off her coat and blouse, her breasts pointing and bouncing as they came free. She opened his coat and shirt, flaying them, then gripped the pockets of his jeans. He touched her arms. Shouldn't we go slow this time? She shook her head, lips parted, dark hair sweeping forward. After this one we'll go slow. She yanked down his jeans, scalding his skin with the force and speed.

Philip saw her in the earliest of morning light as he lay deep within the sheets. She perused the bookshelf, tracing her fingers over the spines, the only real colors in the corroded light. She stood naked before the books, her hair lifted and bundled, the single white lock swept up from her nape. In his sleepy flutter, she appeared tentative before the books, as though she were showing herself to them, ready to step naked into the secret passage behind them. Which one to pull? He closed his eyes to relieve their dryness. When he opened them, she had vanished and his room was filled with a clean yellow light and the sound of Eleventh Street traffic. Four books were gone from the collection, the spaces distinct as missing teeth.

He walked naked to the books, as she had done, imagining her path, almost expecting to find the shelf slightly ajar. Drafts—one colder, one warmer—moved about him and it felt as if she had just left, just rushed off, leaving her heat, taking some of his. The Borges was missing; that one he knew and it made sense she would take it, as something promised. One other was from the *D*'s, another from the *R*'s, and another an *S*. He put his fingers in the spaces and could not help thinking that Lucia knew better than he what to do with Irma's books. Comfort, understanding, direction. She must have laughed inside. She might still be laughing.

Philip had visited Philadelphia many times before moving there to be with Beatrice. Irma liked the city, as well. She saw it as respite from New York. As undergrads they took a special tour of the East Coast offered by the history department—neither were history majors but the deal was irresistible. The two of them strayed from the group too often, got lost, held up the bus, set off museum alarms by leaning too close to the paintings, and consistently failed to attend the evening seminars. By the time their tour, crawling south, reached Philly, Irma and Philip were hardly showing up for anything except the bad meals and free transportation. One evening in Philly they ran together and she led him down a very narrow brick alley with no doors and no windows and it could have been Ionic Street. It was dark and cold, but then a warm breeze billowed up the alley, as though someone had opened an oven somewhere. She stopped him, pushed him back against the bricks, and kissed him hard, cutting his lip as her teeth struck his. She pulled her sweatshirt off, an unfurling sound, a pop and whisper. It was the only time they had sex on the trip, though they were certain the entire tour believed they were screwing behind every statue and monument they passed. When the tour was over, back in Santa Cruz, Irma turned in her paper to receive seminar credit—they were both informed that if they did not pass, the university could bill them for the entire trip. Irma's paper was entitled "Banging Philip Behind Carpenters' Hall" and it received a high pass. The one she wrote for Philip, which received a simple pass, was entitled "Common Senses" and it emulated the style of Thomas Paine's pamphlets but did not use his connotation of sense and it built a strong case for sexual freedom as an underlying cause for the Revolution. Later she told him—maybe it was ten years later—that she also wanted to screw him in the Betsy Ross House but just couldn't figure out any way to do that. He told her he felt the same way about Franklin's grave.

He worked that morning in his running clothes, first on his consulting, then on his story in numbers. He was beginning to feel irresponsible. All he had for consumption in his apartment was coffee, bourbon, and tap water. All he had for cooking was the coffeemaker and a little dorm-room fridge, which he used only to make ice. He tapped away on his laptop, a tall glass of ice water, a hot mug of coffee, and a full bottle of bourbon beside him. The bourbon was there just to catch the morning light and remind him that today he would actually begin the Cervantes. Two e-mailed invitations to run waited in his toolbar: one from Nicole, three words long, loquacious for her, implying a new route; and one from his friend Isaac, reminding him of their monthly run, Philip's turn to be the visiting team. Philip felt dressed for the day.

His feeling of irresponsibility toward his consulting work dissolved quickly as he moved through the figures sent him. He still had trouble believing that they could not see what had to be done with the numbers. Sometimes he felt guilty in accepting their money. But he learned long ago, largely with the help of Irma, that people did not think as he did, did not understand and misunderstand as he did. This went beyond the language barriers he learned to hurdle as a child. Language and our relationship to it, she explained, forever shapes the way we think and react. It creates pathways that we can't help but follow. What you read, what you pile into yourself, shapes everything you feel, sense, and understand. This goes for everyone, even for people who say they don't read. Even for most people in the world who just watch TV. *Your* paths are different, Pip. They're worn deeper and rutted where they shouldn't be and they're overgrown and almost indiscernible where they should be clear.

The insurance company work came so easily he had to be very careful not to overanalyze anything. The story in numbers presented a much greater challenge to his sense of responsibility. He mentioned it to Lucia, partly in jest. But jesting, as Irma explained to him, usually revealed truth, like the quick swordfights in Shakespeare. Yeah, those, he replied.

He decided to write the story first in mathematics, then translate, or have it translated. The title and opening came easily, like the beginning of a chess game. But then the game slowed considerably as countermoves became evident. The blank page equaled responsibility cubed. The messages from Nicole and Isaac sitting in the blue toolbar at the bottom of his screen multiplied this exponent. And they began to stand for all the other messages lurking within his own understanding of his self. Responses to Rebecca and Beatrice, to Sam and Nicole, to his steeplechasing parents, to Irma, to her parents, to Isaac, whom he now spoke to only once a month, to Cervantes, whom he had yet to read one word of but whose pages had provided cushion for Lucia's knees and his pleasure.

Do you think people love having jobs, Sylvia asks Peter in *Theory*, because they offer a condoned but false responsibility that masks, at least for eight hours a day, true responsibility? Only someone who never keeps a real job could ask that, replies Peter. Admittedly, she says. But the question is still valid. They swim in Lake Pátzcuaro and Feli is with them, the Mexican actress who looks like her, who looks also like the woman Peter is trying to find. The two women circle Peter, whom they have drugged, creating a swirling current that disorients him even more. And the low sun glittering atop the ripples blinds him to understanding which woman is which. And he even begins to believe there is a third there, too. And he cannot tell which one is causing him to feel the overwhelming rudder of desire that is making it difficult for him to steer in the cool lake. Later, dry but still smelling of lake water, he makes love to one of them, but cannot figure out which woman it is because of the lighting and her threat to stop if he even tries to remove her slight mask that does not really seem to hide anything.

His story in numbers, Philip decided after the title and the opening, was really about how the most valuable numbers only reveal themselves through what the other numbers all around them are unable to describe;

e, i, and π reveal themselves this way, for example. But those three particular numbers were too important and historical and well trod to be main
characters in a little story. He learned that much from listening to Irma
and her friends. He wanted to compose *Sketches from a Hunter's Album*,
not *Carmody, Tough Bullet*. In his opening, it became clear to him that
his main character was the rectangular hyperbola $x^2 - y^2 = 1$, and that she
somehow had to free herself, in some respects but not all, from e^φ and $e^{-\varphi}$.
Initially, within his opening, he became thrilled by how free he was to
create his own math, one unfettered by true mathematics. His opening
complete, he struggled within the fictional rules his story established as it
went along. He must invent the rules as well as follow them. Everything
must still add up.

A new message slid into his toolbar. From Lucia, it was as sparse as
those from Nicole and Isaac: Something, it said. He eyed the spark of
sunlight in the amber depths of the bourbon bottle.

His train crossed downriver from the Trenton Makes bridge. Philip
saw the steel bridge and its sign strangely in sunlight, though the morning was gray. Trenton Makes. The World Takes. Maybe along with it
he saw Lucia's orange sundress and the way she opened her arms and
herself as she said, The World Takes. He wore his long felt coat over his
running clothes and pulled the collar up as he leaned his head against
the cold window glass. At the Trenton station he bought a coffee and
sipped it on the bus that took him halfway to Princeton. The bus let him
off somewhere on the edge of the Princeton woods, and from there he
found one of the paths that led to the Institute for Advanced Study.

Isaac stood on the edge of the Institute pond in his running clothes,
tossing pebbles into the center and watching the ripples. He wore running clothes even when not planning to run. He slept in them. When
he was not in them, ready for lecture, he looked like a man dressed for a
first date. His windup was like a kid's, beginning too far in front of his
shoulder. Philip noticed as well that Isaac's lips pursed as he threw, bitter
toward his target. His dark eyes, however, remained doubtful. His black
curls always seemed wet in some way, lending his pale skin and red lips
an overall dewiness, a deceptive callowness. At the start of a race, if you
did not know him, you could think he would win or come in last.

He studied shapes. He wrote a formula that explains the shape of the universe. Flat. It remains in contention, out of favor beside the formula that explains the universe as flat but with stitching, a deflated soccer ball. Most people, seeing Isaac at the edge of the water, here at the Institute, would think that he was considering the ripples, perhaps their imperfections, their measure. But Philip could tell that he was thinking about his children, because Isaac was tossing the pebbles overhand, trying to kiss hand to ear before his release the way Philip had shown him, the way you try to teach a kid more inclined toward chess openings. Isaac did not reside at the Institute, but, as he always humbly explained it, they let him have a desk there, while he taught at Rutgers, which he always noted was really only the University of New Jersey.

Isaac slept with Irma five nights in a row just before he met his wife Melissa for the first time. It was while Philip and Isaac were finishing up their grad work in Ann Arbor and Irma was doing her apprenticeship in Chicago. Irma took the three-hour train ride north to run with Philip and stayed for a week, as she often did. "Are you sure this is okay with you?" Isaac asked Philip after each night. Then, at the train station, Isaac met Melissa for the first time, almost immediately after he and Philip had walked Irma to the platform. When Irma boarded the train, she paused in the car doorway. She braced her hands against the metal frame and kept one foot back on the platform, and her skirt wrapped her straightened leg and her waistcoat lifted to show the curve of her hips. She looked over her shoulder. She looked at Philip, not once at Isaac. She remained there for a moment. The conductor approached to shoo her along but then paused, hand lifted, and let her be. In the race that had become their friendship, Philip thought at that moment that Irma had gained the largest lead either of them would ever achieve. Her hair, growing out from a short cut, was just long enough to tumble about her face. And to him she looked like an actress from a black and white movie with heavy dialogue, and that here, now, was the one second where nothing was said, where ascension and doubt would combine in silence. She was an apprentice bookmaker who was beginning to earn the envy of her mentor. Philip was a mathematician about to abandon his doctoral pursuit.

It is the cover of a paperback that should have been written. Air released from the train brakes lifts her clothes tightly about her form, lifts her hair so that one dark lock sweeps across her cheekbone. Her lips are parted as though she is or is not about to speak. Her hands are braced firmly against the doorframe of the railcar as she looks over her shoulder. Your viewpoint as you hold the book is cast over the man's shoulder, framed by the side of his face, the muscular slope of his neck, and the sharp cut of his coat. His jaw seems slightly clenched. Because she is paused midstep, one black high heel up, one still on the platform, her calf muscles are long and delineated, offering. She could be heading home to Algiers or to do business in Istanbul. Steam billows overhead.

Five years later, Isaac (whose form remains outside the frame of the paperback cover) married Melissa. In five more years, they began to have kids. Philip knew—knew absolutely—that Isaac's love for his kids would prevent him from ever figuring out the exact shape of the universe, to the precise point where it would have to be accepted over the soccer ball. Maybe he was counting the ripples in the Institute pond, noting their shapes, the aberrations from circular perfection; but only because such processes occurred automatically and independently below the surface of his thoughts, his concerns regarding his son's inability to make the throw from short to first.

He seemed startled to see Philip step from the woods to the edge of the pond. He paused midthrow to eye Philip in his long coat and running shoes.

"You look like one of the inmates."

Philip shrugged and opened his coat to show Isaac that he was dressed ready to run.

"I'm working on Jake's throw," he told Philip. "He doesn't want to play second. He wants to play third. But he can't make that long throw to first." Isaac flipped the pebble into the water and shook his head. "He can't really make the throw from second."

"Let's hit him some infield sometime," Philip replied. "Soon. The fields should be nice."

They ran the Institute woods. Philip held back for a while as they raced wordlessly through the intricate web of paths beneath the maples,

oaks, and hickories. The blackberry leaves were emerging and the awakened shoots reached into the paths, snagging the runners' sleeves. It's
bizarre, Irma told him sometime after Isaac and Melissa's wedding, to
go through an entire friendship and never be angry at that friend. *Never.*
You can't possibly do that, Pip. I know what I'm *supposed* to be angry
about, he explained. Isn't that enough?

He gauged Isaac's effort as they ran the outskirts of the Institute
woods, as they finished a brief speedplay near the Quaker meetinghouse.
On a horse trail that traced the outer circle of the woods and eventually
looped back to the pond, he kicked away from Isaac. He kicked away just
as he sensed that his friend was about to begin a conversation and warm
down into a jog. Philip did not care that he had a later running date with
Nicole. He ran hard, bracing his back muscles into a near-sprint. Don't
forget to sprint, Irma always warned him. Especially as we get older.
Your body can lose the ability to sprint. The nerves along the spine begin
to atrophy. You lose the ability to even trigger a sprint. You can feel it in
your back. It's like trying to come. You try to come? he asked her. Never
with you, dear Pip. Never with you. She sprinted away from him.

The leaves on the Institute trail had been packed by a winter's worth
of snow and they lay smooth and slick as freshly rolled parchment. The
sassafras roots and oak knees curled in clear relief against the flat of the
path. These little hurdles intensified Philip's speedplay away from Isaac.
They forced him to concentrate on each rapid stride, to adjust. After his
parents defected, they continued to train for the steeplechase in the Palo
Alto woods, where the soggy trails eased the impact on their joints, but
where the redwood roots offered a constant array of hurdles and cupped
pools of water. They took turns with little Philip, watching him when
the other had to be on campus. And watching him meant running with
him, holding his hands when he was just learning, letting him go on
ahead when he found his footing and could fly, it seemed to them, over
the rutted trails. Even if Isaac could have mustered another speedplay,
even with his runner's body and his wind and determination, he could
not catch Philip, who was too tall to be a true runner, but who had been
taught how to pace the 3,000-meter steeplechase in 2,333 well-thought
strides.

Isaac was gaining on him in the clearing between the woods and the Institute pond, but cursing him between gasps. Philip pulled up at the stone bench where they had left their water and their winter things. He wrapped himself in his long felt overcoat as Isaac walked around him, picking up pebbles and throwing them into the water with a yanking motion. When Philip had regained his breath, finished heaving within his felt cocoon, he spoke to his friend softly.

"Two months ago we were skating here. The ice was perfect. That was the nicest Melissa has ever been toward me. Probably because of the kids and because I showed Jake how to skate backward."

"Melissa has always liked you."

"She has never liked me."

"It's true," admitted Isaac, nodding as he stared at the water. "But she doesn't really like any friends I knew before her."

"She always liked Irma."

"I don't know why," said Isaac. "She's the one friend who deserves her envy."

He offered Philip a slightly distant look, an unusual expression for him. Even in his doubting expressions Isaac's eyes appeared quick and ready, present.

"I still think about her," he said. "Then. I mean. Her body. Her contours." He flicked his head slightly to one side, but kept his eyes on Philip. "That's near fifteen years."

"Sixteen," answered Philip. "Almost exactly. But time really isn't a dividing factor in such memories."

"Such memories?"

"Memories of shape and feel," Philip answered. "I think that along with fragrance, they're the most composite of memories."

"You should write a book on contour mnemonics."

"No," Philip replied. "You should."

Philip leaned over, hands to knees, and took some more recovering breaths, inhales that cooled his lungs. The adrenaline of the sprint was descending in stages, as always. He gazed down at the edge of the green water, watching it fit itself against the gravel and mud.

"There is something going on with me, Isaac."

On his shoulder, he felt the gentle weight of his friend's hand.

"Irma's gone," said Philip, still bent and resting.

"I know. Beatrice spoke to Melissa." He clasped Philip's shoulder. "But Irma's almost always gone. Isn't she?"

"This is different. She left me her books."

"Are you reading them?"

Philip nodded. "And there seems to be some sort of design to them."

"You're too suspicious of design." Isaac kept his hand on his friend's shoulder as Philip straightened himself. Three geese slid onto the pond and floated to its center, sending an angled set of ripples to the shore. The birds' colors—green, black, white—appeared matted in the gray noon.

"I assume you're going at them with your usual sampling method."

Philip nodded. "Did you ever show her how to use it?"

Isaac laughed, then, as he usually did, he shaped the end of his laugh into the first words of his reaction. "Phil, *I* don't even know how you use it."

Nonetheless, Philip explained to his friend. There was something going on. In him. Her books teetered in the center of his life, the motley center of his brown life. He'd met someone. That someone felt like a character from Irma's books, or Irma's life or his life. Their life. His stepdaughter contacted him more now than when she was actually his stepdaughter. She ran with him without talking. Later today, he would run with her and they'd go an easy five without speaking. When she did speak, after, she spoke more about my little troubles, while I could see that hers were not little. They pressed her into digression—and silence. A silence that sharpened her. A silence sad to me, but beautiful, too. He noticed for the first time, as she ran beyond him under streetlamps, how she looked like her mother, even though she didn't have Rebecca's red hair and fair skin. He noticed this in a kind of relief, copper on red. But he also noticed a change in her stride, a gait adjustment very familiar to him. And something drains from him. Something is draining from him.

"Beatrice had lunch with Melissa," said Isaac.

"Yes. Beatrice, too."

"She said you just had the best sex ever."

"We always had great sex."

Isaac shrugged. "Then she was saying a lot."

Philip eyed him. "What else did Beatrice tell her?"

"She did tell Melissa that Irma was missing. That you might be look-ing for her. That seeing you look—*start* to look, is how she said it—made her wonder about the divorce. Made her wonder about you."

Philip marveled a bit that Beatrice would offer this small revelation. It made it easier for him to remain discreet for her sake. The celery taste of her breath grazed the cold air.

In Trenton for their postrace lunch, Philip and Isaac walked by the downtown graveyard. The old headstones, lichen-covered and tilted, reminded Philip of the Borges story. "Why are most headstones arched?" he asked his friend, the expert on shapes.

Isaac's answer was quick. "They emulate gateways."

They had lunch at Gus' Restaurant, where Isaac traced arches on the Formica tabletop and used the ketchup bottle, salt-and-pepper shak-ers, and paper napkins to indicate the imposts, springers, voussoirs, and keystones. "The Etruscans were the first civilization we know of that developed the arch. But that's typical Western ego at work. The arch is a natural formation. Gravity forms it. Other civilizations probably enhanced and even emulated natural cave openings. Humans simply didn't find the arch aesthetically appealing. The Etruscans didn't. But they used it for gates, bridges, and drains. The Romans, after they assim-ilated the Etruscans, used the arch for the same functions, then added it as a symbol of victory. Of course, it symbolizes victory only because it implies a bridge to conquered lands and the passageway to the afterlife, all the death required to achieve the conquest."

For Philip, there was no way to cool Isaac once he achieved this degree. But you could momentarily redirect it, move the flame from can-dle to candle. "Could we, you think, figure the shape of her world? And then find her in it?"

The calculation quickly outgrew the table, the shakers and flatware crisscrossing to the edges, the napkins covered in inked equations from the pen borrowed from the waitress. Isaac remembered belatedly to insert P (Philip) into the equation predicting direction from S (Seville). "Of course you'd be a factor. Toward or away is the question."

"Try both," Philip replied.

Isaac halted his pen, looked up to Philip. "You realize she'd expect this. Of us. Wherever she is, she's already pictured this scene, or one pretty much like it."

"Get used to that," said Philip.

Isaac continued to compose the shape of her world, transforming the arches. Philip offered whatever factors and variables he could.

"Her hiding place would have to include anywhere books must gather," Philip told him. "That I've decided. But she is different. She is resigned somehow. I've never known her to be that way. Her mother read me the note and there was so much resignation to it. Irma doesn't resign. You know that. So we have to account for that difference. That difference in her."

Isaac shifted two forks aiming outward from the center. He wrote resignation into the equation and fit it into the shape of her world. He blinked at what he had done. He rolled his tongue inside his cheek. "Maybe it isn't resignation," he said. "Maybe . . ." He slid a pepper shaker into the space between the forks. "Maybe it's invitation, Philip."

For a moment, Philip only looked at his friend. "I think you lend too much value to me. You've made me too singular in all this."

Isaac turned his hand above their mess and shrugged.

"Whenever you do look for her . . . ," said Isaac. "I mean physically. It's pretty clear to me you're already searching—you ran like you were in another time. You look like you're seeing things. But when you go physically, begin here." He pointed to S. "S," he said. "S for Start."

When the waitress returned to clear their table, she asked them if they wanted to keep any of it. They told her no, thank you, and she told them that at least it looked more interesting than the law stuff left all the time by the courthouse people.

They left the restaurant and returned to the Trenton cemetery, on Isaac's suggestion, where they kicked around the gravestones. It was cold in the oak shade, the grass soggy and deep. Philip clutched his felt coat tightly and raised the collar. Isaac seemed unaware of the damp chill and unaffected by their hard run as he searched, darting and hopping, for the most perfect arches among the stones.

"Why didn't they find arches aesthetically appealing?" Philip asked.

"*Because*," Isaac told him. "Because the arch seemed too natural. They weren't interested in repeating nature. That was weak, self-defeating. They wanted to reshape the world. Isn't that what art is? A great, intricate, ongoing reshaping of the world? Those precious books of Irma's. Aren't those all great reshapings? And then her own reshapings of reshapings?"

The softest rain fell and Isaac held his arms out to all the arched gravestones, beckoning them with his hands.

"But look at us now."

S I X

Sylvia describes his transition to adulthood in *Theory*, just before she seduces him in the lake: In high school, his language barrier still kept him from understanding the words of seduction, provocation, admiration, invitation, adoration, and rejection that filled his school days. Physically he was tallish; in demeanor, birdlike, pausing in complete stillness as he tried to comprehend, then moving in small increments. He played all sports and did well enough to make the starting teams, but did not socialize with the other players. They liked him for this, appreciating his willingness to play whatever role needed: decoy, wallflower, rebounder, specialist, our troubled starter, our Bad News Barnes, rube, secret weapon, moody scholar, someone to keep the team's GPA high enough. Steeplechase, of course, was his sport of choice, but few high school track meets featured the race. Few coaches knew what it was exactly. Peter would often have to petition opposing coaches and meet officials to stage the race. Opposing distance runners and hurdlers were usually intrigued enough to try it, primarily because of the water hurdle, but only after they had spent themselves in their respective specialties. So he usually won. When he competed in the rare meet where the steeplechase was included, he did not win, but grinned through the entire 3,000 meters.

He sought rest on the high jump mats, relaxing his eyes on the contrast between the green infield and orange track, the straight and curve of the oval. The steeplechase requires an unusually high level of visual concentration, a constant governing between a close and far range of vision while running as fast as you can. Eventually he would lay back in the deep mat and gaze at the sky and listen to the final blares of the meet, not shaping in his mind any of the metallic words, names, times, or finishes announced over the PA. Once a girl high jumper from an opposing team found him sunk deep in the mat. She asked him for a cigarette and was surprised into smiling when he actually procured one, a bit crimped and bent, from the hood of his sweatshirt. You're the steeplechase guy, she told him as she began the cigarette, lifted her leg, and placed one heel on the edge of the mat. My boyfriend ran that race. After he lost the mile. He was curious. We watched you set up the course. You looked so serious, so persnickety.

How did he do? he asked her.

He beat you. It was his first-ever steeplechase.

He nodded. Almost everybody beat me today. How did you do?

She smoked and leaned forward with her heel to the mat, one leg remaining straight, one bending, her shorts lifting to expose more of her thighs.

I came in last. I don't really jump very high. I just like falling into the soft mats.

The high jumper found him at three subsequent meets, and only managed to seduce him at the last. She pushed aside the cigarette he offered and instead slipped her fingers up his shorts and gave him a hand job. She then slid on top of him and managed to work his erection inside her without removing her clothes or his, twisting his shorts and her shorts just so. They kept their movements, as best they could, below the deep horizon of the mat and beneath the radar of the PA announcements that sounded like the lonely squawk of a waterbird. The binding and friction of their clothes stayed their eagerness and abandon, prolonging and complicating their sense of pleasure, prompting them to be more aware, more considerate of each other. When she climaxed the first time, she bent herself upward, eyes closed to the sky. He quickly pulled her by the shoulders back down into the cover of the mat, then rolled over. They remained locked together, tied by her ingenious this way/that way twist of their shorts. On top, he slowed their pace even more. It was his first time and he wanted to savor it. Forever, he began to think, feeling the warm brush of wind along his back and neck, breathing the cut-grass smell. Oh, this is good, she told him. This is good. This is a good way, she said every time he slowed to save himself.

Finally, he lost control and drove her deep into the mat, until he had pressed the foam to its limit and she was able to thrust back. They almost suffocated each other in the depths, and in unison sprang into the air to gasp for breath. We will definitely be doing this again, she said. But she was not looking at him and almost seemed as though she were speaking only to herself. They met three more times, in a motel with a wagon wheel fastened to its flagstone wall, before she left to go to the University of Texas with her boyfriend.

Sylvia's narration continues as she circles him in the lake, letting her leg sometimes brush his, noting how soft flesh feels in water: If his demeanor in high school was once birdlike, it had softened into something else by the time he met me in college. As we exchanged tales of lost virginity, I at first assumed his, like mine, was entirely fabricated. But my assumption was wrong. You could see him carefully gathering words before he spoke, lifting his face gently to the sun, then directing his gaze to you as he began to speak. He would then look down and blink softly as he continued, making so sure—too sure—of his words. We met on the sidelines of a Frisbee game and exchanged our lost virginity tales, and by the end of his, I was already beginning to realize that he probably was unable to fabricate anything because he had to concentrate just to render the truth. There was a moment when I even asked him what his native language was. He smiled, almost generous, but I could easily see it was an attempt to disguise hurt. His features, because they were so tautly rendered, the muscles and bones barely veiled, expressed emotion readily, instantly. I wondered how it would feel to be that exposed, unable to lie, unable to feign. You would have to learn—somehow—to glide between the inevitable moments of exposure.

When it was time for us to rejoin the Frisbee game, I declined with the intent to watch him. I pretended to do stretches on the grass as the game resumed. He did seem to play with a kind of suppressed grace, jerked loose by flashes of revelation, or perhaps I was already projecting my conceptions onto him. He played defense like a basketball player, shadowing his mark everywhere and at all times, staring at the oppo-nent's shoulders, triggered by their movement. It seemed he could run at any speed, at all times, and I knew right away he was still a runner (and that I would invite him to join me soon). He was easily faked by his mark, but would always doggedly recover, regaining his shadow posi-tion. He did not throw the disk particularly well, but he always held it delicately at the tips of his fingers. He had a funny way of catching it, of watching its flight and spin for too long, as though fascinated every time, endlessly, by the physics of it. Then he would pluck the disk from the air, just as you were sure it had escaped his reach (which was longer than anticipated). His marks could always make him smile or chuckle, even as he focused intently on their shoulders. The dumbest jokes broke his concentration, momentarily at least, so that after you watched him for a while, he looked like a serious man always about to break into laughter, like Gregory Peck in a comedy.

Love, I have always known, is an evolutionary trait. It is a delicately tuned, intricate, sensitive impulse, but a trait nevertheless, a reaction honed by millions of years of an ever-changing and complex mating instinct. You can act on it, as almost every human does, or you can resist its nature. I believe that the most noble human endeavor is to resist human nature and to find—to learn—ways to fill the resulting gaps and reconstruct the pathways between us.

So, yes, I admit to falling in love with Peter Navratil during that Frisbee game and loving him still as I circled him in the waters of Lake Pátzcuaro. Loving him, even though he did not even know it was me cir-cling him, even though he could not see me through the slightest of dis-guises, even though he could not clearly distinguish me from the other woman who circled with me, who helped me stir the waters. Feli, my Ofelia. But love to me is a trait, like the desire to kill, something to be utterly denied, made irrelevant for the sake of enlightenment. If enlight-enment happens to return you to that same, instinctual point of love, then perhaps you are lucky.

It was almost like that for him, too, I could tell. But in a different, mathematical way. Love was a key equation in a longer formula, one that might or might not be hindering connection and understanding. As a mathematician, working on hunches, he had to test the equation once, twice. How many times?

On the train from Trenton back to Philadelphia, Philip fought off muscle cramps from his run with Isaac. He found it difficult to extend his legs until an older woman, someone's sophisticated grandmother in navy blue, helped reverse the unoccupied seat in front of him and create a booth. She sat across the aisle and held a book in her lap, petting it, it seemed, rather than reading it. She smelled of dark cigar. She nodded to the book in Philip's hands, *The Theory of Peter Navratil.*

"That's a beautiful book. I've not heard of it. Is it a new release?"

He turned the book over and back, showing its color and sheen. "There are only five in print."

"May I?" she asked.

He passed it to her and told her she could hold it for the remainder of their train ride. Then he pressed his forehead to the cool window and watched the green and gray smear of the Pennsylvania landscape. In the pockets of towns and satellites of Philadelphia, he searched for Isaac's arches, finding them to his surprise in the borders of communities, in the way towns and small developments encroached on the thick woods. And in the cemeteries, their gates and their tombstones. He fogged the glass with his breath, traced an arch with his finger, then watched it evaporate. Look at us now, he thought. Look at all I've learned. Quickly, before you miss it.

The woman across the aisle did not read the book he loaned her. It rested in her lap, its green leather gemlike against her navy skirt. She lay one hand on it and gazed over the tops of the train seats, pursing her lips from time to time as though she had already read the novel and was now considering its intricacies and implications. Books aren't just for reading, Pip, Irma told him when he discovered her passion for them, for their physicality and content. They are loaned, borrowed, and stolen things. Pepys once borrowed a friend's book on human oddities and returned it fifteen years later saying: Thank you, I enjoyed it. They bind and revive friendships. They are caressed for comfort. Their spines cupped for coolness or warmth. Their covers lingered over. I still love to slip my fingers between cool pages, like finding the fresh creases of bedsheets with your bare legs. They are portable, the most efficient of vessels. You can carry an entire country or civilization in the crook of your wrist. Hold open a life or the expanse of a relationship with the gentle crimp of your thumb. They are incredibly light and manageable for what they contain, what they can induce.

The first one she ever gave him was a re-bound eighteenth century edition of Napier's *Canon*. One of her early projects, when they were still undergrads, it came to her coverless and spineless, but with all the pages present. He saw the thing, first, in a plastic bag and helped her order the pages, the exponential tables. The next time he held it, it was bound in ochre linen—his. It remained in a box of his things at his parents' home in California.

The sophisticated grandmother departed the train one stop before Philip's, at the university station. She returned *The Theory of Peter Navratil*, passing it to him with both hands. Her navy suit remained creaseless, sleeves folding neatly at the elbow. He meant to greet her thanks with a welcome, but instead let slight confusion lift his brow.

"I can't read any more fiction," she explained. "I vowed not to, until I have fully understood everything I've already read."

"But wouldn't new work help you construe the old?" This was simple math for Philip.

"I'm still considering that," she replied. "You know? Is the new burden worth the treasure it holds? But I do love holding new novels. Especially those weighted so nicely as this."

The train swayed to its stop and she disembarked. The train then finished its brief spur into downtown, sliding into the tunnel beneath the river and becoming part of the subway system. Lucia was there to greet him at the East Market Station. She kissed him as though he had returned from some kind of front, not of war but of expedition. She spread the lapels of his long felt coat and touched her nose to his chest.

"You're rank," she said, then looked up to him. "How far did you run?"

"Ten k." He thought to translate. "A little over six miles."

"And you plan to run again this evening?"

He nodded. "With Nick. I'll try, at least."

"Come." She pulled him by the pocket of his coat as he slung his bag over his shoulder. "I have that something to show you. But we have to go to your books. It's in there."

An absurd spring snow was falling by the time they reached his apartment. The mannequin family in the Baum's window wore lime-green beach outfits, ready for the Jersey Shore in a church picnic sort of way. The snow dropped across the display. Inside, Lucia did not allow him to shower right away. On his laptop, she clicked on Theatre of Voices performing Arvo Pärt's *De Profundis*. Then she opened the window to his apartment, letting in whips of snow and cold air. She undressed in front of the window, then clutched her arms about her waist and shivered on tiptoe. "Come feel them," she said.

Cold drafts reached them as they made love, finding pockets in the tousled sheets. He felt the drafts as tongues of metal along his back, then along his shoulders and stomach as she rolled him over in order to be on top. She spoke calmly to him as she shoved gently and adjusted to his thrusts. "Afternoon light is best. I can see the texture of your skin. The line of your collarbone. I can see that you are happy, but still thinking."

She increased her rhythm slightly and leaned forward. She put the tip of her tongue to a line of salt that had crusted along his sternum. She paused astride him and said more. "In the afternoon we can see, hear, smell, feel, and taste. We can leave nothing to imagination. Fucking imagination." She tried to begin moving again, hard; but he stopped her by reaching up and taking hold of her hair, firmly, with both hands. She closed her eyes and let him pull her head back. He turned her head slightly, side to side. She smiled, eyes still closed. She could not possibly be Irma. She could not. He was only going crazy. Her lips were fuller, her eyes a different brown, her skin fundamentally darker. Her face was broader, her cheekbones more prominent. Her hair felt different in his hands, a pleasant coarseness. She was just more. He pulled her face closer.

"What?" She opened her eyes. "Who do you think I might be?"

"I'm just delirious," he answered.

"Not me," she said. She lifted, almost off him, then lowered herself deliberately. She shifted angles slightly as she continued, smiling down on him, knowing that she was making it impossible for him to speak or interrupt. She moved and adjusted according to his gasps, not her own. When she found a particularly effective angle or thrust, she would laugh softly and then repeat the movement immediately, then search for another. She bit her lower lip in concentration. "Close your eyes." But he was afraid to close his eyes, to shut away an afternoon that appeared and felt to be entirely, intricately balanced. Snow fell through the window in horizontal whirls that spun to vertical, then collapsed on the floor just short of the bed. Lucia, moving gently over him, followed his gaze to the snow patterns and smiled at them as though they were familiar, recognized, expected, invited.

"Now close your eyes." He was afraid to close his eyes. She stopped moving her pelvis and began to wrap her hair into a loose bun. Her breasts rose with the lift of her arms and she laughed as she felt him flex inside her. She kept her arms up for a moment. Then she lifted herself off him and knelt between his legs. She took hold of him with both hands, twisting slightly, bringing her lips close. He could feel her breath. "Close your eyes," she told him. She waited, caressing, breathing softly.

"That will kill me," he said.

"I can certainly try." Looking up, waiting, she opened her mouth.

So he closed his eyes and the afternoon slipped away immediately, in a slow spin and yaw. He gripped the sheets, fearing he was about to slide into a black sea flecked with white sparks. That was what he saw. Then for a moment she was off him—no mouth, no hands. Then he felt her brace her legs against his hips as she returned with much force and speed, her full weight over him. She covered his mouth with hers, not letting him breathe, so that he was in a panic when he climaxed. He would have lost consciousness if she had not pulled her lips from his in order to breathe and sob as she followed him.

Together, unfolding in the cold air, they caught their breath. She lay quietly at the edge of the bed, reaching for the snow that tumbled lightly through the window. She spread her fingers and twirled them as though trying to gently guide the flakes. Philip rose from the bed and walked carefully to the shower, keeling against dizziness.

When he returned to the room, showered and dressed, she was sitting at his table. Her hair was up and she wore one of his shirts and her reading glasses as she paged through his books. She had closed the window and warmed the room. The Borges she had taken now lay open on the table.

"What were the others?" he asked, maintaining a distance that allowed him to keep her and the bookshelf in view. He walked to the shelf and pointed to the first space. "*Ficciones* . . . ," he said. Then he put two fingers into the next space, at the end of the *D*'s.

"Duras," she said, adjusting her glasses, sorting the flaps of his shirt around her hips. She recrossed her legs. "Just for fun."

He didn't remember Duras. He put his fingers into the next space, then looked at her. She tracked him above her glasses, played with her pen.

"Robbe-Grillet," she said, smiling at him, at the fact that he didn't know. "*Jealousy*. It's about jealousy. Don't you love it when books are about what they say they're about?"

He ignored her and moved his fingers to the final space, an *S*.

"Sarraute," she said. "I guess you put me in a French mood. Then."

"What's it about?"

"You and me," she said. "It's about you and me."

"What are you doing with them?"

"Come see," she said, looking down at the open Borges. She had one hand on the Cervantes, too.

He sat beside her and she touched his wrist.

"When you told me about the Borges, the first time we met, I didn't think too much about it. Only of how much I liked it and that I should read it again. I read it once very long ago, for a translation class. When you didn't call me, I went to fetch a copy from the library and read it. Sort of as a way of conjuring you. And I had not been able to recall the lichen story—along with others. You said there were eighteen stories. I remember, because you said eighteen several times at the bar."

She slid Irma's bound copy of *Ficciones* toward him, pushing it across the table with her fingertips. Then she drew a battered paperback version from her bag and set it atop the hardcover.

"There are only seventeen stories, Philip" she told him. "There is no lichen story. I checked all editions. All Borges collections."

Philip brushed the paperback with the edge of his thumb. The corners of the cover were curled and webbed with brown creases.

"Someone else wrote 'Lichen.' Your friend, I assume. It's a forgery. But a very good one. I went through it several times and she got all the idioms right. She must have written it in Spanish—Argentine Spanish, no less—and then translated it. And she placed it right where it fit best. In Part One, The Garden of Forking Paths, between 'Pierre Menard' and 'The Circular Ruins.' I read it the other morning, while you slept. I would have asked, but I wanted to let you sleep. It's an entertaining forgery. She attended to everything: diction, syntax, rhythm, all possible patterns. It would fool Borges himself into wishing he wrote it. Of course . . ."

"What?" asked Philip.

"Of course, she doesn't need to fool Borges. Or me." With a pinch of her fingers, Lucia adjusted the corner of her glasses. "She only needs to fool you."

She opened the Cervantes and pointed to a very lightly penciled note on one of the empty flyleaves. He hadn't noticed it before. And he could not believe that he would have missed it, given that Irma now had him looking for such notes. But the scrawl was light, just emerging from invisibility. It read, in what could have been her handwriting, *See changes.* Though the last letter in the first word was nothing more than a crimp in the lead, the remaining tail of some hurried vowel.

Lucia closed the book and pushed it slightly away, as though to watch it move. They both looked at the Cervantes, which lay yellow, large, planetary on the table. She smiled at the volume, then peeked at him over her glasses.

"Anything could be in there."

She watched him the way you might watch someone open a prank gift, the tiniest of smiles only apparent in her cheekbones.

"And the others you have?"

She lifted her brow, a yes and a question.

"You've *finished* them?" he asked.

"I went through them."

"When do you work?"

"I'm at the end of that. I leave soon. The Duras was difficult for me. But a nice contrast to the others. Colors turn into sounds, you know?" She brushed the length of her bare thigh as though sweeping away lint with her fingertips. "But you don't know, do you?"

He shook his head.

"Then pick one."

He thought. Colors turning to sounds. Something about the two of them. Jealousy.

"The one about us."

"Pick another," she said.

"The jealousy one, then."

"That one you sort of have to be there. But it's about a guy—you're in his point of view, but it never uses *I*—who watches his beautiful wife from behind a window blind. *Jalousie* in French. Get it? Those clever French. Her name is A dot-dot-dot." She made a pointing motion with her finger to indicate the ellipsis. "He watches her brush her hair. He watches a man who might be her lover squash a centipede against a wall to save her. You watch this maybe five, maybe seven times. He counts the trees on his plantation for you."

"Why did you say the other one was about us?"

"Because it was the one that enthralled me most. And books that do that make me imagine myself in them, with someone." She looked at him too directly when she spoke these words, an alluring lull in her eyes. She shifted her legs, to make him look there.

He felt lied to, but lied to with a condition of understanding, a vow even. Let me lie to you and I will take you to pleasures unimagined. Better truths.

"I promise to return them," she said.

Preparing to meet Nicole for his second run, Philip invited Lucia to stay with the books. She sat at the table, paging through volumes which she slid from a small stack she had compiled. A simple violin solo played from his laptop. She had made coffee and still wore his shirt as a robe.

Her hair was up, glasses on, legs crossed. It was an unexpected look she gave him as he left, a skeptical expression defined by a sharp lift of one eyebrow and a slight tuck in her lips. Her finger marked her spot on a page. As he closed the door on her image, it felt as though he were both sequestering and releasing her. As though she were part guardian, part invader.

The paperback cover would make the shirt a brighter color perhaps, even higher up on her thighs. But not much enhancement would be needed. The backlight from the window would brighten and change to yellow, suggesting a tropical afternoon, an expat bungalow in Mexico. A tin fan stirs warm air that opens the collar of her shirt. Her fingers hold a pen, as if she were about to flip it, play with it, instead of writing. Her glasses and expression are rendered without change, suggesting both guardian and invader, ally and spy. The view includes half the man, from behind, a linen suit with cuffs. His stance is open to her. You can tell he has committed himself, but his wrist crooks softly, as though trying to palm one last card. You cannot be sure whether he is coming or going, but you know the place is his because that is his shirt she is wearing. Either way she has him, at least at this moment.

Books are best when shared, Pip, Irma told him once as he watched her finish breaking down a disintegrating volume of *The Sheltering Sky*. Using only her bone folder, she scraped the binding residue from the book's spine and then delicately separated the quires by running the bone edge through the decaying cloth. The sound was quiet and deliberate, the brushing of long hair. This particular book has passed through many hands. I can tell. Many reading styles have crimped its pages. It's been read in the desert, been rained on a little. It's not old enough to look like this. She parted the last two quires with a gentle draw of the bone folder and then blew softly, producing a curl of dust.

She had a collection of bone folders, gifts from friends. Some were antique, most ornate. But he only ever saw her use one. It was of the simplest design, like a doctor's tongue blade sharpened on one end. Sometimes she held it as you would a pen, then a knife, then a sewing needle, then a bow, then a paintbrush. He once sat in her shop for five hours and watched as she broke down a nineteenth century edition of Goethe's

Faust, using only that bone folder, holding it in various ways to change its function. She used its sharp edge to make an incision along the joint and then through the center of the spine piece, then to scrape away the crumbling remains of the mull. By limiting herself to only the bone folder, she told him, she could ensure that all parts of the book that would show could remain original and reasonably intact. But the spine piece and the mull, for instance, would be entirely new. She looked at him with a skeptical arch in her brow. You wonder, Pip, how I can take so much time with this. How I can spend a day just breaking down the spine. He nodded, stepped into her light, and touched the tip of the bone folder which she held up for him. Goethe spent sixty years writing this. What's most beautiful about it is the way Faust and Margarete and Mephistopheles speak about each other and themselves at varying distances, even as they stand together. The more personal, the more revealing, the more painful their words, the more distance Goethe lends to their point of view, their views of themselves. And in that distance, you find yourself running to them, arms out, reaching, but then changing direction as each one speaks. God, Pip. It's not like reading. It's like hearing music, getting overwhelmed by music. I know you can understand this. It translates to your math, doesn't it?

It did translate. He composed the equation that night and brought it to her shop the next day and gave it to her as a present for her twenty-eighth birthday. He carefully transcribed it to India ink on parchment. By writing small, he was able to fit it to one page. I'll let you do the rest, he told her, in terms of framing it or binding it. He pointed to the italicized d^{x-1}. That, of course, refers to distance. I had to give it an exponent and variable to accommodate the quick and profound changes. Increases and decreases, you know. Then allowing them to bend according to each person's—I mean each character's—view of themselves and one another.

She stared at the page and said nothing. He went on, trying to explain. What can't be avoided is this. He pointed to a parenthetical in the equation that repeated throughout. That accounts for the level of connection that develops in inverse relation to the distance. So unavoidably, as Faust, Margarete, and Mephistopheles reveal things about themselves, they become more attached to one another, even if those revelations intend to inspire detachment. You see? If your brief description of the characters and the narrative that holds them is accurate, then Faust, Margarete, and Mephistopheles would have to draw closer and closer to each other, independent of the distances they construct, *and* independent of any distance Goethe constructs.

Irma continued to stare at the page, holding it with both hands. Did you read it? she asked.

Only a few parts, here and there, to see if the equation held. It seemed to hold, he told her. Faust was most definitely closer to Margarete at the end of Part One, even as he must pull from her embrace and push her away and literally turn cold. And when he asks, How can I get through this misery? he's talking about misery as a physical, palpable thing. And it seems as though Margarete is speaking *of* him and *to* him at the same time and you wonder if she can even see him, if he is genuinely there, but then she does embrace him and kiss him and feels how cold he is physically, but how warm he seems. The warm act he finally performs for her. And Faust and Mephistopheles seem to grow closer all the way along. That was readily apparent, even to me. I know he's supposed to be the Devil, but he definitely becomes a friend, in the most comprehensive sense of that term.

Philip became embarrassed and reached to take the parchment back. Irma pulled it away from him. As he leaned forward with the momentum, she kissed him on the cheek. She spoke softly. You know your devil well.

As he moved along the sidewalks of the city, combining his easy strides with trots, skips, jumps, feints to the walls, you could see that he still knew his devil well. The devils of others, of his friends and ex-wives and stepchildren, mystified him and pestered him. In his running sweats, he hurried to his rendezvous with Nicole, hoping to catch the next subway across the Schuylkill to University City. He drew frequent looks from the many other pedestrians along Eleventh, then Market, because his bodily expression was that of one hurrying slightly against the grain. The workday was ending and the East Market Station was releasing crowds, people swinging their arms in the freedom of the wide sidewalks, pounding their steps, unclenching their wages, baffled by yet another spring snow that spun in contrails above their heads. In anticipation of meeting Nicole, Philip felt a tightness in his chest, a slight nervousness that surprised and confounded him, that gave his face a searching expression, a runner looking for both the distant finish and the immediate opening. If you were in the race with him, you would be wise to keep him in your sights, to be ready to go with him when he goes.

On his laptop, Philip has digital footage of the 5,000-meter race in the 1972 Munich Olympics. He watched the race, as a boy, with his parents. By the middle, it became clear that it was a two-man race, even though those two men were embedded in the crowd of runners. Both ran in the middle of the pack, but they were already marking each other. The American, Steve Prefontaine, stalked the Finn, Lasse Virén. Philip's father showed him this. His mother explained it, too, touching the screen with her fingertips. Prefontaine, she said, her acquired Slovak accent softening the name into something that seemed to refer to some kind of musical interlude. She showed how Prefontaine kept firing quick glances at Virén's right shoulder, even though the American appeared to be running lost in a sea of shoulders. He was shorter than the other runners, and looked different with his long flopping hair, sideburns, and mustache. His parents both tried to predict when he would make his move, but Prefontaine surprised them and everybody when he moved early. He surprised Virén and it was very easy to see on the Finn's usually stoic face. A lift of concern slanted across his brow as Prefontaine, who was younger and less experienced than the other runners, kicked into a sizable lead with still a third of the race to go. Virén hurried to the front of the chasers, then maintained a carefully measured distance behind Prefontaine. He then drew close heading into the final lap, bringing the best runners with him. He passed Prefontaine and the announcers and Philip's parents said that was all for the American and they watched Prefontaine fall back as Virén began to clear the field.

Then they all went quiet as Prefontaine, looking angry, ran down Virén and passed him. Virén gave him a sideways look as he was passed. He used his much longer strides to draw even with Prefontaine, then passed him with disdain and began his final kick. There goes Virén, they all said. But they were wrong again because Prefontaine was running with an expression on his face unfit for a runner. His eyes were wide with fear, as though he were looking into something completely unknown. His arms had a slight flail to them, which did not bode well for his chances. But he somehow overtook Virén just before the final stretch. Virén looked down in horror as he was passed again. This did not happen in the 5,000-meter. If you were caught trying to steal a race, then you were supposed to be finished. But Prefontaine was seeing something new, finding something new. And so Virén's expression changed also, to one of pained resolve, to that of someone heading into the unknown. He overtook Prefontaine ten meters before the finish and as he did, as Virén became the unknown, Prefontaine collapsed into a nosedive, shoulders down, arms back and up. Other runners suddenly passed him and he did not medal. The other runners seemed selfish and uncaring, taking something undeserving, money off a dead soldier. Virén, even in victory, looked back in concern for Prefontaine, who stumbled blindly across the finish, his hands almost touching the track. There was still some fear and confusion, too, in Virén's expression as he seemed to be wondering what he might have done to his body, his heart. Philip's father cried silently, even though he was rooting for the Finn. His mother blew a hard breath through pursed lips, her way of sighing. Sometimes, when Philip watched the race, he rooted for Virén, sometimes for Prefontaine. I suppose it's a question of mood, he told Irma when he showed it to her for the first time.

That was not the way the race actually happened. The younger, inexperienced Prefontaine was trounced by Virén and the other runners who defeated him. But who wants to hear that story? Who wants to see that? Who wants to reduce life to its essentials and inevitabilities?

Nicole led Philip to the tracks just beyond the University City metro stop, where the subway surfaced and blended into the rail yards. The Schuylkill loomed still and bowed as their gray horizon. Her course began there. She pointed to the red clay path between the first two rails.

"It's perfect."

Philip looked at her skeptically. He pretended to stretch and eyed the rail yards, the dim tunnels beyond, the squat, dark trees bordering the far tracks. The walls of the old neighborhoods near the rail yards looked like paper in the oncoming twilight. The snow fell lightly without consequence. It did not appear to make it to the ground.

"This was part of her course."

"Whose?" Nicole asked him.

He rolled his shoulders and grimaced as though he needed to stretch more, stalling, wondering if he could get her to say more than three words at a time.

"Don't pretend you don't know who we're talking about. I see the way you run. It's new to you and it's very much the way she runs. Every time I run with you I end up thinking of her. Longer strides, lowered arms, gliding straight as if you're on a rail. I would guess that you've seen a lot of her. Lately. At least before she disappeared."

"I haven't seen her."

"Don't pretend, Nicole. It doesn't suit you." He shook his head. "When you told her about your sea changes, I bet she loved that. Did she tell you something about them? Correct you somehow? Did she tell you that sea changes aren't real? That they are only what we make of things afterward? That *we* make the changes and then blame them on the sea?"

She shivered slightly and hugged herself. She looked away from him and the twilight shone on her coppery ponytail.

"Let me make some guesses," he said. "You've quit. Basketball and everything. Maybe you've joined cross-country. You've joined the Frisbee team. You're thinking of changing majors. You're always thinking of quitting school."

"Don't do that, Philip," she said softly, wiping away snowflakes from her cheekbones with the sleeve of her sweatshirt. "I don't like people invading my mind."

"I'm sorry," Philip replied.

Nicole sniffed, though gave no other evidence of crying. But her body seemed rigid with it. "And you didn't quite get it right," she told him, her voice quivering, then recovering. "She didn't say that we *blame* the sea. She told me that we credit the sea. It was the nicest, softest thing I'd heard in a long time."

She hopped three times to keep warm, to show him she was anxious to run. To show him she was not crying, not going to cry.

"When you came into our lives, we hated you. Sam and me. Your stupid gifts, Philip. The way you and Mom sometimes held each other, like you were huddling among ruins, hiding from a world gone crazy. But we couldn't hate you that way for long. How could we? You were so unbelievably strange to us. We always thought Mom was strange. But you . . . And Irma. You came from another world. And even though we were small angry children, we could see that Mom was better. Dad was better. Even after you had to leave. Then you were gone. And we'd miss you."

She crossed her arms and faced him plainly. She was her mother, Rebecca, with all the red removed—and instead all the colors of an almost new penny, with just enough luster in the nearing dusk. The directness of her look was meant to be a show of strength, but it opened her to him, revealed measured angles to him that showed she was trying hard not to collapse—a little too high of a lift in her shoulders, wrists and knuckles sharp and white.

"Let's just run, then, Nick. But just promise you won't ever run here alone."

"I never run here alone. Someone is always with me." She shrugged and widened her eyes at him.

He wanted very much to ask her at least one more question. But he remained quiet as they began clipping along the red clay path between the rails and as aimless flakes of snow drifted around them. She let him set the early pace. Old snow huddled black and furry against the rails. The heat pots at the rail switches had all been lighted, and their blue flames leaned forward as Philip and Nicole ran by them. He wanted to ask her how many times she had run here with Irma.

Nicole took a half-stride lead as they approached the first under-pass and the choice of paths increased. But Philip remembered Irma's route and knew which way they were headed. The damp clay path had a pleasant give to it, and he ran well despite the pains in his hip and heel from his first run with Isaac. Nicole led him diagonally across the rails through the first underpass and they hurdled the ties and the small, half-frozen puddles and were quickly through to the other side.

In some ways, he admitted, it could be a wonderful place to run, with a clear path, occasional hurdles, and a surrounding crash of shapes and colors in the twilight—the gray bowl of sky, the rounded tops of the black trees, the cement buttresses and walls with curlicues of graffiti, the expanse of ties and rails. They could hear the comforting hush of traffic coming from I-76. The first bloom of sweat passed over him, despite the chill, and he began to enjoy just running with Nicole, imagining they marked each other midway through a 5,000-meter race. He took the lead to show her he knew Irma's route, slanting across and hurdling three sets of rails. But he slowed as they approached the next underpass, which he knew was a long bending tunnel. Its black arch loomed.

It's not necessary, he wanted to tell Nicole, as he had tried to tell Irma. You don't really have to run here. We don't have to run through such places. We could be running beautiful Kelly Drive, like everybody else. The river there is so serene in this light.

Whenever they would pass the first shadowy forms curled against the tunnel wall, Irma would glance back over her shoulder and call to him, the echo of her voice sounding waterlike. What are they going to do? Run after me? *Catch* me? *You* can't even catch me, Pip.

As he and Nicole neared the tunnel entrance, Philip slowed, hoping to drag Nicole back with him. The sodium light inside the underpass only enhanced the darkness of the archway, spilling shadows across the rails. But Nicole increased the pace and her lead. Philip stopped abruptly, believing she would wait. She ran. Her bright form glided against the black maw of the entrance, his entire view seeming almost two-dimensional except for the swing of her ponytail. He called to the girl but she did not stop. She seemed to hurry into it, to be pulled into it as she disappeared into the shadows. Before vanishing, she turned to look back at him and said something. But she underestimated the distance she had gained and he could not make out her words. *You* can't even catch me, Pip.

Feeling slow and lumbering, he ran after her. Inside the underpass, the air smelled of machinery, of ozone and diesel, not the rag and urine smell of humanity he anticipated. The overhead sodium light at the tangent of the curve made it difficult to see the pathway between the rails or the gray exit beyond. He felt movement and life in the darkness pooled low against the walls. A ragged, drunken voice called out, chanting. "Run! Run! As fast as you can!" He could hear the echo of his own breaths as he labored to increase his pace. Can't catch me, I'm the gingerbread man!

When he emerged, Nicole was gone. He backpedaled and called her name, echoing it hard in the tunnel. He forwarded himself and opened up his stride and called for her again. He felt wet, cold, heavy. If he trotted back into the tunnel to look, he would lose her completely if she had gone on ahead. He paced himself as best he could, determined to run her down, but knowing how far he had to go and knowing that he was in the final kilometers of a day of running, of running more than he should. The railway lights were pink in the dusk. The snow had almost ended and the city glow reflected on the slick tops of the rails. The sky between the clouds still had some blue in it. He thought he caught a glimpse of her veering off the rails, but it could have been a low-flying bird, a heron seeking the river. He followed Irma's loop, burning his reserves against a cold film of panic. It was the best he could do.

At a bend in the tracks, where the river went straight for a brief stretch, rail and water forming a hyperbola, he did something that Irma could never bring herself to do. Because it was one of those geographical points where math ran counter to perception and intuition. In Colima once, they finally made it to the place called La Ilusión Optica by locals, a place where the road traveled over lava fields and seemed to go up while actually going down. The cabdriver cut his engine and let his taxi roll. To Irma and the driver, they seemed to be rolling uphill. Philip, on the other hand, felt liberation as the sharp line of the asphalt sliced measured angles through the lava beds. Hoping to cut off Nicole, he veered from the tracks and dipped into black woods and icy swamp. Here it seemed already night and the cold muddy trail was lined with litter and crisscrossed by paths and hollows fashioned by the tunnel dwellers. But this is a *shortcut*, he told Irma the first time she took him here. The line passes through a group of exponential curves. You can *see* the equation in the landscape. It's routine: $dx/dy = ay$, where the constant a determines the rate of change on each curve. She looked at him as though he were crazy and stayed her course while he cut into the woods. He emerged from the trees later, waiting, arms folded, well ahead of her.

Philip, running erratically from exhaustion, still managed to emerge from the woods and onto the tracks just a few strides behind Nicole. The weak snow ran like light static across his vision of her. She ran with the confidence of someone approaching the finish line alone in victory, shoulders high, head lifted, hands fisted. He caught her from behind, startling her, almost making her fall.

When she saw it was Philip she clutched her stomach and cried out in relief. He tried to put his arm around her shoulders, but he had to lean over and breathe. He grabbed his knees and pulled in hard, shuddering draughts. He was near tears himself.

"I'm sorry," he finally said when he was able to straighten somewhat. "I couldn't call out. I was out of strength. I'm sorry."

"No," she said softly, recovered. "I'm sorry, Philip. I'm sorry I did that to you. I don't know what I was doing. I don't know what I'm doing. But I wanted to show you. Really show you."

"Show me? Show me what?"

The snow dissipated just above the rails, like fireflies.

"I wanted you to feel how I feel. All the time."

"All the time? About what?" he asked.

"About everything, Philip. About all the people I care about. Everyone who matters to me. Mom. Sam." She paused to stare at him, to let him think. "Irma," she sighed forcefully and then continued. "And you. You. Don't you ever feel like that about *somebody?*"

"You mean afraid?"

"Yes, afraid. Afraid they're gone. That they will all soon be gone. But not just afraid for them. Afraid for yourself because they're gone. Really drop-cold afraid?"

Afraid, he thought, that they will slip away because you choose, just for a moment in your life, to delay, or to wait, or to pursue another direction, one you feel more ready to follow. He grimaced as his legs seized with exhaustion.

"What are you trying to decide, Nick?" he asked.

"You made Mom different. You even made Dad different. You made us—Sam and me—different. *Me* different. You . . . you and Irma showed us a kind of life we could live. I don't know if you live it now. But you showed us."

"That was years ago, Nick."

"You're so stupid. Sometimes. Just like she says. But you can know. The version of Mom you left us. It's better. It's still better. Dad, too. After all these years. But *I* want to be better. We—Sam and I—want to be better. I could go on with how I live. I can just follow what Dad says. It's good advice. It makes me happy. But it's just one version of me. I can be another. But I might be alone there."

"Look, Nick. You're exhausted. Whatever Irma told you. Whatever she's done. Brought you here and showed you her . . ."

"Her?" Nicole put her hands to her mouth and jogged briefly along the tracks, getting ahead of him. If she ran, he could not possibly follow. She turned back to him and stopped, hands prayerlike to her lips, shoulders straight. "It's not *her*. She didn't bring me here. You brought me here. You did it, Philip. I run here because of *you*. She showed it to me because I asked her. She just helped me find it."

They walked the rail yards back to University City Station. He put his arm around her shoulders and dusted the snowflakes from her hair. Inside the subway station, other runners mingled among the commuters and he felt comforted by them, by their fatigued expressions and their damp gray clothes. He stood with Nicole as she waited for her train. When his arrived first, she tried to make him go, but he refused and told her it was nice just standing with her like this. When hers arrived, she touched his shoulder, looking once to her hand, then to his face, before she passed through the train doors along with a few other runners. He walked home in the early night, taking care to keep his strides long in order to resist the tightening in his legs. The mannequin family in the Baum's window display waited for him in their lime-green beachwear. Then they stood guard for him after he passed them on his way to his flat two floors above.

You have a way of crying, Irma writes in *Slip*. You shed what you can, what you have at the ready. Coat, gloves, watch, a piece of paper, pen—anything but tears. And then you turn your head to one side and look down, away from whatever you've let crumple to the floor. I figured this out only after knowing you for a long time and wondering how a person—a thoughtful person—could never cry. It's certainly pretty, if nothing else.

He showered, fixed a whiskey, and was just about to select a book or two and ease into his recliner when someone knocked at his door. Two light indecisive taps, soft enough for him to pretend they were only imagined. He was ready to put this day to rest and he had no physical strength available for anybody. But one more tap drew him to the door.

It was Nicole, still in her sweats, a wool Rutgers cap pulled down to her eyes.

"Nick," he said as he motioned for her to come in. "You shouldn't be walking around out there alone. This late at night."

"You do. She does." She looked around his spare little flat. "Besides, I can stay on the beaten path. Believe me, I'm very good at that."

She looked at his recliner, its aqua-blue tilt, the soft reflection of the reading light along the worn contours. She saw his whiskey on the tin stand. She softened.

"Forget about what I said about hating you. I shouldn't have said we hated you. I had to come back to tell you that. That's all."

"It's all right." He fetched his winter coat. "Come. I'll walk you to your train."

She held up her hand. "Wait." Her Scarlet Knights cap was still pulled down to her eyes and she had to tilt her head back to see him clearly. "I had to show you. What I tried to show you. If I just said it, if I just told you, I would sound stupid. To you. I would have sounded like all freshmen sound. You would think I'm going through what everybody goes through. What you went through. Maybe I am. But maybe if I *showed* you—took you there—you would feel it. Understand it."

"I don't think you're like everybody else, Nick. I won't do that."

"One more thing," she said. "I came back for one more thing. I changed my mind about seeing the books. I want to see them."

She stepped close to the shelves. She reached up and put her fingers to the uppermost row, almost brushing the spines. Then she stepped back and looked at the collection as a whole, eyed its colors. Seeing her with the books like that, watching her pull the cap from her mussed hair, wipe her cheeks with her sleeve, be at ease in front of the collection, he understood the kind of things Irma may have passed to her. Why you have to take him to rail yards and ruins and lake isles and forgotten alleys and maybe the ends of the earth, where words and pages blow away in the wind. Why you have to take him. Why you have to take everybody. Everyone who matters.

"You can borrow them whenever you like," he told her.

SEVEN

Philip awoke in the night after only a few hours' sleep. It was a particular kind of waking, one that he understood well, one that let him know that a return to sleep would not soon be possible. It was not unusual for him to wake like this in the middle of the night after a day of hard running. Something explosive in his dreams throws him upward into sudden consciousness and his heart thumps and his thoughts glitter hard and clear. The dreams, he knows, are without image or sound and can only be recalled as emotion and impression.

He dressed and walked to Ludwig's, where he had a bourbon, ate smoked almonds, and watched part of a black and white Samurai movie. Some German techno-pop played softly, a woman singing in French with a Teutonic accent. The Samurai movie had a windmill in it, which was featured in the background of many of the shots. It was a Japanese-looking windmill, with origami bends and points in its sails, but a windmill nonetheless. A black man in a silver and green Eagles jacket sat two stools down from him, the only other nighthawk.

"Hey," he said to Philip. He pointed to the TV screen above the bar. "It's you."

They both looked at the screen. The weary bartender looked, too. They watched Toshirō Mifune eat a rice cake with his dirty hands as windmill shadows pass over him.

"I don't look like that," said Philip. "Do I?"

"Not exactly," the man in the Eagles jacket said. "Not physically."

The bartender nodded. "I see it." He poured more smoked almonds into the fake wood bowl.

Philip returned to his flat, resisting an urge to walk in a night which was beginning to warm and mist. He reshelved the books Lucia had left on the table and brought *Quixote* and *Slip* to the tin lamp stand, trying in vain to create some balance between the huge Cervantes and Irma's little novel. He eased into the Naugahyde recliner, sipped from a glass of ice water, and read *Slip* out of sympathy for its diminutive size and total obscurity. He also hoped it would quickly lead him to sleep, as it had done on many occasions. But for the first time in his life, he read it from end to end, all the while sipping ice water and resting his muscles and pains.

It was precisely 200 pages divided into ten 20-page chapters. Philip was pretty sure that each chapter had the exact same word count. The sentences were controlled and metered. The story was structured according to a 100-drawer specimen cabinet and a Ravel sonata, and each structural device appeared physically within the story and arose on cue to play its role, take on its weight. When he became aware of this interplay, the sliding and elusive nature of the prose grew more appealing. In *Slip*, Irma is Alma and he is Simon and they are fifteen years married, with an eight-year-old daughter named May who loves to ice-skate on the frozen ponds, canals, and lakes in the Jersey woods. Alma, the narrator, is an obscure photorealist painter doomed to teach art history at a nearby music college and Simon is a painter who must work as an art book editor at a nearby university press. They live in separate dwellings, he in their home, she in a rented attic loft to which she has banished herself for several reasons which become clear or obfuscated, depending on how you interpret things.

It seemed almost written for herself, full of reminders and iterations. She would keep inserting the same sentence or same series of sentences into different scenes and contexts. The two main characters, Alma and Simon, appear to be living the wrong lives—but fulfilling and thoughtful lives to some degree. When they find time and opportunity, the two painters sketch and resketch their charcoal studies, paint and repaint their canvases, until they look as real as photographs.

She bound *Slip* almost immediately after finishing it. She ceremoniously submitted it to New York, aware of its imminent rejection. The

number of readings it received and the lengthiness of the apologies surprised her, though. I feel kind of passed around, she told Philip. Like
the best-looking whore at an Ivy League bachelor party. They want me,
but no way in hell will any of them marry me. They talk about me, but
only among one another. She remained flip about it, but he watched her
as she meticulously stitched the bindings in her shop. She would bite her
lip thoughtfully, blink her eyes, or look aside for moment. She glanced at
him, sheepish, knowing that he could tell.

The final chapter, titled "E20" after the last drawer on Alma's specimen cabinet, circles the earth, telling you where every character travels after leaving Alma's loft. It swells with revelation, but then quiets at
the very end as you follow Simon on a snowy walk to the holding area
behind MoMA, which is being renovated. Alma physically vanishes
from the page midway through the final chapter. She ice-skates alone in
a winter fog. The mist gathers white on her long felt coat and gradually
erases her against the snowy landscape and winter sky. She also vanishes
as a character through the remainder of the story, but remains as the
voice, consciousness, and narrator. And the book manages to finish naturally without her. The reader sees everybody everywhere through her. In
the final image we see Simon, alone in a light snow, walking to MoMA,
forgetting about the renovation, then finding the art (minor works he
needed to see) in a holding tent in a back alley, ready for shipment. Philip
could not yet see the math in all of it, but after finishing he felt he could
at least begin to compose it—that it could be done.

He read through the final image one more time before easing out of
the recliner. He took the Cervantes to a Georgian teahouse, where he
ordered a bowl of borscht, plain yogurt, and very strong, smoky tea. It
was late morning and warm enough for the owner to prop the door open
and let in the air and the smell of the wet bricks of Sansom Street. For the
first time in years, he craved tobacco, specifically a crumpled cigarette.

Finally, he began *Don Quixote*, taking care not to spatter any beet juice
on the pages bound so carefully by Irma. The owner, a licorice-haired
Georgian man who never really smiled but instead practiced smiling over
and over when he wasn't looking at you, brought Philip a bronze book
prop shaped like a Rodin hand. He was accustomed to Philip coming in

to read math and physics texts. In the Cervantes, Lucia had left Philip a note, a yellow Post-it stuck on the second page of the story, with a tiny arrow pointing to the line, → With these words and phrases the poor gentleman lost his mind. The note, also begun with an arrow, read, → Cuidado. . . . Love, L. He had expected something from Irma, along the lines of her Borges insertions, but everything seemed in order through the first pages. Yet how was he to tell? He was surprised to feel lonely as he began the novel, wishing that Lucia were reading over his shoulder, her glasses slid partway down her nose, her breath against his ear.

On page four, where the second chapter begins telling of the mad knight's first adventure, Lucia had pasted another note, which read, → Because Cervantes is timeless, it will be impossible to tell when she is interfering. I marked a few possibilities for you. But the book's so damn big. . . . Love, L. To fit all the words on the little yellow note, she wrote small and neatly, on both sides, producing a miniature calligraphy, intimate and caring. But he also realized she probably used such notes throughout her work. A stylized arrow on the note, with a curl of seventeenth century filigree to it, pointed to the first line of the second chapter, → And so, having completed these preparations, he did not wish to wait any longer to put his thoughts into effect, impelled by the great need in the world that he believed was caused by his delay.

He finished his borscht and yogurt and ordered more of the smoky tea. It was fun to eat and drink as he read this chapter, because Quixote's adventure, such as it is, involves his sating of an extreme hunger by eating leftover salt cod and black grimy bread and sipping wine through a hollowed reed that must be poked through the visor of his makeshift helmet by "two young ladies of easy virtue" whom he takes for nobility. What struck Philip most distinctly was Cervantes's elegant math, his ability to create two simultaneous protagonists—himself and Quixote—through prose that seemed to transcend the concept of point of view. There was Quixote, and Cervantes the writer, and Cervantes the Spaniard, and Cervantes the person—what Irma would call, in Portuguese because no other language she knows captures it, *consigo*—and even a Cervantes imposter. In math, you often begin book-long proofs by attempting to achieve this type of collective quantification, which must nevertheless remain singular and not rely on omniscience. It is rarely achieved. Einstein could do it. Napier, too. The woman whose shape for the universe competed with his friend Isaac's was pretty good at it—better than Isaac.

At the end of chapter four—the chapters are brief—where Quixote lies on the ground, immobilized by the weight of his armor after falling from Rocinante in midcharge, Lucia left Philip another note, → I leave for Madrid on Tuesday. Reading this made me choose Spain over Argentina (which would have been much cheaper). You have my e-mail and I have yours. But this is more fun. . . . Love, L.

He looked away from the book and stared at the sunlit brick and pavement beyond the open door. He counted the days to Tuesday, though he was not quite sure what today was, not without first squinting at the date on the newspaper held by a nearby diner. The owner let him use the phone behind the bar to call her cell. But her voice mail greeting let her callers know she was ending service in order to cut expenses. She had explained this to him during dinner at The Joint. You can easily fool yourself into thinking that you need something, especially anything concerned with technology. He counted the days. What was the great need in the world, the one caused by his delay?

Mentally he desired a run, but he knew he was physically incapable today. It felt good to just walk. On the warm brick of Sansom Street, however, he found himself searching for direction.

I needed to make you feel how I feel. All the time. I needed to show you how I feel about everyone who matters to me. All the time. Don't you ever feel like that about somebody? That they will slip away because you choose, just for a moment in your life, to delay, or to wait, or to pursue another direction, one you feel more ready to follow? He felt that way now, but he could not be precise about the somebody. Irma, Lucia, Nicole, even Beatrice? Isaac? Sam? Everyone who matters to me?

From his flat, he sent a message to Lucia: I look forward to reading the Sarraute. About us. He felt a bit like a librarian, meekly reminding a borrower about due dates. But this small trace of contact also made him feel complicit with Lucia, an accomplice in her kind of theft, her kind of aggressive borrowing. This tumbled forth thoughts of her, brushes of her on his skin, images of her body, his cheek to the inside of her thigh, his hand to the outside, the sounds in her throat. The delicacy of her yellow notes giving him something against Irma, maybe no more than one of Quixote's pathetically imagined talismans, but at least that. At least that she could give him. He left his laptop and went to the shelves. He saw a tremor in his fingers as he reached for Irma's books, stole from his own library, cheated against his own formula. He chose by title and color. *The Rings of Saturn*, a primary blue that looked deeper because of delicate striations in the odd material of the cover, like something in a tidepool. Then *Ava*, emerald green, the color of a towel Irma used to seduce him the first time. And finally *The Unbearable Lightness of Being*, black felt it seemed, what you might find on a very nice hat. Freed from the shelf, away from the colored regiment of spines, the three books slid comfortably in the crook of his wrist. His fingers no longer trembled. But he was taking these books, he believed, somewhere. And he would tell Lucia where, after she left for Madrid. He hid them in his travel bag.

He then called Nicole and told her he wanted to treat her to a nice afternoon meal—no running. He took the train to New Brunswick, enjoying the New Jersey stops, their strange, time-warped names. At Cedar Café on George Street, he and Nicole shared a plate of Middle Eastern food set between them. She seemed playful and bemused, dismissive of their last encounter. She held her food delicately in front of her mouth, her eyes on him at a slant. She was between afternoon classes and he knew his time with her was limited. But he could in no way pry. She seemed worn to tears from talk and question. But he also knew, better than anyone else in the world, that most sums could be reached through numerous solutions. Any quantity revealed through addition could be revealed through subtraction. He subtracted her.

"How are Sam's times?" he asked her. Sam ran the 400-meter low hurdles for his high school and Philip knew he had just begun to break through at the end of this, his senior year.

Nicole held an olive to her lips and squinted softly at him, almost smiling. She put the olive down.

"Sam disappears, too. Like your friend."

"Disappears?" He felt a sliding kind of dizziness begin, an almost pleasant feeling of weakness that often occurs after days of running too much. *Cuidado.* "What do you mean, *disappears?*"

"Disappears. I can't find him. Mom and Dad can't find him. School can't find him. Then he reemerges, usually in time to make the next meet. School lets him come back because he's so smart and they want so desperately to prove to him they're not wasting his time. Coach lets him stay on the team because no other geek runs the four-hundred hurdles."

"You should have told me."

"Don't tell me what I should do, Philip. What I should think. What I should feel. I showed you how I feel. All the time."

She picked up an olive and pointed it at him. "Besides, what can you do? You don't even know when he's gone. If you were in his life more, you'd have known."

"I can only be in his life so much, Nick. I must step aside. That is my position, pretty clearly drawn out for me. And understandable."

"Yeah. But you could have helped him with his times. You're good at low hurdles."

"I didn't want to intrude." Philip shook his head. "It's frustrating."

She chewed an olive and eyed him.

"When did he last slip away?" he asked.

"Two weeks ago. Then came back." She stretched her arms wide, made fists, brought one to a yawn. "Do you miss her?"

Though it was the question he was waiting for, the question he carefully refrained from asking *her*, it caught him unready at first. He sipped water, then:

"I do. But it's strange. I see her much more, more sharply. I think about her much more now than ever before. So in a way, I don't miss her. I want to find her and get rid of her."

He saw Nicole pale swiftly at this, though she maintained her informal posture and chin up. He immediately regretted the words. He was only trying to follow Nicole's whim.

"*I* miss her," she said, straightening her shoulders, setting her gaze on him. "I would go find her. Even though I don't know where she's gone.

I would just go to where she's been. But I don't know that, either. Not much of it, anyway."

"It's not that simple, Nick. She's gone in time as well as place. It's not like hide-and-seek. She hasn't just tucked herself into book stacks somewhere, waiting to be found or called free. Her message had no beckon. This time, she didn't say catch me if you can."

"What? How did you read the note? 'To hell with you: here are my books. Take good care of them'?"

"Yes," he answered. "Pretty much that way, Nick. She put that nice veneer on it, because all her friends and family were addressed. Not just me."

"You just got *all* her books." Her tone sounded envious. She used it to reestablish distance. He tried to keep her near, to keep her from dismissing their last run in the rail yards. He wanted to catch her between tides, see what might be there, what might be exposed. Would he see it? Would Irma?

"What are you trying to decide, then?" he asked.

"Everything."

"Everything equals nothing."

"God, I hate mathematicians." She waved her fingers beside her ears, as though cooling away sound and thought. "After class, we're playing Frisbee. Come join. We can talk more then. But not now. I have to get to class. I have to concentrate on that."

"I can't run today."

"Just play a couple of points. Old players always drop by in their street clothes and ask to play a couple of points with us."

"I'll come watch. Maybe."

"You'll play."

"How do you know that?" he asked.

"Because you want to find out about Sam. I invited him to come play after school."

"I didn't know he started playing Frisbee again."

"You don't know a lot of things."

He walked Nicole silently to campus, crossing the bridge over the railway which divided Rutgers from the city like a river. He walked her all the way to her class. Outside the lecture room door, she spun toward him, her notebook clutched to her breast, her ponytail flung over one shoulder.

"See you on the field."

She flashed a very quick smile, stood on tiptoe, and kissed his cheek before slipping into the lecture room.

You don't know a lot of things.

Philip made his way to the math department, his sore joints loosening in the warm sun. Passing students seemed to give off their own sunlight, dangling unsmoked cigarettes, jackets tied around waists or thrown over shoulders in celebration of spring's return. He remembered himself like that, and Irma, too, finding her between classes, listening to her complain about some writer or boyfriend he did not really know, fielding her challenges concerning running, Frisbee, maybe sex, loving the way she spoke of some current book-binding project as though he knew everything about the craft. He wanted Sam to be walking among those students, to at least get the chance to see if that's what he wanted.

He had attended two of Sam's meets this season. Sam almost won the second one, lunging the tape together with the winner, a 400-meter low-hurdler who had already committed to a Temple track scholarship. Sam looked short and washed-out among the other runners, his shoulders bony and freckled, his shorts baggy, on loan it seemed from some bygone era when accountants and doctors set world track records. Don't be intimidated by all that height and muscle, he told Sam once before a meet. It's just extra weight they have to carry. He showed Sam a 1967 black and white photo of the great decathlete Bill Toomey throwing a javelin. Toomey's tank top is tucked into his shorts, his white socks are pulled up to his thin calves, and his expression is one of a boy playing right field. He won the gold medal at the '68 Olympics, Philip told Sam. He set the 400-meter decathlon world record then, and it still stands today. Which is absurdly amazing. Sam only stared at the photo.

He could be even more reticent than his older sister, but it suited him better than it did her. Where it made Nicole seem pretty and aloof, content and undesiring of anything you could possibly bring to her world, it gave Sam a searching air. It made him appear distracted by profound thoughts, so that when he flicked his look of recognition at you, you felt suddenly and intrinsically included. He had his mother's dark red hair, but his was less curly. His freckles faded as he got older, but they were still there, dark and small as pepper.

I have a crush on him, Irma once told Philip after the three of them had tossed a Frisbee on the Sourland fields. He's kind of like you—but without the math. And the twenty-five years.

Only once could he remember taking Sam alone to the fields, when the boy was ten. Sam had planned to run away. Nicole showed Philip the loaf of bread and the jackknife he had stashed beneath his bed. Philip responded by taking Sam that evening to Sourland, man to man. They threw a baseball, best for talking, but as twilight approached over the woods of the Sourland ridge, threatening an end to their play, Philip's words eluded him. He had planned to tell the boy there were better, other ways of escape, of finding your own trails. And you could share these ways with those you choose—Nick, him, a friend, a girl. But Sam's throws grew harder, almost elevating their tossing to a game of burnout. Some of Sam's throws frightened Philip, coming at him in the waning light as hard sliders, spinning and hissing, stinging his palm. What have I taught him? Philip thought as he concentrated on the approaching fire-balls, defending himself against their speed and spin. But the next day the loaf of bread and jackknife were returned.

Philip weaved among the students as he made his way to Rebecca's building. How do you give twenty-five years to someone? Sam never seemed to take anything more from him than incremental, here-and-there athletic advice. He listened intently, politely, and then you could sense him filing your observation, your bit of wisdom, your praise away somewhere to be considered and evaluated later. Sam's hero was Edwin Moses, the greatest 400-meter hurdler. Austere, scholarly, running alone in his excellence for more than a decade, Moses draped a kind of positive isolation about himself. Is there a positive form of aloofness? Philip once asked Irma. She just laughed at him, paused, then laughed some more, covering her mouth and bending slightly forward. There was a candid photograph of an Italian actress, somebody like Pier Angeli, caught laughing like this, on some movie shoot between scenes. He sometimes put it up as his laptop's wallpaper.

He entered the math building, took the elevator to Rebecca's floor, and learned from her door card that she was lecturing. He took the stairs one flight down to see if Isaac was in and discovered that he, too, was lecturing. Philip bought a coffee from the cart on the first floor and then tried to wait on an outside bench. The coffee was very good, not like the vending machine stuff from his campus days. But waiting proved impossibly fragmentary, abstract, multidirectional.

You could stand beneath the shade of a nearby sycamore, having afternoon coffee alongside students who watched him and wondered if he was their new professor. You could see how he was feeling and say to him or just to yourself that he simply was not working enough. That he was not *doing* enough. That he needed a real job, a real life, a lover, a television. But how much do *you* do? When faced with a day, what do *you* do?

He decided to attend the end of Rebecca's lecture and wait for her afterward. Connections between her kids and Irma were gathering. All the questions in his life were coalescing into one. Where are you? He found Rebecca's seminar and managed to slip quickly into the high back row of the lecture hall. All her students clustered around the stage, the way she always made them, leaving rows and rows of the little amphitheater empty between him and them. Rebecca did not notice him. She wore a green skirt and black blazer. Her red hair was up and she had her glasses pushed to her crown until a student asked something about the equation that filled the board behind her. She needed glasses to see her equations, but liked to keep the faces of her students slightly out of focus.

She peered back at the equation, one foot on heel, twisting thoughtfully. They were discussing the problem of the tautochrone. She considered her equation, as though viewing questionable artwork.

"I don't know," she answered, not looking back to her students. Then she turned on her heel and looked up to Philip and raised her voice slightly. "What would you say, Mr. Masryk? You're somewhat of an expert on pendulum activity."

In unison, the students looked back to him.

He always felt nervous projecting his voice, and Rebecca knew this. She also knew he had the answer without thinking.

"By constraining . . ." He paused to let the wobble in his voice subside. "By constraining the upper end of the pendulum to oscillate between two branches of a cycloid, you cause the period to be the same regardless of the amplitude of the oscillations." He cleared his throat. "Which is exactly how it should be."

The students looked to her.

"Applications?" she asked. She pushed her glasses atop her head and looked at her students.

"Endless in the mechanical field," he called down to them.

"We're theory today."

"Well, for one, you could reverse application and test the constraints. Give the constraints whole and set values."

"Wouldn't that limit the exploration of your theory? Wouldn't that just *end* your exploration in a series of aimed repetitions?" one of the students asked—her, not him.

"It would," Rebecca answered. She looked up at Philip once before continuing. "But it could prove useful in the middle of a problem. An insertion that you remove once it's provided you with possibilities. Thank you, Mr. Masryk."

When they were married, she often asked him to attend lecture. She would call him Mr. Masryk—she called all her students Ms. or Mr.— and he would serve as foil by just following along and answering her questions. This was one of her ways of walking them back through an equation, keeping the tone of her lectures less repetitive. You should teach, Philip, she often told him.

He remained for the end of her lecture and watched her field the after-class concerns and questions of students with kind precision, wordless but sincere nods, no smiles but sharp lifts of her brow. Then he walked her back to her office. He told her she looked great and asked how things were. She told him work was going well, but that she knew she wasn't spending enough time with Andrew, that she could see her husband's concern. He always wants me to cut down on office time.

"But this time is different," she told him after a long pause which involved passing through the double glass doors and into the breezeway connecting buildings. She stopped him at the end of the breezeway by touching his shoulder. She looked around, startled by the warm air. "I stay in my office so much that the kids come and see me there. That's when I'm with them most. And I like them that way. That they are beginning to search me out. I like them more and more."

"They're great kids, Bec. To your credit."

"I know Nicole has been running with you more. Seeing you more." She looked down and toed a crack in the walkway. "I think that's good."

Paused in the breezeway, they let the warm wind blow about them. The russet strands fallen loose from her gathered hair stirred above the collar of her blazer. She lifted her face to the breeze, closed her eyes to it.

"Has Irma spoken with you in the past month or so?" he asked.

Eyes closed, she held very still in the soft rush of air, then parted her lips as if to speak. She then closed her lips and opened her eyes. Whenever she did this—curtailed her first words and gestures—Philip could only wonder what tangent she fought. He wondered, over the course of their marriage and divorced life, what alternate dialogue and relationship formed in the unspoken and unpursued current that ran beneath Rebecca's life with him. Do you think it continues on inside her? he once asked Irma. An entirely different world where we say and do other things, wear different colors? Irma's response was an arched look of amusement and disdain. You're the one who married her.

"Irma," he said again to Rebecca. "Has she asked you for any math help lately?"

"Math help? Irma?" She smiled at him and put on her glasses to look at him, though he stood close. Then she pushed them back into her hair. "No. I haven't seen her. I haven't seen her since we . . . She came to one of our lunches, right? That was more than a year ago, right? Was she the one who sat with us? At the Cedar?"

"That was more than two years ago, Bec. I only asked because . . ." He opted not to explain the book collection and what might be happening with it—in it. "I only asked because Nicole has seen her. Recently."

"Nicole? Really?"

He nodded.

In the breezeway, the warm stream of air strengthened and he turned toward it, away from Rebecca, and told her he didn't want to interrupt her day, that he only wanted to stop by after lunch with Nicole.

"But I did want to ask about Sam," he said. "Nicole told me what he's been doing."

"I think he'll be okay. It's the end of senior year. He's bored. More bored than usual, that is. There's nothing for him there, except running. And at home, he questions everything Andrew says. So . . ." She lifted her arms and let them drop. "I'm pretty sure he stays with a friend somewhere. A new friend. I hope it's a girl. Andrew, of course, assumed that was the case and asked. *That* just made it impossible for any of us."

She gave Philip a quizzical look, slid her glasses down from where they were nestled in her red hair, and adjusted them to her eyes. "I did that when I was in high school. Did you know that, Philip?"

"What? What did you do?" he asked, knowing which story she would tell him.

"I left home for short periods of time and then was vague about it. I don't know why I did it, really. Looking back, I'm glad I did."

"Did you go with a boy?" he asked, again knowing.

She shook her head. "Once myself. Once with a girl I befriended as a senior. Her name was Nilmarie, I remember. How could you forget *that* name? But I imagined the boy."

"What did you and Nilmarie do?"

"Nothing. We rented a motel room and swam in the pool. She had a credit card. It was fun pretending we were on our own. We ordered takeout for the first time in our lives."

Rebecca still seemed befuddled by the spring air. She looked upward, then at Philip, as though he were doing something slightly illicit. She touched his arm.

"Don't leave just yet. I have something to give you. I can bring it to you if you just want to wait here."

She left him in the breezeway, then returned shortly with a disk envelope. The envelope was labeled *With Philip*. Rebecca had a bad memory. More accurately, she had a faulty recall ability for life events. In her field she was brilliant, her memory quick, exact, and comprehensive. But from the life she lived, she usually could only extract memories using elaborate and deliberate mnemonic triggers. Philip argued that her memory was no worse than most others, that her desire for complete memory was what made her feel lacking, but she could never accept that. She often recorded highlights—events and people she believed would matter—with whatever available technology. She kept a journal at first, along with some 8mm footage. The journal was not like most you would read from a teenage girl. It was composed of unlinked sketches, full of exact but random observation, and bereft of interpretation. She often referred to them as bookmarks. The entries read like anthropology field notes, but without focus on any particular people, custom, or place. The experience with Nilmarie at the motel was probably rendered some-where in the journal, telling you what color and style of swimsuits they wore, what they got from the vending machine, what the cloud patterns looked like as they watched the sky while floating on the water. With little apprehension, she let people read it. When they were married, she encouraged Philip to sample it, apologizing for its boring nature. The written journal ended when video recording became cheap and acces-sible. Then she would film herself in snippets of life. Philip remembered one of him cooking her an omelet. You use olive oil? you can hear her ask off-camera as Philip wipes his brow with his wrist while holding the spatula. Now it was digital. She had transferred all her silent 8mm stuff and all her video to disk.

She handed him the *With Philip* disk. He smiled as he took it.

"Is this a copy or are you purging me?" he asked.

She bit her bottom lip with concern and put her hand to her cheek.

"No. No. I wouldn't do that."

He shook his head. She could never tell when he was kidding. "I know," he told her.

"Andrew convinced me that I'm usurping others by recording them for my own purposes. That I owe them. That I should at least share." She motioned to the disk in Philip's hand. "So."

He held the disk toward her, for her to take back. "I will always remember everything about you, Becca. I can recall everything. And I do, from time to time. And I disagree with Andrew."

She pushed the envelope back toward him. "Keep it."

He knew what was on it.

"Did Andrew get to view this?"

She gave him one small nod and a pale smile.

He kissed her forehead, the pink line at the edge of her hair. At that moment, he wanted to kill noble Andrew, to run him through with a lance from horseback. As the warm breeze picked up between Rebecca and him, he wanted them to still be together, to be married, with Nicole and Sam as their happy but usually absent teenagers who hated everything mathematical.

Rebecca removed her tiny silver camera from her blazer pocket and filmed the breeze blowing through Philip's hair. He smiled for her, but remained in profile.

Recorded, he told her how great it was to see her again on this day when spring finally finished off winter, to see her in class, and that he was going to watch Nicole and Sam play Frisbee, maybe join a point or two. He let the kiss to her forehead be his good-bye. He felt her recording him as he walked away.

On the way to the field, he wondered how Irma would ask for help with his formula. Isaac, Rebecca, and he were the only ones who could help. You would have to know math very well—to calculate pendulum activity—and you would have to know *him* very well. Beatrice, too, could have helped Irma. Not with the calculus, but certainly with the approach. And now he knew they had plenty of time for that. He pictured them gazing at ceiling shadows and light, elbows touching. Beatrice would tell her not to waste any time with learning the math or explaining the subject at hand. Just give each book a corresponding number from 1 to 351. Then ask for the calculation. Then he realized that Irma would have come to know Beatrice enough, would in moments be able to think as Beatrice does, without having to ask her.

Before veering to the fields, he stopped in the student union and used one of the computers in the common area kiosk to e-mail Isaac and let him know he was on campus. He added, too, a message for Rebecca, another good-bye, asked again if she was sure Irma had not given her a set of numbers, knowing Bec would be amused by this quick electronic addendum to this afternoon's visit. We have to stop inventing new and more efficient ways for communicating with each other, he once argued with Rebecca and Irma, while the three of them spent a summer afternoon alone together, the kids off with Andrew. We have to leave ourselves excuses, reasons for inaccessibility, reasons beyond our control. We always have to be able to say, "I tried calling, but . . ."

He remembered how Irma looked at Rebecca at that moment, how she stretched and hooked one arm over the back of her patio chair and said, "Don't you just absolutely hate all men sometimes?" It sounded like an invite and Rebecca seemed to take it as one, looking down shyly, her hint of a smile, her red ponytail brushing her nape. Was she shaking her head in commiseration, in disagreement, or in polite, timorous refusal?

The three of them kissed in the pool, drunk, a little high, but still thinking, still knowing. Philip felt their legs brushing his, Irma shoving hard, Rebecca stroking. It was Irma who retracted, back-swimming away from them, a soft apologetic smile in her expression. Later, when she was leaving, she lifted an eyebrow at him, gave him a little grin, which perhaps Rebecca noticed, too. When he and Rebecca had sex very soon after Irma closed the door, she set her camera on the tripod and filmed it all. Philip was aware of the camera, but by then he had grown used to it. Her setting up of the tripod, in fact, sometimes served as effective foreplay. That evening, Philip remained aware that Rebecca closed her eyes throughout, that she was imagining something different, something even better than this. She lost herself on top of him, bending upward and away and stretching her arms high so that her pale breasts were drawn tight. He had to thrust high to stay with her. Her white form seemed to be piercing upward into a vast darkness, like an ascending sea creature.

When Philip reached the field where they were playing Frisbee, he sat down in the shade of a willow oak and watched. Sam was not among the players, but Nicole was. She coaxed him into playing and he agreed to only two points. The players wore shorts and cleats and Philip could not keep up with his mark on defense, and he could not shake his mark on offense. So he ran around on the grass in looping patterns and stayed out of the way, content to enjoy the easy motion, the late afternoon sun. When he inadvertently crossed trajectories with the Frisbee, he snatched it from the air and got rid of it quickly by flicking it to his nearest team-mate. He was beaten by his mark for a score on both points. He retreated to his spot under the oak and waited for Sam. Nicole took a break from the game and sat beside him. She rested with her legs straight out and her arms braced back.

"Sam's not coming," she told him, pretending to be intent on the game. "He's not. He's *really* gone. I know it."

She looked at him. At first she was smiling and then the smile broke into tears, a full cry that shook through her. Philip hesitated, held his hand up as though to stroke her hair. Then he held her and she wept and trembled against his shoulder.

"You want to know what I'm trying to decide?" She sniffed, but remained tucked to his shoulder. Her words puffed against his chest. "I'm trying to decide whether to go or stay. If I go, I might live a life of great wonder. If I stay, I will succeed the way others succeed. But then she will remain gone. And you, too, I think. But then maybe I can keep Sam, if he comes back. And keep Mom. Maybe I can keep them. I wish . . ." She pressed her face to his shoulder. "When you're away, I wish you both had never come into our life. My life. But when you're here, Philip . . . when you're here, I don't think that."

He said nothing and simply held her.

"Go find him for me," she said, her words soft and damp. "Please go get him."

He felt her chin press his collarbone, her forehead against his neck, her tears and sweat dampening his shirt.

He let her stay that way for a long time. The calls of the game rang in the air as he watched the flight of the disk. In *Slip*, Simon ice-skates on the canal with May, his eight-year-old daughter. Their blades make the first marks on the new ice and the feathery tracings reflect the thin clouds in the winter sky. Alma watches secretly from the wooded shore and listens to their laughter ping against the ice and cold air, sees the long white plumes of their breaths.

If you watched from the shade of another tree, disguised among a cluster of other players resting, you would see that he did all he could do to ease her sobbing. He avoided words or strokes and held his arms still around her with a soft steady pressure. He looked away, watched the game. You would be able to tell, by his drawn expression, that he believed good people, those rare and truly good people, were sad all the time, that sadness was their base. That if they released themselves, their self-control, they would fall into a soft but unending cry. All this remained apparent in his expression, in the spare and precise features of his face. And yes, he ran calculations in his mind, but they were no less warm, no less searching than any thoughts, any language you could bring to the situation, to the act of holding someone who was once briefly your daughter, someone you could not comfort or guide, though that was what you wanted to do most.

EIGHT

When Nicole finished crying, she peeled herself from Philip's arms and calmly returned to the game. He watched her play and she played just as he anticipated. She played hard, seriously, intensifying the game around her. The best players on the field followed her lead and their cleats rumbled over the grass. He was struck by how preciously she held her life, how deeply she considered her path. Philip tried to catch Nicole's eye to wave good-bye, but she remained focused on the game. And so he left, his shoulder damp with her tears and sweat.

He sought Isaac and found him in his office. Philip stood outside the open door as his friend met with a student. Isaac waved quickly to Philip, then returned to his counsel. But he must have seen something in Philip's expression, something in his posture, and he cut the session short, ushering the student out and pulling Philip in. Philip apologized for interrupting.

"You're not," Isaac replied. He leaned back in his chair, slouching somewhat in his creased lecture clothes, his jacket looking borrowed from an older brother. He gazed at Philip, letting the quiet of the office collect.

In *Slip*, Irma tries several times to render Isaac and the friendship he has with Philip. They are Bernard and Simon in her story. But their scenes together, which are repeated sometimes with and sometimes without variation, do not appear to advance. You would almost think her a mathematician, exploring tautochrone limits and potentials. By constraining the upper end of the pendulum to oscillate between two branches of a cycloid, you cause the period to be the same regardless of the amplitude of the oscillations.

Thomas Adès's *Concerto Conciso* played softly from Isaac's laptop, only making itself heard in the gathering silence between the two men. The most fascinating thing about friendship, Irma said to him as she sat naked on a squeaky iron bed in Pátzcuaro and smoked a crooked black cheroot, is how it advances even though it is seemingly constructed out of nothing more than repetition. Take us, for instance. You and me, Pip. You are my best friend. My very best friend, whether we're fucking or not, whether you're married or not. Yet basically we do the same things, say the same things, over and over. How does that repetition achieve advance?

Through the accumulation of slight variations, he answered. Over time.

Ah! she said, forgetting she was naked and sliding to the edge of the bed, where she braced her arms and dangled her feet. Ah. For once my math is faster than yours. Time *is* a factor, it always is. But resonation is a much more significant factor. How those resonations play off subsequent events in a person's, a friend's, life. Regardless of the presence of the other friend.

She bounced slightly on the bed. Follow? She put down the cigar, dusted the ashes from her breasts, and opened her hands toward him. We do or say something we've done several times before in our friendship. You notice or do not notice a slight variation. You carry that variation, noticed or unnoticed, around until it resonates against or with something you hear or sense or experience. That resonation then affects both the immediate experience and the friendship. Yes?

He composed it as an equation, a rough sketch on the back of a map to a lake island they planned to visit. It took him less than a minute. When he was finished she slid off the edge of the bed in order to come look. She intentionally held her breasts close to the side of his face as she pretended to read, one nipple grazing his ear. Then she reached beneath the map for the erection she knew was there. Repetition, she murmured, breath thick with tobacco. Resonation. Repetition. Resonation. You are my best friend whether we're fucking or not.

"You're light-years away," Isaac said.

Philip looked up. "Not quite that far."

"Are you all right?"

Philip nodded, though he was not all right, though his stepdaughter's tears still dampened his shirt. "Theoretically, you could come to know someone by moving through every significant person in their life. Profoundly know them. To the point where their innermost thoughts, reactions, *movements* could be predicted. Fashioned, maybe. No?"

"I don't think you'll be able to do that with her," said Isaac. "She's too smart for you. Us."

Philip made no effort to correct Isaac's inversion. Letting him go that way separated Philip, floated him above the conversation somewhat. It made him feel as if he were slipping into her realm, if only infinitesimally, fleetingly. Like leaning in and out of a waking dream, that current that forever streams between consciousness and sleep, full of what we really want to do, say, and believe, free of rationality and order. Full of quiet but close whispers. Philip sighed as though in acceptance of Isaac's misunderstanding and let his friend continue.

"But you should go back to California and talk to her family. I called them. Her mother said you only spoke to her once. To hear the note and ask about the books. You need them, Phil. They need you."

Philip shook his head. "That's where you're wrong. It would be a terrible mistake. They would try to fill me with regret. They would be kind about it. Her mother would be courteous at least. But she would aim for regret. And whether she would succeed or not, she would only give me added burden."

"You really don't have any regrets? About Irma?"

"None. And she would expect that of me. And I think that's one thing she likes about me. If I am in any way a cause for what she's done, I'm not sure yet what that cause might be. But regret plays no part in it. Regret is a fool's game. For her."

Isaac squinted at him. "You're the most important person in her life."

"There are many important people in her life. A trail of them around the world. Readers. Wherever books gather. I have nothing to do with books. Real books. I'm not the most important person in her life."

"Okay. Fine. Then you're not the most important person in her life.

You're one of them. You can't argue with that. And she's left you *and* all of them? ' 'Bye, everyone. I love you. I'm gone. Everything I've worked for was for naught. Is shit. So I'm gone.' "

"Don't mock her, Isaac."

"Mock her? She's mocking us, you fuck. She always mocks us."

"I don't think she's mocking us at all," Philip told him. "This time. I think she's completely serious. I think what she's done is carefully considered and planned out. For years, I would guess. Maybe she always knew. She practiced it, at times. Stepping out of her own life."

"I don't believe it," Isaac replied. "She's definitely seeking profound change. Someone living the way she does would have to do that. Some reevaluation of her life. With work—relationships, too. Thoughtful lives." Isaac shaped a sphere with open fingers. "Thoughtful lives would have to be interjected with hard divergence, turns. Retreats," he said as the word came to him. "She is in retreat."

"No," Philip replied.

"You believe she's permanently gone. Poof! I've disappeared."

"Yeah."

"Won't she have to peek back in from time to time? Out of curiosity? She's so curious."

"Not out of curiosity," replied Philip. "Just out of sheer mechanics. She would have to prompt us from time to time. To keep us all going. To keep her life going. The one she left."

Isaac remained silent for a moment, his one sign of defeat. A kind of tiny fear spread about his eyes, chin dropping, his lips almost parting. Philip wanted to give him something, something to actively ponder.

"Didn't you always wonder where the magician goes?"

"He goes down the steps beneath the stage," said Isaac. "Towels off, has a whiskey, and listens to his amazed audience gasp and murmur. Gloats a bit. Then steps back into a sea of applause. But I never applauded. Everyone disappears all the time. If we're not careful we'll live whole lives disappeared. Unthought-of. Unsought. The real trick is *appearing*. Not *re*appearing. Not finishing your whiskey and heading back up those hidden steps. But just appearing in the first place."

"Is there a name for it?" he asked Isaac. "Is there a term for the kind of appearance that rapidly collects just before disappearance? I figure a cosmologist or magician would know. Do you know the phenomenon? A magician would need his audience to be hyperaware of the object he was about to vanish. His trick would be most effective if that object began to accumulate appearance. A gaudy handkerchief. A scantily clad assistant. A supernova."

Isaac held his hand up in a way that indicated he was about to quote the most current math that explains a supernova's imminent explosion and disappearance. Philip interrupted.

"No. Not the math. The word. The word?"

"The word you may be looking for is eidolon," Lucia answered. She had him in a chair in her hotel room, the last night she would have the room, and was about to slide onto him. She grasped the knobs at the top of the chair and braced her legs on either side of him, on tiptoe. He put his hands on the flexed muscles of her thighs, lifting. He looked up at her, his face in the V of her breasts. "Not the empty meaning it has now. Its real meaning. Real. Ah," she said as she lowered herself onto him and then sought footing, adjusted her grip on the chair knobs. "Ah!

"Now it's used to mean phantom. But it really means the essence— the visible, palpable essence—that gathers just before a life vanishes, into the netherworld or nothingness, depending on what you believe." She moved slowly over him, experimenting, scooting her feet to the best position, then driving a little harder to test. "It's the Western translation of *kama-rupa*. Is this okay? Does this feel fine?" she asked as she clenched herself forward, covering him. "No talk of books for now. Only wordless sounds from our lips for now. Okay?"

She left for Spain and he remained to close out her room at the Latham. She left swiftly before dawn, kissing him on the neck, the only light coming from the open door. She slung one bag over her shoulder and dragged a single case behind her.

"Take anything you want," she whispered to him. "Leave the rest for the hotel. They know."

The Latham delivered coffee and a roll in the morning. He took breakfast as he inventoried the room. She left a few clothes, some hers, some obviously not hers. The terry-cloth warm-ups were there along with a crumpled but nice linen coat which Philip put on and decided to keep. There were three bottles of perfume, in very heavy glass, scents unrecognized. She left two books: the Borges and *The Curves of Life*, Cook's opus about the role of the logarithmic spiral in art and nature. He may have mentioned it to her, he thought. Both were battered versions belonging to the Free Library of Philadelphia. In the Cook, she had bookmarked a page on the sunflower which featured a black and white photograph showing the logarithmical swirl of the flower's seeds. With lipstick, he once drew a logarithmic spiral on Irma's stomach, her navel as center. They were undergrads, cheating in her boyfriend's surf shack. One of the most beautiful aspects, he told her, is that the spiral looks the same from all directions. With his finger, he traced a straight line through the spiral. Every straight line through the center, he told her, intersects the spiral at exactly the same angle. His finger lightly brushed the length of her torso. It's like that in snail shells, sunflowers, filigree, and galaxies.

Don't lend too much to it, Pip, she told him years later when he repeated the spiral on her stomach. They were killing an afternoon in a tiny lodge near the ruins of Tampumacchay, a buried city outside Colima, waiting to explore the tombs in a later and softer light. He traced the spiral on her bare stomach with a fossil chip from a mammoth's molar she had found. Galaxies and snail shells contain the exact same design and math only because we see them that way. It's we who create the design we think we see. It's what we do. I know this better than anyone. I constantly rebind what falls apart. I see, over and over, what people want to do, what they need to do. Bind their thoughts and sensations and share them with others. And so that's what we all do, over and over again, producing a world, a galaxy, a universe that we think is beyond us. When I see your precious logarithmic spiral in a snail shell and a galaxy, I don't think, How grand! How mystifying! How beyond us! I just see the front and back cover of a book.

The people buried beneath us, the Tampumacchayans, wouldn't even see your spiral. If you showed them a galaxy they would see it shaped according to their own, long-lost math. They might see this: using the fossil bit, she traced a shape on his stomach, φ. If I were a great writer, I could rewrite a person's world. I could rewrite and bind your world, Pip. I could make you see spiraled galaxies and sunflowers whose appearances and angles shift when you draw a line through the center.

He left the Latham, found Twentieth, and walked through the museum district wearing the linen coat and carrying the books to return. The horticultural society was just opening its gates, as was the Academy of Natural Sciences and then the Franklin Institute. At Logan Square, advancing through the swirl of traffic, he could feel how warm the day would become. He was anxious to get rid of the books and run. He picked up his stride on Vine Street and was one of the first patrons to enter the Free Library. He slid the Borges and the Cook into the return slot and was about to hurry out when he noticed a bright yellow book on the round display shelf in the middle of the lobby area. The book was brighter than the others on the shelf. Plain, uncovered, it faced the return slots where he stood. He approached it slowly, tilting his head slightly side to side but keeping his gaze directly on the yellow book, as if to test its substance and existence, the way you might approach a beautiful prism on a wall, hoping it would remain long enough to touch.

It was the *Pepys at Table* from Hibberd's, rescued from the dying bookstore and deposited in the library, where it would go entirely unnoticed, even unregistered, but saved. He read the entry for today's date, 1669: And she gave me some gingerbread made in cakes like chocolate, very good, made by a friend. She had read enough Pepys to Philip to enable him to interpret. Pepys was eating dense little bars of gingerbread, probably rock-hard and preserved to last into the next century. Philip craved one. Women are always giving Pepys delicious little bits of food, he told Irma. So? she replied. So is it code for something else? he asked. You said he often wrote in code. What if it's all code? What if his entire diary is in code? What if his written life masks and preserves his real life?

Stick to math, Pip, she told him. Don't try to be like me.

He remembered they were in Mexico, but he could not remember which Irma he was speaking to then. Was it the first Mexico trip, before his marriage with Rebecca? Or was it the trip between marriages? Was it the sporting Irma, honey-colored and running in the dewy mornings of Colima's city park, taken for Spaniard by the locals, yanking him into bed every siesta and every balmy night? Or was it Irma removed, going on secret runs without him in Uruapán's river park, pretending she had forsaken the sport, taken for a local, smoking her *diez minutos*, daring him to touch or not touch her? He felt desire for the latter, but perhaps only because he also knew the former. And there was no difference.

Standing before the Pepys, feeling encased in the white morning filling the lobby, he runs probabilities the way the rest of us breathe. Four possibilities present themselves as savior to this book: Irma, Lucia (if she knew Irma), Hibberd's owner (trying to save it before his store finally, inevitably collapsed), or a book buyer (trying to do the same, and wanting to share). The last two are less probable because of time. The book is here, now. The second is the most probable, rendered so—again—by time. And space. The books he returned for Lucia—she knew he would do that—led him to the one place and the general fragment of time where he would see the book. The first is almost as probable as the second, depending somewhat on the variable which is Lucia's relationship to Irma. Irma could choose to hide within time, rather than space. She knows his habits and preferences well enough to reside within the same locations, but at slightly different times. To complicate matters, if you add the probabilities of the third and fourth possibilities, in unison they become more probable.

He paged some more through the Pepys, then looked at the flyleaves. Irma's penciled inscription to Hibberd's read: *To ensure it stays in good hand.* Why did she leave off the *s*, keep *hand* singular? She was sounding like Pepys. Yes. But she was also writing in code. He laughed as though she were right there with him, watching him finally get her joke.

When he tried to check the book out from the library, the librarian informed him that this particular volume had not been entered into their system. There could be several reasons for this, she explained. Donations often slip through the first inventory without being properly entered. And then, people are constantly trying to slip books—usually their self-published books—onto library shelves, thinking that we'll just take them into our catalogue. But we see that all the time and just trash them. Just because it looks like a book doesn't make it a book. But this one—the librarian weighed it on the tips of her pale fingers—we'll keep. Come back next week and it will be available for checkout.

Philip walked quickly to Hibberd's, convincing himself that he was warming up for a run, but feeling pulled in zigzags across downtown. At the bookstore, the clerk remembered the Pepys being purchased by a woman sometime during the past few days (they didn't sell a whole lot of books). That eliminated one possibility. She was good-looking. That eliminated nothing, but enhanced the first two possibilities. Philip immediately realized that any feature relating to Irma also related to Lucia and did not altogether eliminate the possibility of the third option. The clerk, palming the book he was reading before Philip disturbed his peace, appeared nervous. Philip thanked him and left.

He felt himself breaking from time and place and so he sought refuge, solace, and return by running Kelly Drive. He ran the grassy banks of the Schuylkill at a brisk pace, feeling strong after a day's rest, and breathed the river air in great pumping draughts. Along the curves past the Museum of Art, the waterworks, and Boathouse Row, his mind cleared. You don't know a lot of things. But he was starting to know. On the straightaway toward Germantown, when sweat began to flow in sheets across his back and chest, he felt compelled to cast his thoughts forward. Running teams, men and women, from both Penn and Drexel, passed from the opposite direction, only warming up, chatting, but moving at a pace that astounded him. They divided and converged around him like a stream about a stone.

He believed now that when he first opened the Borges, read the penciled invite from the author and his binder, he somehow knew he would be searching for Sam and searching for a way to reach Nicole, too. He had understood these ventures before he realized the need for them existed. His fear of the dark, his understanding of Turgenev's light, his desire for Lucia, her puzzle, were all him understanding before realizing, the boy pulling the sword from the stone, the mathematician holding the solution before the proof. But this lift, this sudden weightlessness that allowed him to increase the speed of his run, breathe more deeply, also spun the gyroscope of his pace. Was this to be his life? In her books? Swinging back to understand his own prescience? To open *Ficciones* and understand that he would go to Spain, the center of her disappearance, to find his stepchildren, his own fatherhood, his own life?

And fears. To open *Ficciones*, merely peruse pencil scribblings on its fly pages, and wonder deeply about a woman whom he had yet to meet. To desire her, fear her, join her. To read those first stories—they weren't even stories, but little worlds created—and want a woman who actually existed, but who had yet to step from blue light into his life.

And he knew to be wary of Lucia, as he fought to adjust the spin and speed of his run. He could disappoint and anger Lucia by finding her, there in Spain. In Mishima's *The Sailor Who Fell from Grace with the Sea*, the sailor, Irma told him, falls from grace when he returns to Fusako instead of abandoning her and moving on to more conquests. If Lucia had given him a bit of grace, he did want to keep it. Was there such a thing as grace? Something attained without intent or merit? Something bestowed for unknowable reasons? The sailor has the power of the sea, bestowed on him with its capricious nature by the water itself. Maybe the sailor spends his grace in exchange for greater possibilities, a life on land with the beautiful Fusako. That Fusako is a widow gives her some power, too, like the sea, and perhaps also the ability to bestow grace. In his math, grace would be equivalent to π. A number that unquestionably exists, cannot be precisely located, and is known primarily by its effect on others and its crucial role in the comprehension of the single most important shape in the universe, the sphere.

Irma, through her narrator Sylvia in *Theory*, writes: The cover of the Mishima paperback was the most explicit. On it, the man and the woman are naked, coupled, horizontal across the entire picture, forming a human landscape. The curve and lift of their limbs barely obscure what could not be shown. Their forms are blended into the swirl of the sea, her hair becoming waves, his raised elbow becoming an ocean cliff. The woman appears only slightly exotic, her mascara eyes given a tiny lift, her open lips blood-red and full. Her black hair is straight until it begins to blend with the crashing waves. Her powder-white skin contrasts the teak color of his muscles. My mother warned me that my father might ask me to throw it out, or at least to put it away until I was older. But when we brought that first stack of paperbacks home and he flipped through them, he only paused briefly on the Mishima cover and said that we were all that he loved more than the sea. And he made me the abalone bookends from shells he and Mom had harvested.

Philip decided to fly to Spain as soon as he could. His main promise would be to find Sam. He believed if he sought the most difficult solution, the almost impossible solution that was Irma, the lesser equations would be solved. His point of entry into the proof—the proof of Irma—remained somewhat arbitrary. She hides anywhere books gather, could gather. But certain points carried more significance than others. He would bring with him the Cervantes and the three other books he had stolen from the collection, a bag full of clothes, running shoes, and some things that had gathered on his table to be considered; and he would bring his laptop.

From a little bakeshop near Rittenhouse Square, he purchased some gingersnaps which he knew to be very strongly flavored and which he planned to eat on the plane. He was not completely surprised to see Beatrice in the shop, having coffee and pastry with a woman and man he did not recognize. Philip could not tell from their behavior, from their elbow touches and smiles, whether the man was with Beatrice or the other woman. He was very handsome, with a strong neck and straight jaw. Philip approached the table and greeted them and listened to Beatrice's introductions. She half stood and kissed him on the cheek.

"I'm going to Spain," he told her.

"With anyone?"

"Alone," he said. "You look great, B."

He left them with a nod and a carefully aimed wink at Beatrice, and heard the man begin to tell the women about Spain, telling them what they *had* to see. At the door, Philip looked back to Beatrice and she gave him a shrug. Would she tell them how you didn't have to see anything, that you could just close your eyes and feel the air, smell the orange blossoms and heated stone, hear families, the clink of glass and music until dawn? Would she tell them that, with the help of another, she almost killed a man with pleasure there? Would she tell them about getting lost on Calle sin Salida, how one can walk midway down this tiny lane and lose sense of any entrance or exit?

If you lingered and did not follow him right away, you would hear what she says. You would hear how she cuts the conversation. I could go with him. I could, she tells them. And they lean back, stiffly, thrown. The paperback cover would have to visually imply the glass of the large window. The past lover walks by the window. He is almost out of the picture, but you see that his head is slightly bowed in melancholy. The dark-haired woman behind the glass is watching him, is turning away from her table and her company. Her lips and legs are parted and her green dress clings to her form in the steamy café and its color is the center of the picture. Her hair lifts and swirls with her motion and one black tendril lies across the low neckline of her dress and slips into her cleavage. The name of the café, which is painted across the top of the window, is also the title of the paperback.

After ordering his tickets to Madrid, he inserted the disk Rebecca had given him, *With Philip*, fixed a bourbon and ice, eased into his recliner, and opened Cervantes. The lights from Rebecca's disk played across his ceiling and walls as watery reflections. He glanced at the screen in between paragraphs of *Quixote* or when he heard Rebecca moan. At the beginning of the fifth chapter, Cervantes writes: Seeing, then, that in fact he could not move, he took refuge in his usual remedy, which was to think about some situation from his books. He heard Rebecca call out and he looked to the screen in time to catch a glimpse of the S-curve of a back. A back that was not hers, not his, but entirely familiar to him. It was light brown and lean, without a doubt Irma. It vanished into a bright scene, a picnic he and Rebecca had alone somewhere along the Raritan. He did not hurry to the screen, but approached it cautiously. He reversed the DVD, going back to the preceding scene, which was one of Rebecca and him making love in deep orange light. The image of the back occurs for only a second, its S-shape merely splicing the two scenes together. He might not have noticed it had he not looked up the very moment it appeared, immediately after Rebecca's cry of pleasure. There is her cry in deep orange, the flash of Irma's back, then the white of the picnic, the white sky, the white crests of river, the white of their summer shirts.

Philip ran the DVD back and forth between scenes, watching the image of Irma's back flash between them. He tried to determine what time of her life it might have been, but the lighting was dim. The image was hardly more than curve and color, much like the melting patterns that occur on celluloid film. And the scenes on either side of the image were not in chronological order; the picnic was early in his relationship with Rebecca, the preceding scene toward the end, when the sex felt most urgent.

Philip sat at the table and stared at the freeze-frame of Irma's back. He felt foolish: Did Irma ever ask you for some math help? He called Rebecca at her office, though it was late, hoping. She answered and did not sound surprised to hear him. She said hi as though they were continuing an interrupted call.

"You lied," he said.

"Lied?" She spoke the word as though she didn't know its definition. "Is that your question? Your accusation? The best you can come up with?"

"Don't turn things, Bec. I'm not the one sleeping in my office. Is it quieter there?"

"No. No, it isn't quiet. It isn't quieter anywhere. But here maybe Nicole will come sit. Bring quiet with her. Say nothing but 'hi' and 'bye' across a span of hours. How quiet is it there, Philip?"

"When did it start? With her?"

"My life is stranger than people think, Philip," she said. "I get so much work done trying to avoid the strangeness."

"When, Becca?"

"When?" A brushing sound came across the phone, her sleeve beneath her nose. "There's no when. There's no *t* in the equation."

"Where do we start, then?" he asked. He heard her sniff and clear her throat, the brush of sleeve again. "With her?"

"Start? You know where it started. In the pool. Way back there. All through our marriage. I told you there's no when, no time. Time doesn't exist with her."

"When did it end?" He shook his head. "Where did it end?"

"End?" Rebecca paused a very long time. "It really didn't end. We kept seeing each other. Whenever she traveled east. Whenever I traveled west. Sometimes we just had lunch, took walks. I wasn't seeing much of her these last couple years, but that was because she wasn't traveling much this way. We never ended. And I know she's gone. She left me two books. She restored a first edition of Cook's *Curves* and a delicate edition of Napier's *Canon*."

"I'm not asking about the books."

"*It doesn't end,*" she said. "It does not end with her. She'll say anything at any time."

He almost joined her, almost touched his fingertips to the phone. Instead he asked if she was sorry.

"I'm not sorry. I don't apologize. It seemed at first like I couldn't be with you without being with her, too—in that same way. That same way. I told her that. At first, I believed that you and she were doing the same thing. I told her she could. She said no, that she didn't want that."

She paused for a long time. "Do you know why she disappeared? You would be the only one to know. Do you?"

"No." He did not hesitate to hurt her. For the first time ever in their relationship he wanted to make Rebecca suddenly, sharply sad. "Has Sam come back?"

"Sam?" she asked. "Not yet."

He waited.

"*Sam?*" she asked.

"He's gone looking for her."

"That's not true."

"It is," he said. "Maybe you can get Nicole to tell you about it. You can get her to talk."

"No. No, I never could. You were best. Andrew thinks he is because he gets her to talk so much, reveal so much. But I know now that she just makes stuff up for him. To be nice to him."

"She doesn't tell me much," Philip told her. "She kind of told me about Sam. And herself. She's become very astute. She's startling, to me.

She gauged exactly what she needed to give me, and gave me nothing more."

"*Herself?*" The brushing sound across her phone was rougher, bumps and pulses to it. "What are you saying, Philip?" she asked. "What are you telling me?"

"I'm telling . . ." In apology, he paused. "I'm saying that both your children had—have—some sort of relationship with her. Well beyond our knowledge and imaginations."

"Not sexual?" There was collapse in her voice.

"Certainly to them. Certainly with Nicole. And it's a pretty easy guess with Sam. He's seventeen. How much would it take? Irma could get him with a look."

He could hear her breathing, sense her thinking.

"I'm going to Spain," he told her. "I think I'll find Sam."

Philip could not sleep after the call. In the dark, he listened to Górecki's *Symphony of Sorrowful Songs* and stared at the gray window. Then he tried reading Cervantes, but he had reached the chapters about Marcela, the shepherdess whose mythical beauty and wit beguiled every man exposed to her, and this only agitated his thoughts and imagination even more. Cervantes writes: And over this one, that one, and all of them, the beautiful Marcela, free and self-assured, triumphs, and those of us who know her are waiting to see where her haughtiness will end. All the beech trees of the surrounding countryside are carved with her name. Rebecca called back, also unable to sleep or work.

"I'm thinking you're wrong, Philip. You're just extending things unnecessarily. Because of what happened with me and her, with what you've learned. You're extending it. He's just gone to wherever he's been going, off and on, this past year."

He waited. Heard her sigh of realization.

"Oh," she said.

Though she remained completely silent, he guessed she might be crying. She rarely cried, but there was a kind of bend in the silence.

"Bec."

He sensed the bend deepen.

"It might not be a bad thing," he said. "Sam takes care of himself. With the practical things, anyway."

"Practical things? He's almost nothing but pure thought and distraction these days. Have you seen him? When he runs he looks as if he's hurdling toward something terrifying. Throwing himself into an abyss."

She went silent, waited, then ended the call. Before he could dowse the light, his phone rang, still in his hand.

"I'm not as traveled as you," she said. "Distance bothers me. And what if he catches her?"

"He can't catch her," he said.

Even you can't catch me, Pip.

He lay down for an hour, counted the passing of four trolleys, watched their lights slide across the ceiling. He called her back.

"Bec?"

"Yes?"

"If he is in Spain, then he's in one of the finest places in the world. People will be nice to him. They will like his red hair and freckles and even think he's probably from Madrid, until they hear him try to speak. They are nice there, in a real way. They don't say please and thank you and how are you, until they come to know you. They do say hello. He'll like Spaniards, as much as he can like anybody, because they look you in the eye without saying anything. They do not—like Americans—assume everyone is like them. The more I think about it, the more I realize how much it could be the best place for Sam to go. And he'll miss you and Nicole the whole time he's there. He'll be surprised by the occasional redheads and think of you. He'll see the youth—*los jóvenes*—looking so smart and quick and assured and think of his sister. He'll be fine, Becca. And I'll find him. By trying to look for her, I'll find him."

"You should be angry with me, Philip. You should be angry with her."

"I know that," he replied. "At least I know that. But I'm not. It's a good thing we didn't stay together, Bec. Because as I get older, I just get worse. I come to understand everything. You say you are strange, stranger than anyone thinks. You are."

"Thanks," she said. "I think."

There was flirt in her voice, which sounded tired, too. He ended the call there. I used to spy on him in college, Sylvia narrates in *Theory*. From a hidden position, I would watch him in the library or a hall or as he chatted with classmates and professors under trees, on lawns, by fountains. He was lacking in self-assurance, pausing midgesture and midword, looking away from them. And he would not see how they looked at him in those few seconds, with puzzled smiles that grew less puzzled. It was always easy to spy on him, because unconsciously he placed himself for viewing. He centered himself in windows, chose open corners, liked to walk or stand in bright spaces between clusters of things and people. Initially, I didn't plan on spying on him so much; he just seemed to offer himself that way.

In Mexico without him, Feli and I would orchestrate street theater using pedestrians who never realized they were part of a performance. Feli learned to do this on the sidewalks and zócalos of Colima, where her little troupe perfected the technique. The real trick was gaining an audience willing to go along, even help with the performance and deception. I often told Feli about him, about how he would make the perfect mark for this kind of play. We could go on for days, weeks, I told her. He was a legend to Feli by the time she first saw him step out of a taxi and onto Colima's cathedral plaza.

He finally fell asleep in chapter eight of the Cervantes, which includes the long poem salvaged from the funeral bier of the dead shepherd Grisóstomo. The handsome shepherd dies, in effect, from his unrequited love for Marcela. He writes volumes about his love and despair and then orders these volumes to be burned with him at his death. Don Quixote and his traveling companions argue that this request be ignored for the writing to be saved. They win their argument by pointing out that Virgil, too, requested that the *Aeneid* be destroyed at his death, and that much to the benefit of all this will was not honored. But the long poem put Philip to sleep, poetry's usual effect on him. Poets, he told Irma more than once, think they are great mathematicians, but they're not. Here is the gist of their math: if $a = b$ and $b = c$, then $a = c$ and everything else. Their work seems always dependent on unearned leaps. She responded with quiet disdain, forgiving him much later by suddenly saying, "I don't think you really believe that." And he would know what she referred to, no matter what they had gone on to do and say. Once she said it days later, looking down on him after beating him for a score in a Frisbee game, as he lay drawn and fallen in the grass of the end zone.

He woke, as usual, in the middle of the night, feeling ready to go. To go to Spain and find Sam. But there was a great unrest in his center, a twist of nerves, a tight crescent at the bottom of his breathing. This, both his parents explained to him many times before many races, is only your body shying away, hesitating, before committing itself to what you are asking it to do, to going where you want it to go. It's good. This last declaration they always spoke in Slovak. And he could tell by the meter and syntax of the previous line that those words had once been Slovenský, too. But he learned that Slovaks were expert at fashioning good from suffering, misfortune, and mistake. And so he realized that while the first sentence was likely true, the second was only relative or questionable or absolutely false.

Waiting for dawn, for some running light, watching city lights slide across his ceiling, he wanted to call his mother and father and let them know what he was about to do, and how he felt just now. He wanted to hear them explain it all again and say, *Sa dobre, Filip.*

NINE

On the overnight to Madrid, he read *Quixote*. Marcela, the shepherdess whose beauty kills Grisóstomo, makes a sudden appearance at the end of the funeral, stepping from the woods and showing herself to be even more beautiful than her legend contends. When the travelers, their eyes clouded for a moment by grief and anger, berate her for the death and misery she has caused, Marcela defends herself with insight that rivals her physical grace. After explaining herself, she returns to the woods: All those present filled with admiration as much for her intelligence as for her beauty. And some—those who were pierced by the powerful arrow of the light in her beautiful eyes—gave indications of wanting to follow her.

The chivalrous Quixote, hand on the hilt of his sword, warns everyone to abide by Marcela's wishes to be left alone, and threatens to stop anyone who tries to follow. When the travelers go their separate ways, leaving Quixote alone (with Sancho), he of course resolves to seek her out and offer to serve her in any way he can. He and Sancho enter the forest and ride after her: Having ridden more than two hours, looking for her everywhere and not finding her, they decided to stop in a meadow full of new grass where a cool, gentle stream ran, so welcoming that it invited and obliged one to spend the hottest hours of the day there, for the rigors of the afternoon were just beginning. How long would you search, Pip, before stopping?

Philip almost continued to read, with only the trailing edge of his consciousness catching Irma's intrusion, a snag in a stream. The book lay open on his seat tray and he placed his hand on the page. As though caught, he looked around the dimly lit cabin of the plane. Almost all the passengers were sleeping, their snores and breathing blending with the soft engine hum. Pale yellow lights marked those reading their way across the Atlantic.

He continued reading: When I finally go missing from your life, how long will you search? And what will be the starting angle of your search? What will be the curve? How carefully will you draw the formula before you begin? Will you seek help with the equations?

In embarrassment, he pushed the folder containing his composition book and equations deeper into the seat pocket, behind the flight magazines. He did seek help. He did not have the time, really, to swing a pendulum across Spain. Rebecca helped him, out of a kind of amused apology, it seemed. Together they went over his equations in the late hours, in the papery glow of her office. Sometimes they heard the distant tap of a janitor's mop, a clang of bucket. She refined his work, using her own knowledge of Irma to edit unnecessary considerations and to add, Rebecca argued, essential explorations.

She sent an e-mail to Sam. I know you're in Spain, she told him.

I'm fine, he responded. Then he did not respond to any more messages.

"It was odd," she told Philip, to send these messages to her own home. But she felt relieved because it would allow Sam to use his card and not rely on whatever money system he had devised. "But he's not stupid," she said. "He'll take a train a thousand miles just to get cash and hide his tracks. *Can* you travel a thousand miles inside Spain?" she asked him.

"Or he could just take the ferry to Tangier. Or an island."

"Don't, Philip," she replied. She removed her glasses and looked at him for a long moment. Her face was above the glow of her desk lamp and so the light filtered up through her red hair, blushing her pale complexion. He saw and remembered how her lashes were red, too. She replaced her glasses and pretended to look at the equations.

"What does she do with him?" she asked. "With her? Them?"

"You would have to be the one to ask them, Rebecca."

"I know. But you know Irma best."

He shrugged. "She has sex with them. They bring each other to climax, in prolonged and sometimes not so prolonged ways. But that's not what you really want to know, is it? You want to know what she tells them, reveals to them. About us. About you."

She nodded.

"But you already know, Becca. You already said. She'll say anything at any time. Take it from there."

She considered him, sliding her glasses down, then up, biting her lip. "You've changed," she finally said. "You're a bit more engaged than when we were together. You're prickly. It fits you."

He laughed softly, but she still waited for more reply.

"My life is half gone," he told her. "I live in a cheap flat above an old store. I have nothing. I've accomplished nothing, with nothing to show. When I walk these halls to your office or to Isaac's office, I pass mathematicians who do so much more than I do, who have done so much more than I have done, so much more than I can possibly do with what time and talent I have left. And yet they have families and hobbies and amusements. My greatest fear is that when I'm in Spain, looking for Sam looking for Irma, I will have no sense of return."

She touched his temple, then slid her fingers around his ear, as though tucking his hair. "People miss you, Philip. Nicole and Sam miss you. Irma misses you. Tomas and Anna must."

"You mean Stefan and Tessa. Tomas and Anna are Irma's version of Mom and Dad. From her book."

She shrugged. "I get them mixed up sometimes. All the time, actually."

She returned to the equations, but he could tell her concentration was elsewhere. Her eyes scanned the paper up and down, not following any direction. Light reflected and splintered with their movement.

"What are you thinking?"

She smiled down at the papers and then leaned toward him, shouldered in as though to kiss him. She smelled of powdered lavender, a scent from the pink edges of her brow. He looked at the curves of her ear, the pale stem of her neck, all washed in the color of her hair. She bit her lower lip, then let it slide free, and he kissed her there. She parted her lips to his, turned her face more to his. As they pushed harder into each other, her glasses slid off, falling between their noses, clattering between their teeth. As he drew away, Philip caught the glasses. He offered them to her. She took the offer and folded them in her hand, folded herself away from him.

"Things always fall between us," she said. "Everything is falling from me."

She put her fingers to his chin, then pulled her arms about herself, holding her elbows. She drew in a halting, quivered breath.

"Please find him," she whispered, looking down, clutching her arms tightly to herself.

He touched her shoulder briefly as he stood, then her hair, and left her office.

Don't stop me and don't stop yourself, Irma told him the last time they made love. It was the day his divorce with Beatrice was finalized. He went to California to visit his family. He traveled the little ways south to say hello to the Arcuris and was surprised to find Irma there, alone. You have me to yourself, she said. Have me. She answered the door naked. She had let her hair grow long and it seemed fuller. She seemed fuller, younger, but maybe that was because he was seeing her in her family's home. In Spain, with Beatrice, she had appeared so worldly and sophisticated, carrying her looks as easily and gracefully as the Spanish women around her. She ran too much, she said, ran herself thin, but Seville was so nice for running. When he first saw her after their return, in her shop, she looked contrite, scrubbed clean, hair pulled back and out of the way for work. So those images led him to the surprise at the door to her family's home. For him, there was no sense in feigning resistance or seeking complication. She held the door edge, her arm lifted, no skew at all to her stance. No slant of hip, her feet together, her toes lifting and then pressing to the tile of the entryway. Let's see what you're up to.

In her bed, she moved over him intently, kissing his palm while the weight of her spread over him. Beneath him, she hooked her hand behind his neck and pulled him to her, first to her breasts, then pushing him down farther. She rolled her hips, scissoring him. She cried twice when she came, but only wiped away the tears and kept going, laughing at herself, then at him, playfully, as he came. At the end, he told her he was through for the day.

Just one more, she said.

He shook his head and lay on the bed, spent. She put him into her mouth anyway, soft, her hair tumbling about his hips. He remained soft for a long while, despite her efforts. It felt good that way, and he was surprised. When he began to harden, she laughed with her mouth full on him. The vibration of her laugh quickened him. She hurried to get on top, before any risk of losing him. Then she looked down at him kindly, with an unusual smile, soft but quizzical. He experienced an odd but not unpleasant sense of reversal, time sliding backward, keyed by her measuring, assessing expression, and by the afternoon, after-school light. How long would you search, Pip, before stopping? When I finally go missing from your life, how long will you search? And what will be the starting angle of your search? What will be the curve? How carefully will you draw the formula before you begin? Will you seek help with the equations?

He had dinner with the Arcuris that evening, with no one to sit between Irma and him. He had little to say, little to add to his accomplishments in life, but he felt at home with all of them, a nice family friend who could help set the table because he knew where things were kept.

Philip cupped his hands on either side of the open *Quixote* and looked around the plane to see if the eyes of the nearest passengers were closed. He then relaxed his hands and let the book be an open book. No one cares, she once said. No one reads. He continued with the Cervantes, looking forward to Quixote's story and Irma's, too. In the woods, Quixote and Sancho never find the beautiful Marcela. Instead, Quixote's nag Rocinante, left unhobbled, wanders after a group of mares seeking a little fun, and gets Quixote and Sancho into a confrontation with angry Yanguesans. Greatly outnumbered, Quixote and Sancho are badly beaten and left for dead, as they often are left by Cervantes: All his skill and courage were of no use to him. I can only guess how much you know, Pip. How much you know now, how much you've known all along. Sometimes you are so bright that I feel lifted around you, carried along by you. Sometimes you seem lost forever in some mathematical fog, weighted, unnecessarily anchored. We don't wonder the same things.

He bookmarked *Quixote*, then reached for his composition book and tore loose a blank page. He filled the grid with answers to her questions, culling the corresponding equations from the proof composed to search for her. Then he translated them as plainly as he could. How long will I search? He showed her how you can take Newton's binomial theorem to express equations of various curves as infinite series in the variable x. Then apply Fermat's formula, $x^{n+1}/(n+1)$, as Newton did, to each term of the series. This lets me effect the quadrature of many new curves. But I've learned things beyond what Newton and Fermat first gave us. So that's what you're up against. And if you can't follow all this, if you've grown bored and sleepy from it, then just note the word "infinite."

What will be my starting angle? That I've shown you already. Draw a logarithmic spiral. Make it pretty as you can. Trace it on your stomach. Spiral it outward as far as you like, tickle what you want. Draw a y axis and an x axis through its center. Measure all the angles formed. Each one, as you know, will measure the same.

The curve? This is where I have you. The ellipse. πab (where a and b are the lengths of the major and minor axes). This I extend from simple geometry, Archimedes' method of exhaustion applied to a parabola. But you are definitely not parabolic. So it's the ellipse. But the key word for your bored and sleepy eyes is "exhaustion." We do wonder the same things, he wrote in reply. We wonder them in different ways.

Philip almost crumpled the paper. But instead, he inserted it neatly into the *Quixote*, where he had bookmarked his place.

He noticed, as he continued to read and reread earlier chapters on the plane, that she tended to appear most directly in those moments when Quixote lay immobilized by the weight of his armor or the weight of his grandiose decisions—which was often. But she would appear almost anywhere briefly. And, of course, he could not always tell when it was Cervantes and when it was Irma, because he did not know the book and Cervantes frequently addressed the reader and used that collapsing and retracting point of view. Lucia was there to help him intermittently with her little yellow posts. The book felt alive in his hands, treacherous and seductive, the dimpled leather of its cover a providing skin. As its reader, he was outnumbered at least three to one. But then, as noted by Lucia, → You have to consider, too, all the translators involved, all the transcribers and historians and censors. You are vastly overmatched. But that never seems to stop Q. Love, L. She pasted this note within Quixote's ill-fated battle against the twenty Yanguesans.

He tried to sleep, but only ended up in a more agitated state, his attempts to doze merely awakening surface anxieties, those linked to immediate surroundings. The landscapes in *Quixote* and the breadth of Irma's ability to predict him combined to make the plane feel small, a tube insulating him from the world he wanted to search, gliding him over the most oft-drawn path across the Atlantic. The only way to catch her trail was to leave such paths as quickly as she did. She left airports faster than anyone he had ever known. Following her from a plane, stay-ing in her slipstream if you could, was exhilarating. Her main task was to move, to get somewhere, to hop on the next available piece of trans-port, the most battered taxi, a shuttle bus with destinations painted on its windshield. Ask no questions when the way out is clear. Get yourself to a table in the city, a path to a ruin, a drink in a cantina, a piece of fruit or handmade candy from a vendor. The hours gone and the hours to come on the flight felt useless, wasted, nonretractable somehow, the eyes-closed count you take against the tree while all others hide. How fast can you count to one hundred while you think about the one you want to find first? There is always that one you want to find first, hide with later in the game. How fast can you count as you imagine her, eyes clenched shut?

During the changeover in Heathrow his anxiety took shape and pulsed. His count started over, this time to a thousand. Just through customs he encountered walls filled with hundreds of destinations. He found himself skimming down the lists to mark those he had been to with her and then those she had hurried away to, without him. Don't look at signs in airports if you don't need to, she told him. Don't ask ques-tions. Don't ask for directions. Go. A single taxi driver, out *there*, she said pointing, will know more than everybody and everything an airport has to offer. You *moving* will know more.

It was difficult for him to stand, let alone sit, in the gate area for his Madrid connection, over two hours' wait. He felt the heft of the *Quixote*— her *Quixote*—in his shoulder bag, filled with her designs for him and now his plans for her. He began walking the length of the terminal to stretch his legs, to move, to know more. He didn't fear incorrect choices. Mathematicians can't function with that fear. What lay before him was a sea of choices of seemingly equal value, or whose respective values shifted upon consideration. Rebecca had urged him to stay the course, but what did she know? Irma had fooled her more than she had fooled him. And Rebecca wanted him to find Sam, not Irma.

At the rounded tip of the terminal he came upon what the British called the island flights, all advertised with suggestions of the quick and the cavalier. The flights were cheap and frequent from London, several referred to as hops and getaways, poised at this circling end of the terminal. One of the next available was Corsica. The season hadn't quite begun there—Hurry now! Lucia had visited once. And the idea of going there felt much like one of her little yellow posts stuck into the Cervantes. And, too, her finger puzzle, reminding him in all its color and grip to go in to get out. The island was on his list, though much farther down. It stood along the minor axis of the ellipse he had drawn for Irma. The small jet to Corsica had a light, feral look about it as it perched on the tarmac amid the giant airliners. She could be there as well as anywhere, but as he committed himself to the idea of Corsica, he once again sensed that he was acting on something, that understanding before knowing. Something lingered there on the island, just a thought, or image, or feeling he needed to complete. A quieting of her furtive shoulders was how he imagined it. Something he should have done while there, with her, for her. And it was this image that carried him most toward the island, the rightness of it.

In the thrum of the small jet, he recalled Lucia's hands rendering the island for him in a delicate circle, fingertips aligned, thumbs tip to tip. Whether she was somehow with Irma or not, he would make her his ally on this tangent. She had been to Corte, the island's rocky heart. He easily imagined her moving along its broken paths, its stepped walkways, getting what she needed right away from its buildings, navigating directly to the university library to get the books she needed, perhaps pausing once on the remains of a watchtower to catch sight of a mosque broken toylike across a far precipice. In his imaginations her movements, the length of her step, the flicker of her orange dress, her sandals on Roman stones, were all in contrast to his first excursion to the island with Irma, an arduous hike into the stony foothills beyond Ajaccio. They searched for one of the many unnamed crumbling fortifications, trying to stay on a trail that often vanished into thorny scrub, rock juts, or welcomed streams. She wasn't even after the books themselves, but their leathers and clasps, which she heard were rendered from a kind of pygmy goat brought by Moors, then exterminated during the Aragon occupation. The almost unbearable heat of their trek was made worse by their constant view of the sea. We'll swim later, she told him when she turned to find him resting, watching the water. I promise. But they didn't swim. Their search failed and left her angry and defiant in defeat. She stared hard at the wake of the ferry that returned them to Sardinia, as though she were making sure their course remained absolutely straight, knifing the sea.

Maybe that was another reason for his flight to the island. There he could stand on the ground of one of her few failures, reassure himself that she sometimes miscalculated things, overestimated her perception. Perhaps she also would need to return, to correct what she had missed. Pluck Corsica like a book from her library. He closed his eyes and pictured the delicate circle of Lucia's hands again, the pale stretch of her thumbs. It's an island, she said, as though that made it harmless.

To pass the flight, he perused the other books he had taken, avoiding *Quixote* altogether. They still felt stolen. He wanted to tell Lucia which ones he took. *Ava. The Unbearable Lightness of Being. The Rings of Saturn.* He split the Maso in two and read what he estimated was the very center of the book: She wants to convey what is barely felt, never verbalized, fleeting, never arrested, common to all and developing at different states of awareness. He had been thinking of Lucia just before he read the sentence, so by reflex she became the subject. But who was telling him this? Irma or Maso? Was it a compliment or warning? He flipped through the novel and was stunned to discover that he would never be able to find out because it was composed of separate sentences, free of their paragraphs and scenes, almost free of each other, as though she had dropped the book like a treasure box and shattered the content, its order. It was full of crystalline phrasings kaleidoscoped together, enclosed in emerald-green leather.

He switched to the Kundera, someone his parents tried to tell him about when they deemed him old enough. He must have recognized the title from distant memory when he first chose the book. He rubbed his fingers over the black felt, settled his hand to it. He read the opening, sifting through it for her. He was able to push aside what could easily be her musings on life, on eternal return, on the perversity of a world that rests essentially on the nonexistence of return. But he fell across this passage, read it three times, a mere image that immediately became an event for him: But this time he fell asleep by her side. When he woke up the next morning, he found Tereza, who was still asleep, holding his hand. Could they have been hand in hand all night? It was hard to believe. Philip remembered something like this happening once with Irma, in a hotel in Pátzcuaro, an old convent across the street from where penitents dragged themselves on their knees over the cobblestones. She claimed she awoke, too, like him, hands held. Why is it so unbelievable? she asked later, in the same bed, astride him, her thumbs probing beneath his ears, his breathing pushing against her breasts.

In the Sebald he avoided the words. It looked opposite the Maso somehow, all spaces filled, paragraphs brimming. But it had photos and he could flip through it and pause on them, as if going through one of the flight magazines. He suspected one photo about two-thirds through. It seemed more in focus than the others. It showed a doorway fronted by stacks of papers and books, bound and unbound, teetering before a room dimly lit by leaded glass windows, a place they had searched together in Prague. Or so he believed. And unlike the other pictures, he couldn't find direct reference to it in the surrounding text, only a description of a pantry. And it was easy for him to see one moment ahead in the photo, when he had emerged from the room to look back for her, then ducked back in to dodge her camera.

In the breezeway of the Corsican airport, getting to the first taxi he saw, Philip was broadsided by a hard wind off the Mediterranean.

Because he had flung himself farther east than originally planned, his sense of time and light listed, and the wind, which he had forgotten about, dizzied him. He forgot which color taxis were the safest, the quickest. The one he crawled into was burnt orange, with sticky black seats and a wet dog smell. The driver, hunched over his wheel, was much too tall for his little car. He appeared distracted, never fully turning to face Philip in greeting, only showing him the jagged brown coastline of his profile.

"Ajaccio o Bonifacio?" the driver asked as they reached the coast road—the small but sleek airport left them nowhere. The vowel sound between the two destinations was indistinct. Irma described the language as sounding like French people speaking Spanish using Italian words. Philip didn't answer right away and stared at the Mediterranean, which struck the coast directly here, no beach, no cliffs. The rough waves broke among the rocks and scrub, looking as though they were flooding the foothills. You could imagine rabbits and lizards running to avoid the encroaching water.

On the road to Ajaccio they passed ancient forts and lookouts that appeared fused to the rocks. It was not unusual for the edifices to jut beyond the edges of the escarpments, an anxiousness toward the sea about them. Philip tried to remember which one marked the trailhead he had taken with Irma. It wasn't that all of them looked strange to him; it was that each looked familiar. He had seen them all before, with her. Here in his woeful search, she had elbowed aside all attempts to clear her image from his thoughts and senses and stood victorious, hands on hips, waist cocked forward. She had cleared away his visions of Lucia, foiled his attempts to cheat on her library, and tricked him into returning to a place where they had failed together. Brought him to a hall of mirrors.

Passing the ancient parapets, one after another along the rocky coast, reminded him of how long the ride to Ajaccio was. The taxi felt suffocating, with its furry smell, giant driver, and gummy seats. Philip rolled down the seaward window and the wind tore through, a surprisingly chilly force that threw papers across the windshield and had the driver cursing everything in jangly Corsu. A cold sweat of wrongness fingered up Philip's neck. Along one of the smoother inlets near Cap de Freno, where there was some semblance of a little beach and where he could see campers had left fire rings, he had the driver stop. "Please," he said in English, then Spanish, then French, then Italian, finally making the driver laugh. Philip pantomimed the breaststroke, puffed his cheeks.

The driver leaned on his taxi and smoked a cigarette as he watched Philip go down to the water for a swim. He seemed uninsulted as Philip hauled his shoulder bag and case with him. Philip found a sandy crook in the steep tumble of rock and scrub and took off his clothes. The wind instantly dried his sweat. He waded into the shallows, where the waves were broken and weak. There was a leftover chill to the water and the sudden drop-off caught him unaware and he fell into the sea.

He meant to swim in order to rinse her away, but when he surfaced his longing was nearly painful, a kind of swimming cramp low in his gut. More strongly than ever before he felt her gone, torn away. She should have been there, right now, beside him, laughing at their collective mistake about the water, about how cold it would be, how rough, how perfect it would feel to embrace each other in it, skin as soft as the anemones beneath their feet.

He paddled low into the waves, his chin dipped into their salty churn. The water was the kind he had learned to swim in, the cold rough Pacific, and he let its slap against his face bring him around a bit. He closed his eyes to the blue sky. He could undo this mistake, retrace the same return they managed the first time and get back on course, to Madrid. Fuck this island, Irma told him. I want to get off it right away. We take the ferry to Sardinia and catch a plane there. He arced into the water, pulling himself deeper into a green darkness. The colder water down there seemed to shear him, peel away a dead layer, the husk drifting behind him like smoke. And in the cool depths, arms rotating for balance, he thought to do one more thing denied him, the other thing besides this swim. He thought to return to Corte, to the home of Irma's friend Miriam Haupt, the collector who had first brought them here.

On shore, he dried quickly in the wind and let the chill punish him for being impulsive and creative. He dressed, shivered by the salt pinpricks beneath his clothes. The driver took him the rest of the way to Ajaccio and Philip stared at the dying light over the Mediterranean, the sea turning ink-blue under orange light. They drove straight to the station in Ajaccio and Philip—still moving to know more—was able to catch the last evening train to Corte. The Chemin de Fer was Irma's favorite rail in the world. With its little cars and narrow-gauge track, it looked like a child's model come to life. But as he boarded, he was sad to see that the old flat-faced cars had been replaced with sleek bullet-nose shuttles, quicker into the foothills and mountain tunnels.

Twilight was fading to night as his train climbed into the high mountains, but the car's rapid ascent allowed Philip to gain on the sun a little while longer. You had to convince yourself the train was going somewhere, following something, because the path disappeared into mountain curves, and weeds and wildflowers grew between the narrow rails, and rock faces seemed to clash together, closing off passage. Before all light faded, Philip caught a glimpse of the highest, most distant peaks, still tipped with snow and making the island seem as though it had broken from the Alps somewhere and floated into the middle of the Mediterranean.

In Corte, he always felt as though he had been taken to the top of the world. At night the effect was even stronger, as the chasms surrounding the village dropped into blackness and the old walls teetered above streetlights, all crashed together and upward, lifting thoughts just to the crest of dizziness. But the cafés around the main plaza were busy, as though everything were level, tables shoved out over the stone walks, students and professors having wine in summer clothes, toasting the occasional warm breeze rolling through the cool mountain air. Philip stood in the light of the Paoli statue and tried to catch his breath. No one else in the night crowd seemed to struggle with the thin air and slanted ground. Again it was easy for him to imagine Lucia here, moving along the tables, taking her pick of what she wanted, who she wanted, her brown shoulders catching the glow of the streetlamps, her sandaled feet light on the slant.

He wanted to stay where she might have stayed when she was here. With enough time and daylight, he believed he could figure out where. But he was tired and feeling lost again, far away from where he was supposed to be, astray from solving the great need in the world caused by his delay. He took the first inn he found, where the old couple who owned the place insisted—in Corsu, then Italian, then Spanish—on first showing him the linoleum floors of his room and the new fiberglass shower in the shared bath. The old man wore a burgundy jacket with yellow epaulets that had several tassels missing.

The bed was too short for Philip and he slept and dreamt in bits through the night, each dream of another place waking him in a jolt, leaving him to wonder where he might be. He read himself back to sleep each time using *The Rings of Saturn*, going over the same passage about a farmer in Yoxford building a miniature replica of the Temple of Jerusalem in his barn, using a multitude of textual evidence to get the details exact, devoting his final years to the task. The passage is split by the largest photograph in the novel, a two-page, blurring picture of what could be the columned interior of the temple—its miniature replica or the actual one, had it still been in existence. The vaguest figure of a man stands dwarfed by the columns. You don't see him right away. Philip's longest stretch of sleep was filled by a dream walk among the columns, himself the miniature, flickering man trying not to disappear. *Cuidado*, Lucia whispers above him, her voice as big and quiet as the sky, hushing the word into an invite instead of a warning.

In the morning he had a coffee at the only open café on the plaza. None of the chairs or tables were out and he had to stand at the bar with men and women who were getting ready for work by drinking anisette, their perfumed breath hurling forth on cigarette smoke. Philip then walked upward, toward the Citadel—the castle in the sky, says Irma—in search of Miriam Haupt. He veered toward the Paoli schoolhouse and knew he was getting close. The entire neighborhood there collapsed at an odd series of pitches, almost like a collection of rooftops coming together, with each respective slant joining the others to form new angles and planes. You were always walking up or down, often steeply. But these angles, along with pines and junipers here and there, provided shade and cool walls.

Miriam Haupt loved Irma. She brokered antiquarian books, but in her retirement had become exclusively a collector. She and her husband owned a small apartment building, painted blue alongside the many other apartment buildings mortared together, all left to fade to the colors of aging paper along one continuous wall. Each flat in the Haupt building was filled with books. The Haupts themselves dwelled on the second floor, every room lined with bookshelves. The other floors were occupied exclusively by books and a wandering cat to fend off mice. Each decade of Miriam's retirement seemed marked by the ousting of a tenant and the designation of another floor for books. Her husband Vlad Ballestreros, a professor of mycology at the university, often got himself lost in the stacks. He loved their smells, the breath of the molds and fungi he studied. Whenever Philip went with Irma to visit, Señor Ballestreros could be heard thumping around on one of the floors and he would eventually call down, or up, in his shaky Castilian croak and say he would be right there to join. He would only appear hours later, blinking and out of breath as though he had just surfaced from a dive or dream.

He began his scientific career studying the migratory methods and apparatus of fungi, but after he met Miriam and began helping her with the collection and storage of her stacks, he focused on the fungi and molds specific to paper and cellulose. He collected and studied *Aspergillus*, *Stachybotrys*, and *Chaetomium*, trapped and examined the lice and silverfish that carried their spores about Miriam's volumes. They are the only ones reading your precious books, he would tell her. They are the ones who care most. They are the descendants of those who feasted on the great collections in Alexandria. He published enough papers on the physical and genetic migration of cellulose-specific fungi to fill a book, which was published by the university despite his own resistance. *Food for Thought* was the title he wanted, but did not get. They can make it as dry and unpalatable as is humanly possible, he said of his editors, but *Chaetomium* will still devour it.

It was often claimed that Miriam and Vlad would go days without seeing each other in their house, one carefully assessing and cataloguing acquisitions, the other on another floor, or just around the corner, meticulously brushing microscopic powder from the pages and creases. Miriam traveled the world and Vlad never ventured beyond the Chemin de Fer to and from Bastia. Once Philip and Irma came by for a visit, waited for a long time on the stoop for Vlad to appear, only to be invited inside to wait even longer for Vlad to search the floors and stacks for his wife. They sipped sherry and glanced at the ceiling as they listened to him shuffle and thump, floor to floor. Clutching a note, he returned without Miriam, and informed them she had gone to Istanbul. She will be back . . . he peered at his crumpled note . . . tomorrow.

When invited, Irma would arrive at their building with her simple bone folder and set to work on Miriam's acquisitions. Philip and Miriam would watch Irma for hours during a summer afternoon as she crimped and lanced with her bone folder and transformed a flayed and warped bundle of papers and leather back into the book it once was. If it needed more work, Miriam would deliver it to Irma's shop. If it was beyond restoration, Irma would tell her so, waving the bone folder above the decayed volume like a wand.

He rang the bell to the apartment building, leaned back on one heel, and peered upward. His laptop and *Quixote*, too valuable to leave at the inn, hung in a satchel from his shoulder. He looked like Jude Fawley on the cover of the New Wessex Edition of Hardy's last novel. On this cover, a photographer stages the scene of Jude standing outside the college walls, looking up to the windows of the lecture halls he cannot afford to enter. A shoulder bag, meant for books, carries his stonemason tools. The photograph is bleached and then splashed with bright yellow, giving the scene a backlit quality, with Jude dark and angular. If you were to see Philip standing on Miriam Haupt's stoop, waiting, one foot back, tilted, you might mistake him for the dusty phantom of the building's first tenant, a stonecutter, one of Paoli's rebels come to chisel the Moor's Head. You might see this not so much from his features, but from the expression of his stance, one of someone lost in a familiar place. His relationship with Miriam Haupt was one of evolving forgiveness. The first day Irma brought him here, not long after they had finished their respective graduate studies—not long after he and Isaac had seen Irma to her train in Ann Arbor, and Irma had looked back to Philip with that expression he never quite deciphered—they toured Miriam's collection and then sat quietly around some sherry and olives. Philip looked at Miriam Haupt quizzically and guessed that there were over 50,000 books in her collection. A person would have to live 60 years, reading 20 hours per day, just to read 43,800 books. This observation, innocent on his part, and in fact hinging on his own self-doubt, seemed to hurt and offend Miriam greatly. She left the room. Irma, after a time, had to go find her somewhere among the stacks. They left without Philip seeing Miriam again that day. Each subsequent visit proved to be one more step for Philip in an ongoing reconciliation, though he never quite comprehended the offense.

She's read every book in her collection, Irma tried to explain. Every edition in every language. Some more than once. Many studied exhaustively.

That doesn't seem possible, he replied.

You've made that view clear.

It's not my view. It's my fascination.

This helped, at least in Irma's perception of him. But there are those, she explained, who never want to hear of their accomplishments, or lack of accomplishment. Who detest any quantification of what they have done, what they have left to do, what they will not be able to do. When they would come upon Miriam within her stacks, she would be crouched under an old gooseneck lamp she dragged with her from shelf to shelf, floor to floor. She would be sitting on an oak milking stool, one hand grasping a book edge, the other resting gently on a page. Sometimes a section of text from the book would prompt her to kneel from the milking stool and reach for another volume that she could almost find without looking, by just feeling and counting the spines with her fingers. Irma told him that Miriam obtained clues of a book's existence from allusions in other books. She sometimes dashed off, midbook, to a library or university or house in another country. She took Irma when it was possible and Irma told Philip she felt like nothing more than a mechanic carrying her bone folder. Not a bad feeling, she told him.

But outside Miriam's home, out of earshot, Philip could not drop his wondering.

How can someone who will stop midway inside a particular book and travel halfway across the world to find another book ever finish reading 50,000 books? He held his hands up to her.

I don't know, Pip. Have you ever read a book backward? Have you ever read a book inside out? Have you ever read a book one random sentence at a time, choosing them here and there for their sound and look, until you've read the entire work? And it all comes together in a way—you fear, you hope—the author never intended? Have you ever read a book outside of time?

He rang the Haupt bell again and waited, looking up and hoping Miriam or Vlad would appear on one of the four tiny balconies. The narrow street was deserted, with only squares of sunlight forming patchwork along the cobblestones and scorched paper walls. A quiet heat seemed to partition the neighborhood from the cool rest of Corte. The door suddenly opened with the sound of a seal being broken. A young woman answered, a Spaniard, a student. She held one of Miriam's books in her arms, an artist's brush propped behind one ear. Vlad used these brushes to collect his powdery specimens.

Philip explained who he was and asked to see Señora Haupt or Señor Ballestreros.

The woman changed to English, after some thought, a pursing of lips and a clicking sound.

"They're away." She pronounced it, *Zhe're away.*

"How long?" he asked.

"A year."

"On vacation?" But he knew they did not take vacations.

"For reasons of health," she answered.

"Who is ill?"

She shook her head.

"Where did they go?"

"I can't tell you. You're not on the list."

"What list?"

"The list they gave me."

"But I'm with Irma. Irma Arcuri. She must be on the list."

She leaned her head through the doorframe and looked up and down the street. *"No la veo."*

"But she's on the list," he said. "May I see it?"

She tapped her temple. "*Está aquí.*"

He could not explain why he wanted to enter. Maybe he just did not want to fail at another small attempt to track her, in this fragment of investigatory action, this foray ahead of the equation.

"But she is on the list?" he asked. "You know who she is. She *has* been here."

"Of course I know who she is. Her picture is on the"—she drew a horizontal with her hand—"*la repisa.*"

He thought for a moment. "*Sí. Mantel.*"

She wrinkled her nose. "*Mantel?*" She mimicked the way he pronounced it as though speaking Spanish. "*Mantel?* Why would they put her picture on the tablecloth? Like some kind of Shroud of Turin? They are not that crazy. What are you doing here?"

"You're a student of Señor Ballestreros?"

She nodded.

"I'm a friend," he said. "Of both. A longtime friend. A good friend."

"But not on the list."

"Yes. Not on the list. I was never on the list. I counted all the books. Once. I can do that. Up here." He tapped his temple. "I can't help doing that." He tapped his temple some more, perhaps too vigorously. She recoiled slightly, but seemed to gather what he was trying to explain.

Not really knowing why, he drew the Cervantes from his satchel. She looked at the book and then back to him, waiting, it seemed, for some secret phrase to accompany his showing of the book.

"I wanted Señora Haupt to see this. I wanted to ask when she last saw Irma."

"Then you're out of luck," she replied. "You can do neither. I can't help you with the book unless you want to know what kind of ascomycete might be eating its pages. And I have never seen Irma Arcuri here, in person or as an apparition on any tablecloth."

"Has anyone else come looking for her?" he asked, hoping, at least, to catch Lucia.

She lifted her brow in surprise, the paintbrush behind her ear lifting. He did not wait for her to establish any front.

"Another woman, yes? With hair like yours?"

"No," she said. "Just a boy. *El rojo.*"

"*El rojo? Sam?*" he asked. "When?"

She wrinkled her brow. "Almost a week ago. He wanted to see the books."

"What books?"

She shrugged. "All of them. It appeared. He wandered the shelves."

"You let him in?"

She shrugged. "He seemed kind."

"Did he ask you anything? Tell you anything? Do you know where he might be?"

She shook her head, a thoughtful, wistful look on her face. "He just came in, walked among the books, lingered in some places. He reached, but did not touch."

Philip sensed a physical drop, the awful realization that he had much less inside him than he needed, and nothing outside him, here in the high mountain village. He wasn't granted passage and he wasn't privy to whatever codes Irma passed to Sam. His lungs couldn't draw enough from the thin air. He would do better turning in the depths of the cold green sea, where he could at least surface, choking on salt water. You're cheating, he thought. You're drowning me in air instead of water.

Philip handed her a card with his e-mail address. "Will you let me know if he comes back? Please."

She shrugged. "Only if he agrees."

He nodded. "You guard the castle well," he told her. In Spanish, he wished her luck in her research.

"His Spanish is better than yours," she replied.

He caught the first train on the Chemin de Fer back to the Ajaccio station and from there flagged a taxi to the Bonifacio ferry, Irma's getaway, the one that always kept you moving, hardly waiting, knowing more. Train, taxi, ferry, plane. At the ferry landing in Bonifacio he bought some dates and a halvah square from a vendor. He gave the halvah, which looked too neatly cut, to a boy on the ferry and ate the dates on the ride to Sardinia. The ferry had a fountain in the middle of its aft deck, but it stood dry for most of the ride. Then an old man wearing a black ball cap and a khaki jumpsuit opened a flap under the stern rail and switched on the fountain as though the boat had just crossed some geographical timeline indicating the start of the season.

Finally in Madrid, he took the subway from the airport to the Atocha station and found he had three hours before catching the evening bullet to Seville. Swinging west from Corsica, he had convinced himself he'd rewound part of a lost day, gone momentarily into tomorrow, then come back. In the glassy expanse of Atocha, amid the thousands of passengers coming and going, he saw three boys who could have been Sam, with their gawky frames, red hair, and sparse freckles. Even passing close, he had to scrutinize them to make sure they were not Sam, only Spanish versions of him, making their way about the country, exploring their youth. Philip spied two women he mistook for Irma, two he mistook for Lucia, and one he mistook for either. This one he had to trail until she stopped at a ticket kiosk, where he could then step close and see for certain that she was neither. But even with her standing still and close, he could not decide if it was Irma or Lucia she resembled most. When she had completed her purchase, the woman did something Philip found distinctly Spanish. She looked him directly in the eye, then down to his shoes, then back to his face, and then walked on, leaving him feeling as though he had just been entered into some Castilian equation.

Just outside the station, where two streets converged into a sharp point, he found the café with the stale pastries. The place stayed open through siesta and there were students around the outside tables with their laptops, taking in the Wi-Fi. Philip found a table and ordered a coffee. With the coffee, the waiter brought him two small pastries which looked as dry as the breeze drifting across the tables. Even their colors were fading like paint in sun. Philip opened his laptop and found that a message from Lucia awaited him. Like a good sweet, he saved it for later. He sent brief messages to Rebecca and Nicole, telling them he had picked up Sam's trail and that people said he was all right. Sad but kind.

He considered, not for the first time, sending a message to Sam, letting him know he was here in Spain, if he needed anything. But Philip could not figure how to say this without sounding in any way like a bounty hunter. Rebecca warned him. Just find him, she said. And ask him to go on a run. Ask him to throw a Frisbee, find a game somewhere.

His coffee, at least, was good—hot and frothy. He looked at the other tables, each occupied by a single person, all students, all staring at their laptop screens, all ignoring their faded pastries. Do you think these are the same ones they brought us last year? Irma asked, pointing at the pastries, during their second trip through Spain. Back then, well before wireless, the café drew students with cheap absinthe, served straight and harsh, often gratis with a coffee. What he wanted to do most, before catching the bullet to Seville, was run. But Madrid was terrible for running. There were the trees and water and expanses of El Retiro, but little else. Traffic was ruthless, the air breathed harsh, and the altitude was considerable. Irma quoted from the lesbian travel book they used on their first trip: Ever wonder where all the runners in Madrid have gone? They're all dead.

He pushed the pastries farther aside and opened Lucia's message: Promise to read another version of the Sarraute. Before reading hers. For my sake?—L. At first he thought to reply, a simple Why? But then he realized that would be asking her to explain and reveal that which troubled her about the book, about herself, as she explored further. That might push her away more coldly than Mishima's sailor, returned and fallen. Promise, he replied. He couldn't even remember the book's title, but he remembered everything about Lucia, from the way she circled around to him in the blue light of the bar, to the way she left him strewn at dawn in the covers of her hotel bed. Take anything you want.

Instead of running, Philip walked to the Prado and then doubled back toward Atocha, counting redheads. Kind and sad. Reaching but not touching. The pretty guardian must have followed Sam through Miriam's books, keeping watchful distance in the moth-wing light between shelves. He must have lingered near titles he knew, heard Irma men-tion. He must have reached for those she restored, afraid to touch. Would their softness be unbearable to him? Would it brush his fingertips with a palpable futility? Or was he saving that touch, that softness, for another time? Was his hope that strong? "Where are you?" he asked aloud, ambling the wide sidewalks approaching Atocha. How did you get him to go so quickly to Corte, to the top of the world, the castle in the sky?

He did not appear as mad as you might think, though his satchel, weighted with the laptop and the Cervantes, did add to the slightly itinerant look about him. He needed a meal and shave and he had been running too much of late. The coffee contributed to his furtive steps. In Philadelphia, pedestrians would have given him more room. But this was Madrid, the city of La Movida. And so he moved along, garnering only a few extra glances.

Across from Atocha again, he checked a clock tower and saw that he still had plenty of time before his train; he was enjoying all the movement—his, the city's—and so made his way to Puerto del Sol. Irma liked the *pensiones* there best, which added some reason to his wandering. Near the bear monument, he bought some fried almonds from a vendor who mistook him for German and said, *Danke schön*. Even in siesta Sol was busy, and he was able to watch hundreds pass by his bench in the shade of the bear.

A black man crouched over a toy harpsichord at the entrance to one of the pedestrian malls. He played Bach, in pale dusty chords that echoed beneath the shade tarps. He played well enough to slow the crowd, to collect coins. Then he switched to Górecki, playing the second movement of *Symphony of Sorrowful Songs*. Because his instrument could not create enough sustain, the piece was tinny and almost unrecognizable. Lucia took the symphony from Philip's laptop, the same way she borrowed his books, only telling him and thanking him later, the same way she expected others—him—to take from her. Had she—Lucia? Irma?—somehow passed the Górecki to this busker? She would come here, to the bear, no doubt, whether she was passing through Madrid or staying. Did she hum the second movement for him, then drop euros into his instrument case? Philip let the busker finish his version of the Górecki, in which he repeated the opening phrase several times without venturing much further, but lent it variations, much like Górecki. Then Philip gave him some money. He asked him where he learned that piece, but the man did not seem to understand English or Spanish. Philip pointed to the little harpsichord and said, "Górecki." The busker smiled up at him, patted his own chest, and said, "Jonny."

Philip nodded and walked away. Standing between the two central fountains, he scanned the vast semicircle of Plaza del Sol, wondering if he could pick Lucia from the swirl of pedestrians, feeling like the lost rather than the seeker. Would he fall from grace if he found her? If he even sought her out? If he sent her another message? Could he convince her, or even himself, that he had not come after her? I am in Spain, he finally wrote. Just to warn you.

TEN

Descending the escalator to the trains at the Atocha station, one drops from the cacophony of travelers to the polished quiet of the granite platforms, where the attendants, their black hair in neat ponytails, stand and politely notice you. They dress like executives in dark blue skirts and convince you with their straight shoulders and folded hands that they command the trains. And though the cars are almost always full, the passengers between trains are sparse and soft-spoken. In the station above, travelers are coming and going, eating and drinking, buying tickets, finding trains and destinations, hurrying and calling out in the sultry giant greenhouse that is the terminal. But all that vanishes in the subdued underworld of the train platforms. Philip walked between the train to Seville and the train to Barcelona, counting down the cars. Both trains waited, silent except for the intermittent gasp of air from their brakes. They smelled clean, of ozone and metal, and they were pearly and beckoning above the burnished granite platform.

It was impossible for him not to notice the yellow book, which bobbed like a spark against the blue-skirt hip of one of the travel attendants as she hurried to deliver it to one of the cars farther down the track. He hurried after it as you might a friend spied in a crowd, not thinking what to say, only thinking to put your hand to her shoulder, swimming in her sudden turn and recognition. So he followed the book, the yellow appearing the same color as his Cervantes and the same color as the Pepys, fashioned from similar skin. It was easy to imagine that it rode upon Irma's skirted hip. But he could not draw close enough to this book without drawing attention. He could only hurry disguised as a man anxious to get to his train, not as a man trying to catch a lover, at a speed that would draw suspicion. He followed the attendant to one of the cars on the Barcelona train and drew close enough to see the pebbled texture of the yellow book cover. He watched her hand the volume up to someone inside the car, and he let himself be swept along with her gesture, watching the book almost float free of her fingertips, a feather blown from her palm. But then she politely noticed Philip and composed herself in front of the door before he could see who had taken the book. He stepped to the center of the platform, gazed up and down the length of the Seville train. He saw other swatches of color now. A green bag, a red fan, a yellow hat. His math did him little good. Thinking the way he thinks is sometimes easy, sometimes not. You see a triangle and you think: three. He sees a triangle and he thinks seven: the three angles, the three distances that define the lines between them, and the single plane formed in between. He may even go on from there.

He found his car and boarded the train to Seville. He sat for a moment, tapping the back of his knuckles against the window. Eyes closed, he saw blown and scattered bits of paper rising from her cupped hand, floating into yellow sunlight. In the whisper of her breath, the stream of air passing from her lips, he chased his thoughts. He could run after shape and color and feel, an object that sliced across the vision of his search, a bright yellow dare that cut into his senses more intensely, immediately, than the thoughts that led him all the way to Corte. This book he could see, touch—hold. Maybe he *had* held it once. Maybe he had even witnessed its creation or salvation, seen it bound in a press, its very insides sewn. He jumped from his seat and secured his satchel as he left the train. His chest hammered as he hurried across the platform to the other train. Moving to know, moving to keep balance, he found the car with the yellow book. He spoke to the travel attendant before she could speak to him.

"Barcelona?" He leaned toward the car.

"Which number?" she asked. The train released a stunning gasp of air.

"Sixteen," he said, which he hoped was several cars down.

"Go on here," she told him. "The train is leaving. Then you walk that

way through the cars until you get to sixteen. Hurry yourself." She raised
her arm, pointing.

He hopped on, as ordered, and the train slid toward Barcelona. In her
shop, on a rare day when she could let in the sea breeze, Irma showed
him a recent acquisition, a red leather volume of *Jude the Obscure*. Sometimes, she told him, this is my favorite. She said this about several novels.
The volume's red leather had darkened to a blood color, mottled and
even darker, black almost, at the edges. The title was branded on the
spine; otherwise the edition was free of ornament. A scar ran diagonally
across the front cover, a pink, ruining slash. A shame, he said when she
pointed it out to him. Wordlessly she stood, gazing just above his eyes,
and stepped close as though to embrace him. She raised her hands to his
forehead and began to press her fingers along his hairline. She pressed
firmly, forcing his head back, lifting his scalp. Then she lowered her
hands to the book and rubbed the scar with the oil from his forehead.
She ran her fingers along the diagonal and then massaged the line with
the edges of her thumbs until all traces of the scratch disappeared. He
leaned close to the volume, peered at the now-smooth surface. Will that
last? he asked. Will it cause damage?

It's the best thing for it, she replied. Short of actual excretions from
the poor little goat who gave his hide to this book. She eyed him at a
bemused angle. Why? You think I'm a charlatan? Con artist? Thief? I
might give it back to the family who sold it to me. At least they thought
the book deserved respect. They didn't try to fix it themselves. But if
they'd read it, I don't think they would have sold it. If one of them read
it—really read it—he would have run his hands through his hair and
then pressed his fingers to the scratch. No?

Is it a first edition?

She nodded. And then specially re-bound right away, she told him.
Probably as a gift. I'd guess that scratch was applied in 1895, by one
angry reader. Hardy told his publisher—she lifted her fingers and pantomimed quotation marks—that it would be a tale that could not offend
the most fastidious maiden. I'd say this particular book found one fastidious maiden to offend.

Maybe she scratched it just to throw people off, he said. Her parents, her husband. Maybe she loved it.

I don't know, Pip. Books like this are usually better than the people who buy them and have them done up in fine leather.

Philip moved through the cars, heading against the momentum of the train as he glided down the aisles, each stride feeling like a stretch in time and space above the train's speed. He vaguely pretended to be checking for his seat as he scanned laps and tables for the yellow book. He feared it all swiftly becoming like his search along the Corsican coast, the familiar ruins yearning toward the sea, he lost in her hall of mirrors. Walking every car allowable—first class was off-limits—he counted only 18 books out of the 605 passengers. Almost every traveler had reading material, but most consisted of magazines, newspapers, and laptops. None of the 18 books were yellow, only 3 were hardcovers. But he vowed, even against the cold lick of error between his shoulders, against the wild spin of the compass breaking inside him, that he would not let every instinctive search plunge him into a desperate swim, left to climb for air through dark waters.

He came upon an unattended game of solitaire dealt on a tray table over an empty seat. Cards always beckoned Philip, numbers with personalities. He crouched down to the game, caught the book-smell. He calculated the potential for this hand, saw the next decision facing the absent player, pictured the right moves.

An elderly man wearing a starched *guayabera*, with heavy glasses pushed atop his speckled head, watched Philip from the next seat over. His flat expression matched the glide of the train, a poker face in the evening light. A skeptical lull fell over the man's eyes as Philip raised his hand to the cards. At first he thought the old man was guarding the game for the absent player, his wife perhaps. The man glanced from Philip's hand to the cards, then back.

Philip paused. "This is *your* game."

"*Sí.*" The man held his gaze.

Philip played his move, electing to pass on the seven of clubs and con-

tinue the deal, choosing also to delay an obvious carryover. The snap of
the cards felt good against his thumb, the puffs of air. He sensed something from the old man and looked up in time to catch an oblique shift
in his stare, as though someone stood at Philip's shoulder. And this is
what I'm good for, thought Philip, fixing people's card games while they
recall better moments, losses, past loves. When Philip stood to go, the
man leaned away from the cards and gazed intently out his window, an
unexpected youthfulness to the lift of his shoulder and the bracing of his
fist to his chin.

Philip finished his search through the length of the train, then managed to find an unoccupied seat in the smoking car that also backed up
against the bar, the final car. Passengers heading through the smoking
car to the bar were momentarily overwhelmed by the tobacco haze. The
collecting smoke, settling in a shoulder-high layer, added to the quiet
dread gathering inside him. He could not find the book that led him
here. The train to Barcelona was not a bullet and would take nearly
eleven hours to reach its destination, which was not his destination. He
could do nothing but let the train rush him farther off course through
the expanding twilight of the plains.

He worked as much as he could on his consulting assignment, but
was unable to send it out and acquire more. Which he could have used,
because the work offered what little comfort he could find. They sent
him one of those assignments that asked him to identify and resolve an
anomaly in an investment. Why aren't these numbers adding up the way
we anticipated? Why aren't we making more money here? He began
with Newton's second law of motion, $F=ma$, where $a=dv/dt$ is acceleration, the rate of change in velocity over time. Philip went after the anomaly by separating v and t, expressing them as a ratio of two differentials,
putting them neatly on each side of the equation: $dv/g-av=dt$. Then
he integrated each side of that equation in order to uncover its antide-
rivative, where $\ln$ would stand for the natural logarithm. Here, in the
natural logarithm, was e, whose appearance led him to that which was
apparent but incalculable. It's what he loved most about his first language.
Math is not so proud as to believe it can explain everything. It allows
for the realm of the apparent yet unfathomable, but it cajoles you into

drawing on that realm, finding things through its lens, actively accessing it. And yet unlike people—even people you love—it does not allow for lying, withholding, or deception.

If he had more work, if he had not done such a swift job in identifying and explaining the anomaly (which turned out to be a kind of legal, even condoned, embezzlement collectively practiced by the first tier, the tier Beatrice had recommended for elimination), he would have felt less foolish on the train. He and Isaac once developed an equation to measure the depth of foolishness. A particular act's level of foolishness, they discovered, corresponded geometrically to the time necessary to reverse the act or at least compensate for it. Accelerating the dive was the ever-increasing anxiousness linked to the passing of this time. Foolishness and anxiety inevitably produced dread and Philip could taste its bitterness at the back of his throat, could feel it slide him off-balance as the train wheels clicked beneath him. Don't count the rails passing beneath us, she told him. Feel them, hear them, but don't count them. They're taking us away from ourselves. Far away from ourselves. We get to keep only our eyes and minds, but the rest of us falls away. She brushed her fingers along his brow.

He tore another sheet from his composition book. The only shape that allows us to be taken away from ourselves, he wrote, is the ellipse. The shape I have attributed to you now, the curve and shape of my search for you. $\bigcirc$ An ellipse is the locus of two points on a plane where the sum of the distances from any point on the curve to two fixed points is constant. In other words, it requires two foci.

He drew one for her, freehand. He marked the two foci. He drew arrows to each focus and labeled one $I+P$ (Irma with Philip) and the other $I-P$ (Irma without Philip). Then he caught himself, corrected himself. They had known each other for more than twenty years; now $I=IP$. He let her see the correction, all the math, as he changed the labels to $IP+P$ and $IP-P$. He continued. It was something Nicole said, when trying to describe the state she was in. The state I—we, $IP+P$—had put her in. How she could see two desired versions of herself. How she had to choose one and sacrifice the other. But someone a bit more wily, wily with age (he could not resist the dig), might figure a way to live both, one literally, one figuratively—maybe even inverting them from time to time. Kill yourself in one to create the other. So that, dear, is where I have you, right or wrong, in my proof. An ellipse. But don't get too confident. It is much more complex than it first seems. And I know *all* of its properties, applications, and weaknesses. I know them the way you know your ABCs.

As he had done with the other page torn from his composition notebook, he tucked the gridded sheet into the Cervantes, marking his place at chapter nineteen. Then, feeling a little better, he began reading the chapter. The distant lights across the dark expanse outside his train window reminded him of the lights Don Quixote and Sancho confronted at the beginning of the chapter: When they saw coming toward them, on the same road they were traveling, a great multitude of lights that looked like nothing so much as moving stars. Quixote, believing the light carriers to be demonic phantoms, attacks them all. The light carriers, peaceful unarmed priests riding mules, believe Quixote to be a demonic phantom, and disperse in fear. Philip knew he should have been amused by the scene and its physical humor and its irony, but instead he was saddened. He did not know why. Maybe the lights over the vast blackness beyond his train window prompted him to take the words in the wrong way. He imagined a hard, dry wind out there, the kind that builds up swiftly over the sage, day or night, seemingly from nowhere under a cloudless sky. Irma writes in chapter nineteen of Quixote: You shouldn't be surprised that I know, by the time you read this line, that you are in some way searching for me. Because, for one, you are outside of real time and inside the time frame of the collection I left you. That time frame began at whatever point you started reading the collection. You've realized by now that Rebecca calculated the order for me. And you realize also that it would be foolish to stray from that order and ruin the beauty and intricacy of the collection designed just for you. And this time frame, unlike real time, is elastic and forgiving. But even if you go backward and forward on whims and prompts, you still must unavoidably proceed along the given line. Because without that given line, you would lose all sense of time and self—just as you would in reality. Isaac would certainly agree, no?

He tore another blank page from his composition notebook. But you underestimate the ellipse. It goes far beyond geometry. It has, in your terms, character. Specifically, it has eccentricity. In fact, the shape of an ellipse is usually expressed by a number called the eccentricity of the ellipse. The eccentricity is basically the distance between the foci, and the greater the eccentricity, the more elongated the ellipse. I will determine your eccentricity, Irma. Then I will be able to fix the elongation of the ellipse that is you. You shouldn't have left me all the books. He bookmarked the Cervantes with the page and then set the volume down.

He walked the train's length again, searching for the yellow book, seeking within himself the vow to trust his instinct, an instinct cradled in a math that flattened anomalies, easily covered distances between any given stars. This time there were even fewer books out—twelve—and again none were yellow. Most of the passengers slept and all of them remained in some sort of suspended state, stilled by train-lulled thoughts and meditations. He felt some power as he passed between them, picking his way through a drugged, moonlit army. But he also felt things closing behind him, the way he felt with Irma on the Corsican trails that vanished in the thorny brush they had to push through, that fell away beneath their feet as they scaled crumbling escarpments. He imagined the yellow book flying out the back of the train, a spark over Quixote's night. He stepped unnoticed to his seat, the very last one on the train, where he could easily conjure the momentum at the tip of its unfurling across Spain. And only when he leaned his head against the window and closed his eyes did he suddenly feel the exhaustion that must have been the backdrop to this foolhardy trip to Barcelona. Once again he slept well on a train. Irma once gave him a tape of train sounds to help with his insomnia. But she ruined the tape's effect by later blowing him while they listened to it at full volume. After that the tape only made him restless. She thought this funny.

He awoke in Barcelona on a still and empty train. One of the travel attendants stood formally beside his seat. Maybe she had done something to wake him.

"More careful next time," she told him. She pointed to the Cervantes in his lap. "Someone could steal your book."

He thanked her for watching his bags and left the train shaking the ache from his limbs. Without surfacing from Sants-Estació, he caught the Metro to the Provença stop, climbed the stairs instead of using the escalator, and stepped onto the avenue toward La Gràcia. The city, like so many others, was rushing to work. Behind each red light waited a small army of motor scooters ridden by young men and women in business suits. Behind them were the cars and taxis. When the light changed to green, the scooters accelerated into a collective roar, like a chorus of cicadas, and moved in a wave up the broad streets. Neckties and black ponytails whipped over shoulders. The speed and focus of the riders made Philip feel even more dislocated as he pulled his travel bag along the very wide sidewalks of the avenue. He loved the corners, which were all cut at a diagonal to form wide squares at each intersection, opening up the city. He stopped at one of the corner cafés and had a coffee and then a very thick cup of chocolate for breakfast and gazed across the intersection at the Gaudí apartment building, which appeared to be forever melting in its blue and green tiles. He wondered how it would be to just keep moving like this, sleeping on trains and boats and planes, eating confections, pulling what little you had, reading, watching. How would you feel after a week of it, a month, a year, a lifetime? Would you feel sharp and cleansed? Would you feel light, unsubstantial, properly insignificant, irretrievably befuddled?

He finished his breakfast and continued up the avenue. After crossing Diagonal, he reached La Gràcia and the grid, and the motor traffic and the wide sidewalks promptly disappeared. After the coffee and chocolate he felt a strong need to run. His drawn, disheveled, unshaven appearance fit better in the narrow and crooked lanes of La Gràcia, where he often passed street vendors selling fruit, clothes, books, and kitchen pans. The vendors sat calmly reading their morning papers, some chatting with neighbors, none hawking. Along the narrow Travessera, vendors pushed their tables together to form an informal market, leaving little room for any cars to scoot through. He found the narrow side street, marked by a Gaudí dog head jutting from a wall, and headed up the lane to Tom Salgeiro's. This was his only planned stop in Barcelona, and it was calculated by Rebecca as a tertiary possibility, a place to go if Seville and

Madrid came to nothing. Thomas Salgeiro was Irma's first cousin on her Portuguese side. He was a tax attorney, but became interested in acquiring and providing cover materials for books after Irma—without ever having met him—asked him to buy and hold some kid skins for her. The skins themselves were common enough, but she had heard they were tanned in Tunisia by a process that turned them a unique ochre, the color of the Maghreb sunset, she was told. The skins turned out to be fakes, so badly forged that the dye rubbed off on Tom's fingers. He felt bad for his young cousin, only then an apprentice book conservator who was crossing the Atlantic to come see him and collect the skins. So, beginning without any knowledge as to how one goes about acquiring heirloom leathers, he tracked down some genuine skins on the crowded, hawking streets of Tangier. The toothless vendor who sold them barked in Tom's face when he questioned their worth and then gummed the brittle edge of one of the skins to demonstrate how the color did not run. For show, he stuck out his pink tongue at Tom and growled. Tom then had a very difficult time getting the skins through British customs in Gibraltar, but made it back to his office in Madrid just in time to introduce himself. Only when he examined the leather through her eyes, followed the trace of her fingers, did he see the marvel of the skins. They were stiff and light as cardboard, but their surface was soft as burnished copper. Their color changed beneath light, deep ochre under his desk lamp, amber in the sunlight streaming through the blinds. When she bent them gently, they made no sound and held their shape. He moved his office to post-Franco Barcelona to make enough money to support his new hobby. He never married. He rarely spoke. He bought his place in La Gràcia, which had a small courtyard, a house, and some goat pens. Over the decades he transformed the place into holding sheds for his acquisitions and rooms and spaces for family and other travelers. His family, all extensions, were his friends. He acquired linens, gauze, papers, silks, metals, barks, mats woven of straw and grasses that you would think were satin.

Though bookmakers and conservators from all over the world sought his covers, he sold them at cost, or gave them away to apprentices and mentors who worked in humble shops and labs. Whenever Philip and Irma visited, he put them up in the same room, one opening onto the courtyard where a little spherical fountain gurgled. He spoke a few words to Irma, mostly showing her new and interesting cover materials with proud smiles and disbelieving wags of his head. Tall and handsome, he lived alone, though his place was rarely unoccupied by traveling siblings, cousins, aunts, or uncles. He almost never spoke to Philip, getting by with smiles, handshakes, and simple gestures. He enjoyed, Philip could tell, sitting in rooms where others were chatting, eating, drinking. He conducted his tax business in this spare manner, and it served his practice well. Spaniards loved him. *Dígame* was all he had to say to clients, and they told him what they needed.

The first time Irma walked Philip through the holding sheds and then showed him some of the smaller pieces kept here and there around the house, he asked her what it was all worth. She shook her head and smiled, much like her cousin. But then she answered, because she knew Philip, knew the question was not as crass as one might think, coming from him. A small fortune, she told him. Of course, it forever fluctuates as he sells it, passes it on, acquires others. But, yes, on any given day it is worth a small fortune. Priceless to conservators.

Tom moved through the rooms and halls of his modest three-story like a housekeeper. He wore white linen shirts and continuously checked to see that the bedrooms and bath were tidy and amenable to his guests. He kept the kitchen stocked with produce from La Gràcia's vendors and stores, often hurrying off to get something a visiting cousin needed, wanted, asked about. Philip had seen him go through entire days without speaking. First, the younger generation of Arcuris and Salgeiros discovered this open house in Barcelona, where everything necessary was provided, no questions were asked. They could travel to Spain, make it to France, the Mediterranean. The older family members then learned, too, that perhaps they could afford a bit of travel, a bit of Barcelona, at least. And they could get lost in the little stucco halls of Tom's house, follow its sprawl, find company or be left alone among the hides, weaves, and parchments. If they asked him how they could repay his hospitality, he said, "Come back." And those could very well be the only words exchanged. Philip would notice how he would read in a room where his guests might be drinking, playing cards, conversing, laughing, and telling each other about their travels. Tom would look up from his book or paper and listen to moments of the conversation, glasses removed, a corner of their frames pressed to his lips. Irma was the only one who seemed to have any extended dialogues with him, and those always involved book covers. Where and how one might obtain this certain bolt of linen, this sheaf of flax, this piece of hide. How might it be shaped, plied into a workable material. But from these exchanges with her cousin, she gleaned his experiences and adventures. She showed Philip an oval piece of pigskin hanging on a wall like a medieval shield. He got that from a family in Turkey who lived in a cave. The cave was full of everything modern—carpets, cable television, a toaster, plumbing. It was bright and airy, with white stone walls. A natural chimney channeled away the smoke from the oven fire and kept the home ventilated. The family lived alongside other cave dwellers, with ladders and hewn stairways connecting the neighborhood. The entire community, whose history went back thousands of years, was about to be condemned by the Turkish government out of safety concerns in the earthquake-prone region. The oval of leather was from a breed of swine brought to the New World by the Conquistadores, who acquired it from Moors. The breed had almost vanished from the Americas and Spain. It was prized for its lard, which collected in generous layers beneath chocolate-colored rolls of skin. Tom found one of the few remaining herds back where the pig was first bred, thousands of years ago. The pigskin was thick and dried hard and, by varying its thickness through careful flaying, it could be worked into hinged plates perfect for armor and books. Irma removed the oval hide from the wall and with it struck Philip firmly on the head. See?

Philip buzzed Tom's doorbell. A boy holding a soccer ball watched him from the sidewalk. Philip waited a long time. The boy dropped the soccer ball and kicked it so that it ricocheted off the wall across the lane and returned to him. He kicked it again, several times, before the door opened. A tall young man answered. He rubbed his black hair with both hands and yelled in Italian at the kid with the soccer ball. The kid stopped kicking the ball, but braced it at the ready beneath his foot. The young man who answered the door wore only jeans, pockets pulled out. He eyed Philip's bags, cocked an eyebrow at the Cervantes, and nodded for him to come in. He put a cigarette in his mouth, winced at its taste, and did not light it. He let it hang from the corner of his lips as he spoke to Philip.

"Are you Arcuri or Salgeiro?" he asked in English.

"Salgeiro," Philip answered, trying for as much ancestral distance as possible.

"You don't look Portuguese. You look like a Croat." He waved Philip along, shuffling bare feet across the terra-cotta floor. "Tom's out getting us stuff for coffee. Some churros. We could smell them from our beds. He said if you showed up to put you in one of the milking sheds behind the courtyard. It's a full house."

"If *I* showed up?" Philip asked. "You know who I am?"

"No. He just put the word out that if a guy who looks like a Croatian basketball player shows up, put him in the pen. He told us that as soon as we all arrived. And if he actually tells you something, you better remember it and you better do it." He removed the unlit cigarette from his mouth and offered it to Philip, passing it backward like a runner's baton.

"You want this? I don't even smoke them. My cousins are trying to get me to start. But look at them. They're all crashed in bed, smelling churros and groaning. Look at me. I'm up and ready. Almost."

Philip took the cigarette.

"But maybe I do know who you are anyway," he said as he continued shuffling along, leading Philip around the square of the courtyard. "You're Irma's friend. She's the greatest. We all love it if she happens to be here. She shows us the best places. She once took us to a place, right near here, where Borges used to drink. We saw Kundera there once. He's Croat—or something, no?"

Philip stared at the cigarette, now bent. "No. Czech or Slovak. Like me."

"Ha. Czech or Slovak. That's good. CzechorSlovak. Czechorslovakian. They should just use that one. Prague's a great city."

He waved Philip toward the double door of the milking shed. "I'll start making coffees. You really look like you could use one—or two."

The top half of the door to Philip's quarters hung open. He had seen the room before, and knew that Tom converted it according to how the Franciscan missionaries, following in the Conquistadores' wake, changed barn stalls into rooms, complete with bunk and reading lamp. When I show up alone, Irma told him when she first opened the room for Philip, he puts me in here, because he knows it's my favorite. It still smells like hay. Philip sniffed. It still smells like goats.

He tossed his bags on the bunk and arranged the Cervantes and laptop on the plain wooden table. The blue glow from the screen stained the room into stillness, a cell captured on a slide. The color cast the room into a deeper antiquity, darkening its corners and shadows, aging the whitewash in gaslight. A message from Lucia appeared quietly on the screen, melting forth like secret ink: Why warn me? Will you know me better when I see you again? I counted 351 before I borrowed. Such a delicate number. Have I thrown it all out of balance?

He replied calmly, finding strength for that in the old room and its quiet light: All numbers are delicate. I'm in Barcelona. Soon Seville. I would love to meet you there. He recalled her counting the books, stepping naked before them as he watched secretly from his bed. What he hadn't seen, but what he imagined several times, was her counting the spines with the graze of her fingertips, chin lifted. Then her taking the ones she wanted, tilting them free with the gentle tug of two fingers, cradling them beneath her breast.

He pulled a page from his notebook and described for Lucia the equation his e-mail could not contain, one that might complete his fall from her grace. He could not yet compose it because it wasn't complete, but he could explain some of it by beginning with a kind of syllogism. I warn you because I fear you. I fear you because you give me balance, control it. All numbers are delicate. You either broke or tuned the one she gave to me—351. Her understanding of numbers is simple, a literary one, a number is just a word. So she turns to the most literary of mathematicians, the Pythagoreans. They frolicked on the beaches of Sicily with their mentor and worked on their most famous equation, just as an excuse to be together in the Italian sun. That was her theory anyway. To them, 3 was harmony, the most beautiful number, the *only* one that

equals the sum of all those that come before it. 5 was marriage, 3 + 2, harmony plus opinion. 1 was first, first implying all others, infinity. Always
put a 1 at the end if you want to keep them thinking, like Sheherazade.
351. It is a delicate number. Have I made it more mysterious for you, or
less? Now you know how it feels.

He started to open the Cervantes, then stopped. He searched his
satchel for the other books, decided on *Ava*, which held that one sentence,
dead center, that contained Lucia. Just five sentences below that one, he
found this one, alone and untagged like all the rest in the Maso: We've
invented it all. He marked this page with his composition for Lucia.

He stepped into the courtyard to watch the fountain and think. We've
invented it all. The little courtyard sequestered him more than usual,
with its simple, spherical fountain, bubbling knee-high and softly, once
a Moorish space for absolution, where you washed your feet of the sins
through which you walked. More than usual he sensed the noise of himself, like a jittery projection, shadow the quiet walls. He sat on a blue tile
bench. If Tom expected him, then either Irma or Sam had been here very
recently—or were still here. He cursed his math. He cursed Rebecca's
math. He cursed all math and wished he could, just once, delete it from
his self. Someone who knew people, the way Irma knew people, someone who thought in simple English, would have come directly here to
find Sam. An open place, where one did not have to speak or be spoken
to. Even Quixote's romantic, deluded, and rambling reasoning proved
more effective than his.

Philip needed to run. He found himself envisioning his route, through
La Gràcia and uphill to Parc Güell, where he could get lost on the packed
dirt trails through trees and along Gaudí's tiled walls, fountains, structures, and sculptures. He changed into his running clothes and then
began searching unobtrusively through Tom's house. In the smallest,
quietest, most solitary downstairs bedroom, what had once been the
cook's quarters, Philip found Sam's backpack. He spied it through the
open doorway. The bed was neatly made and the shutters were open to
the morning sun. He knew it was Sam's backpack because the scarlet
Rutgers Frisbee Nicole gave him and a pair of cleats were stacked next to
it. Sam was here, but Sam was not here now.

In the kitchen, Philip found Irma's young Italian cousin again. He was pulling the crank to a second cup of coffee. The coffee flowed thick as ink from the spigot, foamy, and its aroma made Philip dizzy.

"I'm not waiting for the churros." He passed Philip one of the little white cups.

"Sam's here?" Philip asked as he took the cup.

"Tom sent him somewhere. He's been sending him to places. To get stuff. I wish Sam were here. We've been using him for translating. He doesn't do much at the places we take him. But his Spanish is real good. He even does Catalonian. Which really puts us in good with the bartenders and door people. Then Sam disappears into the night."

"Stuff?" Philip asked. "What stuff?"

"You know. The stuff Tom collects. Leathers and cloth. I usually don't know one from the other."

"From Barcelona?" Philip asked, but he knew.

"All over. I think he's in Tangier now. Or on his way back."

"Tangier?"

"Yeah. It's—"

"I know where it is."

He nodded at Philip and looked at him intently. "Yeah, you look like you've been to it and through it."

"I just need a run and a shower. You know when Sam comes back?"

The cousin shrugged. "Has to be soon. He left traveling pretty light. Toothbrush, folder, and a book. We thought it was pretty suave, the way he just nodded and took the folder from Tom and went out the door to Tangier. Like a spy. Except for the red hair and . . ." He dotted his finger across his face.

"Freckles."

"Yeah. *Pecas.* He looked like he was just going out to get coffee." He took a sip of his coffee. Bared his teeth against its heat and strength, then took another sip. "He asks a lot of questions about our cousin. I think he likes her." He made a face, a sort of knowing grimace. "*Really* likes her."

"Did he ask you where she is?"

He shrugged. "We don't know where she is. How could we even tell she was gone? If she's not here, she's in California, or somewhere else in the States. Or anywhere. That's what we like about her."

"Did he tell you about how she disappeared?"

He nodded, more a series of chin thrusts, the way one nods to dance music. "We have our ideas about that. We think she did it for love. Like Aida."

"You know *Aida*?"

"Sure. All Italians know it. We have to study it in school."

"But Aida really dies."

"That's what you say. But who's to say for sure? She hides in the crypt to suffocate with her lover while everybody dances above. But maybe they're having fun together in that crypt. It could be a big crypt, with pillows."

They heard someone at the front doorway and then Tom entered the kitchen carrying churros which were bundled in waxed paper and smelled of grease and sugar. He looked at Philip with little surprise, as though he were a guest who had risen a bit earlier than usual.

"Philip," he said. "Did Henry take you to your room?"

"He did. Thanks. He told me about Sam."

Tom nodded and waved for Philip to follow as he walked to the courtyard. He stood over the small fountain and held his hands above the water.

"You sent him to Tangier?"

Tom shrugged, what Philip thought would be his only reply, then said, "He was going there eventually. This way, he will at least come back. I wish I'd gone to Tangier at seventeen."

Philip stood across the fountain from Tom. The water rose through a hole atop the sphere, then flowed smoothly over the stone in a glaze that fell gently about the bowl. In his thoughts, Philip asked Tom several questions, about Sam, about Irma. She writes, in *Slip*: When they sometimes stand together, not speaking, you must think them brothers. One is slightly taller. Their heads are bowed, but the two men still look at each other in a kind of silent vying. If brothers, then both circled the world, one heading west, the other east, crossing paths once near the midway point—the taller one moves somewhat faster—then experiencing the same lands and peoples from opposing directions and in reverse order. Even if they choose to say nothing, they will always be able to anticipate one another's thoughts, actions, decisions, responses, because their courses, though combing opposite grains, have been similar. You're like two old uncles, she once told them. Come on. Let's all go out. Let's go find a new place.

Tom continued to hold his hands above the fountain as though warming them. Philip thanked him. "For keeping Sam. That was very clever. To keep him around by sending him away. I would never have thought of that."

Tom nodded to himself. "It was one of those things you figure only as you do them."

"You sent him to Corte."

"I actually needed him for that. Irma left me a book riddled with little tunnels. A book by Charles Fort. Something was worming through it, covers and all. You could only see the holes, not what made them. But every day there were more little tunnels. It had to be taken carefully, by hand."

"When did she leave it?"

Tom shook his head. "I only found it in her room. I couldn't say when she left it. Maybe three visits past. Maybe the last visit. The room is hers."

He started to turn away from Philip.

"Thanks for letting me stay in it," Philip said. "I appreciate that."

Tom raised his hand in a simple wave of acknowledgment as he left the courtyard. In his room which had once been a milking stall, Philip sat at his table and sent messages to Nicole and Rebecca, letting them know he had found Sam and that he was all right. But he promised them nothing. Then he ran. It felt right to hurry against any thought to wait quietly for Sam, instead to stride along La Gràcia's narrow streets. Fueled by resolution, a steady three-day diet of strong coffee and sweets, and the sense of release you receive by just being able to drop your bags on a bed and go, he ran fast. He clicked off the first three miles in near-record time. Irma marked the first mile when they were twenty-five, a water fountain in the shade of La Sagrada Família, Gaudí's forever-unfinished cathedral which looked like a child's teetering, dripping sandcastle. The second mile was a sewer cap embedded in the asphalt of Lepant, and the third was a stone hitching post along the initial rise to the park. She liked to put hills in the fourth mile. And so from the hitching post you ascend sharply to Parc Güell, the strain made more difficult by the uneven stone sidewalks and the café tables and chairs which teeter on the incline like brightly parked amusement rides. And so the fourth mile, which is always his worst mile on any course, slows his pace, his sense of accomplishment and release. But seeing him pass, perhaps from one of the slanted bars across the street, you could take him for a gracefully aging athlete, a former track star, steeplechaser. Though his face and neck strain with the effort imposed by the climb, there is a bounding length to his strides, a churn and hop. You almost want to join him—it seems more dance than run.

You would not guess that his thoughts were anxious, tortured even. He worries deeply about the boy who was once his stepson, worries that he will not be able to do the right things for him, show him where to go, what to do, how to do it. And as he plows up the hill, following a route laid out by his oldest and dearest friend, he is weighted by the ever-deepening sense of her loss. Her image is with him more than it has ever been with him. It drops in, at any given moment, from the periphery of his vision, where it always hangs like a water drop trembling. She is beginning to cloak him, to bind him. He is mad with her. He feels his breathing tighten, where instead it should be opening, as he nears the plateau where Parc Güell begins. She writes in the twenty-third chapter of Part II of *Quixote*: I felt my head and chest to verify whether it was I myself or some false and counterfeit phantom sitting there, but my sense of touch, my feelings, the reasoned discourse I held within myself, verified for me that, there and then, I was the same person I am here and now.

I am the same person I was the first time I ran this hill with her, and the last time. He thought more. A person's value is attached to a variable exponent. But this did not convince him. He easily imagined her laughing. Standing at the crest of this hill, waiting, laughing as soon as she heard what he had to say. Laughing again like that photo of Pier

Angeli as she bends slightly inward and covers her mouth with her hand. There is a great need in the world caused by my delay, he pleads. Pier only laughs more.

What runners can do, when thoughts reach such points, is drive their bodies to the upper limits of exertion and purge all digressions. Philip ran a speedplay up the final rise and into the expansive dirt plateau just above the park's entry. His lungs burned with the effort and pushed a harsh blood taste into the base of his throat. Stumbling into the dirt expanse, he released what he thought would be a groan of pain and completion. Instead it heaved from his throat as a loud sob. The sweat pouring from his brow hid the tears as he bent over and tried to catch his breath. The Catalonians and tourists meandering close by turned briefly to him with looks of fleeting concern, then left him his privacy and turned to gaze over the city and out past to the pale Mediterranean. Philip looked there also for solace, but found the expansive view saddened him further. She could be out there, at any place they had experienced together, and he would never find her. She could be resting in this park, from a run similar to his, thirty seconds ahead of him. And that would be enough to make her a ghost to him. He could triangulate position points, covering the ellipse, but he could not triangulate time. At this particular age, in this particular state, he felt even less in control and understanding of time.

ELEVEN

Philip waited for Sam, reading Cervantes, working, sending messages. He shifted between the milking shed and the courtyard, sometimes reading beside the water, sometimes working there. In his quarters, he would lay for long intervals and listen to the cousins rattle and laugh their way through Tom's place. One played the oboe, practicing for hours, usually the prelude to Bach's Concert Royal, but sometimes adapting some of Hindemith's viola sonatas. Never before had he realized how Spanish the oboe could sound, even when playing very un-Spanish music. Or was it the air of the place, the Barcelona street noise in the background, or the Cervantes in his head, that bent the music for him? He wondered about the oboe-playing cousin. He would see them all at different times as they passed through Tom's kitchen or one of the gathering rooms and Philip would try to guess which one played the oboe. They were all young, and all, men and women, bore some resemblance to Irma: an eyebrow's dark curve, a bite of lip, an earlobe's tiny shadow, or the thumb-press hollow behind the jaw. He could easily have asked about the oboe player; they all spoke openly to him, treating him somewhat like Tom's other, a host who actually talks, granting him too much personality and value because he was Cousin Irma's friend. They invited him out and he answered, "I would like that," but they never specified when or where and they left it at that. He enjoyed the hum of their activity, their sudden appearances and disappearances, their jokes and songs. He could eliminate those who could not be the oboist, those whom he would see while the music drifted from some other room. Again, he could have simply tracked down the player by retracing the path of the music all the way back to the room from which it emanated. But this he felt—knew—to be against the rules of the house, to wander too much and look among the halls and rooms and nooks and tiled recesses. With the kitchen, courtyard, and *salas*, common areas were abundant. And he knew that in Spain, homes were domestic sanctuaries and that you gathered and met primarily outside the house, in this country of parks and cafés and *places*.

He had the oboist down to three possibilities. One, a pretty cousin who looked very much like Henry's sister and who treated Henry in a very corrective manner, telling him to just smoke or not smoke but to quit making such a show of it. Another, who was the palest of them all, acted and looked Spaniard instead of Italian or Portuguese, the way he nodded and brusquely said *dígame* as greeting. He did not move or behave as you would imagine a musician, someone who could play that Bach prelude or Hindemith sonata as though both were written for the oboe. But Philip knew, perhaps better than most, that talented individuals were often little more than vessels for expression, that nothing in their comportment necessarily reflected the beauty, precision, and delicacy of their art. His favorite for the oboe was a niece who bore a marked resemblance to a young Irma. To Philip, Irma had grown much more attractive as she aged, her features crystallizing into an unnerving starkness, her voice attaining a torn huskiness, her body finding a swift grace, her gestures confidence. This young niece very noticeably lacked all these and her movements seemed as brittle as her voice, which often remained unheard among the conversations in the kitchen or outdoors. Philip wanted her to be the oboe player, to be able to tell her that she would become so beautiful because of her vocation that she would be rendered unforgettable, invasive even, in the thoughts of others.

One siesta, when he believed himself to be alone in the house, the sound of the oboe surprised him while he was working beside the fountain. Its music seemed to seep its way through every opening in the courtyard, from every direction, a musical smoke finding its way to him. Again it was one of the Hindemith sonatas for viola, calling for the oboe to be wrought differently, more drawn and haunting than usual. He imagined Irma's niece sitting like a snake charmer in her room, eyes closed to her music, elbows resting on crossed knees. Philip quietly pulled free a page from his composition book. When does $I+P$ become IP? Where do we put t into the equation? And how? Do we divide ourselves over it, or multiply ourselves within it? Here I am asking you, for the first time, for math help. We were $I+P$ when we stood beneath the volcanoes together, watching the one steam, feeling it shudder. You wanted to run up that one first. I wanted the other. We were together, but apart. As you said, as you wanted. When we raced down, breathing the sulfur, sweating in their steam, is that when? Is that why I had to try to run just a little farther, while I still had the chance?

He inserted the page into *Quixote*, and then stopped working altogether, lying back on the tile bench to listen to the burble of the fountain and the lift and drop of the oboe. He closed his eyes, like the rest of Spain, he imagined, and saw the shell colors of the volcanoes, caught traces of her mineral smell and the taste of sugared coffee.

A following morning, Tom brought Philip a recent acquirement he had intended to give Irma. He found Philip in the *sala* just off the courtyard that caught morning light best, feathered it about the terra-cotta floor. When he saw Philip, Tom's quiet expression became more knowing, recognizing an accomplice, finding him where he first expected. He held the acquisition like a tray, lifting it smoothly toward Philip. One meter square, the rigid cloth looked like linen, but with a tight, almost indistinguishable weave; and it remained stiff, as though heavily starched, and its color shifted from gray to blue, like spider web, depending on the light.

"It's spun from swallow nests. The kind used for soup."

"May I?" Philip asked. Tom shrugged approval as he left and Philip brought the piece to the light of the courtyard, to the sound of water. Why? he asked her once. Why is it so important for you to have your books published? You print and bind them far better than they could. Your books are beautiful, inside and out. More lasting. No one could throw one away, because they are so fascinating in look and feel alone. I just happen to love what's inside, too. This he told her even though he could not finish *Slip* and, to that point, had no plans to finish it. But he spoke the truth. He loved holding the books, caressing them, tossing them aside to rest while he attended to work, carrying them in the crook of his wrist. Long after reading them, he loved dipping into them, randomly choosing a passage and then surrendering to both the anticipation and surprise contained in words he had read and reread countless times before.

I don't know, was her answer. I don't know exactly. Every book is a performance. The performance involves others reading it. Others reading it and hearing it in unsolicited manners. Reading it, thinking about it, talking about it because you somehow happened on it. You picked it up because you were bored and the color of it, the texture of it, seemed so inviting. Because your mom or dad or friend bought you a stack of nine of them for a dollar and they were just the right weight for the strength you had at just that moment. You don't write a book because you have to. You don't write a book because you have something to say. You don't write a book because you have a story to tell, a story that must be told. You write a book because you need to bind it and watch it come unbound. That's the only decent, honest reason.

He held the parchment—leather? cloth?—that Tom had given him, bent it slowly, and raised it to the sunlight of the courtyard. He once read, in a travel magazine on a plane, how bird's nest soup was made, how the nests were gathered from the walls of natural cave chimneys. And how the birds made them in the first place. Tom was wrong; they weren't swallows, but swiftlets, small cave-dwelling birds that flitted around in the dark and used echolocation, like bats. The swiftlets spun their own gummy saliva into nests and fastened them to the high cave walls. And the nest harvesters climbed the chimneys by straddling the high columns and bracing and scooting their way up. The travel writer, Philip recalled, said the soup had a rubbery taste and texture. But throughout Southeast Asia, it was believed to be an aphrodisiac and was therefore quite popular. For what kind of book could she use this?

He tasted an edge.

"You don't know where that's been." It was Irma's niece, the one with the glass stem of a voice, the one who he was now almost certain was the oboe player. She sat on one of the stone benches, on the shady side of the courtyard. Philip was not sure how long she had been there. Beside her was a stack of three books—Irma books, with bright textured binding.

"Actually, I kind of do know where it's been," he told her as he continued to hold the parchment to the sunlight. It was slightly translucent.

"It's bird spit," she said, recrossing her legs in a way that folded her closer to the end of the stone bench, closer to the wall, more in shadow, taking her voice with her.

He lowered the parchment and nodded to the books beside her. "Which did she leave you?"

"*Jude the Obscure, Slip,* and *Of Human Bondage.*"

"Have you read them?"

"Only the one she wrote. She once had me check it for her, when it was only manuscript."

"For the music," he said.

She lifted her chin.

"I wondered how she got that part right," he said. "She doesn't really know that much about musical structures. Especially something that complex. But when you read her book, it seems she does."

"I only told her to change a couple things," she replied. "She pretty much got it right the first time."

He remained in sunlight, she in shade. He was about to introduce himself.

"I know who you are," she said. "You're Sam's stepfather."

"I used to be his stepfather."

"Does one stop being a stepfather?"

"One does," he answered. "I looked it up. You know Sam?"

"He went out with us a few times. We spoke. He has a crush on me."

"How can you be that sure? People don't usually talk to the objects of their crushes. At least not right away."

"I slept with him."

Philip nodded. He smiled, then shook his head and chuckled.

"That's somewhat disgusting," she said. "Your reaction. Like something in a locker room. As though you're keeping score for him and giving him ten big points."

"No. No," he replied. "It's not like that. I'm not thinking anything like that. Your aunt—"

"My aunt?" she asked. "What about my aunt?"

"You are more like her than I thought. At first."

"What does *that* mean?"

"It's your voice. I thought it was pale and brittle. But it's not really. It is when it's among loud and disposable words. But it's getting to be like hers."

She angled her look, squinted.

"Your English has no accent," he said. "Are you from Portugal or Italy?"

"I have an accent," she replied. "It's the same as yours. I'm from California. Why are you trying to be an expert on the sound of voices?"

"I'm not trying to be an expert on anything. I'm just hoping to see Sam before I have to leave."

"He'll arrive today," she told him.

"That's what everyone tells me. Each day."

"But I'm the only one who really knows." She gathered up her books and stood. Clutching the books to her chest, she looked up at him. "I see you reading the *Quixote* all the time. Is that the only one she left you?"

"She left me all of them."

She drew back. "All of them." She walked to the edge of the courtyard, then turned back when she reached the wide open doorway. "You must be . . ."—she looked to the tops of the courtyard roofs—"forlorn."

"Henry says you all believe she did it for love. That she vanished herself for love. Like Aida."

"Henry's a silly boy." She lifted her books at Philip. "The person in these is smarter than Aida. Aida's a captured princess. A slave. Falls in love with a *guard*. Typical stuff. Aida's a soprano. My aunt is no soprano, someone who stands around trilling about her trials in life. I saw her a little more than they did. In California. To them she's just a wonderful breeze who comes and goes. Sometimes she's here, sometimes not. To me she is a person. I will miss her more than they will."

"Did you see her a lot?"

"Once or twice a year." In the wide doorway she hugged the books close to her, swayed with them a little. "Can you tell us what she's done?"

"I'm still trying to figure that out."

"Are you the reason? Did you do something?"

"Why would you think that? You said yourself she's not Aida."

She bowed her head, rubbed her chin against the edge of the books cradled in her arms. "That was rude of me. I'm sorry. I just know Sam's trying to find her. But I can already tell he can't do it. He's too easily drawn to things."

Philip nodded. "That would put him at a disadvantage. With her. Dealing with her. You're very astute. You know her well."

"Not well. I just know she's smart. And not nice just to be nice."

"When did you see her last?"

She thought a moment, leaned a shoulder to the doorframe, and looked above the courtyard. "About a year ago. Here."

"When did you last hear from her?" But he knew the answer.

"About a month ago. When she sent me these." She raised the books slightly. "But they only came with a note: *Thanks for all your help.*"

"Just wait till you read them."

She gave him a skeptical look, one eyebrow sharply raised.

"She bound those herself," he explained. "Those might be her versions. For you."

Her skepticism increased, a retreat against the doorframe.

He waved his hands. "Nothing *that* strange. Like your music. You play pieces composed by others. But you sometimes put extra notes and phrases into it. I hear you. And you might add and change phrases according to who is or who is not listening. And unless they knew the piece well, your listeners would never know."

She seemed better inclined to this and turned herself more toward him. But still there was a wary lock to her stance, a musician poised for a cue. "Watching you, I decided you couldn't possibly find her. Like Sam. But maybe I'm wrong." She took one step back. "I'll see you around."

Philip waved to her but she had already turned to walk away from the courtyard.

He used up the rest of the morning running to the beach at Castelldefels. There and back would be too much distance for him, but he planned to catch the Metro somewhere along the return. He remembered most of

Irma's distance markers: the last Metro stop before the water, the first shower wall along the beach at Barceloneta, the crumpling tower sculpture along the boardwalk, the end of the boardwalk. Beneath the edge of the boardwalk, he removed his shoes and socks in order to run barefoot on the sand. The beach here became much less crowded and much less pitched toward the sea. When he scooted under the boardwalk joists in order to hide his shoes in the rafters, he was surprised to find another pair of running shoes there. The shoes had dried and curled into gray crescents and cobwebs were strung across their mouths. He lay in the cool sand beneath the boardwalk, striped with thin lines of sunlight passing between the planks. At first he believed the shoes to be hers. Then he believed they could be his, forgotten and shriveled. But they were only the abandoned shoes of some unknown runner, a Spaniard or traveler who ran the beaches barefoot, someone who perhaps decided that there was no other way to run than to forever fly barefoot along the banks of the Mediterranean.

When he reached the shore of Castelldefels, he was happy to find the noon Frisbee game. They called themselves Patatas Bravas, the Wild Potatoes, and they played barefoot on the sand and cooled off by running into the surf. Anyone who showed up to play became a Patata Brava. Most were students, but some of the players were the older ones, the ones who had kept the Castelldefels game going for decades. He recognized a woman who had been there the first time he and Irma happened upon this game. She was an ecology professor at the university. He recognized an older man—his own age—they called Mailman, because he was a mailman. Philip knelt in the sand and watched them play on their long rectangle of beach marked by red ribbon. Mailman and the professor, he could tell, were going back to work after this game. Most of the others, too, he assumed. Yet just for now, they were on the unpopular beach, kicking up sand, chasing a plastic disk, chasing one another. The sand stuck to the rivulets and patterns of sweat on their skin and clothes. They wore visors against the sun and squinted in concentration most of the time, always trying to catch their breath in the frenetic pace of the game. But they laughed readily, too, even at comments that were not that funny, as though they were all privy to an ongoing joke. In Spain, you could not find a busier city than Barcelona. But here they were, at high noon, playing in the sand.

They invited him to join, but he waved no thank you and began his return run. He stopped to retrieve his shoes at the edge of the boardwalk and then ran along the planks toward Barceloneta. He ended his run at the tower sculpture. The usual collection of wayward-looking youth sat on the concrete base, smoking pot and cigarettes, listening to a type of music he could not name. They did not wear beach clothes—in fact wore checkered sport coats and jeans. The girls wore sneakers and the boys wore clogs. Above them the tower, a teetering stack of four rusty cubes with windows, appeared postapocalyptic. Joining the kids in the tower shade, he caught his breath and rested. He swallowed, his throat parched by the long run and the wafting tobacco and pot smoke. One of the boys offered him a joint and Philip took one polite hit, said *Danke schön*, and left the beach. He was high by the time he reached the Metro stairs, and had to pay great concentration to every step down, then follow every color-coded line to find the right subway back to La Gràcia.

Once aboard, Philip watched the reflection of his subway's interior in the darkened windows. He could only see a sliver of himself among the passengers, half of them standing. The reflected image of the car would abruptly vanish as they slid into the brightly lit hollows of a stop. When they sped right through a stop, the disappearance/reappearance was even more abrupt. What did you hope to find there? she would have asked him, had she been riding next to him, as was usually the case whenever he rode the Barcelona Metro. He had half hoped to come upon Sam, but only because he knew that he probably had played that game at Castelldefels. Sam would do something like that on his return from Tangier, continue on the Metro to the noon beach game, make it all seem part of the continuum of his escape, his release, his exile, his runaway. And he had vaguely hoped to find her, somewhere along the ellipse. To surprise her, stun her, and then run into the surf with her, as he had done many times after the Castelldefels game or after a hard 10k to the beach.

On his return to Tom's house, he showered and then took one of Henry's coffees back to his room. He left the milking shed's double doors swung open to the courtyard and pecked at his keyboard, toggling between work and messages. Work was amazed at how precisely and thoroughly he had uncovered the last anomaly. They wondered if he could show them how to directly configure that anomaly into other investments. He relayed the request to Isaac—a serious breech of contract on Philip's part. My friend, he wrote to Isaac. My brother in arms. They want me to shape a formula whose final sum appears less than the sums it generates internally. He added the first equation of the formula, again beginning by splitting Newton's second law of motion.

Still a little high from the hit at the beach tower, he sent a quick message to Lucia. I've come to Spain on a sort of business, but now I feel like I'm here for everything. Then a new message from Nicole alarmed him. Why did you tell? was all she asked.

A tether snapping and the tiny spin afterward—the spin of understanding. He felt that and then suddenly very alone in Spain, with no point of return. He turned to his math, drawing on kinetics theory. To Nicole's four words he applied the catalytic equation:

$$dy/dt = -k_1(T)y - k_2(T)y\,(1-y)$$

where y is the fraction of the unreacted reagents, T the temperature, t=time, and k is the rate constant. This did not attempt to answer her question. It was his best attempt at calculating what had happened to prompt her question. Wouldn't anyone naturally turn to a catalytic equation? Tell Rebecca about Irma, Nicole, and Sam. Put Nicole, Rebecca, and Andrew together, the unreacted reagents—y. He could only make a calculated guess at the temperature, but it was easy to reach the possibility that all three of them knew everything. Andrew, the innocent, would be angry and hold the most power by nature of his innocence. Rebecca would choose to hold Andrew, hold him tightly—she would have to. Andrew would choose Rebecca then, too—he is smart and kind and life could go on. They're gone, he would say to them. At least they're gone and we are here together, as soon as we get Sam back. The variable Philip could not accurately predict was Nicole. Who would she choose? To understand that he would have to devise a way to isolate her variable from the other unreacted reagents, because going into the situation her value was definitely not unreacted. That, he believed, he knew better than anyone.

He stared blankly at her question on the screen until a new message prompt slid into the toolbar. He expected it to be Nicole, offering follow-up. Instead it was a very long letter from her mother, which played out his catalytic equation. Rebecca had no doubt composed her long message the night before, in the quiet, solitary light of her office, and only sent it now, early morning in New Jersey. She was asking him to just please send Sam home. To use the authorities if he had to. That she would use the authorities if she had to. I will, she wrote. We will. Including Andrew established it as a threat. She told him that Andrew now knew everything. Everything Sam had done, everything we had done. And that Andrew was incredibly understanding, and that everything he said and understood about what Sam must be going through amazed her. It made her realize what made Andrew exceptional. She asked Philip, respectfully, to deliver Sam and stay out of it.

Everything Sam had done. He composed the equation for Rebecca. It utilized several variables, hinged on a series of hypotheticals, and involved no equal signs. He titled the equation "Everything Sam Had Done," and offered no other response or reply. He composed another equation entitled "Everything Rebecca and Irma Had Done." It was long and elegant and intricate, centered around the problem of the tautochrone, driven by pendular arcs. He felt duped by Rebecca, seduced into her guilt. Did you use me to spare her some of the blame, he asked beneath two possibilities in the equation, or to join me to her in the blame? He sent neither equation at first, registering them as self-indulgent anger. Irma's niece, the oboist, appeared in his doorway, leaning her shoulder against the frame. She wore a flowered dress and espadrilles and looked far away from numbers and formulae. "Come have lunch with us?" she asked. "Just Henry and some of us. Somewhere close. We want to buy you beers and hear stories about Irma."

Seeing her in the doorframe, backed by the light of the courtyard, looking more like her aunt than ever before—the confidence of her posture; the way she toed one foot perpendicular—eased his anger concerning Rebecca's message. And the chance to defend Irma now, to any audience, appealed to him. He looked back to his equations, still on his screen, and saw them differently, too, free of any anger.

"Please come," said the niece. "It's important. If you want, it can just be Henry and me."

"I'll join you," he said, looking at his screen. "Do you think there's hope for Sam?" he asked, turning to her.

"It's not the first word that comes to mind. When I hear his name."

"If you could save him," he asked, "would you?"

"Sure. Wouldn't anybody?" She bounced her shoulder against the doorframe. "Come. I can tell you need to get out. *Dar curso libre*, as they say around these parts."

"The Hindemith sonatas," he said.

"Mm?"

"I've never heard them played that way."

"I water them down."

"No, you don't," he told her. "They work well that way."

"I cheat in parts. It would never pass assessment. But I'm on vacation, so that's what I play. Sonatas for one instrument, on the wrong instrument."

"How did you discover them?" he asked.

"She gave them to me." She continued bouncing her shoulder against the frame. "She put the CD into one of the books. Into *Slip*, like a bookmark. I didn't think she really listened to that kind of music. Maybe just for research."

"She doesn't," Philip told her. "I gave that CD to her."

"Mm," she said and turned to go. "We're leaving. *Das curso libre.*"

He sent the equations to Rebecca.

O Knight of the Sorrowful Face, Irma writes in Part II. When you get together with my young Capulets and Montagues—and you will—be sure to tell them. Even though you will look and feel like the phantoms we have seen many times throughout this book, be sure to tell them the other things, too. Tell them how I seduced both your wives. One during the happiest time of the marriage, one in the dark passageways of Sevilla, during a kind of second honeymoon. And how I seduced your best friend and your stepchildren. I have, like Marcela and Luscinda in Part I, earned my way into this book with beauty, strength, guile, and a certain kind of honesty. I was not completely honest with you, but you are my book. Honesty in a book cannot emerge fully until the end, until contemplation. So if you tell my story to those who would listen, to those who might request it, to those who would pass it along, promise to lend me those attributes also—beauty, strength, guile, and honest persever- ance. Alongside whatever others you choose to bestow on me.

They took him to nearby Salambó, the café Irma had once shown them. They sat him between the niece and Henry and ordered him *cañas*, the little beers served very cold in barrel-shaped glasses that fit to the curve of your palm. Altogether, six cousins sat at the round table. He was never comfortable holding court and so he tried to bore them by opening with the story of how they met at school, at the Frisbee game, where he and Irma exchanged tales of virginity lost. But then he was coaxed into elaborating on those tales, both his and hers, and that got the table laughing, and little side conversations started up among two or three of them, speaking Italian or Portuguese or Spanish or English or all of them at once.

And so, on his second, third, then fourth *caña*, he told them tales about her beauty, strength, guile, and honest perseverance, and how she seduced both his wives and his best friend. The laughing quieted but did not vanish, and the side conversations continued, also, but at a measured pace and volume. The café brought them little plates of food, some ordered, some not: olives, manchego, hard-boiled eggs, fried squid, spiced potatoes, pimientos, whole shrimp, fried almonds, translucent slices of dried ham. He told them how she gave him 351 books, but that they might be changed in ways that he could never discern, so that when he read them, he was at the mercy of both the author and the book- binder. He knew enough from his math, and from what Rebecca had told him about lectures, to stop before he was finished, to stop when they still wanted him to continue. They went on rendering their own tales, involving Irma in at least some small way, while Philip quietly gathered together a small plate of food from the wide selection at the table. He caught bits of their stories, most in languages he could not understand well. With that type of enlightenment that can only come with melan- choly, he realized how little he still knew about the person he knew best.

Henry, on one side of Philip, shouldered him. "I believe you will find her."

The niece, sitting on the other side of Philip, pointed at Henry and glared at the others sitting nearest him. Her light voice, for the first time, carried the table. "Why should we want him to find her?" She glanced up to Philip quickly, before continuing. "Why root for him? Why not for her? I think she's the one who's doing something brave. Something beautiful. Why hope that he wrecks it?"

Henry looked across to her, opened his mouth, then looked to Philip. Those sitting near followed his gaze. Others passed glances to one another.

Philip turned gently toward the niece. "I know," he said. "I've thought that out. I won't wreck what she's doing. Whatever she's doing. I promise you that. I promise myself that."

She sipped her beer.

"You sound sure of yourself," one of them said. Though it sounded like a male voice, he thought it came from a girl, one who arrived late, wedged herself in, and sat across the table opposite Philip. She wore a ball cap pulled very low and tight over her ruddy tufts of hair, whose short locks had leather strings tied to their ends. She wore a billowy white blouse, the kind sold at the outdoor markets in Madrid, and a woven leather bracelet the colors of the Maghreb. Philip could only catch glimpses of the dark bottom crescents of her eyes, and even the angle of her nose was obscured by the hat shadow. She spoke mostly to the cousins on either side of her, and Philip could not really hear her voice.

"I'm not sure at all. I'm only looking for her as best I can," he told them. "Mostly up here." He tapped the soft skin at his temple. "But she often outsmarts me, even in my memories. And what can I do? I'm just a mathematician."

The new girl across the table straightened in reaction to Philip's words and then removed her cap before she spoke, showing herself. It was Sam. He wore eyeliner, his hair was chopped and twined with those leather strings, he had lost weight down to only muscle and sinew, and he wore a long silver earring. His expression was none Philip had ever seen on him, one inclined toward disdain, reflective of one of his sister's looks. But it was Sam, quite clearly, revealed to him with just the removal of the cap.

There was no hiding from Sam his failure to recognize his own stepson, but Philip did his best to hide it from the rest of the table. The niece knew. She knew all along. She shouldered Philip, with some remonstrative push.

"Do you love her?" Sam asked across the table.

"I don't know if I can answer that, Sam," he replied. "Someone my age can't see love the same way you do. To be deeply in love, do both have to love the same kind of life, to love the same kind of pursuits? At your age, the answer is no. A resounding No! Let's run away together! But at my age it may very well be yes."

"You're not very Spanish," said Henry.

Most of the table laughed. The niece did not, giving him instead a hard look, straight from Irma.

"Let me be more Spanish, then," he told them. "I believe love is a madness. Two people grow mad together. Mad for each other, mad for each other's body, mad for each other's feelings. They want to get caught in the same paths, feel the same cuts and scars. But what happens if they also each find divergent madness? And another, and perhaps another? Because one madness always leaves you set up for others."

"That's a lot of madness," said Henry. They laughed. Again the niece refrained, the student who would not accept the cover of the joke. Sam's look joined hers.

"This world easily hides its madness," Philip told them. "Every culture I've seen hides great amounts. You could almost say it's what they do best. It almost becomes the reason they exist."

Sam leaned back in his chair, but kept one hand on the table, arm extended. He looked flatly at Philip.

"*Sin embargo,*" he said. "*¿La quieras?*"

The rest of the table followed his look to Philip. Sam chose the exact word in the right language. In English, love dissipates because the word lacks precision. Spanish calls for types and conditions, giving someone three choices to express a particular kind of love. Throughout Philip's math, $q = querer$, the love connected most deeply to desire, physical want, total craving.

Philip fought the urge to throw the question right back to Sam. Do you? Philip knew what this would accomplish and knew he wanted to spare Sam that humiliation, the sort of self-revelation the boy had always needed to avoid. Or perhaps he feared Sam's answer, the violence of the boy's affirmation. Either answer might make Sam better in their eyes. He felt a bloom of anger, a bile from the *cañas*, directed at Sam but spreading in tendrils over the table.

He turned away from the question, clenched his jaw so they could see, left Sam open to their looks, which were changing and turning to him. He could endure the silence better than all of them, save for the musician.

They all left Salambó together, then dispersed from the busy sidewalk outside. The long run, the beach, the single hit beneath the tower, the meal, and the *cañas* left Philip almost groggy, only ready to continue with siesta. La Gràcia was one of the few neighborhoods in Barcelona that maintained at least some sense of traditional siesta. He was grateful to just stand for a moment in the sunlight, nodding quick farewells to the cousins as they paired up and went their separate paths. More people walked on the shady side of the street, carrying canvas bags for siesta or work. Philip kept an eye on Sam, who stood chatting with Henry and the niece. The niece did not act intimate with Sam, except for the one moment when she slipped two fingers beneath the leather Maghreb bracelet on his wrist. Philip expected Sam to head off with them and was surprised when the boy waved them on and turned his full attention to him.

"You heading back?" he asked Philip.

When Philip nodded, Sam turned to walk with him, looking very much a traveler anxious to find a stop. His skin had darkened and the bones of his hands, wrists, and jaw drew sharp lines. His red hair was sun-bleached along its chopped, ornamented ends. As they walked the sidewalks of La Gràcia, he kept a sidestep distance. When oncoming pedestrians forced him nearer Philip, he quickly returned to that distance, a racer's kind of gauging.

"Run with me?" he asked, finally looking at Philip. But the words, almost exactly his sister's, did not have Nick's plea, only challenge.

"Maybe in a bit," replied Philip.

Sam walked beside him with a kind of sideways gate, almost beggar-like, with tiny hops to keep slightly in front. Philip became aware that he was being boxed in.

"You're limping?"

"My hip's a little sore," explained Philip. "It's nothing. I've been running a lot with your sister. She's getting fast."

"I want her to come here," said Sam. "I've been asking and asking her. She needs to get away from New Brunswick. Right now. It's no good if you tie up all the loose ends first. It's not the same unless you just bolt."

Near the plaque commemorating the 1868 revolution, Philip took hold of Sam's elbow and stayed him, bringing him beneath a small awning. He could tell, from Sam's question to the table, from his challenging air, that he was serious about his search for Irma. Perhaps more serious, more intent than himself. Tom must have sensed that, too, before he began sending him on errands, began giving him purpose, direction and return. But Philip could also sense that Sam's understanding of Nicole—and home—did not balance with his intent to find Irma. For the first time since her disappearance, he felt a real anger toward her. The pain in his hip sharpened. How dare you, he wanted to say to her, to write to her in the *Quixote*. I regaled you. To your Capulets and Montagues, I regaled you. How dare you leave me with this.

In chapter fourteen of Part II, where her request was written, Quixote defeats the Knight of the Mirrors by charging his adversary as he fumbles to secure his lance into its leather pocket. In fifteen, it is revealed that the Knight of the Mirrors is really Bachelor Sansón Carrasco, a friend in disguise sent by Quixote's village to rescue the old knight from his madness—by defeating him. But Bachelor Carrasco underestimates Quixote's commitment, his madness. And, from practice, Quixote has gained some strength and purpose. He does not hesitate to drill the Knight of the Mirrors when he sees the chance. He is tired of being knocked off his nag.

Beneath the awning, Sam appeared puzzled. He looked at Philip's hold on his elbow. Philip waited until Sam lifted his gaze to him.

"Or maybe Nick's just smarter than you. Maybe she's better at the game." He paused. "Maybe she's more than Irma was ready to handle." Philip gripped Sam's elbow. "See? I can recognize that possibility, Sam. Things like that. Flaws in her. Because I have seen them. Felt them."

He almost let go of Sam's elbow, then regripped.

"I told your mother," Philip said. "Everything. You understand? Maybe things you don't even know."

"I know about Nicole. About her and Irma. They don't hide things from me."

"Did you know about your mother?"

Sam nodded, but weakly.

"I told her without thinking," Philip said. "I told her because I just found out about her and Irma. And I made the mistake of thinking of Nicole as a child—and you."

"So?" replied Sam. "So it's good you told Mom. I have nothing to hide."

"But that's how we left your sister, Sam." He finally eased his hold on the boy. "In all of that, do you see? She wanted me to come and find you. But I left her in all of that. Think. And think which one of us is free. You don't just bolt. When you do that, you bolt right where she points you."

Sam went quiet and began walking beside him, his gaze aimed firmly ahead, shoulders even, the way Philip had remembered him. The way he ran the 400-meter low hurdles, trying to defeat better athletes, nearly passing them at the finish. Philip remembered how the tall, muscular hurdler with the Temple scholarship looked down in sudden fear at the scrawny redhead who almost nosed past him. Sam, who flailed his pale arms, desperately seeking balance, before he stumbled and then fell to the orange, rubberized track. Only then did the winner's expression transform into a look of disdain that barely hid relief. When Philip approached Sam to congratulate him after the race, he pretended not to notice the tears. Tears come easily to any runner entirely spent at the end of a race. If, in fact, you drain yourself completely, run yourself out of all reserve energy, expend all muscle strength, then you can do nothing *but* cry. It is not an emotional reaction, but a physical one, a kind of falling and release.

Philip let him remain silent during their return to Tom's house. As they stepped among the lulling siesta at the small Plaza de la Virreina, that silence took its place comfortably between them. They looked at the same people, the same faces, the same things as they passed among the benches, and did not speak or feel compelled to speak.

When they reached Tom's—quiet except for the lapping of the courtyard fountain—Philip led Sam to his desk in the milking shed. Sam remained in the doorway as Philip motioned toward his notes on the catalytic equation.

"I was going to show you these. Explain them." Philip looked at the pages as though they were ashes. "But you can imagine better than I can. What's going on back at your home. What Nicole must be going through."

"Nick's strong," replied Sam. "And she's not at home. She's on campus."

"Your mom and dad are angry with me. They know I've found you. They've asked I deliver you. They can force me—and I really couldn't blame them."

"I won't go."

"You can't find Irma, Sam."

Sam centered himself in the doorway, the light of the courtyard at his back. "I need to. I *have* to find her."

"And what about Nick?"

"She'll be fine. She can hold her own."

"She can—maybe. But as I said, she doesn't feel the same as you. She isn't as convinced." Philip almost said *impulsive*. He almost told Sam again that she was smarter, more thoughtful, more knowing, further ahead. Irma has taken her further ahead. But he sensed he was about to lose him, in the twilight, just in front of the rail yard tunnel.

"Don't try to use Nick that way," Sam told him. "I know her. A lot better than you do."

"I'm not using Nicole. She didn't just ask me to find you. She asked me to *get* you. But I'm not asking you to go back. I'm not sending you back. Okay?"

Sam nodded.

"But I am asking you to come to Seville with me."

"I've already been there. She's not there. She won't be there."

"I know where you've been," Philip said. "In some ways you've gone ahead of me. Still—I have to go there. Think how you'd feel if you had not looked for her there. Or here. Or Corte. Or Tangier. If you had just let her disappear without following whatever traces she left, whatever shimmering trail remained. Come with me and maybe I can show you some things. Things you may have missed."

Sam stared hard at him. He looked like a runner at his peak, honed, perfectly aquiver, ready to fire. "Do they know where you found me?"

Philip shook his head softly, feeling some relief. "I didn't tell them that."

Sam leaned against the doorframe. The lapping of the fountain sifted behind him. Philip shut his eyes, breathed, knew Sam would still be there. He opened his eyes.

"I sent your mom messages. Two equations. One about you. One about her."

"What did they say?"

Philip shrugged. "Not a whole lot. But she'll be even angrier."

Sam toyed with the split door of the milking shed, moving the top and bottom flaps in syncopation. "I'll think about Seville," he said.

The last time Philip was their stepfather was a kind of agreed-upon moment. He took them to the Sourland fields. They brought everything, everything needed to play whatever sport they chose. They lugged footballs, Frisbees, baseballs, and mitts. Everything looked like such toys to him, the foolish stuffed animals you give your grown niece or nephew. Andrew was coming back and Philip was leaving their home. But this was supposed to be their day. They, all three of them, had planned a longer time of it, a late picnic, a full afternoon in the Jersey sun, pauses in the shade to decide on new games. But all of them found separate ways to delay, or just leap past the moment, and the afternoon got away from them. They only arrived near evening, separately, and knew they would not have much time in the encroaching shadow of the Sourland ridge. Backhoes, come to widen the roads, loomed above the outfield fence, their heads painted green and purple, colors meant to seem less menacing but which only brought the machines more to life. He bought Sam and Nick new mitts, gloves good enough to use on junior high teams.

They briefly tried each sport, but even the easy glide of a Frisbee appeared too cutting in the darkening air. It was Nicole's decision to race, to attempt the simplest, purest of sports, barefoot over the outfield grass. They marked off their usual course for the 100-yard sprint using their shoes. It was the perfect event. Sam was just young enough—twelve—to still compete with his sister. And Philip was old enough to have lost enough steps in such a short sprint. Philip took the first race, lost in the release, safe in the twilight. Nicole took the second, laughing at them both. Sam, already showing the stamina that would eventually make him the best runner of them all, took the third. Brother and sister huddled briefly before the fourth and final race, the deciding heat. When they broke ranks and headed to the start, Sam's head down in earnest determination, Nicole winked at Philip. What did it mean? It was a gesture so unlike her, one he had never seen coming from her. To be safe, he eased up slightly at the end of the sprint and Sam won. But it was the fastest they had all run together, each of them throttling up in response to the other, their gasps spun forward into the twilight, their muscles quivering on edge, their toes skimming the grass. At the end they felt good about it. They had something to tell back home.

Sam continued to flip the milk shed doors, the top half one way, the bottom the other. He was anxious to run, but Philip needed to gather some more strength, more wind, somehow.

"Have they cut into the fields yet? At Sourland?"

"I never go there. I don't want to see. Do you?"

"Only in my thoughts," said Philip. "Your field of victory."

Sam halted the doors, lulled his eyes like a runner before a heat showing the others he is not nervous, could take them in his sleep.

"You were supposed to win that last race, Philip," he said. "That's what Nick planned. Let the old guy go, she said. Let him go find his pretty friend. Let him just go away."

It was like eavesdropping and hearing what you weren't supposed to hear about yourself, something you wanted to discover about another. Philip spun back to his screen in order to hide his face. The twist inside him was small but deep, drawing on the nerves about his neck. But when he glared forward into the equations on his screen, his aim, he found, was not toward Sam, but toward an image of Irma dressed to run, but barefoot in another twilight.

"I'll go away later," he said. He turned to Sam. "After Seville."

Before their run, Philip told Sam he needed to take a few notes and get ready. Alone in his room, he repeated his anger toward her, calculating it carefully on the grids of his composition book. He translated: $x^2 - y^2 = 1$. Play fair. I regale you and you leave me with this? You have him looking one way when he should be looking the other. You gave her more. You left him unfinished. Why? Did you see what you had done? With her? Did you grow afraid? Is it frightening out there? Do you need me with you?

He placed this page between chapters fourteen and fifteen, where Quixote fells the Knight of the Mirrors, and where you discover (but Quixote does not) that the Knight of the Mirrors is really Bachelor Carrasco. It is wonderful and brilliant math, Philip thought, on Cervantes's part.

They ran together toward Parc Güell, following the path Irma laid out seventeen years before. Sam held back in order to stay with Philip. After mile two—the sewer cap on Lepant—where they could easily see the street heading up to Parc Güell, Philip told Sam to run ahead and then catch him on the return. Even rested, Philip could not keep up with Sam. But worn out from his first run to the beach and drugged by siesta, Philip could barely manage a jog. Sam made no polite protest and bounded quickly ahead, in what to Philip looked like a sprint. If it were not for the measured power of his gait and the tanned and pronounced muscles of his calves, Sam could have been mistaken for a street thief, on the dash. And as he turned the corner, he held that expression he always raced with, the look of astonishment and fear.

When Philip reached the base of Carrer de Larrard, he paused for a moment. He could see the entire street slanting over a quarter mile up to Gaudí's park. Sam had already made it to the top and disappeared into the twist and plateaus of forest, sculptures, buildings, and fountains. The incline to the park was forty degrees. Philip showed Irma how to measure it. Forty degrees? she said. I don't trust you. That sounds too neat. It's not an arbitrary number, he explained. When they built it, they measured it. She peered up the length of the street, its ridiculous slant. The café tables and chairs running the length of its sidewalks all seemed about to come tumbling toward them in an avalanche. At any rate, she said, it's one hell of a climb for us. They raced to the top, she catching and passing him at the lip. They were young. They were each in love with someone else, back in the U.S. When she passed him, though he had already known her for years, traveled with her, done everything with her, become a part of her family, he saw her, finally, unequivocally, as beautiful. The grueling run up Larrard, the draining of his physical strength and his desperate breathing, left him wide open to her, entirely unguarded, without armor. When it was clear she would win, she looked over her shoulder and smiled as though she had caught him admiring her legs.

The incline heading up to the park now looked twice as sharp and twice as long. The clutter of chairs and tables and other hurdles along the sidewalks looked thicker and more precarious than before. Tourists and other visitors trudged up the hill like pilgrims bowed against the climb. Philip took in one deep breath and began his run up to the park's first plateau. He was not sure why he ran the hill so hard. Maybe it was simple training. Runners are always training. So maybe he was trying to dip into that unknown reserve of strength and stamina that every runner must prove he possesses. Or perhaps he was trying to reach once again that state of physical and emotional baring, the end of math, that paring down of everything that had first led him to the possibility of her beauty, first in Mexico, but now conclusively, here, in Spain.

When he crested the hill and reached the park steps guarded by the dragon mosaic, he felt a surge of energy, exuberance. But that strength, like a shooting star, dropped suddenly from him and his sweat went cold, his muscles lax. He recognized, with some dread, that he had reached the runner's true state of exhaustion, that sudden clammy bloom across the body that hearkened paralysis and unconsciousness. He pictured himself, absurdly, as one of those marathoners often seen being carried from the finish, held like collapsed marionettes by the crooks of their arms and knees, ignoble and defeated. Foolishly, he veered to the left and ended up staggering amid Gaudí's incomprehensible Sala Hipóstila, a

galley of eighty-four (he counted them once) twisted, dripping columns
that collectively looked like a huge cave beneath tree roots. In a niche
between stalagmites, he fell. He lay in the cool dust, only his head and
neck reclined against the stone, so he could gaze between the many columns and see the bright Spanish sky.

He remained half conscious. He could hear passing tourists make
quick comments about him. "*Borracho*" and "*que temprano*" and "*pobretón.*"
And the sky between the drippy columns seemed to keep getting brighter
until he closed his eyes.

In Part II, chapter sixty-four, after the Knight of the White Moon
has dropped Quixote with his lance and left him sprawled on the sandy
beach of Barcelona, she writes: The armor that often saves him, just as
often pins him to the ground. Get up, Knight of the Sorrowful Face. You
are defeated, almost slain. The Knight of the White Moon who dropped
you to the Barcelona sand forced you to renounce your beliefs and honor.
But you remained true to the one claim that matters. Even with the point
of his lance at your throat, insisting, you would not renounce the beauty
of your Dulcinea: "Dulcinea of Toboso is the most beautiful woman in
the world, and I am the most unfortunate knight on earth, and it is not
right that my weakness should give the lie to this truth. Wield your lance,
knight, and take my life, for you have already taken my honor."

And the legend of her beauty only grew.

TWELVE

Sam accompanied him on the twelve-hour train ride south to Seville. They took a day train so they could see the countryside. Irma had bequeathed Sam *The Magus*, *In the Skin of a Lion*, and *Tracks*, and these he stacked on the table in front of him on the train, keeping them out even though he had finished reading them. He would look to the passing landscape for long stretches of time, then dip into one of the books. Philip could not tell whether Sam reached for random passages or sought specific ones, but he always pretended at least to know immediately where to go in each of the books. Outside, the scrubby foothills of Aragon were patched with olive and orange groves, and on the occasional rocky overlook stood the ruins of a castle. When Sam noticed Philip craning his neck to keep the last castle in view, he said, "I always imagined them as gray and enormous and mournful. But they're the colors of the sun. And small and vulnerable-looking."

Philip, sitting across from him, with the window and table between, eyed him for a moment, then said, "You're different. It's why I didn't recognize you at first. Is it because you're here?" He looked at Sam's three books, stacked zigzag. "Or because of her?"

"Her," Sam answered plainly. The train rolled through foothills whose slopes were covered by dying, wind-pressed grass, and by evenly spaced oaks, young and dark and still close to the ground. He told Philip the story.

She found him at a Frisbee game—thinking back, here in Spain, he realized that she probably was looking for him. It was the game in

Princeton, the one played on the Broadmead field, which lay unused
except on the few weekends the eating clubs set up their vast lawn par-
ties. It was a better game than the Rutgers one and it was an easy train
ride south. Nicole had taken him there many times. He already knew
about Nicole and Irma. And both he and his sister had wondered about
Irma and Rebecca, speculated, hoped. His sister told him almost everything, even though he told her almost nothing. He always wanted to stop
her from doing this, from telling him so much, because he worried that
it would one day make her disdain him, distance herself. And because
it made him feel too singular and responsible. But when Nicole began
telling him about Irma, he felt happy for her—happy that she had someone else besides Mom and Dad and him. Happy that she had somebody
smart and different to talk to.

The field was covered with a thin layer of snow, the sky clear and
the air frigid. The players would often pause and heave their breath to
the sun, clouding it. The ones who wore their hair long, like him, were
startled by the icicles that formed on the ends of their locks and clattered
when they stopped and started and flailed over the snowy ground. Irma,
whom most of the players greeted and welcomed back, played for a long
while without seeming to notice him. Then she matched herself across
from him, ran toward him over the snow, marked him at arm's length,
then grabbed his sweatshirt when he tried to cut away from her and get
open for a throw. His cleats skidded on some packed snow and he fell on
his back. She almost straddled him, like Ali over Liston. She breathed
down on him and did not reach to help him up. She wore knee-length
stretch pants, exposing her brown calves to the cold. His back pressed
to the snow, the wind knocked painfully from his lungs, her breath
clouds blurring her silhouette against the winter sky, his sweat freezing
to his temples, Sam for the first time felt her desirable and accessible.
On the balls of her feet, she stepped around him, as though avoiding a
puddle, while staying keen to the game. He gazed at her calf, close up,
at his leisure, at the impressions on either side of her Achilles and the
specks of frozen mud clinging to the rims of her cleats and her smooth
brown skin.

"Stay away from my sister," he said, trying to prop himself on his elbows.

She pressed one cleat firmly to his chest. She smiled, full of menace. "Don't threaten someone while on your ass. Especially when that someone just put you there."

With her cleat, she shoved him back to the snow. "Get up and chase. I'm getting cold."

His erection, which was the hardest he had ever felt, confused him. He was glad it was hidden beneath the layers of his winter sweats. But he wanted her to fall on him. He wanted to put his mouth to her Achilles. She wiped her nose with the sleeve of her sweatshirt and sniffed. She crossed her arms and tucked her bare hands beneath her biceps, feeling her own breasts, seeking warmth. Everything she did, everything he saw, made him harder.

After the game she apologized to him and shared her thermos of very hot coffee. "I've always been a dirty player."

The intense cold and their sweat left them little time to think. They bought more coffee at the Princeton student union and hurried together across campus to catch the train, their winter coats wrapped around their rank sweats, their cleats tied and looped about their necks. They had their wool hats tugged down to their eyes so that they had to tilt their heads back in order to see. They went arm in arm over the icy patches on the campus walkways. His erection, which never quite went away, grew whenever her sleeve even brushed his, whenever he smelled the coffee on her breath, whenever she sniffed and wiped her runny nose.

On the northbound train, they sat together and sipped their coffees. She removed her winter coat, but he remained wrapped in his. It was Sunday and passengers were sparse.

"Certain physical expressions are more apparent to women than men realize," she told him, speaking softly but steadily. "At least to women who have been around the block a time or two. And we do appreciate your attempts to be discreet about it, to be as polite as possible. That tends to make your claims of helplessness more believable. But I wouldn't expect a man to have to let himself cook on a Jersey train."

He fought off a smile, stared at the winter woods blurring by.

"There was this movie star, well before my time," she said. "His name was Robert Taylor. Legend has it that he always had to be filmed from the waist up when he was on the set with Elizabeth Taylor. He wasn't necessarily in love with her. Nor did they have a relationship. She just made him hard and there was nothing—he claimed—he could do about it. They were in *Conspirator* together. And *Ivanhoe*."

The image of Ivanhoe, perhaps in medieval tights, with an erection did make him laugh.

"I know what you're trying to do," he said. "And I appreciate it. But you're only making it worse."

"Worse, better," she said. "Depends on how you look at it."

She turned fully to him, bracketing him to the window. "I invite you to stay on this train with me. Skip your stop and come to my hotel room. I won't make it *that* easy for you. You will have to converse. You will have to listen. But you can leave at any time. You can leave this train at New Brunswick and that can be the end of it. If you are bothered by whatever relationship I had with the others, well, I would understand."

"Nicole doesn't consider the relationship over."

"It isn't over at all," she said. "It's changed."

He did not know many women or girls. Even though he had seen Irma many times before, he had no idea what she was really like, and he had no idea that someone like her could exist. She cut through inhibition, indecision, and self-doubt with the quick use of words. It seemed to him as though she threw them out there first, and then made sense of them, backfilled the cuts and holes they made. At that moment on the train, gazing at the swampy, icy Jersey woods, viewing through her transparent reflection in the glass, her steady dark-eyed look, he suddenly wanted to travel somewhere far and unknown to him. He wanted the train to take him to Mexico and Spain and Argentina and all the places he heard Irma and Philip talk about. He wanted it to bullet him to the same volcanoes they had climbed, and to new ones. Ones they had never even seen. Places they had never seen. Until that moment he had always defensively argued against that kind of superficial exploration, that kind of predictable expenditure, rich kids with backpacks. To his sister and his teachers, he always argued for the virtue and heroism of hermits, of putting together the kind table that saved travelers and wayward souls. But that moment on that train with her, even before they passed his stop, he explained to Philip, put him on this train to Seville.

He felt the weight of forever justifying his life, of forever self-righteously justifying his unrelenting, undirected sadness and anger, blow away behind him in the rush of the train. It was even better than running, racing and beating the field, almost flying beyond yourself. He imagined the weight of it all, the mass of it all, snagging in shadows between the bare trees and sinking into the ice-crusted swamps and ponds. When the New Brunswick stop was announced and the train slowed, he took hold of her hand. "When you are binding a book," he asked her, "where do you start?"

When the train veered from the coastal foothills and headed into the drab stretches of La Mancha, Sam, apparently already experienced at riding the Spanish rails, tucked himself into the corner against the window and slept. He appeared older, singed by his errands and searches, too easily comfortable in the hard crook of his train seat. There was new menace to his appearance, simultaneously appealing and resistant. But Philip could still see the boy he hit infield to, and the nervous, doubtful runner defiantly racing against track stars, and the little brother brave enough and foolish enough to spy on the dark friend his stepfather brought into his home.

Philip considered reading *Quixote*, but opened his composition book instead. The ellipse can be covered completely by an infinite series of triangles stretched around the double foci. The base of the triangle is fixed by the eccentricity of the ellipse, the distance between the two foci. The shape of the ellipse is drawn by the moving tip, which follows the path of elongation. He felt he was getting a better fix on the eccentricity, the distance between $IP+P$ and $IP-P$. As a variable in calculating that eccentricity—the eccentricity of her ellipse—Sam was becoming more clearly defined. Others might panic in trying to work with an ellipse whose foci are not quite fixed. But he relished the challenge this presented, felt in fact that this accommodation for sliding foci made his search more valid, added the necessary complexity to at least track her, if not ultimately find her. And he would only need a small section of the perimeter to determine the precise shape of her ellipse, the way an astronomer can accurately measure the vast orbit of a comet through just a fraction of its curve around the sun. The challenge that unnerved him more was moving between the eccentricity and the perimeter; he didn't always know if he was sliding along the perimeter or sliding between foci. Sometimes, as when he listened to Sam's story and then watched him nap on the train, he felt as though he were experiencing both at the same time. Continuing with his notes to her, he calculated a hypothetical, forcing solipsism, learning from the *Quixote* what you can do with protagonists: You do not only pursue them to compose me, you affect them to compose me. But you affect them differently. Or do you affect them the same and produce different results? Sam is here, vagabond, yet more free and vital (if not more happy) than I have ever seen him. Nicole is there, in crisis and transition, losing the identity her brother gains. Yet she blames me, not you. Me. Sam also challenges me, not you. They *love you.*

Again I ask you for math help. You're the one who's broken the equation that could define us, shape us, *hold* us. He drew the snail shell of the logarithmic spiral, then put the cross of the two axes through its center. He broke its equation beneath the shape, crumpled figures, betrayed and meaningless in their positions. Who are we now? What are we now?

After slipping the page into *Quixote*, he leaned into his own corner between window and seat and watched the dun flats and swells of La Mancha. Beatrice was with him the last time he was in La Mancha. They were on the train with Irma, taking a roundabout path to their Seville rental. When Irma, like most of the passengers, dozed off gazing at afternoon over the endless farmlands which looked much like central California, Beatrice invited him to the bar to drink *cañas*. He knew the windmills were coming and he told her. You don't see them at first. The train hooks up to Alcázar de San Juan, stops at the surprisingly large junction, then backs up for a few miles into a spur, confusing first-time riders. When it pauses at the end of the spur to aim itself toward Córdoba, if you look atop the nearest rise in the plains, you see them. You see them much like Quixote first sees them, according to Irma, except that their sails have been stripped from their arms, leaving them sleeveless and shameful, especially in the wind.

The other men and women leaning on the bar watched Beatrice in that direct Spanish way, lifting their eyes from their newspapers and beers. Her dark hair was shorter then, parted on the side so that the lighter wisps just around her face swung forward, and she was already filtered and colored by the Mediterranean sun. She wore a dress from Barcelona, gray and simple but cut sharp at the waist with small red wedges, where you would put your hands.

"Let's get off and go see them," she said to Philip. "Let Irma sleep. We'll catch the next train behind her. We'll leave a message for her. She'll like it." Beatrice leaned over the bar, putting her elbows to it, sipping her *caña*.

"They're not your style, B. There's not much to them. All you do is walk among them and kick a few stones." It puzzled Philip that she wanted to see windmills up close. He knew she would want to see them from the train, to see how they looked sagging but still sentrylike on the rise overlooking the farmlands. She would want to seize their image with her photographic memory, see instantly and forever that there were eleven of them and that it was not so far-fetched to see them as giants. Beatrice understood delusion, particularly that brand of cultivated willful delusion she came across frequently in her work, in her studied estimations of who was and wasn't necessary. She was not so exacting as to automatically remove windmills from people's lives, from the systems they designed in order to function, create, produce, flourish.

As they stood at the bar holding their beers, she leaned against him. She nudged him with her hip. "It might be romantic. I'll go change. I have a skirt you can hide under."

They exited the train and watched it pull away from the platform, taking the sleeping Irma with it. Was she still sleeping? Was she looking back at them through her window, craning her neck to keep them in sight as long as possible? Perhaps she said to herself: I will do the same to you, Pip. But I will do it in spades. Or perhaps she said: He is saved.

Philip watched for any flinch in Beatrice's expression as the train abandoned them on the rather desolate platform. He remembered how startling it was, how the purring, sleek Spanish train left you on a slab of dusty concrete shaded by a thin metal roof. It was difficult to convince yourself that such a train would ever return to this quaint stop. But Beatrice smiled as she shaded her eyes with a fan purchased in Barcelona, and she turned immediately from the train to the windmills along the ridge.

"We can take the road up," he told her, "or we can cut through the brush and walk straight to them."

"Let's go straight at them."

They found a narrow goat path through the low brush, then clambered up the ridge through scrub and rock. She lifted her skirt and wrapped it high about her hips so that it would not snag on the brittle sage tips, and so that she could lift her knees high as she sought the best footholds along the rise. The sun reflected in elongated ovals along her thighs and calves. Though she could never show remorse for the results of her work, she felt it. And she assigned practical value to the most human elements: loyalty, years of service, family, camaraderie, sense of humor, self-awareness, self-deprecation, emotional intelligence. She gave Philip credit for being the only person she knew who understood this about her. She craved the catalytic equations he showed her, wished she could apply them as readily as he. But how could anyone not understand this about her, watching her climb the ridge to the windmills, forgoing modesty and openly displaying her eagerness to reach the top and see?

They had the windmills to themselves. Philip had never seen people there before and he was not surprised by the abandoned ridge. The Manchegan siesta, ancient and steadfast, hung over the surrounding farms and ranches on the flatlands below. He watched her examine the windmills, with her eye for expedience. Their pointed caps were black streaked with remnants of blue, their fat whitewashed bodies pocked with stone windows and tiny vents, their skeletal arms stained black by the sun and wind. A couple of the mills were propped up by wooden buttresses. The last one, on the end knob of the ridge, had lost two of its arms and the remaining two hung apelike in an inverted V, making it the most real, the most sad. She leaned against its sun-baked wall, facing the expanse of La Mancha.

"What's it like at night?" she asked.

"What makes you think I would know?"

"*She* would take you here at night. *That* I can tell."

He nodded, leaned next to her against the wall. "We came here at night with a book collector from Corsica. Miriam Haupt. She and Irma wanted to show me how the lights scattered over the plain and up the hills blended into the stars. Just like in the book. But I have never read the book."

"Did you ever return with Irma alone? At night?"

He nodded. "At dusk."

"Where did you screw her?"

"We didn't. We thought about it without saying anything. Sometimes it's best to go back to the hotel."

"Sometimes," agreed Beatrice. She knelt in front of him. She undid his jeans, flipped back her hair, and watched as he grew hard and lifted. She clutched his erection with both hands and put her mouth over the tip. She sucked firmly, nursing with her tongue. He cried out, almost needing to stop her. Then she pulled away, keeping one hand on him, pumping. She aimed him and fired him and he closed his eyes feeling himself go over the ridge, over the plains. She stood and leaned back against the wall and lifted her skirt, inviting him in with a quick downward nod. He knelt and she draped her skirt over him, spreading her legs, bracing herself to the wall, tenting him. He hooked his arms about her legs and grasped the backs of her thighs, pulling her to his mouth. Rocks dug into his knees as he pushed upward. The light inside was the sun filtered through the green of her skirt. Her hands cupped the back of his head and held him to her, guided him. She told him, between breaths, where and how fast and when to stop and when to start again. When she told him to stop for the third time, he ignored her and listened as her directions and words lost coherence. He stood, taking her skirt up with him, lifting her against the wall. For a while it was good like that against the wall, her knees pushed under his arms. But neither of them had the strength to maintain the position.

"I can stop," he told her. "I don't need to keep going."

"But let's see what we can do," she said.

She found a long shelf of stone just over the lip of the ridge. She patted it with her hands and got him to lie down. With one hand she gripped him firmly, keeping him hard, and with the other hand she arranged her shoes at either side of his hips. She put her knees into the shoes and straddled him, pressing him to the scalding rock. She smiled and laughed above him as she fitted him inside her. "Can you stop now?" she asked.

On the platform, they waited for the train. They stood arm in arm beneath the shade of the roof. An afternoon wind had picked up, hot and dry coming over the dead grasses, but with the smell of oranges in it. From atop the ridge they had seen the train, miles away, snaking into the valley, and they had hurried through the rocks and scrub to meet it. She looked back to the windmills, once. "It's not so far-fetched," she told him.

They rendezvoused with Irma at the Córdoba station, where she had figured things out and stood waiting on the platform. Beatrice got to her first, ahead of a hesitant Philip, and the two women grasped hands. Irma said something that made Beatrice laugh softly. They returned to the train together, remaining ahead of Philip, bumping shoulders as they ascended the stoop. Irma looked back at Philip once, silent, her gaze flat. The ellipse widens one way, narrows the other.

When their train backed into the spur out of Alcázar de San Juan, the change of direction woke Sam. He rubbed his eyes and looked out the window to gain his bearings. He seemed startled to see La Mancha instead of New Jersey, and then he looked at Philip and this confused him a bit more. His brow furrowed momentarily and then he blinked himself fully awake. Understanding exactly where they were, he peered upward through his window in order to catch sight of the windmills.

"You abandoned her there," he said as he nodded toward the ridge.

Sam's clairvoyance unnerved him, as though he had not simply wakened from a dream, but had returned from another time or place where he could look down on Philip's story, from the castle in the sky. When Philip realized Irma must have told him the story, this sense, rather than passing, only intensified.

"She might have exaggerated," he told Sam. "I did what we often did. With each other. Without the usual notice, I admit. That time."

"How could you do that? How could you abandon someone like her?"

"It's almost impossible to explain," Philip answered. "I've written it out for myself, several times, as an equation. I showed it to Isaac a couple of times, and he kind of got it. We could at least talk about it in understandable terms. It begins with a paradox. In order to be with her, I had to not be with her. Irma and I both understood this, very early in our friendship. So the paradox is actually: In order to be together, we could not be together. We understood this from two very different approaches, which I think enabled us to endure"—he paused to lean toward the window and glance at the ridge—"for as long as we did."

"Is it really over?"

The train released its brakes, and they felt that floating sensation just before it began to purr westward.

"Not if I can help it."

Sam tapped his stack of three books. He knocked the zigzag one way, then the other. He looked flatly at Philip.

"I think I may have found her."

Philip offered a skeptical smile. But Sam's words bothered him.

"When I got here," said Sam. "When I landed in Madrid and took the Metro and surfaced in Sol, I felt sick. I thought I was going to die. I had all these plans mapped out, starting at her *pensión*. I had all these notes I took. I wrote down so many things she told me. After being with her, I'd write them all down. And on the plane over here, I listed them, highlighted bits of information, the way she spoke of certain places, certain people. On the plane, doing this, I felt even more sure that I was doing the right thing. Even that I was doing what she expected me to do. But Sol was fucked, a punch in the gut. It was afternoon and there were so many people and cars, all swirling around the plaza. Suddenly I couldn't understand Spanish and the sun felt so fucking bright and hot. I couldn't get my eyes used to it. My lungs felt like lead. My hands were shaking and I didn't know why. I took out the chart I'd made. My chart of possibilities. And it looked like some kid's scribblings and drawings. I almost threw up, right there beneath that bear statue. I heaved and hyperventilated. People thought I was a stupid drunk American and they were calling to me, 'Not by the bear! Not by the bear!' Those were the first words I understood. I did not want her to see me that way. It's funny. Right away, I believed she might be there, on the Sol plaza, because of course that's where I was beginning my search. I feared, more than anything, that she'd find me like that."

"What did you do?" Philip asked.

"That's hard to explain." Sam tapped at his stack of books again. Then he spaced them out on the table, squared them. "This one"—he put his hand on *The Magus*—"is you." He moved his hand to *In the Skin of a Lion*. "This is me." He lifted *Tracks*, which was an extremely deep blue leather. "And this is her."

He looked at Philip for a moment.

"Have you read them?"

"No," answered Philip. "But they're on my list."

"They're all real good. Each one is different. I just went to the nearest hostel and holed up and read for a few hours. I read from each one. It was stupid. My first time ever in a place like Madrid, and I go to some room by myself and read. I took a break, walked around the corner, walked into the first place I saw, and asked for a beer. I really just wanted a beer and didn't know or care if they could serve me. The guy behind the counter drew me the coldest beer I've ever felt and then slid me a plate of bread and these red shrimp cooked in garlic with their heads still on. I ate them whole because I asked him how. I asked for another beer and he told me he would only give me one more and I said that would be fine. With that beer he sliced me this piece of ham that was so thin and dry you could see through it to the street outside. It tasted like ocean air. When I left that place to go back to my books, I was dizzy— from the food, I guess—and Sol felt like it was giving off this sort of, I don't know, this sort of weird energy. It didn't feel nice or comforting.

But my lungs felt good and there was a little bit of a thrill—like before a race, you know. And that evening I went for a run around Retiro. The altitude—I forgot about that—got me, but it was beautiful. The people looked so beautiful, because they ignored me. I went back to the hostel, even though everybody else was going out, and read myself to sleep listening to the foot traffic and the taxis. The next day I started looking for her, according to my original plans."

Philip opened his hands to Sam. "But you said you found her. You said you think you may have found her."

"Yeah," Sam replied. "I really think I might have. I mean, I haven't exactly found her yet. *Here.* I think I know where she'll *be.*"

"Are you going to tell me?"

Sam restacked the three books. "I went to Seville. Made all my stops there. Then back to Madrid for one day. Finding nothing. Bullshit. Just people who knew her or saw her. It was like I was only *verifying* her existence. Then I went to Barcelona and stayed at Tom's place right from the start. I told him what I was doing and he said that I might as well run these errands for him since they took me to the places I needed to go. It was after I got to the Haupt house in Corte and stayed there for a while that I started doing another search. To go along with this planned one. I saw all those books. The smell, the way the light shone through the stacks. I walked through all of them. I sat among them for hours, looking at their spines. I fell asleep in them. It was there I figured something out. I started doing a real simple thing as I ran Tom's errands and my own stupid little investigations. I started running Web searches for news stories about books. I don't know. I didn't—I didn't know what I was doing, really, I just searched Spanish, English, and Portuguese, because those are her languages. I only looked for stories that were current. New ones came up every day. Five, six a day, from all over the world. People buying rare books, finding rare books. People banning books, burning them. Reading them together, reading them aloud together. Whole towns acting out a book or organizing a tour according to a book set there. I just made it a little hobby, you know. Something to do in the cracks of my schedule. It's real easy to find wireless in this country. In the big cities, at least. Even Tangier. I didn't think it would really get me anywhere. But I also thought about the note she left. She sent copies of it to me and Nicole. Along with our books. Any mission she could do would have to involve books. Right?"

"Yeah," Philip said. "Anywhere books would gather."

"In Tangier, I found this." He dug into his backpack and removed a printout, which he handed to Philip. "I mean, it's not from Tangier. I just went online in this café there, while having tea. I could have found it sitting anywhere. Even New Brunswick."

Philip read the printout. It was a news story, a few days old, from the L.A. *Times*. It was about a man in São Gonçalo, Brazil, who had started collecting books and cramming them into his little home. Carlos Leite was an illiterate construction worker. He was fifty-one and poor. On a job site one day, he found six thick red encyclopedias on the rubbish heap. The foreman told him he could take them. From that point on, he began collecting free books from people. He asked everybody about books they wanted to give away. Leite shelved the volumes in his São Gonçalo home in the poor outskirts of Rio de Janeiro. Then he opened up his house to anyone who wanted to come in and read or borrow the books. Schoolkids flock there. They learn to read there. Professors find volumes not available at their universities. Leite has everything. After just two years, he has over ten thousand volumes, all catalogued and organized by Maria, his companion. He still cannot read. His cycling club calls him the Madman of São Gonçalo. But in his sleep, every night, he claims, he dreams that he is reading his books. The volumes are still coming in and he does not know how he will keep up with them, care for them.

"If she's not in São Gonçalo," said Sam, "I think she will be. If I could find that story, she could."

"There's some probability to it," Philip replied. "Maybe enough to travel to Brazil."

"Enough for you."

Philip eyed the article again, but did not read it. He could tell Sam how many places like the Haupt home there were in this world. He had been to others, here, in the States, in Mexico. Irma could find them. Money and education did not play necessary roles in their formation. Throughout the mountain state of Michoacán, Mexico, she followed an interconnected chain of informal libraries dating back to the Revolution. The libraries were in homes, cafés, inns, churches, bars, and hotel lobbies. Some were modest and informally organized, while others were gargantuan and rigorously catalogued. They remain somewhat underground. In *The Theory of Peter Navratil*, Peter tracks Sylvia along this hidden string of libraries. Books have to be protected from a lot of things, she told him. From molds to regimes, zealots to publishers. She no doubt knew about the Leite house in São Gonçalo. Maybe one day she would have to go there, because each book house had its interesting traits; this one appeared to have more than a few. Carlos Leite dreaming he is reading the books would intrigue her, perhaps remind her of how she read those first ten novels, at the age of nine, without actually *reading* them. But to her, the Leite house could only be one of dozens she knows in more out-of-the-way places than a town on the outskirts of Rio de Janeiro. For Philip, the article had an effect opposite the one Sam intended. It did not find Irma. It lost her even more.

"Will you go there?" asked Sam.

"Yes."

Sam looked away, stared out the train window. They were climbing into the Sierra Morena and the mountains were covered in live oak and yellow and orange wildflowers and velvet patches of crocus. The rocks were darker, wet-looking. Sam folded his arms low across his waist, as though gripping a stomachache, and began rocking slightly.

"But not right away," he said. "Not with me."

"Look, Sam—"

"No. It's okay," he said, still rocking stiffly, arms pushed across his waist. "I'll find a way to go. I'll find her. I think . . ." He looked at the passing mountains. "I think she is the most remarkable thing on this earth. She keeps herself free, Philip. And not in a way that hurts others. She ignores the rules that should be ignored. She lives by what she learns and she learns by feeling. Being with her anywhere would make that place beautiful. I think you know that. I like to think you do. And knowing that should blow away anything to do with probability. I can find her."

"You can't find her. Not like this. Not like how you are now." As he watched Sam hunch into silence, jaw tightened, the cords of his neck drawn, face turned toward the window, Philip cursed Irma again. Not for what she had done to Sam and Nicole, but for leading him to this point, to where he felt he had to hurt someone he cared for, hurt him *for* her. He cursed her but he held himself short of blaming her. He wasn't sure there was any blame. And he kept that possibility—that possibility of blame—to himself, for himself, believing it might be his, and believing it might be of value to him. The way you hold back the values of e, i, or π until the point where they are most revealing in the equation.

"You can't find her, Sam."

"Why?" Sam asked without looking away from the window and the mountains beyond. "Look how far I've gotten."

"But look how quickly I got you. To where you are." Philip censored all the befuddlement, tangents, and luck involved, convinced himself somewhat that he knew all along what he was doing, that it took insight to follow a little yellow book onto the wrong train.

"And you *can* find her?"

"If you'll let me. If you help me by sending me what you find. Like the Carlos Leite house. And by being with your sister."

"You want me to go home to avoid trouble. Trouble for yourself. Trouble from Mom and Dad."

"No. I honestly don't fear that. Maybe I should, but I don't. I want you to go home because you are not valuable enough."

Sam glared at him. Philip, for the first time, knew what it was like to stand directly in the path of Sam's race, to be the object of that wild yearning gaze that fell over his expression as he looked past the finish, past mere victory.

"Irma," said Philip, as though invoking. "One thing she does not understand well is how deeply her vocations run, compared to others. And how much they are a value to others. If you really want to follow a path similar to hers, then first increase your worth."

"Like you?"

"Like I failed to do. I was given value. By fortune. And by my parents. By strange, wonderful parents. She saw that value in a different way. She tried to get me to carry it in a different way. Maybe I finally let her down. Let go and dropped it. Maybe that's why I didn't get to go with her."

"Would you have gone with her?"

"In a heartbeat. Wouldn't anyone?"

"No," said Sam. "Not anyone."

Philip tried to soften the air.

"I'm not sending you home. I'm taking you back to Seville. Back to her, no? Her passage? I want to show you those things you missed. To show you what you may be up against. How long the race really is. So stay with me a little longer. Then go your way. I won't prevent you. I won't even object."

They read their books in silence, letting the train keep them together, letting their mutual destination be enough. In chapter sixty-five of Part II, Philip discovered a torn page. He realized it was from Lucia's knee, from when she knelt before him in the darkness of Ionic Street. The tear was small, but it changed direction and cut into the words. The first time Irma ever made any serious effort to demonstrate book repair, she explained to him the rule of reversibility. Some labs—most university labs, for instance—abide by the rule without exception. You do not make any attempt at repair that cannot be reversed. Undone. She waved her bone folder over an open book that had a severely torn page. But I don't abide by the rule, Pip. For one, how can you discover what can and cannot be undone without trying new things? Also, if you happen to alter a book, what's the true loss? They're not fossils. They're not relics. They're more alive if you treat them the way I do. If you see what can be done with them. No? I mean, what kind of lives would we all lead if we could live by the rule of reversibility?

Even in math, he agreed, it doesn't work. She lifted her brow in surprise. He explained. Everyone thinks you can back up in an equation gone wrong. That you can erase your way back to a certain point in the equation. But it doesn't work that way. Instead you have to observe the equation as a whole and retest specific bases and borrowed formulae and precedence. If you tried to poke your way through an equation following the rule of reversibility, you would discover nothing.

She kissed his cheek, giving him a good grade, marking one of those rare moments when his science and her craft converged.

Again, she waved her bone folder over the torn page. The torn page is by far the most common repair. Yet it is one of the most challenging, especially if you want to abide by the rule of reversibility. I get stacks of children's books with torn pages. You know, some family heirloom an overexcited toddler rips. I think I've repaired page thirty-nine of *Ferdinand the Bull* at least fifty times.

Each piece of paper, she explained, has a specific grain which generally follows the direction of the print. But not always. So you have to determine that first. You can only repair in one direction at a time. Even the slightest turn, for one or two millimeters, must be done separately. Each repair takes a half day's drying time. Then you must determine the stability of the ink. If the repair paste, or even water, causes the ink to run, then you have to resort to archive tape and feature the repair rather than hide it. Or you just leave the tear and honor the rule of reversibility. Or you can do what I like to do. I like to try and re-create the words. That's why I photograph each torn page before I begin. I might even change a word or two, if I thought I could get away with it. I've never been caught.

She slipped wax paper beneath the torn page, then carefully brushed two strips of Japanese paper with paste. Working from the center of the page outward, she ran the two strips along the grain of the tear, ending at the point where it changed direction. She placed two pressboards over and under the page and then looked up. When I'm done, you will not be able to distinguish this page from the rest.

In chapter sixty-five of Part II, he discovered that the Knight of the White Moon was, once again, actually Bachelor Sansón Carrasco, the friend sent by concerned villagers to save Quixote from his own madness. When Bachelor Carrasco first posed as the Knight of the Mirrors, he was overconfident and careless. His well-intended disguise backfired, as his defeat at the lance of Quixote only fueled the old knight's madness. In the guise of the Knight of the White Moon, Carrasco drops Quixote and brings him near death on that Barcelona sand, where he tries to no avail to elicit Quixote's renouncement of Dulcinea. But you do not discover the Knight of the White Moon's identity until this chapter. Until this chapter, you share some of Quixote's madness. The tear in the page hooked across the paragraphs depicting this revelation, and Philip had to carefully piece and hold the paper together in order to read it.

THIRTEEN

Siesta had ended in Seville and they were in the labyrinth of Barrio Santa Cruz, the old Jewish Quarter. This was only Sam's third time here and already he knew it was best to throw away the map. In fifteen hundred years, no one had successfully mapped the quarter. They passed students with backpacks holding limp brochures and looking skyward, uttering to each other the names of the streets so carefully inlaid in tile on the ochre walls. Sometimes they would see five names, but only four streets. Sometimes it could be two names for five streets. The walls, like the stone walkways, were clean, the only uniform aspect to the neighborhood, which just added to the confusion. You could ask directions, and that would only get you to another point inside the labyrinth, where you would then have to ask someone else for more directions. And that would get you to another point. And so on, until you found the place you sought, or until you just gave up and wandered your way to the cathedral plaza, or to the boulevard Menéndez Pelayo, or back to where you entered at San Esteban. But you could just as easily find yourself running into the impenetrable wall of the Alcázar, or bottoming out on Juderia, or caught in the small wonders and gazebos of the Jardines de Murillo. Often, on maps of the city, the quarter was depicted as nothing more than a triangular mosaic mortared by unnamed streets. Irma once pointed out to him what she called Franco's widows, old women who opened their doors to release their lapdogs for brief runs on the stone walks. These widows survived Franco and their husbands, seemed happy enough, and haunted the empty churches in flowered dresses. If you asked them directions, they smiled kindly and spoke rapid Spanish that led you to the nearest bakery or market, where you would then have to ask for further directions. If you listened closely enough, you would hear just a tail of bitterness over the fact that they had to survive Franco and you did not. They're our guides, Pip, she told him. You ricochet from one to the other until you find your way in—or out.

Philip and Sam, toting their bags, stood at the base of a church tower.

"Which one is this?" Philip asked, gazing up at the belfry where the orange eye of sunset shone.

"I thought you knew."

Philip shook his head. "Maybe Bartolomé."

"Do we really have to go there?" Sam paused, looked back down two divergent alleyways, and said, "This'll be my third time there, Philip, asking questions. They were nice the first time."

"I need to show you the books."

"The books?"

"You mean you didn't look at the books?"

Sam squinted, pretended to peer down a third narrow street named either Ashes or Happiness. "I noticed a few here and there on shelves in the halls and entry."

"At last count, there were twenty-eight hundred and forty-seven volumes there."

"Oh," said Sam.

"She's restored several."

A very small boy with a soccer ball wedged beneath one arm passed them. Philip asked if he could show them how to get to Plaza de Las Cruces. *La pensión*. The boy looked at them once, quickly, and kept on walking without answer. He then looked back from twenty meters on, seemingly disgruntled that they had not moved, and waved for them to follow.

"You fit right in here," Philip told Sam as they began following the boy.

The boy led them to the entrance to an old monastery and told them to ask the woman behind the rope which plaza they meant. The woman, who wore a long red apron, told them to turn left at the next street and to keep walking that direction. The next street looked like a dead end, but when they entered it, they found that it turned sharply and became a slender passageway. They had to twist their shoulders in order to walk it. This took them to the wrong plaza, where they stopped to have a sherry and olives. They could see the last rays of the sun cutting across the tips of the surrounding buildings, giving a painterly caul to the rooftop anten-nae and clotheslines. But where they sat, in the walled depths of the tiny plaza, a warm evening had already settled.

Philip could sense that Sam was anxious to move. To either return to his own chase or to return home to save Nicole. He could tell that Sam's thoughts, which always gathered like birds in the sky, shifting, then swirling into one direction, were all heading one way. It was the same way he ran his best races, with the first laps as a sort of gathering of strength and will, then with the final laps marked by an almost ter-rifying pace, relentless expenditure and focus. But Philip could not tell toward which direction Sam would ultimately spiral. He wanted Sam to return home—not for his own sake, not out of fear of Rebecca and Andrew, and not out of any embrace of convention. And part of him did want to see Sam continue on his trajectory toward Irma. But he wanted Sam to return home to save Nicole. Not by comforting her, but by keep-ing alive in her all that Irma had given her. To be in conspiracy with her, brother and sister. To not wreck what Irma had wrought so far, though what she had wrought angered him.

"Stay with me a bit more," said Philip. "I want to show you things. One we have to find in the *pensión*. Another I can take you to this eve-ning, but it has to be at a very specific time. Then you can leave whenever you need, okay?"

Sam stood from the table, shouldering his bag. When Philip began to stand with him, Sam shook his head, waved him back with his hand. "No," he said. "I feel I've gone backwards. I've let you take me back-wards. Here we are, trapped in this tiny plaza. You can't see anything from here. I can hardly breathe here."

He lifted his arms to show Philip how small the space was, how big the coppery sky above them, how soon he could fly.

Philip took him back. "Do you know who really won that race?"

Sam dropped his arms slowly, turned his head slightly, suspiciously. He remained standing above the table, looking down.

Philip answered. "There was no way you could have run with me that evening. Over the grass. I could have beaten the greatest of runners that evening. I took what you and Nick gave me and crushed it further. I ran with relish to my pretty friend. To Mexico with her, to the beginning of worlds that have now passed. From your mother, Nicole, *you*. Not like a coward runs, Sam, but in the way a victor runs."

Sam sat down, not to listen but to point, to wrestle, it seemed, putting an elbow to the table. Philip continued before Sam could say anything.

"But I didn't win that race, either. Your sister did. She knew before any of us what it was all about. She was starting to learn way back then what would happen here, now." Philip pointed to the middle of the table. "She told you to let me go away. To go to my pretty friend. Then over your head she winked at me. I see that wink now. For what it was. So unlike her. Where do you think she got it? Who do you think gave it to her?"

Sam slouched back in his chair, leaving one hand to the table.

"I'm not taking you backwards," Philip told him. "I'm taking you to her. The best way. The way only I know. Your little searches and excursions and errands, grand as they may seem, will start to feel worn very soon. You won't even be going backwards. You'll be spinning in place.

"So come or don't come."

They eventually asked their way to Plaza de Las Cruces, where Irma's favorite *pensión* formed one of seven corners that came together around a little knoll of roses, shrubs, and wrought-iron benches. Many Sevillanos and tourists were out now that the sun had set. The air remained just as warm, the stucco walls baking. On the far corner of the quaint plaza, a vendor dressed like Carmen sold fans, marionettes, and souvenir castanets. She took turns demonstrating all three in brief performances.

Inside the *pensión* they did not ask any questions. Philip secured himself a room and they left their bags there. Then they walked the halls and perused the alcoves, looking at the books on the shelves. The books were

not organized. Some were lined up neatly, some were stacked haphaz-
ardly. They were for guests to borrow. It was easy to spot those Irma had
re-bound; they looked newer and were dyed with deep colors. The ones
she had merely repaired were much trickier to spot, but Philip showed
Sam how the spine bowed outward more on those volumes.

"If she repairs a book, in any way," he told Sam, "she'll always renew
the hinges. That returns a new bow shape to the spine."

One of the most discreet repairs you can make, she told him during
another of her demonstrations, is to secure the hinges inside the spine.
She waved her bone folder above a hapless-looking volume, one that
stood crippled and skewed. Everything happens inside, she explained.
She withdrew a long knitting needle and coated it with a very thin layer
of paste. This she inserted along one hinge of the spine. It took precision and strength to guide the needle firmly between leather and paper
without tearing either. She capped the end knob of the needle with her
thumb, her knuckle whitening with the exertion. With the needle fully
inserted, she then spun it delicately between thumb and forefinger, infus-
ing the paste behind the very edge of the spine. She repeated this proce-
dure for the other hinge and then placed the book in a lightly set press.
When it was cured, the book balanced straight on its end, like a new
volume with a tensile spine.

"But we're not looking for those, either," he told Sam. "We're looking
for one she didn't finish."

"Maybe there isn't one," replied Sam as he gazed along a shelf in an
alcove. "Maybe she finished the last one and that's when it was time for
her to leave."

"Maybe," said Philip. "But she always had at least one more to do. In
places like these. It's true that she liked, in general, to leave things finished.
But she liked messing with books even more. So . . ." He shrugged.

It was difficult to see in the dimming halls and alcoves, but they
slid the most tattered-looking volumes from their perches, flipped
through them searching for notes or blank, crisply cut bookmarks. They
found three on which she had done some preliminary examinations.
Maybe she had already prodded and creased them with her bone folder.

One had a note written on a bookmark: *Not 1805—older.* Philip could see the effects of Irma's handwriting play across Sam's expression—first sad, then bemused.

"I can find these in just about any city I know she's been to," he told Sam. "I wanted to show you that. I wanted to show you that I could do that. That I was not just a buffoon pretending to search and talk stupidly about love to her young cousins. I needed to show you that I am not taking your discovery in the papers lightly. That I am not taking Brazil lightly. I'm just taking it in a different way. Okay?"

Sam nodded, still looking at her note.

"But there is probably more," Philip told him. "Here."

"More?"

"These are nothing. She's only grazed these. Marked them for later. It's probable that she's really dug into one or two more. Somewhere on these shelves."

"Couldn't we ask?"

Philip shook his head. "They let her work at her discretion. And she never believed in taking books out of circulation. I can find what we're looking for faster than they could. They could help a little. But I figured you wanted to stay out of their way as much as possible."

In a hall corner illuminated by streetlight through stained glass, they found the book they wanted, stacked with five others on a simple night-stand beside a reading chair. Bound in linen, both coverboards were cracked down the middle. The spine had been torn away. Several quires and pages had come loose. The entire volume held together much like an overstuffed folder, with pages beginning to slide in different directions. Irma had bookmarked it in five places. They did not open it for fear that pages, notes, and bookmarks would fall out, their order lost. They brought the volume back to Philip's room, where they set it carefully on a small writing table. The title page was gone and Irma had replaced it with a flyleaf entitled *Zed.* Some of the loose pages and quires seemed to be of different size and texture. All the pages were not in numerical order and some page sequences were repeated, but Philip and Sam were careful to maintain the order she had left (unless, of course, some

careless guest had dropped and regathered the whole thing). The language was Portuguese. Margin notes, by previous owners, were scribbled throughout in different-color pen, much like you would find in an
undergrad's used textbook. Most of these margin notes were written in
Spanish. Irma's margin notes, all in light pencil, were written in English.
Sam read bits of each. The Spanish marginalia he could read with con-
certed effort; he could, like Philip, understand only those brief parts of
the Portuguese text that resembled Spanish; Irma's penciled notes were
clear and neat, scratched in fine calligraphy. From it all they gathered
that *Zed* was a biography, or a novel written as biography. The name
Zed appeared a few times and only inside dialogue. They could surmise
that Zed was most likely a woman and that she was the book's narrative
voice, but they could not determine if she was recounting her own biography or someone else's. The names Adão and Fatima appeared often
enough to be biographical subjects.

"It could be about both," said Sam. He held a segment of the book,
while Philip held the rest.

"Or all three. There's someone I can show this to."

"Can you take the books out?" Sam asked.

"I think as long as you're checked in here. But really they like to keep
them in the building. Taking them to a café for a coffee or drink would
probably be okay. But it doesn't matter," he told Sam. "I think Lucia will
come here."

They took a night run along the Guadalquivir. Philip, feeling rested
and relatively free of pain, was able to go fast enough to stay with Sam.
The river was bent and deep, walled like a harbor. They could easily
imagine the black silhouettes of Columbus's ships, furled, waiting to
finally set out for the New World. They passed the Torre del Oro and
then the bullring. To their left, the dark river reflected the lights of Tri-
ana. Enough pedestrians filled the walkway to make the run feel like a
race. Philip could sense Sam testing him, seeing how fast he could go,
how hard. Philip called out Irma's mile markers as they passed each. He
stopped to turn back at mile four, the Barqueta Bridge. He told Sam that
if he really wanted to go ten, he could run all the way to the Alamillo
Bridge, then turn back. Sam waved and ran onward, increasing his pace.

He had the colors of his sister about him as he ran in the river light, with the sparkle of a city around him, the burnished innocence of a penny. Philip dripped sweat in the hot air, which already felt thickened with the breath of night comers. He weakened halfway back and rested at mile six, a stone bench hollowed into the river wall. She writes in the margins of *Zed*: If you've made it this far, dear Pip, then I do owe you an apology. I'm sorry I had to leave like this. I wasn't sure how hurt you'd feel. But if you are this far, then you are hurt. And I am sorry. I shouldn't underestimate your math. How far it takes you. How far it takes your feelings.

How many times had he rested with her on this bench? He knew the answer. Dozens. The salt of their sweat was soaked deep in the stone. Across Paseo de Cristóbal Colón, crowds gathered outside the bullring waiting for the evening fights which featured apprentice matadors. He braced his hands to the bench and leaned forward, taking in full, measured breaths. She wasn't going to come and rest beside him. The one thing he needed to ask her in order to discover the full equation of his life was this: What did I do to deserve abandonment?

He understood that he had sought the conventions that she dismissed. But he never hid that intention from her. He agreed that he was like her, that convention was more than just bothersome—that it was crippling. They lived their lives behind a thin veil of decorum and compromise. They had each been born with a gift that might allow them to function in that position, disguised, pressed to that thin veil, their profiles outlined, their breath fluttering through. You are the only other one I have ever met, she once told him, who so deeply and compulsively sees *anything* and automatically begins seeking alternatives. I test through words, Pip, and you test through numbers. But we both see a corner of a building and think: Why does that have to be a corner, a right angle? Running through Seville with you, at least I see evidence of many more who must have thought somewhat as we do. I don't want to change the world, Pip. And you certainly don't. So maybe together we can find another. Live in another.

As the city's bullfights faded and night fell, Philip led Sam past the tourists in the river cafés, past the crowds about the Plaza Alfalfa and Alameda de

Hercules, past the films projected on high stone walls, through the music played from plywood stages, finally into the route of shadows. From the narrow streets flamenco wails carried through the night air, lifted on the thrum of guitars. The voices floated as distant howls, sometimes a man, sometimes a woman trembling out words of love and pain and impossibility, threatening, luring. A few horse carriages still waited on the Town Hall plaza, fishing for night stragglers trying to make their way to the river, but even they appeared phantom, driverless, out of time, haunting rather than existing. Sam had showered and dressed for travel. His bags were packed and propped on the floor of Philip's room. There was a late-night bullet train to Madrid. He was barely with Philip as they approached the Town Hall from the fountain. The cajoling flamenco more than anything seemed to be leading Sam now as he looked up trying to gauge the direction of the calls, the traipse of their echoes. Sam took the lead as they approached the archway at the near end of the building, the filigreed passageway between Plaza de San Francisco and Plaza Nueva.

"I've already come here." He spoke over his shoulder. "Several times. Daytime, nighttime. Early morning."

He walked into the dark archway while Philip stopped before the entrance. "She told me all about it once. Cervantes's arch. Where novelists come to get their ideas. Where he got his, or so they say." His words echoed in the stone hollow.

Philip spoke from outside the arch. "She claims it's the only place in the world where her vocation and mine come together. Cervantes's words and Napier's spirals. Stories and logarithms."

He reached into the archway and gently led Sam by the arm, backing him out. "But I could have shown you that anytime. Come stand with me and wait a bit."

Sam flexed his brow in confusion as they stood in the light and sound of the nearby fountain. One of the horse carriages gave up and clopped off toward another plaza. The remaining horse huffed in its sleep. A man passed through the light of the fountain. His hair and beard were dirty and uncombed. His broken sandals flapped on the stone walk. He wore a tattered coat in the very warm night and even from a distance they could smell his sweat. He paid no notice to Philip or Sam as he walked toward the archway, paused once, then entered. He leaned against the wall, near one pillar where he was absorbed in shadow. In the tongue of light that fell across the archway floor appeared the man's black stream of urine making its way over the stones to an iron drain. Then he passed through the far end of the archway and disappeared into the darkness of Plaza Nueva.

"We used to come and watch him arrive," he told Sam. "If we ever needed to find one another while we were in Seville, we could come here, at this time. He doesn't always piss. Sometimes he just leans against the wall, resting, thinking, waiting. She claims it's Cervantes."

Philip sat on the lip of the fountain. Even this late into the night, the granite still carried the day's heat. The water smelled like boiled onions. Sam started to head toward the archway as though that was where he was off to. Philip touched his arm.

"Wait. There's more."

The street cleaners arrived in the plaza. With the sound of their truck, the last horse carriage awoke and trotted away. The cleaners were one woman and two men dressed in jumpsuits decorated with reflective geometric patches and stripes that glowed silvery green beneath the streetlamps. They connected their fire hose to a stanchion on the Town Hall wall. The woman held the nozzle, one of the men worked the valve, and the other man held a large broom. They began blasting the stone with a powerful jet of water while the broom man brushed and scrubbed the well-trod areas. The almost sweet scent of wet paper filled the air. They cleaned Cervantes's arch, blasting its floor and walls, moving through it on their way to Plaza Nueva, dragging their canvas hose with them. Philip and Sam looked over Plaza de San Francisco, now wet and sparkling beneath the streetlamps.

"Come," said Philip. "I'll walk you to your train."

But they missed the last train to Madrid. Sam checked his bags in a locker and, instead of returning to the *pensión*, they walked the Sevillan night. They returned to the Jewish Quarter, to its very bottom, where darkness pooled on Juderia, and where the intermittent flamenco wails

converged against the ancient wall of the Alcázar. From its shadow they
watched formally dressed wedding stragglers spill from beneath bright
canopies, their metallic dresses and tuxedos seeming angular and somehow fitting in the night music. They walked upward into the Quarter,
following the rough Moorish wall of the Alcázar until it breached into
the Jardines de Murillo, throwing them suddenly into the soft white
light of a garden concert where a small, formally dressed crowd of Sevil-
lans listened to eighteenth century pieces played on oddly shaped, oddly
strung guitars. Fireworks from the river burst high over the patio, mildly
distracting the crowd. Sam looked upward again, not toward the lights
in the sky, but to the flamenco calls that still made it past the wall. His
eyes seemed to calculate the direction in what Philip was surprised to
recognize as mathematical thought.

Would she have taken him to the bar, the nameless one on Levies,
one of the real ones, the ones that Lorca tried to save before he was disappeared? Did she tell him about them, how the people in them did not
smile, wear flouncy dresses and boleros? How they hissed at you when
you first stepped among them, to see if you could be one of them?

They slid back into the Quarter. Philip could not tell who was leading, Sam in the pull of the nearest flamenco wail, the most palpable guitar strum, or himself following Irma's sure path through the dark streets
to Levies, in the very heart of the old and tragic barrio. They found their
way to that unnamed flamenco bar, that real one, marked only by the
open jaw of light from its doorway, where people outside conversed only
in rehearsed steps on the cobblestone, their heels clicking in the music.
A man in a Mexican wedding shirt, standing guard just inside the doorway, stopped them at first, then appeared to recognize them, a leather
talisman dangling from Sam's hair or the crimp in Philip's worn boots.
He waved them in with a low swoop of his arm.

Philip and Sam moved across the wooden floor, through the sparkle
of a cheap glitter ball to the bar, and ordered beers. Two guitarists played
in syncopation. Someone deep in the crowd clicked percussion sticks,
intermittent tocks in the muscular strumming. Several dancers hammered the floor with their nailed heels, all dressed in street clothes. When

the song ended, the two best dancers remained on the floor as the rest found seats and drinks. The two dancers were young. The man wore a checkered sport jacket and black cowboy boots. His white hair was cut short and combed earnestly forward. The woman wore jeans and a white T-shirt. Her black hair hung loose, still damp and tousled from the previous dance. They began searching the audience. Everybody in the bar seemed to understand what was occurring. The guitars played lightly, but building as the search continued, the dancers moving as a couple from table to table, then snaking along the bar toward Philip and Sam.

Philip put his arm around Sam's shoulders, something he had never thought to do even when Sam was a boy. He didn't care what Sam would do. He pulled Sam to him, watching his profile, feeling his shoulders curl in his grip. Sam looked down into his beer, his eyes glittering with movement as though watching what was to come. Then he looked at Philip, his head still lowered, like someone softly betrayed, delivered.

The dancers moved along the bar, toward them, swaying more, making it even more of a dance. The crowd was watching those few left to choose. The guitars were quickening, raising heartbeats, spinning the glitter ball, it seemed.

"I lied," Sam whispered. "About the fields. I returned there alone. I went there alone, all the time. I ran faster each time. Barefoot even when there was snow on the grass, even when it was too dark, even when I hated you. Nicky won every time. Saved me every time, from hating you."

He straightened out of Philip's embrace and let the dancers finally select him, each gently touching his arm. Wordlessly, clearly seeking permission, they looked at Philip. Then the young woman, who had a mild overbite which heightened her Castilian accent, asked him if they could borrow his son. Philip did not check with Sam and said yes.

The guitars' tempo lifted as the dancers positioned Sam in the center of the floor. An old singer, a woman sitting beside the guitarists, leaning forward against her cane, began the mournful flamenco trills and calls. As the opening part of the dance, the couple circled Sam and then bound his hands behind his back with a red silk scarf and blindfolded him with a black silk band. Their dance circled Sam. Sometimes they faced him, sometimes they shouldered away from him. The rapid clicking of their heels must have sounded frightening behind the blindfold. The dancers' arms stretched high, kinetic and dangerous, and their fingers twitched, miming flames. They whirled around Sam, their hips sometimes glancing him, trembling through him. Sam, as though he knew, looked upward, stretching his throat, exposing it to the dancers and the crowd. Philip could not understand the words to the song, if they were words and not just cries of anguish. Mesmerized, locked by the music, he could not even bring himself to lean forward. Sam's shoulders were stretched back as though the scarf were lashed tight, and the long silk trails flickered blood-red in the wind of the dancers.

He held him closest, just before this, thought he had him for once. He closed his eyes to try to hear the thrum and percussion of the guitars the way Sam, blindfolded, must have heard them, felt them. Instead he found himself knowing, in the raw cry of the song, what it was like to run to the depths of such an ancient place, to throw yourself forward with broken heart, to race against spirits that barely touched the earth, to face return. When he opened his eyes, the dancers appeared more arrogant, knifing their steps, taunting Sam with their bodies, their stomachs even touching him, the man's arm hooking around Sam's exposed throat, the woman's hair whipping his face as she whirled, arms raised, fingers together. When Philip tensed forward to save him, the old singer's cry warned him back with words of pain and broken vows. He could feel the witness of the crowd, waiting to see what he might do.

Sam stretched higher. He parted his lips as though the dancers were spinning the air from him. Each dancer, still in sway, took hold of the ends of the red sash that bound his wrists, pulling tighter under the commands of the singer and the pizzicato and strum of the guitars. Then the song and the dancers fell away from him, together like veils tearing. Like matadors, the dancers took their bows. The singer hunched over her cane. They treated Sam as though he had been vanished by the magic of their dance. Philip stood and loosened the sash from Sam's wrists as the crowd slid around the bar and the dancers and the guitarists. He did not give it back. In his hands the silk was heavy, liquid, and warm with sweat.

I fear our respective, intersecting worlds are about to spin from our grasp, she pencils in the margin of a loose section of *Zed* that falls to the floor of his *pensión*. I've always carried that fear while you have shrugged it—the primary difference between you and me—but it has come on stronger of late. I even saw it once, in the black archway at the left end of Juderia, the one that no longer leads anywhere. I saw it as a dark figure moving within the even darker arch, like a swirl in oil. I ran from it. Maybe I need to run to it.

He writes in pencil, on the same page, an equation. In the margin of the next page, he translates the equation: I need—need unto death—to see you at least one more time, to hold you at least one more time, to say a sad and awkward good-bye.

He finally parted with Sam in the scatter of dawn shadows in the courtyard of the old tobacco factory—where once Carmen worked but which was now a central hub of the university. The city was finally quiet, the streets empty. When Philip moved to continue along with Sam toward the station, Sam stayed him with a touch to his shoulder.

"Stay here," Sam told him. "I want to walk to the station alone. I want to leave you here. I'm going to come back right here. Or Salamanca. Whichever will have me."

He backed away, keeping his eyes on Philip, taking him in. "Thanks for this night. I'm glad you made me miss that train." Then he added just before he turned away, "Find her."

Backpack slung over his shoulder, he crossed the tobacco factory courtyard, passed through the columned entry, and hurried into electric strips of sunrise which shone along the edges of the shop windows and Plexiglas bus kiosks of Menéndez Pelayo. Philip remained in the courtyard, watching Sam's lone figure hurry up the boulevard. He forgot the words and explanations he had gathered, feeling muted by Sam's sudden good-bye, pillared by his final two words. "Find her" was the opening sentence of *The Theory of Peter Navratil*. He finds her in the last sentence.

Philip rested in the Pensión de Las Cruces throughout the rest of the day, sometimes reading *Quixote*, sometimes perusing the marginalia of *Zed*. To take some air, he would shamble out to the tiny plaza and read on a shady bench, in the overripe smell of the roses wilting in the sun.

For siesta, he had a beer and sandwich at a place he knew by Jardines del Valle, where a section of the old city wall still remained. He returned to the *pensión*, intentionally walking the sun-baked sides of the streets so that he was drowsy enough to fall asleep immediately upon reaching his bed. He dreamed chapters sixty-nine and seventy, not yet knowing if they were written by Irma or Cervantes. The beautiful, mischievous, independent, roguish Altisidora, whose strange love for Quixote goes unrequited, returns in these chapters. First as an apparent corpse, borne on a catafalque, illuminated by torches. Quixote and Sancho find her even more striking in death: displayed on the catafalque was the dead body of a damsel so beautiful that her beauty made death itself beautiful. Her head, crowned with a garland of fragrant flowers, lay on a brocade pillow, and her hands, crossed on her bosom, held a branch of yellow triumphant palm. The events that occurred were so surreal—Altisidora awakes on the catafalque, reclines, shoulder lifted, addresses the funeralgoers and Quixote—that upon waking Philip could not sort between what he had read and what he had dreamed. Until he reread the chapters and discovered that his dream made more sense than the book.

He showered, shaved, dressed in his freshest clothes, and staggered into the late Sevillan afternoon, along—it seemed—with the rest of the city. He made it to the train station on Avenida Kansas City in time to meet Lucia, but he refrained from greeting her. Instead he remained hidden and he followed her to Maria Luisa Park, where they had agreed to rendezvous by the frogs. She carried a shoulder bag as she walked the busy sidewalk of Menéndez Pelayo. Traffic was loud, making it easier to track her without being noticed. He believed that in the cover of the street noise, the many quick horns and buzzing scooters, he could step closer. It was the first time he had done anything like this. I like to pick random people, Irma once told him, and watch them, follow them. Not necessarily interesting-looking people, just some individual I happen to see. I follow them and see the little things they do that make them different. The way one particular woman looks at the ground around a parking meter, checking for dropped coins, before spending any of her own. The way a man might happen to look sadly at a mannequin, her smile reminding him of somebody. I track them, watch, until I get to know them just a bit. Sometimes I follow people I know. Sometimes I follow you.

At first he found it somewhat fearful, watching Lucia walk to their meeting place without knowing he was behind her. He felt self-conscious, a distinct sense of trespass. Men and teenage boys looked at her as they passed, then looked at him with an implied wink in their gaze. But when she crossed the boulevard—it was so busy one could hardly make it even using the crosswalk and lights—his feelings shifted. There was no clear reason for her to cross. The park was on the side where she had been walking and the sun was low and its light seemed scattered at all angles across either side of Menéndez Pelayo. He stayed with her, wondering if she first planned to meet someone else or if she would make a call at the phone kiosk. She paused to look at her reflection in the Plexiglas window of a bus stop. She raised her hands as if to adjust her hair, which was gathered into a chignon, but then halted and did nothing. She continued walking, nothing hurried about her. When she reached the Moorish gardens, she veered in and strolled among the small fountains, pathways, and playgrounds, still heading in the direction of their rendezvous. Children played hide-and-seek among the shady hedges and some played a condensed game of soccer on the clay patch beneath the Columbus fountain. From the gardens she passed into the grounds surrounding the tobacco factory and walked there, continuing in the same direction. University students smoked cigarettes just outside the huge open doorways. Their postures were collapsed, still bent over their desks, but they watched her pass and their faces, men and women, lifted like flowers. From the tobacco factory, she led him to the tree-covered theater complex and then crossed the street to the park.

Inside the gate, he let her vanish into the maze of the park. He realized she simply chose to walk the more interesting, slightly less direct route. This roused an odd, undirected envy in him. He would have taken the most direct path, thought exclusively of getting to her. He still could not convince himself that she was not acting in some way, performing. Performing not for him, but for someone else, under someone's direction. In *The Theory of Peter Navratil*, Sylvia leads Peter by tricking him into believing he is leading her. She and Feli—the actress who reminds him of Lucia, who looks and moves like Lucia—continue to use this method once they get him to Michoacán. When Philip first read the novel, he only realized this after reading the final sentence. He had to immediately reread the entire book, delicately holding that realization like the precious variable that allows you to complete the equation.

Maria Luisa Park was sprawling and beautiful. It contained palaces, museums, canals, fountains, and maybe a hundred different gardens—even he had not counted them. It was ungridded, angular yet amorphous, its roads and pathways exploratory. There were long trellises covered in vines and hundreds of statues of authors, thinkers, animals, insects, amphibians, reptiles, gods, and goddesses, all waiting to surprise and confuse you even more. Most of the fountains were shallow, playful, beckoning. Irma pencils in the margins of *Zed*, noting a particular passage with an arrow, If he entered, he would be heading into her world.

The park was at its busiest. People getting off work were cutting through it or meandering into it as a diversion. In the small playgrounds tucked here and there among the trees, kids called to grandparents who sat on benches watching doves. When Philip reached the edge of the clearing around the frog fountain, Lucia was there sitting on one of the tiled benches watching a group of young German travelers, probably students, splash in the water and call to each other. The fountain was a large circle with eight giant frogs sitting on the lip watching a white goose in the center. The students redirected the fountain sprays in order to splash each other. Even though two were women and two were men, they did not seem to be flirting and appeared most intrigued by the water, by their ability to aim it with their thumbs, and by the unimpressed frogs they sometimes hid behind. Lucia turned her gaze steadily from them to Philip. She smiled and patted the space next to her on the tiled bench.

"So young and already so tired of each other," she said to him as he sat down.

He gave her a confused look as he sat next to her.

"Them," she said, nodding to the German students in the water. "I'd say they've been traveling together for about a month. Began as friends, tried each other out, and now are here in this fountain, just barely friends again."

"You can know all that?"

"Sure." She put her hand to his shoulder and then slid it to the back of his neck. Her fingers were cool in the heat of the park. She lifted her face to his, but only to look. Her breath smelled of wet hay.

He kissed her gently and held her wrists, his thumbs caressing the tendons. Her lips had a quick, passing coolness, as though she had just eaten an apple. He backed away just as he began to sense falling into her.

"I ask myself," he said, "if I traveled to Spain to see you. The answer is no. But I wouldn't have come here if you were not here."

She looked askance, her smile lifting.

"I could say it better with an equation," he explained. "In it, you would be a conditional cause."

"Is that all I am?"

"That's a lot."

"I know something about conditionals." She looked down at his hold on her wrists. "From the text I'm translating. Without the conditional cause, a situation could not be. However, the conditional itself does not predict the situation."

She kissed him and pushed her tongue inside his mouth, tucking the tip in the soft pocket beneath. She drew her tongue out slowly, released his lips, and leaned away.

He touched her lips with the edge of his fingers. "Please. Before you beguile me further—"

"Beguile?" she laughed. She pushed the back of her hand against his erection. "Is that what this is?"

"It's a lot more than that. After we have sex, then I'm even more mystified. You're even more beautiful. When I see you in my thoughts and dreams, I see you looking over my books, your lips mouthing certain words. And so, before you completely cloud all my thinking, I need to ask you some things."

"That's funny," she said. "When I see you in my thoughts and dreams, your back is to me and you're facing someone else. I only ever see her black hair and the corner of her bare shoulder."

"Then you'll understand my questions."

"About the book you've found? The one only I could translate?"

"No. No books." He touched beneath her chin. "Do you know Irma? Did you lie when I first asked you?"

He felt some of the German students watching. Their calls had ended and less water was splashing.

"I did and I didn't," she said. She smiled at him, talking directly to him, holding herself to that. "She is my friend. We've been friends for fifteen years. We met in Michoacán. But we are not in cahoots. We were never really in cahoots—against you. She's told me a lot about you. A lot. But she did not send me to you, after all these years."

Philip nodded, bit his lower lip. "There is a character in one of her books. Ofelia—Feli. And another in that fake Borges story—Sefi. Those are you."

"Again," she replied, "yes and no. Those are fictions. She had me pose as her a couple of times. Just to see if you could be tricked, for only a moment. Once, while the two of you were sitting at a café in Pátzcuaro, having beers, we dressed exactly alike and switched places. She told me how to continue the conversation. It was outside, at night, and a lot of people were pushing by. You were watching some street performance involving a bunch of tumbling children in skeleton masks. I had to pretend to smoke this really awful black cigar she had left in the ashtray. You and I talked about the Days of the Dead."

He looked at her, noting carefully how she was different from Irma. Her hair was much the same, but her hairline was rougher. Her mouth was fuller, her nose almost the same. Their eyes were not the same shape or size, but he could not say whose were bigger, whose were more round, whose were darker. "I remember that moment very clearly. She said she wanted to have sex wearing a mask. But that I couldn't wear one, too."

Lucia remained silent, watching the German students in the fountain.

"*You* said that?" he asked.

"Then I choked on my cigar," she said. "And excused myself. And that was it. Then we switched back. She told me about the mask later. How wonderful it was with you. And how you got frightened in the middle and thought that maybe it wasn't her behind the mask. But she wouldn't let you take it off."

"She told you that?"

"We're friends. She always told me intimate stuff. With you. It was very easy for me to fall for you. Sometimes, in Mexico, we would watch you together, from a little distance. And she would note things about you. Predict your movements. 'Watch how he asks for the check.' And you would pantomime the writing of a check even though your Spanish was fine. 'Watch how he lifts his arms a little as he starts looking for me. Why do you think he does that?' And you would step into the plaza where you had agreed to meet and then lift your arms a little. As if seeking balance."

"When was the other time?" he asked.

She raised her brow in question.

"The other time?" he asked again. "You said you posed a couple of times."

"Couple, to normal people, means I'm really not sure. It doesn't mean two. It's intentionally vague. For purposes of conversation."

He shook his head. "But it means, without a doubt, more than once. You said couple."

She sighed and smiled. "The next time involved touch. Her idea. I kissed your ear, from behind. You were on the shore of Lake Pátzcu-aro, at night, watching the lighted fishing boats come in. I remember the boats looked like pieces of light breaking off the island city, like icebergs floating away. Again, I had to take a pull on one of those awful cigars. To get the smell on me, the taste on my lips. I walked up behind you, after switching with her. You were sitting on an overturned boat. I didn't say anything. I wasn't even dressed like her. I put my hands on your shoul-ders and, from behind, I kissed your right ear."

"I put my hand in your hair," he said.

"Yes. Then I left to switch back with Irma."

"How far would you have let it go?" He let go of her wrists and leaned away. "What if I had kissed your lips? Pulled you to the sand?"

"I honestly don't know. It was a very romantic-looking night. The air felt like silk. It was all a kind of a sexy thing to do. And it wasn't as though I didn't know you. I knew you a lot better than I knew many other men. So, honestly. I don't know."

He realized that they were now alone in the clearing, except for the frogs and the goose. The students had left and the sun had gone down. City light streaming through the trees lay flat on the glassy water of the fountain, which, at some point, had been switched off.

"Do you know where she is?" he asked.

"No." She swayed her shoulders slightly as she looked at the frogs. Then she looked at him, holding still, her face still, all as though realizing she must remain that way for him to believe. "I set myself up in Philadelphia, knowing where you'd be, Philip. Wondering about you. And wondering if I could somehow find her through you. A part of her, at least. But I didn't really have a plan. I came here not quite ready to give up. I knew if I came to Spain, you might eventually come, too—bringing her in some way. But I'm not really looking for her."

She leaned toward him, paused as though expecting him to lean away, then kissed him on the chin. Her kiss was light, but she held it there for a long moment, until he could clearly sense the warmth and part.

"I want to see her at least once more," she said, her breath on his neck. "Almost as badly as you." She looked around. "It's getting dark. We should leave."

She stood and he remained seated, gazing at the dark and quiet fountain, the frogs just silhouettes.

"Listen," she said softly, resting her fingers on his shoulder. "The way I live. The way I am. With people I like. I sometimes seem deceptive—but I don't mean to be. She was really the only friend who understood that about me. I just don't like trying to explain everything about myself—certainly not right away. I believe that only creates more deception. Because I only end up proving myself wrong.

"If I had told you up front who I was, when we first met at the TLA, you would not have gotten to know me at all. We would not know each other the way we do now. And we would not have accomplished anything. The only thing I withheld—lied about—was knowing her. If I had admitted to that right away, then we would have joined perspectives. We would have lost that advantage. That advantage of approaching her from two distinct angles."

"You sound like me," he said.

"I'm trying to sound like you."

He stood, turned toward her. "Were you going to tell me? This time?"

"Only if you asked. Because if you asked, then you had pretty much figured things out. Or thought them out. At least enough to make you hesitate with me. But see? Nothing's really changed. Either way I still want you. And either way I'm still one of her characters. Still one of her characters come to life. And either way you still want me. Want. In the Spanish translation of that word."

"You know that?" he asked.

She pressed her hand low over his stomach. "More than you do."

It was full dark and they had to stand very close to see each other's face. Hers lifted, everything upward.

"Listen, Philip. It's clear to me that, for you, I am her in many ways. One of her creations, perhaps. A part of her left for you. That's okay. That's good. I like that. I like that very much. For me, you are much the same."

They walked arm in arm, quiet along Menéndez Pelayo, looking much like many other couples along the sidewalks. In his *pensión* room, she wanted to shower after her trip, and so he waited on his bed, in low-slung reading light, watching angled shadows on the ceiling. She returned to the room naked—she walked that way down the common hall, to his door—with her hair up, her towel and things over one arm. She asked him to remain still as she undressed him, removing his pants first. When she reached to spread his shirt open, her breasts fell over his erection and he had to concentrate to keep from coming.

"It's all right," she whispered. "In the shower, I thought about what I want to do. So just hold still for a moment and then you'll figure it out."

She climbed onto him and straddled his face. Her knees folded on either side of his head, her thighs brushing his ears, she took hold of the headboard. He put his tongue to her, pressing with it, but holding it still.

"Ah," she said. "Just like that. Keep it just like that." And she began rotating herself against his tongue, slowly, with deliberate, incremental shifts. She began to come. As she continued, he felt her hand reach back and feel its way down his stomach. She took hold of him, pumped once, and he came in five intense pulses.

"It's okay," she said. "It's good. It feels good. But don't stop yet."

After a moment, she climbed off him and went back to the hall shower without dressing. She returned and crawled under the covers with him, smelling like olive oil soap. "Now we take our time. *Te quiero, te amo.* Figure things out."

FOURTEEN

"You haven't quite finished," she said, noting his copper bookmark.

"No," he replied, looking up at her from his pillow. The *Quixote* was open before her, the reading glasses low on her nose, her thumb against the closed pages of the book.

"How can you pause so close to the end? I can never do that."

"I'm not quite reading it that way," he said. "Straight through." He touched the edges of the pages as she let them fan open. "I mean, I am going through in order, but I fold back every so often. I'm also not finishing because I know he's going to die."

"He died in Part I," she said.

"But that was different. The deaths were told in poems and epitaphs, on moldy, worm-eaten parchment sealed in a lead box. This time it's going to be different. There isn't going to be any kind of fade-out into poetry and epilogue and promises."

"Are you really that sad about it?" she asked.

"Yes."

He raised himself, resting on his elbow to get a closer look at her.

"What?" she asked, removing her glasses to look at him. "Are you still wondering about me? Wondering if I was sent. Like the Knight of the Mirrors or the Knight of the White Moon. Come to battle you back into sanity."

"The Knight of the Mirrors and the Knight of the White Moon are the same person," he replied.

"I know," she said. "I finished it. And it made me very sad. But I don't have this special version. Maybe she'll spare you."

She let the book remain open against her inner thigh. He drew his finger along the curve of her jaw.

"That time Irma and I made love and she wore that mask," he said to her. "When I worried in the middle that it might not be her?"

"Right," she said. She smiled. "It was her, if that's what you're asking. Your doubts came from the moment hours before. When I posed as her, with the cigar, in the night. I translated a book on facial recognition once. It's interesting. Most people see faces in a series of descending generalities. There's actually an equation for it. You see me, you see her. You see dark hair, dark eyes, light brown skin. You see attractive. We both have Lusitanian features, though mine are filtered through Brazil. Our noses are almost the same. But our mouths are different. And so on."

She looked back to *Quixote*, perusing. "We could only ever trick you for an instant. Now that you know us separately. Now that you know me as a separate person, we could not trick you, even for an instant."

She read him chapter seventy, the one that reveals many of the deceptions planned against Quixote and Sancho, carried out in earnest concern by Bachelor Sansón Carrasco, orchestrated in curiosity and amusement by the Duke and Duchess, and dramatized with a combination of mystery, sincerity, and enthusiasm by the alluring Altisidora who is, Cervantes writes, more willing than wise. The chapter rewinds time, and you see Altisidora climbing onto the catafalque as the stage is set to fool—teach? help? redeem?—Quixote. Though Philip had already finished the chapter, it sounded new to him as Lucia read it. She pronounced the names and archaic terms with a genuine accent, a softness at the back of the teeth, intricate curls of the tongue. Catafalque. Watching her, listening to her read that way, made him hungry. And when Altisidora spoke, Lucia's voice grew whispery, dark, with a slight rasp. Altisidora tells of her trip to Hell's gate, where she watches the devils playing jai alai, and where the pelota, struck hard, splits open and out spills the story of Don Quixote. As she tells her audience the story on the pages that burst forth, she emphasizes her love and Quixote's unawareness and coldness. When she is cut short, she calls him "Don Codfish, with a soul of metal." She is vexed and angered and she is not acting. When Lucia was done with the chapter, which was only seven pages, she closed the book and rested her hand on it.

"That part about the pelota splitting open and spilling out the story," Philip said.

"Mmh?"

"She wrote that, didn't she?" he asked. "That's one of her inserts."

Lucia shook her head. "No. That's Cervantes. I'm sure of it. It all seems in order, to me."

There are several approaches to replace missing or badly damaged text, she once told him, waving her bone folder above a tattered volume which lay like a patient on a table in the center of her shop. The traditional approach, according to the rule of reversibility, is to mark it as missing and provide, if available, a separate note on the contents. But I don't do that. She squinted at him, tapped the bone folder against her lips. I try to re-create as much as possible. Scraping or bleaching away the old, messed-up words is easy. People did it all the time, way back when parchment was more valuable than the words written on it. It's actually harder for me to disappear the oldest stuff. I use what they used to use— nothing fancy. I start with the softest abrasive possible, oat bran. If that doesn't work—though it usually does—I move on, all the way to pumice. I use tincture of gall for any needed bleaching. You know, for that finishing touch. She waved her bone folder. If I have to re-create paper, that's easy. A child could do it. In fact, children do it all the time in art classes. I'm as innocent as they are, Pip.

"Would you like me to read the last chapters to you?" asked Lucia. "I like reading to you, glancing over to see the expressions on your face. You *will* be sad at the end. I can tell. I could accompany you. The last twenty pages."

"Later," he said. "And maybe just a couple of the chapters. I should read the ending alone."

"You mean alone with her."

"No," he replied. "I . . ."

"It's okay," she said. "I think it's sweet."

She took him to dinner, saying it was the least she could do. For deceiving him. They ate at Café Cesar, in a small clearing nestled deep within the old Jewish Quarter. She talked the owner into bringing an extra table

into the little plaza—all the others being taken. The owner, an austere
man in a dark suit and horn-rimmed glasses, carried the table himself,
the waiters following with chairs. It was near midnight, and the heat had
receded enough to leave the air almost balmy, though the brown shoulders of women glistened. The owner brought them a bottle of red wine,
slid it into a damp terra-cotta sleeve in the center of their table, and then
disappeared into his café without saying a word.

"What did you say to him?" Philip asked Lucia.

"Nothing," she replied. "I only went in and told him we needed an
outside table."

"Does anyone ever say no to you?"

"I avoid yes/no questions."

The wet terra-cotta kept the wine cool, adding a taste of rain. She told
him she had been working hard in Madrid and that this was a needed
break. I feel lucky to have you here, she told him, to make Seville even
better. She told him she was translating a textbook by a Spanish astronomer who had identified the Star of Bethlehem through a painstaking
series of calculations. "I didn't know you could study history with math.
I didn't know you could triangulate positions and time that accurately."
He replied, "If only people moved like stars."

At the *pensión*, the wine and food and lack of sleep combined to make
him very tired, a pulling kind of fatigue. He lay down on his bed and
apologized to her.

"Rest," she said. "I like going out alone. I want to."

"You don't have to look at *Zed*," he said softly. "That's asking you
to work."

"No, it isn't. I want to look at it. I want that, too. I came here for
that, too."

Sometime in the night, she returned to the *pensión*, letting the sounds
of Seville flash briefly through the opened door, hushing him awake. He
awoke again later, and she was sitting at the reading table, the desk lamp
pushed low so as not to disturb him. She was studying *Zed*. She had set
the broken covers aside and arranged the loose pages and quires into
three stacks. But she had also found his other books, too. With her fingers to her forehead, she read, her silhouette still against the lamplight,

her hair, in moments, falling loose from its chignon. Her lips were parted and sometimes they mouthed the words. Later in the night, she was gone again, then, in a blink it seemed, returned to the desk. In a waking dream, he saw her silhouette at the desk and at the doorway simultaneously. When he called to her, she came to him—from the desk and doorway, it seemed, at the same time. She put her cool hand to his forehead, as though tending a fever, and whispered, "I'm going for a walk." She added in Spanish, "Come with me if you'd like." Warm, her breath smelled of red wine. She laughed softly at his sleepiness and released him back into the covers. When he awoke again in darkness, she was beneath the sheets with him. Her hip was against the side of his face and her feet were tiptoe to the headboard, the muscles of her calves catching vague street light from the window. Her mouth was pulling him into hardness. When she sensed he had wakened, she straddled his face with an easy lift of her thigh and swing of her hips. She had brushed a licorice-scented liqueur wherever his tongue and lips would search, and he knew from the pleasant sting that it was absinthe. "Hurry," she whispered from down deep in the sheets, "or it will burn me."

When she curled around and surfaced, barely more than a shadow, she drank from a tiny coffee cup on the nightstand and then inserted her tongue into his mouth, letting more absinthe run into his throat. It was like tasting a flame. Then, in the darkness, she hung over him, her face hidden in the black fall of her hair. Before he could reach to push her hair aside, she rolled onto her back, guiding him along. Her hair and arm swept across her face. He reached for the lamp, but she put him inside her and he felt the burn of the absinthe down there, too. She pulled him down to her, face to face, the sides of their noses brushing. Her eyes looked blurry in the dark. "I don't want you to die," she whispered in Spanish. She moved constantly beneath him. He smoothed his hand along the back of her thigh and into the crook of her knee, where she clenched and trapped him. Her mouth was open and her eyes were closed. In the darkness, her hair and features seeped and set like ink.

He stopped thrusting, braced his arms, planting his hands above her shoulders, bowed away from her without pulling out. He pushed her hair completely free of her face so he could stare at her features in the deep

gray, against the pale of the bed. He whipped the sheets free to expose
the splay of her arms. Dim stars, like bits of metal, ringed the edges of
his vision. His head did not spin, but rather felt as though everything
were pressing to spin around him, the moment of stillness in a pendulum's sweep. Again he tried reaching for the light, but found he would
have to withdraw, and nothing in him would allow that. It would free
her, leave him uncompleted.

She whispered in a voice that attempted no disguise, but blended possibilities. "It wouldn't help. It would only frighten you more in the light,
brighten us together."

He thrust to stop her words, but her moan taunted him more. When
he thought her eyes were Lucia's, he looked and they were Irma's. He
thrust and her chuckle was Lucia's, the upward bend of her throat Irma's.
He could not thrust again or he would lose himself completely, fall too
close. He tried touch, held her breasts, pushed them together.

"Feel away," she whispered. "By the time you figure out if they are
hers or mine, pull them, taste them, bite them, you'll be senseless and
dying of pleasure." She arched them up to him. He pushed her back
down, his hands around her ribs.

"Where else?" she whispered. "Where else to go? Where can you go
where you haven't been with either of us?" Her breath was warm with
absinthe and wine. He was swimming in it. She moved beneath him,
making herself sigh and breathe more around him, filling the air. Again
he reached for the light, his aim shaking and wide, lost in the sparks at
the edges of his vision.

"Do you really want this to end? Do you really not want to feel what
it would be like to fall screaming into both of us?" She closed her eyes, or
softened them—he couldn't tell in the darkness. She groaned. "It will be
like nothing you've felt before. Or like everything."

He began to thrust, fast, believing he could go too fast to feel her, too
hard for her to withstand. But she took him eyes-closed, staying with
him in easy gasps. He paused to gather strength.

"Besides," she whispered, "you already know."

Below him, pinned, her legs lay flat and spread, her arms reaching for the edges, all of her stretched tight. Beneath her, the milky sheet, the only contrast to the dark, appeared tender and thin, a damp skin holding her to him. What he knew was that with his next motion he would tear them both through, their nerves shocking as they intertwined in the velocity. Their pulses would slam together at an unbearable speed and they would have no breath, no gravity. The only act that would allow them to survive, to keep them from death, a snap into black, would be to grip each other with every part of themselves. To wrap their legs together, crush hips to one another, dig fingers into backs, bite, trusting each other's body not to break.

In the next thrust, he released into her and she cried out just before, as though she knew it was coming. And she gasped with each descending thrust, his weight falling onto her, his scream buried in the damp heat of her hair, her jaw grinding against his. *No quiero que mueras.*

As soon as they were finished, while he was still trembling over her, she slipped from beneath him and went into the hall. In the open and shut of the door, he glimpsed the curve of her back and the angle of her shoulder. He leaned against the headboard, waiting for her, watching the crack of light along the door, which at first seemed left ajar, then closed. He wiped tears from his face, not knowing whose they were. When she did not return soon, he pulled on his pants and went to the shower. She was not there, though steam, ripe with absinthe, hung in the room. He returned, finished dressing, and hurried into what was left of the Sevillan night. He smelled of licorice and turpentine and his lips and eyes were caked and sticky.

Flamenco still thrummed in the murky labyrinth of the old Jewish Quarter. Couples and groups still navigated the narrow and crooked streets. He asked a couple with lots of wine on their breath if they had seen her pass by and they pointed toward the bottom of the Quarter. He tacked his way toward Juderia, his head clearing, but his muscles feeling soft, grasping in languor. On Juderia, in the trickle of the fountain fastened to the Alcázar wall, he washed his face. He stood midpoint between the dark archways on either end of the brief little street. First he went to the black arch of the Alcázar, where she had seen her fear come to life as a ripple in her vision.

The darkness of the arch was deeper than expected, and he fell into it a bit, as on a ghost step at the end of a stairway. The archway was an enormous wooden door, blackened by age, rough and smelling of creosote. He reversed his path along Juderia and went through the tunnel on the other end, which, after two dark turns, led him to the cathedral and its wide plaza. Two young couples sat on the lip of the fountain. The sweepers had left the walkways and street wet and smelling of warm rain and clean stone. One of the couples at the fountain, after sizing him up, told him they had seen a woman heading that way. They nodded their heads together in the direction of the Town Hall. Philip hurried there, running whenever no one was on the street to see him.

Plaza de San Francisco was empty, the horse carriages long gone. The street cleaners had passed through here, too. Only the sound of the fountain echoed off the wall of the Town Hall. He entered Cervantes's arch. At first he thought it was empty. Then he saw a woman step from the corner along the far archway. His heart caught. In veiled light of streetlamps, he saw that it was Lucia or Irma—then, finally, heartbeat subsiding, Lucia. He leaned against the wall beneath the tile plaque commemorating the young Cervantes, the youthful writer who got his first ideas in the shade and solace of this archway. Or so say the books and the tiles, she adds.

"She's not here." Lucia's voice echoed in the passageway.

"Can you tell me what we just did?" he asked her.

"Did?" She drew near him, pressed him delicately to the wall. She put her face to his collar and inhaled deeply. "I poured absinthe all over myself and brought you back to life."

She leaned fully against him and looked at his face. "We still smell of it. All of it."

"But you showered."

"Briefly." She held her wrist to his nose. It smelled of olive oil soap.

"Why did you disappear so fast and hurry away?"

"Hurry away?" she asked. "I returned and you were out again. So

I took this walk. I come here to find her. To triangulate the movement of the stars. Like you."

"I was not out. I was awake. Waiting."

She remained against him and laughed softly. "I like this. It's like nothing I've ever experienced. It's like being two at once, getting banged as two." She kissed his lips gently. "To be succinct."

He held her shoulders to keep her at bay, but touching her, sensing her muscle and bone and flesh, only made him want to gather her against him. "I can't think clearly when you're here."

"Then don't. What's to figure?" She put her hand around his neck, took hold. "Realize. Realize that you are much the same to me, Philip. Very much a character from some of her books. You are Peter Navratil and Simon Bauer and others. I know you as them, probably more than I know you here." She spread her fingers over the back of his head. "In the flesh."

"But I told you who I am. You deceived me."

"You told me a Borges story," she said. "A *fake* Borges story."

The licorice scent of absinthe lifted on the warmth between them, its burn rising in his throat. It still fizzed on the edges of his vision. She kissed his lips, then leaned beneath the Cervantes tiles.

"It was me," she said, but smiled, the same half-smile Irma had drawn in her books.

He stepped to her, much closer than she expected, his body pushing her back against the wall, her face against his neck. Her words brushed his throat.

"There is no better place than here. For two of her characters to find each other. It's where we were created."

When they left the archway, arm in arm, leaning on each other, dawn had begun. The sky shifted from brown to pearl and a halo of bright yellow outlined the spires and towers of the cathedral. Couples in evening wear, shirttails out, shoulder straps fallen, hair mussed, shuffled over the slate walkways, a clucking sound. Everywhere was the smell of orange blossoms, new, peeling open. As Lucia and Philip strolled by the cathedral fountain, swallows darted about the high bells of the Giralda. He could tell by the way she watched the birds, how she kept looking back to them, to see the sunrise flash on their wings, that they reminded her of something past. He did not ask her what.

They slept until noon. She had to wake him, telling him they had little time, that she had to return to Madrid in the evening.

"Yes," he said. "Back to the star book." He felt rested, lifted, ready to run. He considered the route he would take, along the river, in the evening balm after walking her to her train. They took *Zed* to Maria Luisa Park, stopping along the way to buy fruit from a cranky vendor on Menéndez Pelayo who acted as though his produce were too good for the likes of his customers. Beneath the curtained shade of an enormous willow, they sat on a bench near the lion fountain. The fountain lay in two parts, with a long reflecting pool—the one he and Irma would sprint through—leading up to the circle of lions sitting at attention, spitting water. The trickle was the only interruption in the quiet heat of the park. The shaggy willow stood in contrast to the cropped and angled hedges.

Lucia stacked the loose collection of *Zed*'s pages on the benchtop between her and Philip.

She explained. I've only read parts, and most of the margin notes. Her notes, of course, you can read for yourself. The other notes, the Spanish ones, look like they were taken by a college student. Lecture notes following some professor's interpretations. The professor, I can tell, was more political than romantic. The student's notes seem a little frustrated by this—I think she really liked the story. The book itself, from what I could gather, is about two Brazilian athletes who went to the 1968 Olympics in Mexico City along with their young journalist friend. That's Zed. She sometimes passes herself as a young man, to gain access. She clearly loves both Adão—Adam—and Fatima. She hides her love in her interactions with them, but reveals it in her narrative. I can tell by the cultural references and the political notes that it was written not long after the Olympics, sometime during Brazil's Tropicália. It's quite like the love triangle stories set during the Vietnam War protests that came out during that time. Painfully dated, but innocent and sweet.

The writer tries hard to be hip to the movement, all the while struggling under the burdensome conventions of love. Irma might have read this as a kid, when she was reading anything that fell in her path.

Fatima is a pole vaulter with long legs. Adão sprints. Neither of them expect to get past the qualifying rounds and both like to marvel at the great athletes surrounding them. They tell Zed what to admire. There is a lot of music in the book—all of it Tropicália. You know. Gil, Veloso. Os Mutantes, Tom Zé. But significant chunks are missing. And many of the pages and sections are repeats. The ending is gone, so I don't know what happens. I can't tell what Irma wants to do with this. It's rather pulpy, but in a good way. Not like the stuff she usually messes with.

Philip nodded, a kind of thank-you.

"Did you read the messages to me?"

"Yes," she replied. "And the ones you wrote to her."

"Are there messages to you?" he asked. "Embedded in the prose."

"You mean instructions?" She held a strawberry to her lips. "On what to do with you?" She ate the berry whole, snapping the stem free with her fingernails. "I suppose there could be. But how does one tell the difference?"

She sat with arms braced to either side of her, shoulders up, her hair lifted in the heat. According to her habit, she spoke to the fountain, then looked at him to see the effect of her words. Along a near pathway, a family of three pedaled by in a surrey.

"What books did she leave you?" he asked.

"None. But I seem to be reading the ones left to you. I like what you put in *Ava*. For me." She placed her hands gently on the *Zed* pages. "How much design you want to lend it all is up to you. Me? I'm going to do what I want to do. What I'm compelled to do. I like you very much. I like reading your books. I'm already starting to feel like returning to Madrid later in the night, instead of evening. But I'm not going to try to convince you, to prove to you, that she and I didn't switch places last night. Proving things to you, I can tell, is a tedious, frustrating process. And it doesn't matter to me what you believe. If you think me nefarious, duplicitous—*her*, even—then I'll come even harder."

She put her fingers to his temple, along his damp hairline. "Let's find some grass and some good shade. You can rest your head in my lap while I read for you. You can nap if you want. I'll read to your dreams. Tonight, if you want, I'll take you to the end of *Quixote*."

"Do you ever fall in love?" he asked.

"A long time ago," she told him, "in Mexico, Irma and I spoke of ourselves . . . and you. We spoke of rescuing you, rescuing people like you. But rescue isn't the right word. The Spanish word *salvar* is the right one. Because it means to save, but also, at the same time, to except and exclude. We're three of a kind, but the two of us needed to save you. *Te salvamos.* Except you, exclude you from the life you kept falling into. We were young and ambitious. Like knights. And insensitive. Yes, I fall in love."

They found some shade and grass and she read to him, his head in her lap. They reclined on the edge of the shade so her feet could be in the sun. Other couples sat in the shade, too: students bent toward each other and plotting, grandparents back to back like kind statues. Lucia first read some passages in Portuguese so he could just hear the sound of the words. Then she translated, trying to show him Adão, Fatima, and Zed. Their world.

In *Theory*, Irma writes the good-bye scene between Peter and Feli. Feli is dressed as a man in a suit, for a role she is rehearsing. Though she is in costume, she speaks the most genuine words he ever hears from her lips. She explains herself to him, how she feels about Sylvia, him, people in general. Stripped of all pretense and motive, he tells Feli that she is the most beautiful woman he has ever seen from across a table. In the scene, Peter learns from Feli that Sylvia has changed shoes, gone from sandals to hiking boots. The boots clue him to the volcano, on whose summit he solves, with Sylvia, the book's mystery.

He dreamed in Lucia's lap as she read in Portuguese. Somewhere in his dreaming her words changed to English and he was on top of Mount Paricutín with Irma, sweaty and caked with volcanic dust, gasping in the high altitude. The sun shone through the sulfurous mist and the rim of the caldera seemed razor-sharp. Lucia's words, telling the story of *Zed*, seemed to be echoing up from the green lake at the bottom of the caldera. Fatima and Adão, more and more, lost interest in performing well in their respective events, lost interest in being part of the Brazilian team, and instead began joining the Mexican students who protested within the thick crowds who gathered regularly in Tlatelolco. Adão openly joins the Mexican students, swept up in their vision of reform, drawn into their idealism and hope. Fatima keeps herself at a remove, loving Adão for his fearlessness, his affinity to their own country's Tropicália movement, but foreseeing all along the massacre that is coming to Tlatelolco. Zed must record two versions—the real one for herself and the sanctioned one for her Brazilian publishers.

When Philip awoke in Lucia's lap, she was still reading, translating. The shade had receded and half of him was soaked in the Andalusian sun.

"I wish I could tell you how it ends," she said, putting her cool hand to his head. "But all that's missing. Maybe she'll find it somewhere and slip it in."

"Maybe she'll write it herself," he said. "How she remembers the story. Or envisions it. Maybe she'll let them live."

"Adão dies," she told him. "Zed and Fatima live."

"How do you know that?"

She translated a passage where Zed watches Fatima compete in the first qualifying round. She describes her long strides, holding the pole before her, her expression going from confusion, to fear, to wonderment as she sprints toward the bar. "It's those three expressions, feelings that will save her in Tlatelolco Plaza," Lucia explained. She continued. Zed describes Fatima in the air, near the apex of her jump, just after she releases her pole and it springs her upward. Fatima straightens her body, her long legs flexed together, her arms extended like a matador's. She is upside down, twirling gracefully, controlled, then pinned to the sky.

She read a later scene, too, where Fatima and Zed are alone together. Zed is still dressed like a man after gaining access to a locker-room interview session. She remains that way the entire evening with Fatima. "I've already carefully imagined my life without Adão," Fatima tells Zed. "More than imagined it. Constructed it. The same way I envision each stride toward the vault. Even though you see me running full-tilt, with speed and abandon, I already know exactly where each one of my strides will land. I know precisely when I will release the pole. I know what I will see when my body turns toward the sky, then back to earth."

"You can't tell he's going to die," said Philip, "from that."

"It's all quite melodramatic and formulaic," she replied. "So, yes, I can. And I translated a bit loosely when I said *without*. She uses a phrase in Portuguese—Brazilian Portuguese—that's somewhat mathematical. It negates Adão, removes him from everything, erases him."

He flexed his brow, stared at the edges of the trees against the sky, where the sun flickered. She set down the loose page she was reading from and cupped both hands about his face. She bent over him. "Don't see any more into it. It's just a book. Maybe not even a particularly good one. Something for you to find if you happened to miss her more than she anticipated. Something that might bring you and me together. Here. *Como este.*"

"You're like her," he said. "But you're also very different. And you're different in one particularly significant way. You seem more aware of what you and Irma are doing, living the way you do. Living in spite of human nature, not according to it. Your global friendships. Your . . ." He didn't know how to finish.

She smiled over him, holding him in her lap, tucking her fingertips beneath his jaw. "We used to argue about that. I wanted to talk about it more, with her. Because she was one who could understand. But she always contended that it needed to remain mostly unspoken, undefined. We'd kill it if we exposed it to too much light."

"How many of you are there?"

"Don't be so quick to exclude yourself," she said. "Counting you and her, I know four. Irma wouldn't even want me to speak that number, that hard clear quantification. That admission. I know what people— friends, even—say about me. How I can be so uncaring. How I can be in your bed one night, then somewhere way across the world in the morning, not letting you know until later. 'She'll be so lonely when she's lost her looks and energy,' they claim. But I keep my friends, as long as they'll have me. And most other people I know, except very few, have strewn broken relationships across their lives. Ex-wives, ex-husbands, stepchildren, ex-friends, and jilted lovers."

If you saw them, singled them out momentarily from the other couples in the shaded grass, you might at first take them as much younger.

He with his head in her lap, bending back to look more intently at her, she palming his face gently, searching. And if the splash of the nearby fountain were intermittent enough to let you hear fragments of their conversation, their voices would sound younger, too, maybe from the spark off the water, but maybe from the mix of play and sincerity in their inflections. When you realized that they were not so young, you could easily mistake them as lovers in tryst, finding in each other's touch and words a brief escape from their respective lives.

They lay together on the grass and kissed like young lovers. They were not the only ones; it was siesta in Maria Luisa Park and the fountains were all going and the doves, in groups, were dusting their wings in the warm powder of clay paths.

That night, she took the bullet back to Madrid. They had dinner early, watching the sunset over rooftop clotheslines and water tanks. They ate cold food—vinegared potatoes, olives, salt cod—because the café was not really open yet and Lucia talked the bartender into letting them sit and have sherry. In bed, before taking him almost to the very end of *Quixote*, she read him the challenge of the Knight of the White Moon, who is, as we learn later, Bachelor Carrasco in disguise: Renowned knight and never sufficiently praised Don Quixote of La Mancha, I am the Knight of the White Moon, whose extraordinary deeds perhaps have come to your attention; I am here to do battle with you and to test the strength of your mighty arms, obliging you to recognize and confess that my lady, whoever she may be, is incomparably more beautiful than your Dulcinea of Toboso; and if you confess this truth clearly and plainly, you will save yourself from death, and save me the trouble of killing you; and if you do battle and I conquer you, I want no other satisfaction than that you abandon your arms, abstain from seeking adventures, and withdraw and retire to your home for a period of one year, where you must live without laying a hand on your sword, in peaceful tranquillity and profitable serenity, for such is required for the increase of your fortune and the salvation of your soul; and if you should conquer me, my life will be at your mercy, and my arms and horse will be yours, as spoils, and the fame of my deeds will be added to yours. Consider what you should do, and respond immediately, for I have only this day to settle this matter.

She was very forceful in bed, pushing fast and hard, urgently, in a way that was not pleasurable in the moment, but that would become very much so on recollection. When beneath him, she pressed the soles of her feet together and bowed her knees apart so that she was stretched very tightly around him and it was difficult for him to thrust, but possible. She clenched her teeth and shut her eyes and he could not tell if these were expressions of pain or pleasure. When on top, she braced her hands against his neck and chest, locked her arms, and drove herself over him, hurting him, but not enough for him to try to stop her. The room got very warm, and the sheets were wrung and damp about their legs. When she fell over him, their bodies slid wet against one another. This time, she whispered, you know it's me.

Human perception, he once told her as she looked down at the spiral he drew on her stomach, can be quantified. She stared at the red spiral, letting him proceed with the lipstick, knowing it would end at her navel. Irma our perceptions, our senses, follow the logarithmic scale. The equation is quite simple and elegant. Her expression remained dismissive. He persevered. How we react to brightness and color, sound, touch, occurs according to a logarithmic scale. I don't have enough lipstick and your belly is too narrow, but I could write out the equation. Go ahead, she told him. Write it out. Use the rest of me. There's another stick on the nightstand if you need. He wrote the differential equation across her chest: $s = k \ln W + C$, where $\ln$ is the natural logarithm, C is the integration constant, and W is stimuli. W_0 would stand for the lowest level of stimulus required for response. He wrote two more applications, one down each of her thighs. The music we are hearing, he explained, the music that is making you sad, me happy, is written out on a staff. That musical staff is actually a logarithmic scale that contains any possible note imagined, heard, absorbed. The same equation applies to the color spectrum, all our spectrums. He waited for her response, expecting her dismissal of his math, a damning of his culture, an "Oh, Pip" of some kind. But she lay there, looking across the equation covering her body. The music, drifting from the only café in Tampumacchay, across the rattling song of river toads, was a fiddle playing an ancient lullaby. You could figure it all out, she told him softly. You could solve it all.

After seeing Lucia to her night train, he ran directly from the station, down Avenida Kansas City, down Menéndez Pelayo, going fast by the huddled darkness of Maria Luisa Park, easing into the crowds strolling the bright walkways of the Guadalquivir. He felt wide-eyed, going too fast for the distance, like the designated rabbit in a race for better runners. He noted her mile markers along the river, then reached his point of collapse near the Torre del Oro. There he rested, bracing his arms to the Moorish stones of the tower base, breathing downward. Night heat poured over him. The only other runner among the river paseo, a Spanish woman, called to him as she swept by, friendly, competitive. *Andale pues!*

How many of you are there?

He ran some more, but slower, zigzagging through the narrow streets of the Arenal, until he reached the quiet of Plaza de San Francisco, abandoned for the night, even by the horse carriages. He checked his watch and rested on the lip of the fountain. He splashed a little of the warm green water on his neck and it blended with the sweat streaming down his back. The pain between his lungs subsided, as it always did, no matter how sharp it became, no matter how hard he pushed himself. He walked into the archway and sat beneath the commemorative tiles. In the distance, he could hear the street cleaners working their way across the cathedral plaza, the whispery sound of their brooms and water.

Precisely on time, Cervantes shuffled into the archway with his broken sandals, his greasy jacket filling the hollow with its smell, his beard glistening in the lamplight. He looked once at Philip, then took his place against the wall inside the shadow of the archway lip. His urine trickled across the stone and chimed into the iron drain. He leaned in the darkness, only the brushy ends of his beard and the broken edges of his features catching the dim light.

"When did you last see her?" Philip asked him.

"Last night," he answered. "Where were you?"

Philip began to approach him, but the man stood away from the wall and looked upward, eyes glazed in the lamplight. He stayed Philip with a raised hand and cocked an ear to the archway, the hush of the approaching street cleaners. "Listen. They're coming. They're near." He then hurried off, ignoring, or perhaps not even hearing, Philip's questions and pleas.

"They're nothing but sweepers," Philip called to the man, but he stumbled on the Spanish for the last word. *"Barrenderos,"* he finally said in the archway, the word echoing in the empty hollow.

When Philip tried to give chase, the man looked back in fear, began to cry, and so Philip stopped, bowed apologetically, and let him disappear into the black edges of Plaza Nueva.

Then he was alone in Seville. He could not even imagine her watching, spying, as he always could before. Returned to his *pensión*, he showered and eased himself toward sleep by finally reading the last paragraphs of *Quixote*. The final word was the italicized *vale*, Cervantes's farewell to his reader. It is the lightest of good-byes, untranslatable to English, *adieu*, something you bid softly rather than declare. But it was not this final word that struck him, that in fact jolted him far away from sleep, but rather the final letter. The italicized *e* was slightly reshaped—just a mere untucking of the inward spiral—into an ellipse: *o*. From there he paged back immediately to all of his compositions for her, to see if they were still there, or stolen, or changed. He found them unchanged and intact. All he had revealed to her was still there, his intricate plans to pursue her to infinity, past the point of exhaustion. His challenges and renouncements, all gridded clearly for her to see. Yet when he tried to pull them out of the Quixote, he found they were too tightly and too neatly inserted to be removed. They lay evenly, perfectly squared within the surrounding pages, bound with them, and he could not tug them free.

FIFTEEN

In Philadelphia, a cold mist fell. Without unpacking, without reading his paltry stack of mail, without reshelving the Cervantes to its place among the collection, without even reconfiguring the time change, not knowing the time, he ran. He ran along the Delaware, on the terra-cotta pavers of Penn's Landing all slick and chilled with the mist. The river looked wide and gray as a northern sea, with black cargo ships sliding in, lowing. Across the water, the dome of the aquarium rested wafer-light on the Camden skyline. The mist grew heavy on his hair and clothes, graying him into the surroundings. It softened and cooled his breath.

For me alone was Don Quixote born, and I for him, Irma or Cervantes writes in the last chapter. For he knew how to act, and I to write; the two of us alone are one. Lucia reads more, taking him almost to the end, with her voice so careful, her accent tapping the words with lip and tongue, keeping them wet and new, not sparing him in any way. Her pronunciation of the x, from the back of her teeth, a soft and connecting sound instead of the severing English version, would forever make him read it, hear it, and see it that way. Quixote. Irma did not spare him, either, as he and Lucia hoped, killing the Knight of the Sorrowful Face and, even more sadly and cruelly, doing it by cutting out his madness.

At the apex of the Walnut Street walkover, he rested briefly, only to stretch his hip flexor. Below him, the tall ships, bare and still, caught the mist in silvery ropes. Nicole, were she running with him, would notice them as she flew by, how the ships seemed collected and forgotten, draped in cobweb. Across the river, beyond the ships, the insurance building stood at the end of the Camden skyline. He had sent them work from Madrid just before his return flight. He received more, in London's Heathrow, during changeover. Never seeing him, they issued him electronic paychecks, which he would only see if he looked at his monthly bank statement. The bank had one of the tallest spires in the Philadelphia skyline. He never went there. If he went cheap, he could travel the world forever. Or he could stay in his little apartment over Baum's, reading his books, sipping bourbon, listening to Pärt, Adès, Górecki, Sampson; he could listen to Riley's *In C* forever, the mathematician's dream music.

He descended the walkway switchback in full stride, letting the momentum push him along the landing as he continued his run. He could live in Nicole and Sam's silence, the same way he could live in the rest of the world, as a precise but incalculable number, fixed, but only seen by the almost imperceptible ripple it creates, by the math it completes, e.

He knew, before leaving Seville, that something had happened. He received no messages from Sam or Nicole. No two-word invitations to run. No complaints or musings. Nothing. His own messages bounced back undelivered from dead accounts. Fatal errors.

He warmed down from his run by walking up Sansom to his apartment. After Seville, the brick row houses just off the docks seemed wide apart. The mannequins in the Baum's display window were dressed for an evening out, but their gazes were aimed too upward, and the whole family looked as though they were being invaded by flying saucers. His apartment was warm, the windows fogged by the cold mist outside. He had left the heat going for the books and they remained crisp and bright on their shelves. The day was so gray, the window light so weak, that he had to turn on the lamp to read.

On a page stolen from *Zed*, she filled the margins: The three characters in this paper story have more life in them than those who would judge L. or me or you. Fatima struggles to justify the kind of life she wants, imagines, plans. Adão strives to live a life that no one would try to justify. Zed puts herself at the mercy of all who would judge her as she offers her portrayals of Fatima and Adão and her collective and individual love for them. Lucia translated the noted passages for him, but he didn't see what Irma perceived in the words and events. He saw Fatima running almost blindly toward her final vault, pinning herself to the sky.

He saw Adão slipping deeper into the thickening protests of Tlatelolco Plaza, where hundreds of students would soon be shot down by Mexico's Olympic Squadron. He heard some prophecy, sublimation, and yearning in Zed's voice, but he didn't see what Irma gathered. Lucia noticed his expression, touched his brow, and told him that she could only translate.

He reshelved the books he had taken to Spain, fitting the Cervantes last. Though evening light still shone, he went to bed and fell asleep eyeing the books, the colorful spines a spectrogram of his thoughts and feelings of defeat. My valorous knight, she and Cervantes write on the final page, after Quixote dies. For the first time in a very long while, he slept through the night without waking. When he awoke, he found himself in the same position, facing the books from across his room. Morning light and rush-hour sounds streamed through the window. His entire right side felt crushed and numbed by sleep. He made coffee and worked, the math as cold and clear as morning ice.

On loose pages stolen from *Zed*, Irma pencils a note for herself: They appear inverted here, Fatima and Adão. Cautious with the translation. Ask L.

After this he ran the cold, drizzly banks of the Schuylkill, then immediately caught the Metro to Jersey. From the New Brunswick stop, he hurried to Rebecca's office, dressed only in damp sweats against the cold wind that cleared away the drizzle and blew wet paper and leaves across campus. He was shivering by the time he reached her door, criminal. Her first look as she stood from her desk held no recognition of him, took him as stranger. She had cut her hair, shorn it. But she looked somehow fuller, pushed out to the world. Then, as she stepped nearer to the door, about to close it on him it seemed, she looked fearful, her eyes finally acknowledging him. They were wide, facing a broken equation.

"Philip." She was shaking her head. "This isn't good. This isn't a good thing for you to do."

"I miss them."

She hugged her shoulders, pulling herself tightly together, more inside her office. He remained outside.

"Can I see them?" he asked.

She shook her head.

"Then will you meet me one more time?" he asked her. "I just have something to return to them. Some books. We won't have to talk."

"Okay," she said, or something like it, the merest sound of agreement. She rested against the edge of her door, then began to slowly close it. She reached vaguely, fingers raised as though to touch him. She tried a smile, but it trembled and failed and left him sad.

At the university store, he purchased a few bookmaking supplies. He was still in his sweats, his hair oily and stuck to his forehead and temples. A student working as clerk mistook him for professor and asked him if he was teaching the course on bookbinding and told him, before he could answer, that she hoped to take a course like that when she was finished with her requirements. "I want to buy this kind of stuff," she told him. "Instead of all those books." She tallied the little bottle of methyl cellulose paste, the ivory bone folder, the blade, the thick acid-free stock, and three novels.

In the Sebald he purchased for Isaac, he wrote in pencil on one fly page: I think she neglected to leave this for you. Maybe she found herself in more of a hurry. Maybe she just wanted to let you be. The most breathtaking rings are made of ice and dust. —P. He slipped the book into Isaac's door pocket. Leaving campus, he was careful to circumvent the fields.

That night he practiced matching his inserts to the novels. He was able to match the typeface using the fonts described in the end pages. In the Ondaatje, the information he needed was on the very last page, after all had ended. It read: A Note on the Type. This book is set in Fairfield, the first typeface from the hand of the distinguished American artist and engraver Rudolph Ruzicka (1883–1978). In its structure Fairfield displays the sober and sane qualities of a master craftsman whose talents were dedicated to clarity. It is this trait that accounts for the trim grace and virility, the spirited design and sensitive balance, of this original typeface. Philip needed these sober and sane qualities. He would need that dedication to clarity.

Between books, he sent a message to Beatrice. He was surprised at the quickness of her reply. Yes, it had been nice seeing him in that pastry shop, buying gingersnaps. Yes, she would like to meet him there and talk

of Spain. Yes, of course I remember the windmills. It was as if no time
had passed from when he had last seen her in the square.

Both in the Ondaatje and the Erdrich it was easy to find good insertion points. The passages were fragmented and the voices varied. In
both, he found enough white space between segments and chapters to
confidently insert shorter notes by removing the page, printing out his
words in the blank areas, then replacing the page. He practiced with
the bone folder. He could tuck the pages all the way to the spine, snug
enough to remain secure through the tension alone. But he nevertheless
added the thinnest line of paste to the paper's edge, letting it dry almost
completely before inserting it, then resoftening the paste from the inside
by massaging the spine with the tip of his bone folder. I learned this in
Chicago, she told him when she demonstrated this technique. When I
was sort of pining for you in Ann Arbor. When I wondered most about
us, about you and me together. I learned that I could let the paste almost
set, so that it wouldn't smear, and then recatalyze it from inside the mull
through firm, repeated pressure. I thought it was brilliant. My mentor
was appalled. She became appalled by everything I was trying to do. She
called my methods tricks and forgeries. Fakery, not restoration. But it is
restoration. I make them come alive again. Philip found that by lightly
sanding the fore-edge of the entire text block, he could blend the inserted
pages perfectly.

He slept well again, waking only once in the middle of the night,
suddenly, to walk to Ludwig's for a bourbon and a handful of dried
peas. The weather was breaking and he could feel the night beginning
to warm. The moon shone on Baum's mannequins, stunning the entire
family in spotlight.

He ran at dawn along the Schuylkill. Cool dew dripped from the new-
leafed sycamores, but the air was already warm. He worked until noon
and then met Beatrice. She was on time and he knew well enough to be
the same, to be there to watch her enter the corner pastry shop, in pin-
stripe like a spy on the cover of a paperback. She kissed his cheek before
he could finish standing. She considered him silently for a moment and
then looked out the plate-glass window at Rittenhouse Square, where
people were gathering for warmth. Hissing coffee machines, yelling

clerks, and chattering patrons dissolved the music—a low bass and whispery trumpet. A clerk brought them their coffees.

As they sat across from each other he studied her face, thought of her
walking alone in the darkness of The Street Without Exit. Her expression opened. Her hair was pulled back and up neatly, her lipstick clear,
only giving a wet effect. Her eyeliner lifted briefly at the ends, blending
with the upward curve of the lashes. She watched him, tilted her head
thoughtfully.

"You're not as alone as you think, Philip," she said.

"Did you always know what I was thinking?"

"Almost. But I almost always know what people are thinking. No
matter what they're saying or doing. It's worse than having total recall. I
must have been impossible to live with."

"I liked living with you."

"You miss it?"

"No."

"Neither do I," she replied.

She lifted her coffee for the first time, winced at it, set it down. She
looked around the shop, precisely, completely. She looked across Rittenhouse Square, at people removing their blazers and jackets, loosening their ties in the sun, letting their shoes dangle from their toes. She
watched the people beyond the glass as if they weren't real, actors changing backstage.

"I have a proposition for you to consider." Beneath her chin, she
formed a steeple with her hands and fingers, her elbows to the table.
"With my job, I travel more and more. I go places and find that, after
I'm finished with my assignment, there is no reason to leave right away.
Or no reason to return here before going on to the next place. Maybe I
learned that from her, too."

"What are you saying, B.?"

"Do the same. Move your books to a nicer place. You can have your
study back. We'll hardly see each other, coming and going. We'll see each
other less than we do now."

"Why?" he asked.

"We can sit and share our travels over wine. Maybe we'll run into each other halfway across the world." Her expression was sincere and her gaze was steady. "And I want your books. You can bring your ugly chair and your little tin stand and lamp. But bring your books."

"My books."

She nodded. "I have to go now. I'm assessing an American company in Antofagasta. I never really knew exactly where Antofagasta was. From there I'm going to the Atacama Desert. To see those giant etchings on the valley floor. The ones in the last chapter of her book. Where the photorealist goes and walks on that giant waterbird. Think about my suggestion while I'm there. There's no hurry. We have all our lives."

"What if you meet somebody?" he asked.

"He, or she, will have to understand. You're part of the furniture."

"What if *I* meet somebody?"

"*You* already met somebody."

She stood, moved to his side, and hugged his head against her hip.

"27182," she said. "That's the new entry code to the flat. That should be easy for you to remember. I sold both cars, by the way," she said before she offered a small wave and left the shop.

She crossed the street to Rittenhouse Square, to be in the sun. She let loose her hair and shook it across her shoulders, and bowed her head pensively as she walked, before looking straight back to him, knowing she would find him watching. He remained at the table, feeling the way he always felt at the end of a new equation, half stunned by the inevitability, half assured. He imagined her all the way to the Metro on Market, descending the escalators to the subway, gliding, her fingers barely touching the rail for balance. She would stand during the train ride to the airport, knowing she had a long flight ahead of her. He saw her on the enormous rock drawings of the Atacama Desert, lifting her arms to let the dry wind blow through her, not trying to figure out why an entire civilization would devote so much time and resource and permanence to etchings too expansive to see until thousands of years later, when people learned to fly.

He ran for a second time that afternoon, a steeplechase through the center of downtown. The air was sultry, tactile. He began near the stock exchange and ended in the historic district on the stoop of Library

Hall. After resting and cooling down on the steps, he went inside the building, to the branch of the Free Library of Philadelphia dedicated to readers with special needs. Irma donated her services to the Braille books, rebinding and repairing many of them. They break quickly, she explained. You could imagine. The first time she took him there and showed him the walls containing the Braille collection, they watched two women in overcoats move along the stacks and graze their fingers over the spines and the raised labels. They should have a special collection for you, too, she told him. The hall was warm and the sweat from his run resumed immediately upon entering, the dried salt on his skin dissolving again. An elderly woman sat at a table in front of the Braille stacks. Her two index fingers were pressed together in a V, skimming over the lines and pages of a book. Her face was lifted upward and she was smiling at the words she was feeling. She kind of looks like Ben Franklin, Irma would've told him. But without the glasses. No? But look at her face. Look at her world opening up, endlessly. Endlessly. Look at that little exclamation. And that one. What is she finding, Pip? What is she see-ing? What sad words are saving her?

That evening he worked some more on the Erdrich and Ondaatje. Then he ran the calculations for the next swing of the pendulum. Borges, Turgenev, Cervantes. The next, he knew, would bring him toward the back of the alphabet. It brought him to Malcus Rabet. The novel was bound in blood-red leather with hard black lettering. **The Plague.** He fixed his bourbon and took the novel to his Naugahyde recliner. He eased himself into the chair, delicately positioned his bourbon glass on the tin stand, and let the book lay for a while in his lap as he eyed the rest of the collection on the shelves. Then he opened *The Plague* and read the brief prologue: This novel wasn't written by Malcus Rabet. That is just an ana-gram for the real name of the author, whom you should know. But you don't, even though he is about as famous as an author can be these days. You should know the author because it is a great book by anyone's defini-tion. It is a beautiful book. Its story is timeless. Its conditions and ques-tions and answers are timeless and rendered delicately, sadly, perfectly. It is about all of us. I had to configure the anagram so that alphabeti-cally it would fall fourth. However, the anagram is nothing compared to what's beyond it, what spiral it will give to your life. Put the book back on the shelf, before it's too late. But before you do, I'll offer one small reason why it had to fall fourth. It was the fourth novel I read. I was ten. I loved the rats—the dying rats and the dark mystery they contained. And the doctor. Even though I had a good father, I wanted Dr. Rieux to be my father. The next year, when I was eleven, I read the book again and it seemed entirely new. I loved Dr. Rieux and I loved all of his friends, especially Tarrou and Rambert—and Grand, the old municipal clerk with his novel that never gets past an endless revision of its first sentence: One fine morning in May a slim young horsewoman might have been seen riding a handsome sorrel mare along the flowery avenues of the Bois de Boulogne. The next year, when I was twelve, I realized the chapters did not necessarily occur chronologically, that the story sometimes unfolded thematically, according to Rieux's attempt to comprehend. I read this book every year of my life. Each time I found something new to love. And you'll find out that it's a great book. And you will love the rats. And then Rambert and Tarrou. And Grand and his one, perfect, opening sentence. And then, like mine, your heart will break.

SIXTEEN

In the morning Philip awoke in his aqua-blue Naugahyde recliner, his thumb still bookmarking his place in the Camus novel. He reread the last passage he could remember from the previous night, to make sure he had not merely dreamed it. It was the opening to Part II, where the city gates had just been closed to quarantine the population: From now on it can be said that the plague was the concern of all of us. Hitherto, surprised as he may have been by the strange things happening around him, each individual citizen had gone about his business as usual, so far as this was possible. And no doubt he would have continued doing so. But once the town gates were shut, every one of us realized that all, the narrator included, were, so to speak, in the same boat, and each would have to adapt himself to the new conditions of life. Thus, for example, a feeling normally as individual as the ache of separation from those one loves suddenly became a feeling in which all shared alike and—together with fear—the greatest affliction of the long period of exile that lay ahead.

For most of the morning he worked on his consulting assignment, then reviewed some equations for Isaac, who he was sure was up to something regarding life shapes and the Weber-Fechner law of human sensation. When he was done with Isaac's math, he began preparations to mail back some of the pages he stole from *Zed*, apologizing to the *pensión* owner in a note, claiming he had inadvertently gathered the loose papers while packing to leave.

He began that day's run in front of Baum's mannequin family. They seemed cool and collected in their evening wear, neatly separated from the heat and humidity of high noon. Separated, too, in their geometrical

Eisenhower suits, from the complicated world beyond the glass. Despite the humidity, he ran well and was in fluid stride by the time he reached Columbus Avenue. The avenue, like its namesake in Seville, curved with the shape of the river it followed. He clocked two speedplays along Penn's Landing and continued up the avenue past the *Spirit of Philadelphia* and other tall ships, heading toward the Walt Whitman Bridge. He felt he could follow the river all the way to its mouth in Delaware Bay. The high sun banked off the water, dulled to a parchment light by the heat and stillness of the afternoon. Along Paseo Cristóbol Colón, the first sirocco blew across the Guadalquivir, heating the river air, filling his lungs.

Thoughts—our best thoughts, Tom Salgeiro reads from a note attached to a type of linen he has never seen before, are fragile strands, formed of crystals only molecules in diameter. The note, too, is on a small remnant of the linen, and so Philip's handwriting is checkered by the weave. The weave is uniquely sumptuous because the linen threads are produced from one type of Brazilian flax retted by a highly localized strain of *Clostridium*. Twenty-two species of bacteria have been isolated as retting agents for Brazilian flax, Philip writes. The retting agent particular to the flax in this linen thrives only in the wetlands just north of São Gonçalo. Forgive the rough note. All my paper was lost in a downpour and the little postal station has no supplies.

Tom just stared at the swatch you sent, Irma's niece writes in a long letter wrapped around a CD. You should have seen him. He just stared at it for more than an hour. I think the next time you stay here it won't be in the milk shed. The CD contains her oboe variations on the Hindemith sonatas, not yet ready for assessment but getting there. Her note continues: I am confused by some things in one of the books she left me—the Maugham. You seem to be in it (*you* meaning the both of you—Spanish is a better language for trying to explain such things).

He listens to the Hindemith sonatas rendered on the oboe and feels as though he has wasted so much of his life. But then he thinks of Grand's sentence in *The Plague* and its variations. One fine morning in May a slim young horsewoman might have been seen riding a handsome sorrel mare along the flowery avenues of the Bois de Boulogne. He holds her letter and plays her CD and wonders about the character Grand and how he keeps working on perfecting that one opening sentence even as the plague devastates the quarantine city. And how Rieux and his friends live beneath the shadow and whisper of the plague (at night, Rieux can hear the plague whispering overhead as he tends to his stricken and dying patients). And how they listen to Grand's sentence revisions while they learn that the plague is life, life the plague.

One fine morning in May a slim young horsewoman might have been seen riding a glossy sorrel mare along the flower-strewn avenues of the Bois de Boulogne. He wants the first sentence to be perfect, wants the first editor who sees it to say, Hats off!

It is clear to me that we need voices in our heads, Zed declares in a translation Lucia reads to Philip as they sit on a picnic table in a makeshift park in the ramshackle outskirts of Rio. As many voices as possible. Sane voices that ring like music, saving us. The translation is newly bound in dark green linen. They find it with ease in Carlos Leite's mothy stacks. It fairly glows on a high shelf. It is translated to English, but Lucia's accent serves the words best and Philip can close his eyes for long stretches of time and feel the heat and insects, sense the whisper in the background of her voice. I don't know which would be best: for you to be me for a moment, or I, you. And Philip, eyes closed, does not know if it is Zed, Lucia, or Irma who wonders this.

200 meters, Nicole reads in *Tracks*. That is the distance between us. But that has always been the distance between us, even on my best days, even in the races where I had you in my sights right up to the final kick. The page does not completely stun her. Her brother warned her something might be coming, coaxed her, in fact, into reading the Erdrich even though she needed to study for her finals. But don't skip ahead, he added. You'll lose the effect. In a well-paced 10k, she reads, I cover 200 meters in thirty-eight seconds. Thirty-eight seconds is more than enough time for a friend to think of what he wants to say, what he feels, and then come to know whether he should speak or just keep running. It's more than enough time for you to do the same, and to just keep running. You are in every race I will ever run from now until I die. There are wonderful road races in Spain. Sam can tell you about them. Within a 200-meter stretch

in a race in Barcelona, you pass three Gaudí pieces—visions of dragons and dogs and melting castles that will send you flying over the pavement. I will see them, too, perhaps only thirty-eight seconds later. If I inadvertently end up in the same Frisbee game as you—the noontime Castelldefels game, for instance—I will leave at your first signal, your first second of hesitation, the first bow of your head. I will run over the sand, along the blue shore of Barcelona, as swiftly as my old bones and tired muscles can carry me. You will have to forgive me if, for a moment, I need to lie down in the sand dampened by the cool lick of the shore break.

As I begin my fall, Fatima narrates through the voice of Lucia, my hip catches the bar. I don't clear my final jump. But fortune grants me a reprieve, sends me onward in the competition, an imposter athlete among the best vaulters. For the bar bounces hard out of its hold, quivers free in the air, falls securely back into its perch, and allows me to live where I should have died. Lucia senses his head shift against her lap and asks him what's wrong. He pretends to be asleep and so she continues in a softer voice, one that barely rises above the trill of the *cigaros* in the surrounding trees. She pauses to look up toward the sound of the insects, hopes she has really found a spot in the grass where their spray won't reach her and Philip. Sometimes their spray falls like a heavy mist and forms yellowish puddles beneath trees. She puts her hand on the side of his neck, the cool tips of her fingers in the tuck of his ear, and continues with Fatima's narrative. I see Adão in the stands as I open into my fall. He has come after all, to see me jump, watch me rise. He and Zed hold hands and raise their fists together, saluting me. And I am so happy to see them joined together like that, in the crowd, with the crowd. In a crowd that is joyous and not protesting anything.

If you make it to São Gonçalo before I do, Sam reads from *The English Patient*, I'd look toward the upper shelves. Not the very top of the stacks, because dampness reflects downward, too, from ceilings, as well as up from floors. The words jolt Sam from his reclined position beneath a tree on the Rutgers playing fields, where he waits for the Frisbee game to collect. He thinks at first that he has come upon one of her insertions, but realizes, no, hers always emerge more delicately from the prose and theme. And the paper, font, and tone of the ink do not quite match the rest of the book, either. The page number is repeated. This is crude, he thinks, compared to her. And then he knows and reads more.

If I run into you searching through the same stacks, I won't turn and walk away. I'll ask you if you've found anything. And I will tell you what I've found. And if I see you running the same path as I, I will run you down. I'll call out her mile markers as I close in behind you. Don't let me catch you. Remain that much better, that much wiser. There will come a day when the sacrifices you make now to hold your family together are no longer necessary. When you can see me and recognize me as nothing more than a friend who sometimes crosses the same paths you travel. Who searches for the same beauty.

Sam reads from a later paragraph, one tacked into the white space of a chapter ending (the lines are slightly tilted): We were much closer than we thought.

We do need places of return, Beatrice reads from a book she knows Philip has stolen during one of his trips. She reads in the Naugahyde recliner and is again surprised at how soothing the vinyl has become, worn smooth as pearl in warm sun, contoured. She understands why he often sleeps in it, nights at a time, a book across his chest. She clicks her nails against the tin stand, liking the hard quick sound. We do need people of return also. But I think we instinctively place too much value on both. We value too much—horde, in fact—time spent in those places, with those people. If you return to my shop, you will find it much the same, but without me in it. You may come upon one of my three proté- gées, who rotate through it, sometimes overlapping (though I'm not sure any of them likes the other enough to work side-by-side for very long). I chose them and gave them my shop because they believe in my disdain for the rule of reversibility. They are young. They are beautiful when they are working. When they are under the quiet light, pulling thread over wax, tapping the coverboards, adjusting the turnscrews, thumbing the bone folder into the spine. Leave them some of your odd, difficult music if you happen to stop by. They might find it interesting, just the right mood for their work—which changes.

I have no doubt that you possess the math to capture me one day, that you will eventually triangulate time, space, and my desire. You may need Isaac's help with the more subtle anticipations. You will certainly need Beatrice's help with any fundamental decisions (is that why I miss her in such strange proportion?). But understand that *I* possess the language to find you, observe you, move you, touch you at any time I want.

Fatigued from travel, she falls asleep while reading, sinks deeper into the aqua recliner. As her eyes flutter, she thinks she may have dreamed the lines. Reading his books, with Irma's little appearances throughout, has left her susceptible, unable to always discern between what is hers and what is theirs, what she reads and what she imagines, what she believes and what she desires. She remembers to crook her thumb between the pages, to mark her place, before she lets herself fall into much-welcomed sleep. Light from the reading lamp grays over the tin stand and mutes her still form against the background of his bookshelves. The spine colors look best in this kind of light, emerging. It isn't difficult to gently remove her thumb from the stolen book without waking her, to rescue and kiss the knuckle. From the flicker of her lashes and the smile on her lips you can easily tell that she isn't dreaming about the lines she's just read, but about the rest of the book, which tells the buxom story of nineteenth century pirates off the Argentina coast. Feeling reckless, you steal a kiss from her lips and hope that it will not wake her, will only fall into the book she dreams, work its way into the hero's embrace. This allows you to feel confident in removing the stolen book from her breast, lifting it along with the gentle rise of her breathing. Cover her with a blanket, douse the light, and quickly, before he returns, begin your journey to the place where the book belongs.

7/27/08